Dear reader,

I love to write about the West Country, and Cornwall and Devon in particular. The continuing saga of the big cat sightings is custom-made for my stories of the Fifth Dimension. My stories of the shape shifting cats are a never-ending source of amusement to my family.

My daughters have encouraged me to continue the series and they both enjoy reading and criticising my work. They like to check to make certain I haven't embarrassed them in any way. When they considered it good enough for the reading public they allowed me to send it the publishers.

Thankfully the publisher thought the same…

I write for fun, and hope you enjoy this third book in the series. If you spread the word log onto my web site at:
www.jillhowes.com
or e-mail me at:
jill@jhowes.freeserve.co.uk

I'd love to hear from you

Sincerely
Jill

**Other books by Jill Howes**


**The Fifth Dimension Prophecy**
ISBN 978-1-90348 978-9

**The Lost Soul**
ISBN 978-1-84386-118-8

# THE FIFTH
# DIMENSION 'CHOICES'

# Jill Howes

## THE FIFTH DIMENSION 'CHOICES'

Vanguard Press

VANGUARD PAPERBACK

© Copyright 2007
**Jill Howes**

A CIP catalogue record for this title is
available from the British Library.

ISBN 978 1 84386 332 8

Cover illustrated by Matthew Ivey

*Vanguard Press is an imprint of*
*Pegasus Elliot MacKenzie Publishers Ltd.*
www.pegasuspublishers.com

First Published in 2007

**Vanguard Press**
**Sheraton House  Castle Park**
**Cambridge  England**

Printed & Bound in Great Britain

# Dedication

To my new son-in-law Geoff Pope – my
computer guru – a welcome addition to the family.

# FOREWORD

**Middle Earth** – This is halfway between earth and heaven. The only way most humans even know of its existence is after death or a near death experience. However, to heavenly beings and spirits who wander the earth – ghosts, and visitors from other dimensions – it is known as the waiting room. Where it is decided who should go – to be quite blunt – upstairs or downstairs. This is why Lucifer is very familiar with the location. He was summoned there often. It is the place where, on very rare occasions, the members of the Astral Council receive their orders from the Almighty. As, usually, they are given them by Lucifer or a messenger angel.

**The Fifth Dimension** – Home of the First Ones, Angels who were there at the beginning of time. They had become the custodians of all of the knowledge of the universe. These angels who wanted a life outside the confines of heaven had created a haven for the oracles and sages who sought peace and knowledge. The library of the universe, every book ever written or thought of, was contained within its ancient walls. In the twentieth century their sons, the Old Ones, had stepped outside those boundaries and set foot in the mortal world. They had opened a dark doorway. Correcting their mistakes was one of the tasks undertaken by the Astral Council.

## Cast of Characters:

**Elliott Black** – Head of the Astral Council. He is a dark angel and grandson of Alpha the leader of the First Ones. His wife is Natalia a heavenly angel. Their son Nicholas is an angel child.

**Jason Parkes** – Elliott's friend and second in command. His wife, Allegra, son Simon and daughter Riva were recently reunited with her parents in a Prehistoric World. Read the **Lost Soul** by Jill Howes.

**Daniel Jeffries** – The third member of the trio who run the Astral Council. A Druid, he has been given the knowledge of the ancients and has the wisdom to use it. His wife Pauline is a werewolf as are their twin daughters.

**Quinn and Vespazia** – A shapeshifting Dragon recently awakened from a magical sleep and his wife a Primeval witch. Allegra's parents and King and Queen of the Lost World.

**Drago** – Quinn's brother also a shapeshifter. Able to turn into a Dragon and other creatures at will. He had been Quinn's guardian whilst he slept.

**Vern and Charles Fallon** – Shapeshifting cats that can turn into Lynx at will.

**Lance and Diana** – Brother and sister shapeshifting Jaguars with short tempers. Lance is the vicar of Apcombe on Bodmin Moor the home of all of the shapeshifters. Diana is Vern's girlfriend.

**James Purcell** – A shapeshifting Mountain Lion from a long line of mountain lions, including both of his parents. Very laid back but blessed with the eyes and ears of his alter ego.

**Thomas Fallon** – Vern's son, also a Lynx. He is proud of his father but wary of the exalted company he keeps. His brother

**Patrick Fallon** also a lynx has visited the Fifth Dimension and is destined to become a druid. **David Fallon** their cousin is a shapeshifting falcon. His ability to fly has been a great advantage.

**Alistair** – A very human computer genius who has attracted the attention of Lucifer and is the subject of his long-term plans.

**Charalder** – Daughter of an angel from the Fifth Dimension whose evil ways were so abhorrent she was thrown out to wander the universe as outcast forever. She used the millennia of her punishment to learn every evil spell ever cast and every vile potion ever mixed. She became the most powerful sorceress ever known and, still unaware of her existence, the enemy of all mortals and immortals. She is Vespazia's mother. They hate each other.

# PROLOGUE

## Salt Lake City
## July 2002

He stood on a rocky promontory above the western edge of the lake. Silent and predatory he waited. This was like a harvest for him. Below him was the walkers' car park. It was just after sunset. There were always the stragglers, the ones who had stayed too long admiring the wonders of nature in the foothills of the Wasatch Mountains. Those who thought they had plenty of time before it got dark! He had been waiting a while, but now as most of the cars and campers had left, he heard the voices of a small party of walkers heading towards the few remaining cars.

He knew they would soon start packing their belongings and souvenirs in their trunks, and then, whilst they were unprepared, his night's work could begin. He wasn't normally a patient man but he knew, on this occasion, it would pay dividends.

The noise of two parties arriving almost simultaneously gave him a perverse pleasure as he walked towards the side of the cliff. A narrow pathway led downwards, but for him easy enough.

Almost immediately his attention was caught by a slightly different sound far above him and, looking up, he saw an object hurtling earthwards. Being a good judge of distance he realised that the object would land almost where he had been standing moments before and without conscious thought moved back to catch it. Seconds later he was almost knocked unconscious as the object dropped neatly into his arms with such force he fell over backwards, still clutching it tightly. Momentarily stunned he released his hold on the object and got unsteadily to his feet. He took a few seconds to regain his senses and then bent over the bundle lying beside him. The background noise of two cars driving away made him pause momentarily: his quarry for that night had escaped.

Evil predatory hunter that he was, he shrugged off a strong sense of menace and an unaccountable feeling of fear as he started to undo the bundle. He saw first a tiny white hand and then a very small pale face, seemingly unconscious or dead. He put his hand on the child's pulse and found a faint thready beat. He gingerly unwrapped the folds of cloth and found to his surprise that this was no child, but that a very small, yet delicately formed adult female was revealed. The diaphanous, silvery, very revealing dress she wore left no doubt of that. Although not a lot was visible through the ropes which bound her arms to her sides.

He was stunned; almost unnerved that it should have happened in this particular place. The spot he had picked so carefully to watch the walkers returning. He had nothing with him to cut the ropes and the knots appeared to be sealed. Whoever wanted to be rid of her had done a good job of tying her up.

Had he not been there to catch her she would have died as she hit the ground. He hesitated only briefly and picking up the tiny female strode back with her to his car.

A very sensible man, he realised that to involve the authorities might draw too much unwanted attention to himself, which he certainly could not afford. He drove them both to his home on the outskirts of the city.

Sometime later – he hunted some way from his home – he pulled into the covered carport and, easing the body into his arms, carried her into the house. Striding through the kitchen and down a dark hallway, he entered a spacious yet rather dark bedroom and placed her on the bed. He put on the light and, unfolding the wrappings, examined her more closely. He discovered to his great dismay that she had been tied up rather tightly with a binding he was unfamiliar with. It was wound round and round her body like a cocoon. Her arms were bound so tightly to her sides that only her hands were free. He went to the kitchen and returned with a sharp knife to cut her bonds. It was extremely difficult and as he realised that the rope had a wire core, left her again to fetch his tools. With wire cutters, he finally set her free. As he looked up from his concentration on the bonds, he saw her eyes were open and that she was watching him anxiously.

For some reason, which he could never explain he felt as if she reached out to him and asked for help, yet she never said a single word.

"I don't know how you got into this mess," he told her, "but you certainly had a lucky escape when you fell into my arms."

He looked silently at her. "I normally eat little girls like you for dinner," he said quietly. "I can't think why I am setting you free."

He wondered, briefly, if that had been the reason she had

dropped practically at his feet. But dismissed the idea as far too fanciful.

She lay there, just looking at him. He moved impatiently, and rose to his feet. "You'd better get out of here, before I change my mind."

The girl, for she was little more than that, attempted to sit up, but was obviously too weak for the time being to do so. The man hauled her up against the pillows and spoke again.

"Just who exactly threw you out of a plane?" he inquired roughly.

"I don't remember falling out of a plane." She looked puzzled. "I don't think I was in a plane."

"How about a balloon?" he asked.

"I don't think so," she replied doubtfully.

"A space ship then!" he said, running out of suggestions and getting annoyed.

A look of dismay spread across her face. "Please, don't be angry, I really don't know."

He sighed resignedly. "Well, I did say I wouldn't eat you, but I'm afraid I shall have to leave you and go feed on someone else."

Her eyes widened for a horrified moment. "You must be a vampire!" she said. "I must be in America. However did I get here?"

The man was taken aback. "What does a baby like you know about vampires?" he asked sternly. "You shouldn't even know we exist."

"Of course I know about vampires and shapeshifters, and werewolves, demons and witches," she said scornfully. "Where I come from they are commonplace, but they are usually doing good not killing people."

"If you know all that what were you doing flying through the air? I don't suppose you are a witch?" he asked hopefully.

"That's the trouble," she replied sadly. "I know what I am not; I just can't remember what I am."

"If I don't go out and hunt soon," he told her, "I will have to eat you or die."

"Go!" she said urgently. "But promise me one thing, only take enough to live, not enough to kill."

He looked at her for a moment and saw the pleading in her eyes. "Just this once to please you," he said, surprising himself even as he spoke the words.

Outside his home, he shook off the unaccustomed feeling of guilt at his outright lie as he headed into the darkness.

He drove to the lake once more. It took a while, but he found 'food' and had every intention of satisfying his blood lust with a kill; but, with each chosen quarry, he found that he took no more than he needed to be sure they lived. Somehow he had lost his urge to kill.

Whatever his foundling was, she certainly had strong powers of persuasion or possibly even suggestion.

He had been rather disillusioned with life lately, perhaps this new diversion would help to pass the time away. He went back home rather jauntily, perhaps life was going to be more interesting for a while.

He arrived back just before dawn, to find his unexpected guest fast asleep in his bed. As it was the only room in the house that had blackout curtains, he was not thrilled to find his bed still occupied. Not being completely reformed by any means, he took off his shoes and shirt and slid in beside her. He was rather taken aback when she opened her eyes and said rather sleepily, "Oh good, you're back. I feel safer now," and promptly went back to sleep again.

The vampire, for the only time in his long life, could think of nothing to say.

For the next ten days she stayed around the house, like a rather nervous kitten. She had discarded the silvery dress and wore his old shirts with a belt around them as she moved around his home and seemed happy enough, pottering around the house and garden, reading his books and watching his television. She didn't say a lot about herself, but was very eager to hear what he had done in his long life. For some reason he found himself giving her a very edited version of his exploits. After that first night she seemed to take it for granted that they would share his bed and it had not troubled his conscience in the least to do just that, as he quickly realised she found comfort and safety in his arms

She was always pleased to see him when he returned from his hunts, and without actually saying the words he let her know that he had not killed. She smiled at him each morning when he told her and he saw in her eyes that she was pleased with him. Why he should want to find approval in her eyes, he did not know, but for some reason, he found himself gradually looking for other ways to feed than on humans. For some unknown reason he found some sort of peace in her company and her total acceptance of him just as he was.

On the morning of the eleventh day, he found her sitting at the kitchen table waiting for him. She was again wearing the silvery dress, now cleaned and ironed, and he could tell she was nervous about something.

"What is it, little bird?"

As she could not remember her name and had dropped from the sky he had joking called her little bird; the name was as good as any.

"I have remembered who I am and how I got here." She hesitated briefly. "I can't tell you my name, at least not yet. I have to go. If I don't return home in the next few hours, my father will start searching for me. I don't want him to know I have been here with you. He would kill you before I could even offer an explanation. You saved my life, I have no gift to offer you as great as that. I owe you at least the courtesy of saying goodbye. If it is possible for me to return, I promise that I will. I know you have wondered if I am a witch. I am not. But what I am, and what happened to me is beyond your present understanding."

She stood on tiptoe and pulled his face down towards hers, and kissed him; not the gentle peck he was expecting but a firm, loving kiss with what seemed like a promise to return.

Whilst he stood there, stunned, she opened the kitchen door and left.

It couldn't have been more that a few seconds later that he tore open the door expecting to see her on the path, but she had completely vanished. He stood there for a while. He knew he would miss her. He hoped she meant her promise to return.

A fortnight later he returned from his night's hunt to find her sitting at his kitchen table nibbling at a piece of toast, and quite obviously very much at home. She stayed a few days, then one morning kissed him goodbye and left again, telling him she would return when she could.

The vampire was beginning to feel rather bewitched and shook himself out of a feeling of déjà vu and carried on with his life, albeit he found he rather missed the mysterious female.

Towards the end of September he decided she was not coming again, but one afternoon, he woke abruptly as he felt someone slide into his bed, then ruffle his hair to awaken him.

Opening his eyes he knew what he would see and was not disappointed. She leaned over him laughing gently at his surprise.

"I told you I would be back," she said, smiling wickedly.

"We've hours before you need to go hunting, don't let's waste it."

She wriggled her way into his arms and found her vampire only too ready to oblige.

This time she stayed three weeks. He enjoyed her company more than he had thought possible. He was intrigued by her total acceptance of his feral nature. Several times she accompanied him on his nightly 'trips' and urged him to try the animals in the mountains in preference to the humans. He found himself doing just that. But once again she left, this time in the middle of the night. Half way through a hunt, she told him she had to go. She had an important task to carry out, which couldn't wait.

Half way through November he was forced to the conclusion that, this time, she wasn't coming back.

# CHAPTER ONE

*Exmoor*
*October 2002*

Angels, Elliott Black, and his wife, Natalia had been to China. Natalia had as usual got her own way and flown along the Great Wall. Elliott had of course accompanied her to make sure she didn't get into any trouble. The angel Natalia was notorious throughout heaven and their friends for her wayward actions. She was inclined to rush headlong into danger and kept Elliott on his toes. He had repeatedly warned her to stay out of trouble but she was so confident that he could rescue her in the nick of time that she tended to ignore his warnings. Elliott idolized the naughty angel and let her have her way far too often. His friends were waiting for the day when she went too far and regretted her ill-considered actions. However on this occasion they had in fact had a very pleasant vacation. They had such a good time exploring China they were gone two months, and had only recently returned to the Fifth Dimension to collect their son, Nicholas from the care of Elliott's parents, Torquil and Yohanna. They then dropped into the Lost World, under Exmoor, that the members of the Astral Council had discovered earlier that year.

Elliot, a Dark Angel, commanded the Astral Council assisted by his two closest friends, Jason Parkes, a vampire and Daniel Jefferies, a druid. Accompanied by a number of shapeshifters from Bodmin Moor, they had been instrumental in releasing the Lost World from a curse that had hidden it from human eyes for a million years. He'd decided to check that all was well with Quinn and Vespazia, the King and Queen of this world.

The Astral Council considered itself responsible to the continuing wellbeing of this underground world that had disappeared beneath Exmoor a million years ago. It had been known far in the past as Dragonara. Probably because most of its inhabitants were Dragons who could change their shape, not only into human form, but other animals as well. Quinn was the King of this world and had once been known as the Dolonquin.

When discovered the world was derelict and inhabited by

apparitions, the ghosts of his subjects who had been held within its confines under the curse which had left the Dolonquin sleeping for a million years. They lived on the edges of the petrified forest which stood at the entrance to the world waiting for the day their lost princess; Quinn's daughter would arrive to liberate them. She had arrived at last and the world reawakened. Jason had been amazed to learn that his film-star wife, Allegra, was their daughter. He had known since he met her some five years before that she was an Old Soul and had been reincarnated many times down the centuries. He hadn't known, until they arrived in the Lost World, that she was the Lost Soul they had been waiting for or that he was the man considered worthy to return her to her home. After releasing the underground world from its spell they had saved it from destruction by Vespazia's mother, a prime-evil witch named Charalder. Vespazia's mother had been the instrument that had sent the world of Dragonara and Quinn's family into its hibernation one million years before. Elliott, with Daniel, Vespazia and Lucifer, had vanquished the evil witch and she had perished in the Eternal Flame.

It had been shapeshifters who had renamed the Dolonquin. Quinn, although nostalgic about his ancient title, had liked the new name.

Quinn's brother, formerly known as the Grimmon, had also been renamed by the visitors. Drago, as he was now known, had been spared the curse and he had guarded his brother and the Lost World throughout his slumber. He too was a very ancient shapeshifter and sightings of him as a Dragon, a wolf, a troll and a number of other supposedly mythical creatures had been reported down the millennia. Over the years he had built the castle they now lived in. He'd wanted his brother to have a home fit for a King.

Elliott and his wife Natalia, found that their vampire friend Jason, his wife, Allegra and their toddler son, Simon had returned to their home in Winchester. Allegra, being Quinn and Vespazia's newly discovered daughter, Jason had agreed that his family should spend some time with their new relations and get to know each other. The new grandparents had been enchanted with their grandson and would have loved to keep him with them longer, but after a while, Allegra had wanted to go home.

"They'll bring him back," said Natalia. "Jason's a generous man, he wouldn't keep him from his grandparents."

"His generosity has extended to improving the comfort of his wife's new home," Quinn had remarked – he considered the palace his daughters home. He had then shown them around the refurbished palace.

Elliott noticed that Vespazia still looked a little shell-shocked as she showed them around, and understood why. No expense had been spared to bring the place into the $21^{st}$ century. It had been turned into a millionaire's luxury pad.

"Lucifer's had a hand in this, I should think," he said to Quinn.

"I believe he was carrying out our son-in-laws instructions. After the shapeshifters had finished the building improvements and laid down the plumbing, Lucifer appeared with a long list of instructions from a shapeshifter called Vern to finish everything off."

"One of our friends from Bodmin Moor," explained Elliott. "He and his brother Charles Fallon are builders. They built my house. They are both Lynx and work quite closely with us. They were there when you regained your Lost Kingdom, but you were rather busy at the time. You probably didn't realise who they were." Quinn glanced at Vespazia. "We were rather occupied with our reunion and our daughter," he agreed, "but we can still appreciate the work done by your friends. Lucifer was only here for a few seconds," he added with a sly look at Elliott. "I realised quite a lot of it was done with a thought or two and the wave of a hand. Plus of course some good book keeping?"

"That's the general idea," agreed Elliott, "but some of us have wives who like to do it themselves."

"I can see where that might be inconvenient," replied Quinn.

Elliott shuddered candidly. "All that mess to clear up, rubble and paint everywhere. It's a nightmare."

Even Vespazia thought this funny and laughed as she followed them around the shining new rooms.

"I lost count of the bathrooms after fifteen," said Vespazia, "and you should see the kitchen!"

"Actually," drawled Elliott, "I prefer to keep away from kitchens, they can get very messy too."

"He does the washing up with a wave of his hand," said Natalia crossly. "How can I be a modern housewife if he doesn't let me have a dishwasher?"

"Dishwasher?" queried Quinn. "Have we got one of those?"

"If Allegra is going to live here, you most certainly have," said Elliott.

"She has installed a nursery and playroom and all of you have a suite of your own with three bedrooms, a bathroom and lounge. Daniel and Jason have a computer room and there is a TV room, and a heated indoor swimming pool," said Vespazia in awe.

"Just who is going to clean and look after all this lot?" asked Natalia.

"Once my wife got used to the opulence and comfort of our son-in-law's gifts," said Quinn dryly, "it wasn't too difficult for her, as a very superior witch, to master the thought or two and the wave of the hand herself."

"You and Elliott must have been friends in a previous life," muttered Natalia sourly, "he mastered that art centuries ago."

Everyone laughed at this unangelic remark.

They were preparing to depart for earth with Nicholas in his rather elegant pram, a gift from Lucifer, when there was a loud bang and a puff of red smoke eddied in from the hall.

"Good, you are still here!" said Lucifer strolling through the door. "I hoped I'd catch you all. Enjoyed your little vacation, I hope? Pity we can't all swan off around the world to exotic foreign countries and stay there for months." He added to Elliott, who glowered at him.

Lucifer ignored this completely. "Time to go to work again. There's too much evil gaining the upper hand for you lot to take that many holidays. I told you things are going from bad to evil more quickly that I can keep track of. We are on top of the problem in England, we need more help around the world."

"And just what do you propose that we should do about it?" asked Elliott sarcastically.

"I've got my eye on a piece of real estate in North America. I was about to ask you all to go and check it out. It's a very young country, but a significant proportion of the population didn't take long to master the evil arts. There's a lot of demonic activity over there, and it's multiplying faster than I can keep up with it. Of course they have blamed it all on me. I'm not too popular in some parts of the USA. As if I am responsible for all the evil they get up to! Me, when have I got time to organise more chaos and mayhem? I've got enough problems keeping on top of what's out there already.

"That's what I've got you for. That's why I need you to go to New York."

He breathed fire and gestured angrily. "I don't have to get

26

involved with a city that has hundreds of different churches, underground cults and religions worshipping hundreds of different gods and icons. I know there's only one. He's the reason I'm here. I know you English-speaking vampires and shapeshifters call him the Great Entity and to our counterparts in America he's known as the Great One. But to me he's the Almighty, the one who threw me out of heaven and down to earth a very long time ago.

"This is my domain, to rule as I see fit. I like being the Demon King. I've perfected the art of creating just enough havoc to keep everybody on their toes. For centuries I didn't have any trouble balancing the scales. Now the world is getting overrun with violent humans and evil is rising faster than I can keep up with. It won't be long before I have to create a new Hell dimension. Keeping track of all those fake priests, fraudulent healers, false prophets, witch doctors and so-called do-gooders touting for business and trying to muscle in on my territory has got to be brought under my control."

He paused and glanced at his audience. "If I wanted to I could dispose of the lot of them just by removing them from this dimension. However, too many unexplained disappearances can lead to mob rule and vigilantes. Therefore, I need to get rid of them legally. With evidence of their crimes and that's where you come in."

"Anything else?" demanded Elliott.

"Well, I did have this idea, sometime ago, that there must be one or two useful contacts we could persuade to work for us on the Council. So I had a word with the Great Entity about it. I said surely in a country that size the demons aren't all bad. There must be one or two we could use. He told me that there are a few He has had his eye on for quite a while, but they need organising into a coherent unit. He has sanctioned a new mission to get them onto our Astral Council. I want you all to go to America and find out whether they are going to be any use to me."

"Just like that," said Elliott amused despite himself. "I thought you were hiding some terrible secret."

Lucifer looked at him for a moment, considering. "There is something I should perhaps tell you, although you should already know. Vampires in America aren't like those you are familiar with in Britain, and the demons over there are very low class, mostly minor demons with a few serious ones to make it interesting. One of my brothers was let loose there some time ago, but he was disposed of after a lengthy confrontation with the opposition.

"Unfortunately the opposition haven't got your contacts; they have a very loose connection to the supernatural, and none to the heavenly powers. I did have the idea of introducing an angel into their operation. She's there now, trying to find a way to mingle with the demons and vampires. She's fairly new to the job, I hope I'm not expecting too much of her. There are quite a few hazards in America, different dangers. There are only a few shapeshifters over there, nothing to concern you, some cats, a few bears and birds. Most are fairly friendly."

"What do you mean the vampires aren't like the English ones?" asked Elliott, homing in on the one point that interested him.

"Nasty vicious creatures, most of them," Lucifer elaborated, "predators and killers. There are one or two who hide their calling and live an outwardly normal life. A little difficult when you can only go out at night.

"That's the main difference. Most British vampires were born vampires and are descended from the first vampires. Present-day sunlight only weakens their strength and senses, so they wear strong sunglasses and drive around in darkened cars and mobile homes. The oldest ones can walk around in the sunlight with no ill effects. They could hunt in daylight but it's not wise. They get around like normal humans. It's the European-made vampires who are responsible for all the aggravation, of course. They've been migrating around the world for centuries. Transylvania's got a lot to answer for, one day! As you know, the tales about vampires originated in Europe hundreds of years ago when they needed little protection from the human population. They preyed on humans and killed them to feed on and for pleasure, many still do. That's not to say there are no made vampires in England, there are a few left, but in the main they emigrated to America at the same time as many of the European ones, at the turn of the century. Too much danger of being discovered in a small country like this, once the population started increasing and law and order became organised and civilised.

"So they went to America and the result was a population explosion of the blood-sucking killers. There are now so many it is hard not to trip over them every night when you go out. I'll have my work cut out one day to accommodate them all.

"The vampires there are very young compared to most of the vampires on this side of the Atlantic. There are very few who are over two hundred years old, and most of them were originally from

Europe. Most were made in the USA in the last eighty or ninety years or so. They have no inherited immunities to fire, wooden stakes or holy water and of course they are allergic to sunlight, being so young, one glimpse of the golden orb and poof! Gone!"

"It won't make Jason go 'poof!' will it?" asked Natalia anxiously.

"Certainly not," said Lucifer indignantly. "*Me*, jeopardize the safety of my godson's father? *Never*!

"Anyway," he continued seriously, "Elliott knows that Jason is descended from the original vampires, he was born a vampire, his sensitivity to light has decreased greatly over thousands of years. He would be in no more danger in America than he is here. Except that I have heard that many Americans now believe in vampires and demons and actively hunt them to kill, so he'd have to watch his back. Which he's always been good at anyway."

"What about Simon, he's a vampire baby," asked Natalia anxiously. "There can't be many baby vampires around, he may be the only one. We don't want to put him in danger."

"A vampire born now will be sensitive for a short while," Lucifer qualified, "but his inherited genes will soon take over. In any case my godson is half human, he may not be in the slightest danger from sunlight, but of course he is far too young, as yet, to test that theory."

He paused for a moment thinking nostalgically of his favourite godson. Then carried on:

"There are two sure ways to kill an American vampire: a wooden stake through the heart and exposure to the sun. Chopping off the head is also very successful," he added callously.

"Almost all made vampires have no reflection, but digital cameras have solved that problem. What's more, European vampires who now live in America have passed on a thing or two and the Americans are now learning to get around in mobile homes and the latest sunglasses, which are very good; but even with full protection, they have very limited powers in daylight.

"Fortunately for all of you they still prefer to go underground during the day and come out at sundown. You'll have to take your chances with the other demons and unpleasant humans who exist there. Almost every home has a gun of some kind, so you have to watch out for bullets as well. They could kill some of you, especially the shapeshifters, but fortunately not the vampires. Of course the oldest vampires in the West of England have had the protection of the druids, like our Daniel, for centuries – that is why they had remained a secret for so long. Unfortunately all this television nonsense has drawn them into the public eye. Now everyone believes in them and is actually looking out for them. Particularly in America, where they are something of a cult.

"Jason would still have to be very careful. Wood is poisonous to him and a stake to the heart would kill him, whereas a bullet wouldn't. It would be a slow death, and that is why Torquil was badly injured by the stake when he threw himself in front of Jason to save him. Jason is Elliott's friend and his father wanted to save him the anguish of losing him. Torquil healed quickly in the Fifth Dimension and is well again as Elliott can tell you."

Elliott nodded in agreement and turned once more to Lucifer.

"You want us to go to America which is far more dangerous than England and organise a secret society of vampires, and others, to do in America what we do here?"

"I want a little more than that," replied Lucifer. "I want one or two of you to move to America temporarily and get it off the ground properly. Get them used to hearing from me and him," – he pointed skywards – "and make sure this angel has a sensible and very strong protector."

"You don't want much," protested Elliott. "I need time to think about something like this. Why can't you send Lance and James to start things off? A jaguar and a mountain lion shouldn't attract too much attention."

"You're being facetious now," said Lucifer irritably. "I'll give you a month to think it over, THEN YOU can go!"

Elliott just looked at him and Lucifer glanced away quickly.

"I haven't been to America for ages," said Natalia wistfully. "I'd love to see the Grand Canyon again."

"We can fly over it any time you like, we don't have to live there to do that," said Elliott dismissively. "It's safe enough for us. There are very few shapeshifters in America and only a few of them are birds. What Nick wants is for us to go and live there and mingle with the new age vampires, demons and human riff-raff of America. They've probably never even thought about getting organised. We'll get stuck in some hellhole of a city like Las Vegas and be there until he says we've done the job."

He turned back to Lucifer.

"Natalia is far too headstrong to let loose in a city like that, or New York or San Francisco," he told the Devil emphatically.

Natalia made a protesting sound, but Lucifer glared at her.

"You do as Elliott tells you. I need him in America, and he's quite right. It is too dangerous for you."

"I'm not going to leave her behind; at least not for very long," said Elliott frankly. "I prefer to have her beside me. I can at least see what she's up to."

"You can come home any time you want to," said Lucifer craftily, seeing the glimmerings of consent in Elliott's words.

"I'll let you know. I'll talk it over with Daniel and Jason and get back to you," said Elliott firmly. He took Natalia's arm and, with Nicholas in his pram, they vanished.

"Strong minded young fellow," said Quinn as Lucifer looked at the spot they had been on ten seconds before.

"Not that young," said Lucifer dryly. "In earth time he is thirty thousand years old. In dimensional time he is about thirty, but as he is immortal, who's counting?"

"And the angel?" asked Vespazia tentatively.

"In our terms, just a baby," laughed Lucifer. "She's been around about two hundred years, but as you saw she's a handful, and until she fell for Elliott, she was nothing but trouble. One look at Elliott and that was it. Fortunately it happened both ways. The Almighty wasn't too pleased but they got results. He did try to keep them apart, but recently, well... chemistry is the name for it. You can only keep two people apart so long and they were kept apart too long.

"I'd been training that boy for several thousand years, couldn't let it go to waste. So, in the end the Almighty and myself made an agreement, a favour for a favour and our little problems around the world get sorted by those I trust to do it right. The angel comes to join us permanently and before long the inevitable happens." He smirked reminiscently.

"The Almighty blamed me. I blamed chemistry and the result was he married them. Then their son was born. They named him after me you know," he said proudly, "He's my godson as well.

"Of course Elliott's mother is very grateful to me," he boasted, "she told me if it wasn't for me they might never have had a grandson. I'm welcome to visit her anytime. The rest of them are a stuffy lot. I only speak to them in an emergency.

"I'm just giving you a bit of background Vespazia, just to let you know that Jason has very illustrious friends and the Almighty has been known to speak to him personally."

31

Vespazia turned pale. "And I spoke to him so rudely. You said he had powerful friends. I had no idea how exalted they were."

"Never mind, my dear," said Quinn, "you apologised beautifully and as you had no idea who he really was when you first met him, I'm sure he understood."

Vespazia wasn't so sure. "He brought our daughter back to us and allowed her to reawaken our world. I realised right away he was a vampire. I called him a vile monster. A disgusting creature and killer of humans. I feel so sick at the thoughts I had when I discovered that they were married and had a vampire son. For one brief moment I wanted to kill him and his son. My own grandchild and Jason overheard everything I said. How could he ever forgive me?"

Quinn put his arm around her shoulders. "He forgave you even as you spoke, my dear. He has already planned to make life easier for both of us. He knows that you are confined within the boundaries of our world, and it was only your one good deed in helping to save the devil's kidnapped grandchildren, Simon amongst them, that has given you a second chance."

Vespazia brightened considerably. "He and Allegra did seem thankful that I was able to help. Perhaps you are right. He can forgive me."

"He has already invited us to visit his home, and he said he would get permission for you to stay on earth with Allegra whenever you wanted. Hearing of his connection to heaven, I feel he will succeed. Look what he's managed to get done down here in just a few weeks!"

Lucifer looked at them both appraisingly. "I hope you realise that you will both be called up in the future to assist in our work. Once someone knows of the Astral Council, they are given tasks to perform whenever a suitable one turns up."

"I can't wait," said Vespazia. "I owe you this new life, anything you ask in return I do willingly."

"And I," agreed Quinn.

"I too am ready to help," said Drago, who had been listening to the latter half of Lucifer's explanations.

"Excellent. I shall really look forward to our little chats," said Lucifer enthusiastically, "It's many years since I could talk on a one-to-one basis with someone as old as I am. Most of them are in my domain for negative reasons. I am sure we shall get along fine. For now, enjoy the new life and your new family. I will be back.

Just one more thing, I am most partial to afternoon tea and home made cake!" he said, disappearing in his normal puff of smoke.

"It's a shame he's got such a terrible reputation for evil," sighed Vespazia. "He's not at all unpleasant when you get to know him."

"I feel he is rather selective in his choice of friends," said Quinn, "and I suppose that even the Devil can't be evil all of the time."

"I wouldn't like to bet on that," said his brother, "I'd certainly rather keep out of his way and those relatives of Elliott's from the Fifth Dimension. They certainly seem to make free of your world. I'm off, in case they decide to return."

# CHAPTER TWO

## Bodmin Moor, Cornwall
## November 2002

Allegra arrived in the middle of the night. A loud banging on the front door brought Charles and Katya Fallon racing downstairs to answer it. Charles pulled the door open and there stood Allegra, baby Riva in her arms, Simon by her side,

The car stood – doors open, lights on – outside the gate. Charles left Katya to help Allegra into the house and went to park the car around the back of the house.

Charles was worried. Allegra was his sister-in-law. He was only very newly married to Jason's baby sister Katya. Although Jason was a five thousand year old vampire his sister was pretty old herself. Four thousand one hundred give or take a year He was only thirty-five but had fallen instantly and totally for the beautiful creature who had arrived at his home some months ago. Jason had finally had his fill of his four thousand year old troublemaking sister and knowing that Charles was used to the presence of several teenage nephews dumped his problems on Charles.

The teenage Katya had soon got fed up being ignored by Charles and decided to grow-up. Katya thought Charles looked like a Greek God and he thought she was the most exquisite female on earth. Jason made no secret of how delighted he was to get his sister off his hands.

Only a crisis could have brought Allegra to them in the middle of the night. Katya guided them towards the front room and sat them on the settee. Charles, returning, took the children from her and stood watching.

"Allegra!" exclaimed Katya alarmed. "What's up?"

"Jason's gone!" cried Allegra, tears welling in her eyes.

"Gone?" cried Katya shaken, "As in – dead?"

"NO, no! Gone. As in left, gone, no forwarding address, just went." Allegra became almost incoherent and started crying again.

"So, he is still alive?" asked Katya, starting to breathe again.

"Yes!" wept Allegra bitterly. "He's gone, just left us!"

Charles handed Riva to Katya and put Simon into her other

arm. "Put them to bed, I'll sort this out."

Katya hesitated for a moment and left with her nephew and brand-new niece.

Charles sat beside Allegra, placed a box of tissues in her lap, and put his arm around her. "Okay Allegra, calm down and tell me what has happened."

Allegra stopped crying and wiped her eyes with the tissues, blew her nose, and told him:

"Jason went out tonight like he often does, you know, to feed."

"Ummm! So?"

"He didn't come back. Well, sometimes he is late," she said defensively.

"It was so late I went to bed. There was a note on my pillow and a red rose and a white one. I thought he was being romantic," she added and started to weep again. Through the sobs, Charles gathered that the note was not a love letter.

She handed it to him. It was screwed up and damp. He unravelled it and smoothed it out. All it said was: ALLEGRA, I LOVE YOU. I SHALL BE GONE A WHILE. THERE IS SOMETHING I HAVE TO DO. I'LL BE BACK. JASON.

"Not very informative, I grant you. He does say he loves you." Charles hesitated briefly. "I'll check with Elliott in the morning. Meanwhile, didn't he give any hint where he might be going or what he had to do?"

"Except for the time he has spent on the phone lately, and sometimes just sitting staring into space, he has been the same as always: looking after me, making sure the baby had everything, coming to the hospital when Riva was born. He was so excited when she was a girl; he said every man should have a daughter to spoil. He adored her from the moment she opened her eyes. He loves me. I know he does. Oh Jason, Where are you!" She sounds grief-stricken, thought Charles. He tried to shake her out of her misery quickly, wondering how he would feel if Katya had just disappeared.

"I am sure that he does love all of you, and knowing Jason only something terribly urgent would take him away from you now."

"I keep telling myself that, but it won't take!" said Allegra sadly.

"He's been different somehow since we came back from the Lost World. I know he's afraid of losing me, but I don't want to be

35

lost, so we don't have to worry about that yet. I'm still young. There's plenty of time to work something out."

Katya came back. "Both sleeping," she told Charles as she looked at Allegra who had gone from being a happy laughing mother to a white-faced, bewildered and exhausted sister-in-law in need of comfort.

"It was those vampires; they made him go all peculiar. They told him he had to make choices. He's going to do something silly, I know he is!" She started to shake and cry all over again.

"Crying won't solve anything," said Katya firmly. "Pull yourself together, start thinking positively. He must have said or done something we can use to start tracking him down."

Charles frowned at her, and she nodded.

"Allegra, we'll find him. But there's not a lot we can do in the middle of the night. Come and get some sleep."

Taking her hand she drew her out of the room. Once upstairs, seeing Allegra was in no state to talk, she helped her into bed and told her to get some rest.

"Think of the kids, they need you," she said.

Allegra just looked at her. "I want Jason. I need him," she said simply, but she had stopped crying

"We will find him, I promise!" said Katya "We've got some great people working for us."

Nothing like this had happened to Katya before and she had no idea what to say to Allegra. So she relied on instinct and went with a comforting hug and a confident smile. "Trust me, I'll track him down myself if I have to and I'll murder him when I catch up with him!"

Allegra managed to raise a weak smile at this sisterly remark. "I just wish I knew why he went."

"Maybe we can find out tomorrow – well, later today," amended Katya, realising it was now four am.

She stayed sitting on the bed until Allegra went to sleep.

She went back down to Charles, who was still sitting on the settee looking at the note as if willing it to tell him – why?

"Well, that's a turn up! 'Old Reliable', my dear brother, Jason, has taken off into the blue. That's been my game for centuries. It drove him nuts. I am beginning to know how he must have felt. I'm going to find him," she said firmly.

"Of course we are," said Charles, "but where on earth do we start?"

"With her brother, Alistair," said Katya.

"Him first, then Daniel and Elliott," agreed Charles. "They'll be devastated. I'm not too happy myself."

Katya rang Alistair on his mobile. He could be anywhere in the world, he never told anyone where he was going and seldom when he would be back. It was several months since she had heard him tell Jason that the other side of the world might just be far enough away to stop everyone getting him into trouble and keep him out of hospitals for a while. He had kept to his word and after a few weeks' recuperation had departed hastily for the Far East on the first available plane. Except for a brief return to Bodmin Moor when his sister and Jason had needed his talents when they had ventured into the Lost World, he had spent most of his time in oriental countries.

"Alistair," said Katya when she heard his voice, "where are you?"

"Kuala Lumpur," was the terse reply, then, "Is that you Katya?"

"Yes. How soon can you get back here to Bodmin, to Charles and me?"

"You sound upset, what's up?"

"Jason's disappeared. Left a note for Allegra and just went. Goodness knows where!"

"Are you still there?" asked Katya sharply, as the silence from the other end lengthened.

"Yes, I'm thinking. I have access to a private plane. Give me eighteen hours and I'll be with you. I'll see what I can dig up on the Net before I get there."

"Thanks. I've got bad vibes about this."

"I'll be there," said Alistair and hung up.

Alistair reluctantly dialled the necessary number to take him home. It wasn't that he didn't love his sister and her hippie husband; he just wished that, when they dragged him into their orbit, he didn't keep getting physically mauled. They seemed to forget that he was only a human whilst they were all, without exception, supernatural beings far stronger that he would ever be.

He sighed and made plans to re-enter the dangerous world inhabited by his sister and her vampire husband.

Charles took the phone from Katya and started to ring Daniel Jefferies in Salisbury. "It's only just gone 4.00 am; don't you think we should wait a few hours?" she asked.

"No! Hot pursuit is the order of the night here."

37

Daniel answered the phone on the twentieth ring. "This had better be good," he said sharply,

"This is Charles. Jason's disappeared with no forwarding address. Allegra's here very cut up about it. What's more he left a very strange note and a red rose and a white rose on her pillow."

"Oh, my God! What's he done now?" groaned Daniel.

"What's up?" came a sleepy growl down the phone.

"Big problem," Charles heard Daniel tell Pauline. "Jason's vanished, they need help."

A very succinct swearword echoed down the line.

"Pauline!" said Charles.

"We'll be there by breakfast time. I'll have a full English one," said Pauline.

"See you then," said Daniel, disconnecting.

A similar conversation took place when Charles rang Elliott, who only lived a few miles down the road.

"See you for breakfast." Elliott replaced the phone and, gently shaking Natalia awake, told her what had happened.

"Good heavens! Why?" she asked, bewildered.

Elliott shook his head, but he wondered if he and Daniel might be in possession of a clue.

After a few minutes' thought, he called Ward a vampire friend, in Scotland, who had been co-opted onto the Astral Council when his talents as a tracker had been urgently required to assist Lucifer's search for his kidnapped godchildren. The angel Carlotta had been assigned to him as a go-between by using her angelic powers. "Get your computer into gear, we've lost Jason. Can you track him by his credit card numbers?"

Getting an answer in the affirmative, he called Charles and told him to find the numbers and get them to Ward. This was arranged and, shortly before breakfast, Ward was in possession of Jason's credit card numbers, and began a search which would eventually take him world-wide. To begin with it was fairly easy for a man of Ward's talents.

Jason had used a cash machine in Salisbury the previous morning. He had used his gold card and drawn his limit. He had used another machine the previous afternoon in Winchester, and shortly after had used it to buy a train ticket to London. It seemed he was already preparing to leave a good many hours before he did. On a whim, Ward checked the Eurostar passenger list and found a possible passenger who could be Jason, one who paid cash for his ticket; but it all depended on when Jason left his home in Winchester. Ward checked with Charles and, when told that Allegra has spoken to him at 8.00 pm the previous evening, crossed that particular passenger off the list.

"Check the ferries, don't bother with planes. Jason can't go through the airport security checks, he wouldn't register as human, nor would you."

"I forgot that," said Ward.

"If you're dead you're dead," said Charles unfeelingly. "Get used to it."

Ward snarled furiously at him down the phone. Charles just laughed and hung up.

"I don't believe he's ever left the country," said Charles grinning at Katya. "He's never had experience of flying, that's for sure."

"Neither have I," said Katya. "Planes are not natural, if you are going to fly you need your own wings."

"I suppose you have always gone by sea?" he asked her.

"I'm not stupid. Only birds and angels have wings, and I can swim. There's nothing holy about sea water, you know."

"Not in the twenty first century," agreed Charles.

About 08.00 am, Elliott and Natalia appeared minus young Nick.

"Left him in the Fifth?" enquired Charles.

"He'll be fine there. They both adore him," said Natalia.

"He's spending more time with them than with us," said Elliott moodily. "I miss him."

"Only a few days here and there," protested Natalia, conveniently forgetting their recent trip to China.

They sat around the kitchen table in desultory conversation, unable or unwilling to discuss Jason until Daniel arrived. Katya assured them that Allegra and the children were still sleeping.

About half an hour later, Daniel's Rolls drew up alongside Elliott's. Daniel and Pauline appeared complete with their twins, Lucinda and Penelope and matching buggies.

"Cute," observed Elliott admiringly. "More like you every day, Pauline."

Pauline bared her gleaming teeth warningly.

"Careful, she's only one day off the full moon and so are they," said Daniel, frowning at Elliott.

"That's all right, you can lock them in my cellar," he replied obligingly.

"Aw, gee! Thanks," said Pauline huffily. "A lovely cellar for me and mine,"

"I had it done up especially for you," said Elliott, sounding hurt. "It's just you!" he added with a grin.

Daniel exchanged a dismayed look with Charles, Elliott was taking Jason's disappearance very strangely.

Seeing Pauline and Katya start to get breakfast, they both converged on Elliott, and taking him by the arms, hustled him out of the kitchen.

"What's up Elliott?" demanded Daniel severely. "It's not like you to take something like this so lightly."

"Don't know any other way to handle it?" queried Charles, troubled by his odd humour.

"I'm very concerned, but I think he's gone on a search for enlightenment rather than anything on which we need to fear for his safety."

"What makes you say that?" asked Daniel, almost immediately supplying himself with the answer. "The vampires and their damned prophecies? Allegra's future reincarnations?"

"I think so!" agreed Elliott.

"Where on earth could he go for that?" asked Charles.

"Depends on what or who he goes searching for," said Daniel. "He obviously hasn't consulted the Oracle. He'd want Elliott or myself to go with him. The Oracle lives in a temple in the Fifth Dimension. He's not the only Oracle in the universe, but he is believed to have the knowledge of every curse and prophecy ever thought or written. He has in fact got a very ancient book full of prophecies from the beginning of time."

"So he says," said Elliott sardonically, "He hasn't been too accurate lately. Jason's not too happy with him."

Elliott referred to a prophecy regarding the Dolonquin and his awakening after a million years sleep that the Oracle had completely forgotten. He'd excused his lapse saying that a million years was a long time to remember a curse and its probable outcome. As it had involved his wife, Allegra, Jason hadn't been too impressed by the Oracle and his Book of Prophecies. As Elliott had pointed out Jason was unlikely to seek the advice of the Oracle.

"Is there more to this than Katya told me?" asked Charles, getting worried.

"What did she tell you?" asked Elliott.

"She just told me he had decisions to make that could alter lives and wanted time to think about them."

"I'm afraid it is a bit deeper than that," said Daniel, and told him the full story.

"While Jason and Katya were in the Lost World they were contacted by a group of vampire sages. They were, it seems so ancient that they have progressed to a higher plane of existence. Another level of intelligence. I'm not quite certain how it benefits them, but I presume the ability to appear and vanish at will is a plus for vampires. They drew Jason and Katya into their midst and prophesied that Jason had chosen to travel the wrong path and was about to make the wrong choice for himself and Allegra.

"Now that they have two children Jason intends, with Allegra's consent to make her a vampire. The sages warned against it. They weren't very specific so we can't be sure but they indicated that Allegra and her human soul are indivisible. Elliott and I have a feeling they may be right. When he asked our advice we could only point out his choices. They may have been trying to get the two of them to join them which was what Katya felt they wanted. However Allegra is an old soul. Her soul was lost and travelled through the millennia searching for the man who was meant to return her to her Lost World. When she was born, a prophecy came true, and that man did appear. Jason was considered worthy and fate did the rest. Unfortunately, Elliott and I had to tell him that there was no guarantee that her soul would transfer with her to her new vampire form. At the instant of death for a made vampire the soul departs even though the memories remain. Without a soul that vampire is a cold non-human creature without a conscience. Jason couldn't bear to do that to the woman he adores. He's torn between having her with him for her lifetime and searching for her again someday or risking her leaving him sooner if he makes the wrong decision."

"That's the hell of a choice to have to make," said Charles aghast. "Couldn't we have helped him?"

"Only Jason can make it, and Allegra must agree," said Elliott.

"So, where do you think he has gone?" asked Charles.

"To find the answers," said Daniel

"He's not running away from them?" asked Charles.

"Not Jason," said Elliott roughly. "He runs towards his problems not away from them, and from the sound of that note, he thinks he knows where. It's the white rose that is worrying, the red one is for blood or love, the white one is for death or eternity. He

41

knew exactly what they meant and was leaving one message for Allegra and another for Daniel and myself."

"What are you saying?"

"He told Allegra, with the two roses, that he will love her forever. He told Elliott and myself that he would prefer death to losing her."

"Are you sure?"

"Of course we are not CERTAIN," said Elliott harshly, "but that is one of the meanings of the red and white rose symbol in the supernatural world."

"How come I didn't know that?"

"You haven't been mingling in the realms of the supernatural for very long, until just over a year ago you were a shapeshifter who kept himself hidden from the world. Why should you know?" said Daniel.

"We need Alistair," said Elliott decisively. "Until he gets here we can't track him properly. Ward doesn't know him as well as Alistair does."

At that moment Natalia appeared carrying the vampire baby Riva. "Isn't she sweet?" she said to Elliott.

"Yes, sweet," muttered Elliott, his mind elsewhere. "What on earth made him go now, just when Allegra needs him the most?"

"He waited for Riva to be born. When he saw that everything and everyone was okay, he went. Whatever made him go must have taken a very strong hold on him." Daniel was very troubled by this thought.

"He's running on instinct again, I've warned him about that," said Elliott.

They looked at each other and at Charles. They were all contemplating the problem that had so devastated Jason when confronted by the vampire sages. They had listened to his plea for help, but that was all they could do. They had pointed out the pitfalls in his reasoning but had been forced to tell him that the choices were his. Now he had gone. But where?"

"Well, you'd better eat this breakfast now that I've cooked it," said Pauline. "I shall need all my strength if I'm going chasing around the world after Jason, and so will you."

Ward, in Inverness, still working on their instructions, finally got a lead on Jason's whereabouts. He rang Charles:

"He seems to be heading east into Europe. He's in France right now; I scanned the customs' cameras and was lucky enough to

42

catch him on a digitally enhanced one. He passed through Calais two hours ago, but I believe I caught a glimpse of him getting on the train to Berlin."

"Thanks Ward, keep searching and following his trail," said Charles.

"Who have we got in Berlin?" asked Elliott.

"Kurt Danzigger, he's one of Nick's demons," replied Daniel after a moment's thought. "I'll get his number."

Almost immediately Daniel was speaking to him and telling him the situation.

"It's a discreet find and follow for now," said Daniel. "Watch yourself, remember he is a very old and experienced vampire. He's a friend in need at the moment, we have no reason to suppose he is in any danger, so keep with him but don't intercept."

"Description?"

Daniel described Jason as he had last seen him, his usual hippie self.

"I'm on it my friends," said Kurt. "I shall see what I can do."

"We are grateful. Keep us informed."

He gave him Ward's contact phone number and Alistair's mobile number.

Kurt Danzigger had been a member of the Astral Council for a very long time. He was one of Lucifer's better class of demons. He'd been recruited several hundred years before, but had been forced to go into hiding quite a few times over the years. Several Prussian wars and two twentieth century conflicts had caused him to 'disappear' for a while. He had homes in several cities and Bavarian villages, but his preferred headquarters was Berlin. Although he was a demon he had no trouble after all these years maintaining his human form, but very occasionally under extreme stress he reverted to his demon form – a rather peculiar mixture of horn-headed human features and green lizard-like body. He actually preferred his human form, and was quite at home with it. He had moulded himself in the image of the almost forgotten William Tell, whom he had met centuries earlier. He had rather admired the heroic figure and had even joined him in his fight.

He set off to find Jason on the Berlin train. It was quite a while since the Council had used his services and he was pleased to be in action again. He made sure he had plenty of money and credit cards with him.

On the way to the station, he rang Daniel and gave him his

credit card numbers. "Track me by them in case I can't call you," he told him.

"Excellent idea. Good work, Kurt," was Daniel's reply. "The boy's thinking on his feet," he said to Elliott.

"He's been around long enough!"

Whilst they had been doing this, Charles had used his mobile to speak to his brother Vern and tell him what was happening.

"It's half-term," said Vern. "I'll send David, his nephew, over to man the office phone for you. That'll leave you free to help find Jason and look after your family. Shout if you need me."

"I will, and thanks!"

Vern was dismayed at the news. He had admired the vampire ever since they had first met; his strength and fortitude had helped Vern through a difficult time. He also greatly admired Jason's disrespectful attitude to Lucifer and had been present on a number of occasions when Lucifer and Jason had crossed swords and usually the vampire came out best. He felt very sad that Jason hadn't felt able to consult his friends about his choices.

Elliott had taken Daniel with him and gone to consult some of his friends in the demon underworld about the vampire sages, and then they planned on visiting the Oracle for a consultation. They told Charles they might be gone sometime.

Later that same morning...

Natalia and Pauline had their hands full. There were the four children, Allegra terribly upset and Katya pretending she wasn't.

Charles took one look at them and sent for the only people he knew could help. He rang Alex and Faith Lanyon. An hour later, three witches arrived driven by Alex. As they all walked through the door, he heaved a great sigh of relief and handed the problem to Elisande and Felicity the resident witches of Bodmin Moor.

The problem explained, Alex took over. "We'll transfer to my place, it's a hell of a lot bigger than yours."

"Even Alex's mansion, Simba can't hold all this lot," pointed out Charles.

"My parents are away for a few days. Daniel and Pauline and their kids can use the attic flat. Ten bedrooms should be enough to fit in the rest of you."

"Okay, but we'll have to wait for Alistair, he's in transit somewhere over Europe by now."

"I'll wait for Alistair," said Katya. "I need to be alone to think."

44

Charles looked at her appraisingly, substituted 'brood' for 'think' and decided to stay as well.

"I'd better stay," he told Alex quietly, nodding towards Katya. Alex understood.

Without further ado, Alex arranged to transport everyone to 'Simba.' They all knew it well having spent quite a lot of time there during the past two years.

They left Elliott's car for him and Daniel when they returned, as Charles needed his own car.

Charles and Katya had had a harrowing morning and collapsed on the settee, momentarily worn out and glad to be alone. Then Katya started to prowl restlessly around the house. Charles watched her with concern.

Although Jason and Katya had, in previous centuries and right to the present day, fought like tigers, he was aware that they were extremely close to each other. Like most siblings they fought each other, but each would defend the other to the death if attacked. Parents had never been mentioned by either of them and his relationship with Katya was still too new to bring up what might possibly be a taboo subject. However, in the circumstances he decided to risk a tentative inquiry.

"Stop prowling, Kat. There's something I would like to ask you," he ventured hesitantly.

"What's that?"

"You've never mentioned your parents and neither has Jason, did something happen to them?"

"Nothing happened to them; they just got fed up living on earth and retreated to the netherworlds. After all they were both almost ten thousand years old when I was born, they disappeared into the cosmic dimensions when I was quite young, about 4,000 years ago. They've never been heard of since. We've certainly never seen them, but they are probably still alive. Jason thinks he would know if they weren't. I don't miss them because Jason's always been around for me – but now he's gone as well!"

Suddenly she flung herself at Charles, burying her head in his shoulder. "Don't ever leave me Charles, I couldn't bear it. I don't want to be alone!"

Charles was horrified and held her tightly to him. "Katya, I can't make that promise, you are immortal. I am only a shapeshifter, my lifespan is ordained by mortality."

"No, it's not!" cried Katya. "That, I can change if you ever

45

want it."

"We'll see. But for now, let me assure you that I have no intention of ever leaving you."

Katya raised her head, looked into his eyes and was reassured by what she saw.

"I couldn't lose you both, I'm not that strong."

"Yes, you are," said Charles firmly. "You are strong enough to help Allegra and the children through this. Strong enough to help the others, and strong enough to welcome your brother back when he comes."

"I hope I never let you down, or lose this marvellous opinion you have of me," said Katya fervently.

"You never will," said Charles calmly. "I won't let you."

# CHAPTER THREE

## *America*
Two days earlier...

Lucifer was in New York attempting a coup. A difference of
opinion between himself and another demon called Corazan, who
had previously held a minor position in Hell, had resulted in Lucifer
being forced to remove him from his self-styled exalted position of
'Chief of Underworld Operations' in New York. Lucifer had no
intention of allowing some upstart young demon to interfere with
his plans for New York, which were many and varied.

    Corazan Lucifer's nephew had promptly made himself known to
the chairman of Goodman, Goodhew and May, the joint directors of
the business that Lucifer was interested in and had joined the forces
against him. They had lined up a formidable array of sorcerers,
ghouls, spectres and demons to keep Lucifer and his forces out of the
building. A trio of African witch doctors had summoned Balzahar, a
first generation demon, from the underworld to assist the said
chairman, Austin Goodhew. This had been arranged at the suggestion
of the company's sleeping partner, a recent addition to the firm whose
name did not appear on any records.

    The May of Goodman, Goodhew and May had died some
years before leaving his share of the business to his partners, as he
was unmarried with no heirs. But the managing director, Erskine
Goodman, was also involved with the evil being behind the whole
affair and both he and the chairman were completely in the clutches
of this sleeping partner, whose name they were afraid to speak out
loud.

    When raised to earthly existence, Balzahar, whose powers
were almost the equal of Lucifer's when on earth, with the help of
the unholy trio was able to blunt the strength of Lucifer's will, at
least temporarily. Corazan was able to supply details of Lucifer's
interest in the building to add to their successful intervention. It now
had protective spells preventing demons and vampires from entering
and sufficient wards and hexes to keep the Devil from obtaining
immediate entry – they had effectively locked him out.

    Normally this would have been only a minor inconvenience.

His own power could have got him in quite easily. No one on earth had the abilities and powers that he had, although many had thought they had, to their cost, in the past. But he was reluctant to divulge to those inside the building the extent of his knowledge of their evil, at least not yet. By seeming to be unable to enter the building he hoped to put them at a disadvantage.

The Devil had never been known for his patience and this skyscraper in Manhattan, which was causing him so much aggravation, was beginning to try it to its limits. Those who worked in it were almost to a man and woman steeped in evil. He knew they were up to something but was unable to find out what. He went himself to Pittsburgh, the vampire and demon headquarters, to check with one of his agents that no really unsavoury demons or vampires had left the city or gone missing. He liked to know in advance what type of demon was absent from their usual haunts. His agent had made a tour of the local 'hot spots' but, when she returned, she had no positive information about any of them. He was not pleased.

There was a limit to the amount of evil that Lucifer would tolerate in opposition to himself and the amount that one city could sustain. This one was well past that limit and steps had to be taken to balance the scales.

Lucifer, unless granted a short dispensation from time to time, still had only limited access to earth and even less in America than in England, where he had friendly access. So he was unable to penetrate the barriers right away. This made him even angrier than usual, to think that evil was working against him, the Lord of the Underworld.

He had demons in positions of power and, although as yet they were unaware of this, vampires and humans working for him as he craftily directed their efforts towards his goal. They were none of them aware of his interest in the targeted building, and he didn't want to advertise the extent of his interest by forcing entry himself.

This had bothered him for exactly twenty-five seconds, when he had decided the only way in was to use an angel. Surely the detectors weren't adjusted to check for them?

He had a young, very pure angel on loan to him now that Natalia and Carlotta were otherwise engaged. Natalia was with Elliott, who rarely let her out of his sight, and Carlotta was being trained by Ward to be both his business partner and a member of the Astral Council.

When he got back to New York he had summoned his very new angel messenger and sent her to infiltrate the offices of the people he was interested in. He told her to remain invisible and listen to all conversations and report back as soon as she found out what was going on.

He was still most annoyed that he had been unable to persuade Elliott to help him sort out his problem in America, and it was now almost twenty-four hours since the angel, whose name was Bianca, had entered the building. He had not heard from her since. She had disappeared. This was not a normal occurrence. Angels could make themselves scarce merely by dematerialising back to heaven, or at the very least Middle Earth. Known irreverently to the angels as the waiting room, it was in reality, a reception room for the dead. It had a number of entrances but only two exits. A white door led to heaven. No prizes for guessing where the black one led. Lucifer came and went through this door frequently. Because a split second could mean life or death angels sometimes sought refuge there for a brief time to allow a dangerous moment to pass or to wait further orders, Lucifer felt it necessary to look there. He had even had them arrive in Hell to take advantage of his protective custody on more than one occasion. So the absence of his messenger was a catastrophe.

He was by now seriously alarmed at her extended absence. A lot of things could have happened to her. There were so many vampires in America, he was having trouble keeping up with their exploits. As he had told Elliott, they were in a completely different category to English vampires, who were in the main so reasonable and inconspicuous that they were accepted in human society as friends and equals by those who knew of them and as neighbours and friends by those who didn't. In other words they lived completely normal lives alongside mortals. He was very much afraid, however, that his very new angel might fall foul of these evil American vampires, and had instructed her in the art of instant dematerialisation and self-defence. He had also sent her on one or two innocuous errands to make certain that she knew her way around America, where he was intending to use her services to act as messenger between himself and the vampires Elliott was supposed to be recruiting.

American vampires, as he had told Quinn and Vespazia some months earlier when he had begun to plan his assault on the multitude of evil American troublemakers, were completely different to those his agents in England were used to. Other than a few who wished to live quietly and undisturbed, they were mean, vicious killers and preyed on humans, demons and almost anything that moved. The balance was well and truly on the side of evil and had to be changed. It was a great pity that his usual agents were resisting his efforts to get them to work in America for a while.

Consumed with fear for the lost angel he made a final all out effort to find her. He had made several sorties into the vampire and demon underworlds of New York, and tried to find out what was happening in the building he had told her to check, and had found nothing. He had sent a message to a rather unpleasant vampire in Salt Lake City who lately, for some unknown reason, had stopped killing and feeding on humans, to come and search for her. He hadn't had time to research the reason for this evil vampire's change of lifestyle, but was confident that he would come in time. For now he intended to make use of him in the current crisis. As yet he hadn't turned up and quite possibly wouldn't, so Lucifer made him an offer he couldn't refuse and waited for him to arrive.

He had also found a firm of secretive supernaturals who had accepted a fee to find out what was going on in the building. His other contacts were all mysteriously missing and had left messages that there were urgent supernatural occurrences to check out on the West Coast, namely California. Now he was beginning to get really worked up at the loss of his angel and Elliott's reluctance to help.

He made several attempts to find her over the next few hours but without success, what's more the Great Entity had noticed that she was missing and was breathing down his neck for results.

By now he was so seriously concerned at her protracted disappearance that he returned to England to pressurise Elliott and his friends to help find her.

He appeared in Elliott's home to find it empty and promptly visited Jason and Daniel in turn with the same result. Getting himself into a really fiery fury he went to Charles and Katya.

Result? Before he had a chance to open his mouth, he was regaled by Katya on her brother's disappearance.

"He a big lad, he's not made it through five thousand years of existence without learning a thing or two about self-preservation. He can wait awhile," said Lucifer grimly, "I've got a big problem in the Big Apple, and I've got a much greater problem than a missing vampire. I've got a missing angel."

"I need Elliott and Natalia, to help find her and I need the druid as well if Jason is not here," he said cryptically.

"Daniel and Elliott are off looking for Jason right now, and I can't see Elliott letting Natalia go," said Charles. "Not with one missing angel already."

"Tell him to leave her behind this time, I need help. He shouldn't mind helping to find this angel, after all he once needed help finding his own."

"I'd forget using blackmail, if I were you," said Charles, "he's already in a funny mood with Jason gone. What's more he told us he may be gone some time."

"I can't wait for him to get back, tell him to come to New York's Central Park and bring help. Some of you shapeshifters can come. Tell him you are to use a spirit path, it's quicker." He vanished immediately.

"He must be in a hurry," commented Charles. "He forgot the puff of smoke."

Elliott arrived alone in New York about two hours later, and, as predicted by Charles, was not in the best of tempers and in a hurry to return before he even got there. His foray into the demon underworld and a second trip around the surface gathering-places of its various demonic inhabitants had produced no clues as to Jason's whereabouts, and no sightings had been reported of unusual vampire activity. As yet he had no opportunity to consult the Oracles.

Lucifer was pacing up and down in Central Park attracting a great deal of attention as he had forgotten to make himself invisible.

Elliott hadn't, and tapped him on the shoulder, "You are creating a disturbance. You'll have the police here soon if you don't calm down."

"It's about time one of you realised your responsibilities to the Council," fumed Lucifer, as he corrected the situation and became invisible to human eyes. "I've got more trouble than I can handle."

"Who's fault is that?" snapped Elliott. "I'm not the one who caused chaos in heaven and got chucked out to cause chaos on earth. You wanted chaos, you got it."

"I am supposed to cause it, I agree, but I am now the victim of my own training methods. They were supposed to help me, not take over and try to run the world themselves. I won't have it. I'm Lucifer, Satanic Master of Hell and Beyond, my word is law and you have to help me prevent further encroachment on my preserves."

51

"In other words, as usual, get you out of the sewer you've dug for yourself!" said Elliott crudely.

Lucifer frowned darkly, his lips thinned ominously and his eyes turned coal black. An unaccustomed shiver of fear went through Elliott as the Devil seemed to look into his very soul. He sent a vicious thought into Elliott's mind.

"If anything happens to that angel because you refused to help find her, you and the rest of your team will spend the rest of eternity in a special hell I shall devise just for you. There will be no reprieve. I'll give you until tomorrow morning, and if you aren't here so be it."

He showed Elliott a small portion of what awaited them. A dark dank cave with the entire team chained to walls dripping with water. Even the angels were there. The shapeshifters and their families were being tossed in turn into small furnaces. Elliott, Jason and Daniel were pinned to the walls by molten steel spikes, watching, as Lucifer himself was torturing their wives. Fiery flames shot up around the three women. The screams were horrendous and the sight sickened Elliott. He was unaware that his own blood could run cold but that is exactly what happened.

"You've made your point," he said harshly. "Enough of the future prophecies. You have obviously got a personal interest in this angel. What's the problem, and what do you want me to do about it?"

Satisfied that Elliott now realised his place in the scheme of things in New York, Lucifer calmed down.

He told Elliott the truth. "I don't suppose I'd ever be able to bring myself to do that to any of you. But it is within my power to do so. I was showing you what could happen if necessary," he said coldly. "Just because I use your services to keep this world on an even keel, doesn't mean you are immune from my punishments if you cause me grief."

"Okay. I got that part," said Elliott recovering his equilibrium. The shock had been rather a bad one. Even though he knew that he was probably equal to Lucifer's threats. It was by no means certain that he could overcome him in a duel of strength or wits.

"I'm sorry that my attitude to your problems has caused you such aggravation," he said judiciously, "Of course I'll help you find the missing angel. Where do you want us to start looking?"

Lucifer, now he'd got his own way, attempted to rationalise his thoughts:

"The balance of power here in New York is so far over on the side of evil that it is going to be a hard job to even the scales. There is no one in America who could even begin to tackle the problem, and I should not even be here, but the Great One knows I have to find the angel. She's in trouble somewhere, but she is hidden even from me. He doesn't know where she is either. He is as concerned about her as I am.

"I shouldn't have to point out to you the danger an angel can find herself in without any warning. This angel is a baby when it comes to danger; she wouldn't have a clue what to do. It was entirely unintentional but it seems that I unknowingly sent her into danger. Now she is missing and I have to find her."

He regarded Elliott sternly. "You know He expects you to do the right thing. So I tell you what I'll do," he said abruptly. "I'll send a special envoy to track down Jason and find out what he's up to, and you and some of your shapeshifting friends can come to New York and help find my angel. While you are here, you and Daniel can set up my new organisation."

"Nice try, Nick," drawled Elliott, "But I'm not ordering anyone into danger, I'll ask them to come. That way the choice is theirs, and I'm not telling them what you showed me. I want them to come willingly, no blackmail."

"Any way you want to play it." Lucifer was more agreeable, now that he'd won the argument. "Just see that they volunteer."

He told Elliott his two main items of concern, the building he'd sent the angel to reconnoitre which he thought might house the culprits and his traitorous demon nephew Corazan, who knew enough about him to assist the enemy. Then he sent him back to Bodmin Moor to get organised, and returned to his own domain to check that all was in order there.

Since the stressful incident almost six months ago, when he had had to review his security arrangements, Lucifer didn't leave the running of the place quite so much to his minions. He made more frequent checks on his inmates and visited the demonic dimensions more frequently. He also inspected the Elite Guards and their barracks from time to time on a random basis. He didn't intend them to get too complacent about his trust in them. His chief assistant Rannoth was controlling all of this from his computer console in the fortress, but even he had to have time off now and again. Rannoth was too good an assistant to lose. Time away from the computer was essential and Rannoth did enjoy the hands-on approach of visits to the torture chambers from time to time. As Rannoth had told him, computers do break down and personal contact was necessary to reinforce their authority. Lucifer was in complete agreement with him on this and, as today was Rannoth's day off, he had to stay there himself.

Not for the first time, he wondered if he ought to let Rannoth liaise with the earth forces sometimes. He might enjoy the change. He decided to see whether the Great One would consider it.

Elliott arrived back in Alex's home about twenty seconds after the devil arrived in Hell. Everyone was there waiting for his return.

"What's the big deal?" asked Katya, "Surely he can find his missing angel; he's all seeing, all knowing and all powerful, isn't he?"

"It appears that someone has usurped his powers, he's been shut out of the buildings he wants to enter. He can't get in to find this angel, if she is there of course," Elliott reported dryly.

"Someone has enhanced the spell that keeps him from walking on earth without permission?" asked Daniel surprised. "That's a new one! I don't like the sound of it. Only a very powerful triumvirate could evoke that much magic. Possibly three Voodoo Priestesses?"

"To the power of three. I hope you are wrong, that's a very potent combination of spells if they cast them." Elliott and Daniel exchanged grim nods as he went on to tell them of Old Nick's offer to find Jason for them and the urgent need of their presence in New York.

Pauline looked at Daniel and raised an eyebrow, "We could go now, but I'm wolfing tonight as you know."

"We'll all go tomorrow," said Elliott, mindful of the twenty-four hour deadline and not entirely certain that Lucifer was in his right mind over the disappearance of this particular angel. "I need you all there, and apparently the services of a druid are highly desirable."

He caught Daniel's eye and the two of them headed for the door.

"There's something a bit odd about his concern for this angel. There's no hint of humour in his actions. He's deadly serious about this. He threatened all of us with eternity in hell if we didn't come to New York by tomorrow morning. He meant it. I kid you not, my blood almost froze as he showed me what was in store for us. I'm letting you see, but the others can never know." He showed Daniel the same picture shown him by Lucifer of their incarceration.

"Can't say I'm too happy to see that sight, either," admitted Daniel, as shocked as his friend. He was as worried as Elliott. "He's never gone that far before. If it's that urgent, we'll send Vern, Diana and Pauline immediately after sunrise, and tell Katya and Charles to leave as soon as Alistair gets here to liaise with us all. But I still think that you and I should consult the Oracle," Daniel said firmly as they walked back to the lounge. "If they need anyone else in a hurry, Lance and James will have to go."

Elliott nodded his approval of this plan, adding that, "Tally can stay here until we find out whether it is safe for an angel in New York."

Natalia frowned at this but caught a disapproving look from Allegra. She remembered her promise to herself, to think before she acted. "All right," she said reluctantly, "I agree to let you find out first."

Elliott raised his eyebrows questioningly at this instant acquiescence. "I know you worry about me, and it sounds like an unpleasant place for an angel to be," she admitted. "I'll wait until you tell me it's safe to come."

He would have been more than a little annoyed if he had noticed the fingers crossed behind her back.

# CHAPTER FOUR

Bianca had entered the building as directed by Lucifer. She had thought herself undetected and had prowled around the building, quite invisible for several hours but had not overheard one single suspicious conversation, the entire staff seemed hell-bent on outwitting each other to earn more money and the gratitude of the chairman of the board. Finally she had thought it necessary to gain access to the office of the chairman. The only way was to use her powers and whisk herself through the barriers to his office. Unfortunately the chairman, who had a paranoid fear of vampires, had fitted the approaches to his corridors of power with the latest digital electronic surveillance equipment. The angel was detected in the office of two senior accountants who worked on the same floor and became visible on the electronic cameras. A laser force field was activated and the angel was severely injured by the rays. She collapsed unconscious on the floor.

The four security guards and the two accountants who arrived on the scene had, of course, no idea of the true identity of the intruder. When she came round she was lying on the floor and tied hand and foot. She tried to dematerialise and was terrified to find that she could not; she sent a plea for help to the Almighty, which went unheard. She realised that she was cut off from help.

A serious crime occurred. One they would pay for heavily in the hereafter.

They tortured her for what seemed like hours, but, as she knew nothing, she could tell them nothing. Even worse was to follow. Intending to throw her from the window, they had to untie her. She managed to evade them and remove her jacket, which although torn she still wore. She partially unfurled her wings but was again overwhelmed and captured. They tied her up once more, this time face down on a table. They fetched a fire axe from the corridor and hacked off her wings. Deep cuts were left in her shoulders and back and feathers littered the floor. Yet still, somehow, not realising that she was an angel and presuming she was a demonic mutation, they left her lying on the table in a pool of angelic blood, and went to find the janitor to dispose of the remains. They had the sense to know that a de-winged body lying of the sidewalk would ensure unwelcome publicity.

She lay there unconscious for a very long time...

However, help was on the way. A vampire, with judicious use of a hang-glider and darkness, had infiltrated the building sometime after she was captured. The smell of blood and a trail of feathers led him to her.

As evil as he was, he was badly shaken by what he saw. He took one look at the feathers, which remained on the mutilated wing, and knew at once what he was looking at. He hoped the Almighty who commanded her kind was aware that, although he was a vampire, the angel would be quite safe with him and his friends. He untied her arms and legs, removed his long jacket – all American vampires seem to wear long, black leather coats – and covered the broken and bleeding body. He pulled out his mobile phone and summoned the only help he was sure would come at once. Whilst he waited he took out his camera and photographed the scene, making sure to get plenty of the blood and feathers and ensured that the background was recognizable as the executives' offices. He managed to get a couple of family photographs and the chairman's portrait in the pictures. After all, he was an industrial spy. One never knew when a spot of blackmail might be profitable.

He had taken out the alarms to the roof when he had entered. Although he was almost afraid to touch her, he knew it was time to leave and gathering her gently into his arms, he retraced his steps to the roof. After looking carefully at her he had decided that calling 911 was not appropriate. He stood waiting in the shadows, he still held her as he felt unable to put her down. In any case he was, as was most of his kind, very strong. She weighed little more than the feathers that had littered the room. Someone was in for a surprise. He hoped they would worry a great deal about being found out.

About ten minutes passed by and a helicopter approached the roof. It touched down just long enough for him to climb in with his burden. Moments later it bore them both into the air and away from the building.

"I've blown my cover; they are bound to have picked me up on their scanners. I didn't disable the rest of the cameras once I smelt the blood. We'll have to find another way in. For some reason they didn't come rushing to see what was happening either. This is an angel. They've hacked her about a bit. I couldn't leave her there. I know I'm a vampire but I could never harm an angel. They beat her up badly. Bastards!" he reported savagely.

"We'll have to take her to your place," he told the pilot. He looked grimly at the other two passengers. "She's an angel, and needs help. How could anyone even touch an angel?" he was thunderstruck at this atrocity.

"I wonder where she comes from?" asked the female passenger.

"I should think that's obvious," said the other coldly, "if she's an angel they work for the Great Entity."

"I'm not too sure about that," said the pilot, "I've heard a rumour that Lucifer is interested in this building!"

"You means she might be Lucifer's angel?" asked the vampire, shocked as he looked down at the rescued angel. "This will cause a panic in low places."

They flew on in silence to the rooftop landing-pad of the pilot's home.

The pilot's name was Travis. He was also a vampire. He flew mostly at night of course, and mainly flew his friends around the hunting fields. He wasn't a particularly nice fellow either, but fell a long way short of complete evil. The two passengers were Cassidy and Cybel, brother and sister witches from the dark side; they didn't have many friends either, but they did follow the code of witchcraft reasonably well.

The vampire who had rescued the angel was known to his friends as Sebastian. It wasn't his real name or even the one he had used in past times, but he was one of the new breed of vampires who had elected to live alongside humans and lead as normal a life as was possible for the death dealing, bloodsucking monster he had been. The four of them ran a secretive business enterprise. They were industrial spies and they had the best credentials possible to carry on their trade.

He was one of the people Lucifer wanted Elliott to start off the American organisation with. He was already working for Old Nick although, as yet, he didn't know that.

The helicopter landed five minutes later on the roof of Travis's apartment block. Once inside his rooftop apartment, where he lived, the angel was placed gently on his bed. Sebastian gently unwound his coat from the bloodstained body. They were shocked at what they saw.

Cybel moved towards the bed and felt for a pulse, the angel was scarcely breathing, just an occasional short shallow breath. "Faint pulse, no brain thoughts", she said. "This is bad."

Sebastian turned the angel gently onto her side and showed the others the stumps where the wings had been. Cybel placed a pillow under her shoulders so that they wouldn't touch the mattress.

"Less painful," she said as she and Cassidy started chanting healing spells. She pushed the vampires out of the room. "This is witches' work," she told them.

"Go and find the ones who did this. Punish them, kill them," said Cassidy harshly.

The vampires went back to the rooftop. They hardly dared speak the thought in both their minds.

"Did they?" asked Travis.

"I don't know," said Sebastian, "they certainly roughed her up badly. Besides chopping off her wings, it looked as if they tortured her. I don't think they did anything else."

"God help them if they did," said Travis, then realised what he had said. "I don't suppose that he will be very pleased about this. I hope he doesn't think we did it!"

"I think he would know that we didn't," said Sebastian, "and I hope we are wrong in thinking what we are!"

"Even if they didn't, she looks as if she was beaten really badly, she's covered in bruises and finger marks," said Travis, sounding sickened by the idea.

"If they did, I wouldn't like to be them," said Sebastian viciously, "but I'd like to be there when he punishes them."

"I would too," said Travis feelingly.

"If they did do that to an angel," said Sebastian, still unable to actually say the word, "hell is too good for them."

"I have heard that there is a place worse than hell," said Travis cautiously.

"Oh? I hope so!" said Sebastian.

During the night Lucifer had returned once more to England. Elliott and Daniel were both at Simba by now. He woke them both, impressing upon them the urgency of his need. He accepted their explanation that they had to stay until after the full moon and would join him the next day, and that they had already convinced the shapeshifters to come to New York. He expressed his satisfaction, opened a portal to New York for them, and vanished back there again.

While he was away he had thought of a way into the building he was interested in and had inspected the sewer system in detail. As the most powerful being in the universe, bar One, he could have razed the building to the ground, but hesitated to do so as the angel might be inside. He would effectively be killing her if she were. He could have caused a lightning bolt to make a hole in the side of the building, but held back for the same reason. Normally it would have amused him to have a disaster hit the building. A fire, a shift in the foundations, even a meteor strike was quite within his powers. It might however hit the angel, so all these options were out of the question. He ground his teeth in rage and began a search for a weakness in the protective grid.

It was with great satisfaction that he had eventually found an unprotected entrance and made a thorough search of the entire place. On reaching the penultimate floor, he found the blood and feathers and his face changed. His head sprouted horns, his eyes turned red and flames darted from his finger tips. His hair was a fiery halo around his darkened and satanic features, his huge black wings unfurled, and the Lucifer of Legend stood breathing fire as he waved his hand and the blood and feathers were cleansed from the floor and walls, until no trace remained of the atrocity.

Satisfied that the perpetrators would be terrified when they found the mess cleared away and quite possibly give themselves away, he rose through the rest of the building into the night sky. The trail of fire and brimstone lit up the night sky for miles. Whatever the rest of New York may have thought, the people who were still up and looking through their windows thought the end of the world had come and Nemesis was upon them.

Hovering some way above New York, he put an invisible wall around the building, which allowed those who worked there to enter the next morning, but no one would be allowed to leave. There it would remain until he got the names of the guilty ones who had dared to harm an angel. Lucifer would deal with this himself.

He left immediately for Middle Earth, where he faced the Great Entity.

"They are mine," he told Him, courtesies dispensed with on this occasion. "This is personal."

"I know." The Great One looked gravely at him. "I give you leave to punish them as befits their crime."

"They will suffer the torments of the damned forever. But no torment that I could devise would ever be as vile as their crime." Lucifer looked grim. "You can trust me on this one."

"I know I can," said the Great Entity as Lucifer vanished.

Now she was out of the building, Lucifer found the location of his angel quite easily. He was after all THE demon from hell, and the witches and the two vampires who had found her had no reason to hide her from him.

He knew the shapeshifters would arrive shortly and made sure the portal was centered on Travis's rooftop. Remaining invisible he checked the angel's condition and was really alarmed. The two witches looking after her seemed competent, but very young.

He materialised beside the bed, giving the witches a terrible fright, Cassidy reeled back and Cybel almost fainted.

"Don't be alarmed." Lucifer told them coolly. "I've come to check on the angel. Good work you two, keep it up. You keep chanting those healing spells and you'll have her back on her feet in no time."

He leaned over the bed and lifted the sheet, wincing as he saw the poor damaged body and wings. His face had not changed from the moment he realised what had happened and he knew it would not until she was avenged.

He looked at the witches. "Is there anything else I should know about this?" He indicated the purple finger marks and bruises all over the angel's arms and legs.

"We don't know, we won't know until she comes round," said Sebastian harshly from behind him, appearing in the doorway, followed by Travis. "Who are you?"

Lucifer swung around to face them.

Travis sucked in a breath. "It's Lucifer, Satan himself. Now we are in trouble!"

"Not necessarily, my boy, unless you did this!" said Lucifer calmly.

"Good God! We didn't do it," Travis hastened to reassure him. "Sebastian here found her and called us up to rescue them. We brought her here to try to heal her. We didn't know who she belonged to, and we couldn't call 911. Who'd believe we'd rescued an angel?"

"Excellent thinking, my boy," approved Lucifer. "Good work recognising an angel. You have earned the thanks of the very highest realm of all. For now let's just leave it like that. You keep her here until she is well again, and I'll nip off and inform higher authority you've found her."

He left again to inform the Almighty. Afterwards he materialised on Bodmin Moor in the home of Elisande and Felicity, his two favourite witches. This was because some years before they'd saved Elliott's life.

After a short chat they packed and left for Simba.

As Vern, Diana and Pauline prepared to leave for New York, Elisande and Felicity arrived. "Mother's going with you," said Felicity, "she had this premonition that she is needed there."

"Okay by me," said Pauline. "Elisande is a very astute witch. If she says she had a premonition, we need her with us. I have great faith in her powers."

Pauline referred to a time when, after being badly injured in a fall on Bodmin Moor, Elisande and Felicity had saved her life. They had stayed by her bedside chanting healing spells and Lucifer had arrived to make sure no one found out she was a werewolf.

Felicity handed her mother a large pouch. "Essentials," she said smiling.

Pauline nodded approvingly; potions and other witchy things were, in her opinion, absolutely essential.

All four stepped through the portal and were on the way to New York.

"I've never been to New York," said Diana.

"It's nothing special," said Pauline, who had been several times. "A very nasty type of vampire lives there. Totally depraved and evil. It's a good job I'm a werewolf; they don't like us, we taste awful," she snickered.

"Thanks Pauline, we really needed to know that," said Vern swearing beneath his breath.

"They like the taste of lynx," she added slyly. "I'll have to protect you."

"What about jaguars?" muttered Diana.

"You'll be okay, vampires and jaguars are pretty well equal in strength," said Pauline judiciously.

"Thanks for the battlecraft lesson," said Vern sarcastically. "Any GOOD news you can tell us?"

"The food's okay," said Pauline sounding serious. "Providing it's not you on the menu."

Vern growled ominously and Pauline shut up.

Elisande moved forward. "Be quiet, children. I've several spells I can use to shut you up."

Pauline and Vern exchanged a look and both laughed.

"Only passing the time on the journey," said Vern.

Elisande gave him a very piercing look and he pretended to be scared.

They arrived in New York about two hours later, "It seemed

longer," commented Diana, as she noticed dawn about to break.

"It was the entertainment," said Elisande. "Very boring."

Vern and Pauline snickered at her.

"Where are we?" asked Elisande as they stood on the roof of a skyscraper. A helicopter stood nearby – and two men who looked absolutely stunned to see four complete strangers stepping through a black hole in the sky just above their rooftop.

Vern moved easily across to them, followed by Pauline, "Either of you two fellows seen Old Nick?" he asked them.

"He means the demon of the underworld, Lucifer," explained Pauline, as they seemed to be in a state of shock.

Diana and Elisande moved more cautiously towards them.

"He disappeared some time ago," said Travis. "Who are you? Where have you come from?"

"Oh, Dear me!" said Pauline sounding amused. "Didn't the old nuisance tell you we were coming?"

"Obviously not," said Sebastian coldly.

Vern looked closely at Sebastian. "He'd give Elliott a run for his money," he observed to Pauline. "I don't suppose he smiles much either."

Sebastian ground his teeth and vamped. Six-foot two inches of well muscled athlete who worked out, Sebastian was a good-looking man. His coal black hair, copper skin and hawk-like features he owed to his Indian forebears. In his vampire persona he was a dangerous looking demon. Dark skin stretched over a prominent forehead drawing his yellow slanted eyes and slightly pointed ears into a fierce mask. This with his sharp, shining white fangs and clawed fingers would have terrified a normal woman. If he had hoped to surprise or frighten the four of them he was sadly mistaken.

"Ooh, look Vern! A vampire," cooed Pauline girlishly. "Ain't he adorable?"

Sebastian growled menacingly as Vern and Diana both laughed, and shifted into a lynx and a jaguar.

"Nice pussies," said Pauline as she stood hands on hips laughing at them. Sebastian and Travis both glared at her.

Travis had assumed vampire mode fearing attack.

Elisande stepped forward.

"Do stop playing with them, Pauline!" she said crossly. "You know you can't eat them."

Sebastian and Travis gave the elderly lady a second glance.

Seeing the twinkling eyes, and noticing for the first time that Pauline was grinning from ear to ear at them, they slowly resumed their human form.

"I suppose Lucifer is behind this?" asked Travis.

Elisande placed her hand on his arm. "My dear boy! Who else?"

She pointed towards Pauline. "This is Pauline. I should warn you not to annoy her in any way; she's a werewolf, a particularly trying one. Only her husband can control her and he's busy elsewhere at the present time. These two are Vernon and Diana, shapeshifters as you can see. My name is Elisande. In England I am the Crone of the Witches, here I am just another witch."

"Welcome to you all," said an amazed Sebastian, who had never met a werewolf in his very long lifetime.

"We badly need the services of an experienced witch," said a stunned Travis. He led them from the roof to the bedroom where the angel still lay unconscious.

"Help's arrived from England," said Sebastian as they entered.

The shapeshifters remained in the doorway. The witches stood back as Elisande and Pauline approached the bed and surveyed the injured angel. She still lay unmoving on the bed.

"She's an angel, they hacked off her wings and possibly even worse!" said Cybel.

"What's worse?" asked Vern looking at Sebastian.

Sebastian conveyed a soundless message and Vern looked sickened. "To an angel?"

"Bastards!" said Pauline. "Bloody bastards!" She lifted the sheet so that she and Elisande could see the extent of the wounds and gasped as she saw the broken body and bloody wing stumps. Elisande looked away and nodded to Vern, who came for a closer look. "That's worse than what happened to Natalia," he whispered to her.

"You're right, this is a lot worse, but the treatment is the same," she replied.

"This should bring Elliott in a hurry," was his only comment as he turned away in disgust that anyone could treat an angel like that.

He motioned to the vampires to join Pauline, Diana and himself in another room. "Leave the healing to the witches for now."

"The bruises are beginning to fade a little," said Cybel as

Elisande rolled up her sleeves, "but our spells are not powerful enough to heal an angel, we can only ease the pain."

Elisande took a closer look at the wounds and became the efficient healing witch everyone recognised. She took out her herbs and potions and indicated that Cassidy and Cybel assist her in preparing the necessary spells and incantations.

Pauline looked around her and decided she was the senior council member present and would have to take charge in the absence of the others.

"Who did it? Where and when?" She asked Sebastian briskly.

He told her.

"Lucifer," yelled Pauline, "Get here on the double, we need help."

A puff of smoke heralded the arrival of the grim faced Lucifer of Legend, "Oh, good! You are here already!"

"This is a bad one!" said Pauline urgently. "We need Elliott for this. He was going with Daniel to consult the Oracle, but Daniel must go alone."

Lucifer agreed with her, but was mindful that Elliott had proved very reluctant to come to America.

"Tell him a female angel has been badly damaged in an attack," said Vern, "That will bring him in the blink of an eye. You know that."

"Jason can wait," added Pauline, "as you said, he can take care of himself."

Lucifer vanished reappearing ten minutes later with Elliott and Natalia. Elliott had relented and allowed Natalia to come with him when he had heard of the badly injured angel. She had promised to stay by his side, or at the very least where he could see her. Elliott took one look at the angel in the bed and became the Dark One again. Elliott was so vividly reminded of the day not too long ago, that his own angel, Natalia was abducted and assaulted in an attempt to distract him from his purpose in ridding the shapeshifters of Bodmin Moor of the demons tormenting them. Seeing the broken and bloody body of his adored wife he had changed instantly into the dark avenging angel prophesied to save them.

Even he had not known until that moment just what the powers he had within him. The former angels of the Fifth Dimension had long ago given up their wings so he had never expected to have any. Nowadays his huge black wingspan and dark visage was a terrifying sight. He seldom made use of his enormous powers, thought by some to be equal to Lucifer's.

He did however make use of the wings.

Natalia looked down at the angel, great golden tears pouring down her face. Elliott stood behind her, the great black wings almost filling the room. Flames curling around his head, eyes like glowing coals he cursed aloud. He held Natalia's shoulders in a tight grasp. She turned into his embrace.

"Find them," she ordered. "Do what you must."

Lucifer and Elliott stood one each side of the bed, their wings outstretched as they planned retribution. Lucifer leaned over, put out his hand and gently touched one of hers as it lay outside the covers; his face was a raging fury as he held the tiny hand in his own.

"Awesome!" breathed Cassidy, the warlock.

"Those two are related somewhere!" said Vern softly to Diana. "Look at them!"

"His grandfather is the same generation as Lucifer. Perhaps they are brothers, perhaps Elliott is his nephew," whispered Diana.

Vern regarded then narrowly. 'It would account for Lucifer's personal interest in him', he thought to himself.

Elisande stepped forward, "Lucifer, you are wasting time here when you could be trying to find out who did this. You and Elliott start searching. I'll stay here and keep up the healing process."

Lucifer spoke in lowered tones to the witch, "Keep her free from pain, I cannot heal her or give her back her wings, only divine intervention can do that, and only when all who harmed her are dead or in hell can she be restored."

Elliott heard as well. He was only too aware that this was true. Only when those who had harmed his angel had been killed by Jason and himself had Natalia been restored. He held her tightly, remembering.

Lucifer looked meaningfully at Elliott and nodded. He too remembered. He knew Elliott would never forget.

Elisande also knew, she had been there and seen it all through a crack in the door. She had never revealed her knowledge, but she could do a lot to help.

She took over and motioned for Cassidy and Cybel to assist her.

"Now," said Elliott, "where do we start?"

"This is Sebastian, the fellow I want you to persuade to become my chief asset in America," said Lucifer, "and this is

Elliott, my associate," he added coolly.

"Promotion," whispered Vern to Diana, and received a quelling look from Lucifer,

By now both of them had furled their wings and resumed almost human features, thought they still looked dark and deadly.

Elliott looked shrewdly at Sebastian. "Seeing things a little differently now you've seen an angel?"

Sebastian knew when he'd met his match, but didn't give an inch.

"I see you've got one of your own there," he said, glancing at Natalia.

Elliott raised his eyebrows.

"Golden tears, a dead giveaway," pointed out Sebastian.

"This is my wife, Natalia," said Elliott, surprised to know that Sebastian was aware of an angel's ability to cry golden tears, "and yes, she is an angel."

"Demons allowed to marry angels now, what is the world coming to!"

"How did that come about?" asked Travis, intrigued. "Special dispensation?"

"Personal approval," replied Elliott dryly. "Performed the ceremony himself."

"My word!" whistled Sebastian, awed despite himself. "We do have friends in very high places."

Travis eyed Elliott with respect and gave him a wordless salute.

"Enough of the chit chat," said Lucifer, "you've got to find a way into that building for all of us. I realise now that, quite possibly, I got in because they hadn't repaired the alarms that Sebastian cut off. They've probably got half a dozen banshee and scree guards watching the place by now. You'll have a hard job spotting the Scree. They look just like gargoyles, small and ugly, but alive. Probably sitting on a desk like a paperweight or hanging on a wall, watching for intruders and listening to every word you say. They don't take up much room when they arrive in hell, and that's the only good thing about them. I've circumvented the spells they had around the building earlier and replaced it with a far more powerful one of my own. I could get in undetected by using my powers, but they'd soon 'see' you. Even with me, you lot would be detected instantly. The vampires would be eliminated by lasers. Can't have that, I need you all."

67

"I wonder if they've got a defence against druids and shapeshifters?" mused Vern out loud.

"Worth a try," said Sebastian. "I don't know any American druids and there are not that many shapeshifters either. We are more into vampires, demons and witches."

"Well get on with it," said Lucifer snappily. "I'm wasting good vengeance-planning time. I've got to get back to my place. Everything goes to hell when I'm away too long. You know what I mean," he added majestically as they all looked less than amused.

"Moron," muttered Pauline, "we've only just got here."

Lucifer looked daggers at her. "You're here to work, not to waste time chattering." He turned to her menacingly, frowned and disappeared.

"Pain in the neck," remarked Vern as Old Nick vanished.

"He seems very cut up about that angel," said Diana. "Do you think he's going soft on all humans and angels?"

"There is certainly a strong element of personal interest in this one." Elliott sounded surprised. "He doesn't normally get so involved, and he must have had permission to keep coming and going so openly."

"Okay, so he had permission. That means you know who is involved," said Vern. "We'd better snap to it and do as we've been told."

Vern and Elliott consulted with Sebastian and decided that Vern and Diana would take a chance and make a survey of the building and if possible get in to the ground floor.

"They are certain to have replaced the surveillance cameras, and the scree will detect vampires, but they may not detect shapeshifters, after all technically you are human," said Sebastian. "Sorry we can't go with you, but, well daylight and all that."

Diana grimaced. "We'll have to remember you American vamps can't go out by day. Our English vamps only need dark glasses and they can go anywhere."

"Except on planes," chorused Pauline, Elliott and Vern.

"Nice for them," commented Travis. "We'll have to learn the secret."

Vern and Diana surveyed the building Lucifer had directed them to enter. "We are not dressed for this," said Vern, looking objectively at himself and Diana. "We'd stand out a mile."

Diana eyed Vern's jeans and sweatshirt and her own jeans and anorak, and agreed. "We'll have to smarten ourselves up a bit." She dragged him off to the shopping mall she had noticed earlier.

"I hope you brought your gold card," she said looking at the prices.

Vern sighed. "Don't worry, I can afford you."

"And yourself," she added.

Both emerged some time later with all the accessories necessary to pass as successful New York top-floor business executives.

"We need references and impressive sounding introductions to even get past the door," said Diana, having noted that all who entered without passes were questioned and asked for identification. "Let's go back and see Sebastian."

"No problem," said Sebastian. "Travis has excellent contacts for this sort of thing. He can get you some gold-plated references."

Travis took their photos, got a sample signature from each and departed. They heard the helicopter take of a couple of minutes later.

"Thought he couldn't travel by day?" said Vern.

"Specially adapted chopper, and flying helmet," replied Sebastian.

"So, you aren't totally restricted to the dark?" said Pauline thoughtfully, "There are definite possibilities opening up for you. Given some modifications to your vehicles I think we can work something out. What do you think Elliott?"

"I was sure Nick said American vampires were susceptible to sunlight, burned them up in fact," mused Elliott.

"Looks like they conquered the problem," said Vern. laconically, "Cars with dark smoked glass and underground car parking."

"Oh, very useful!" said Elliott. "I suppose that's why they all wear wrap around sun glasses and long dark coats?"

"Extra protection, I guess!" said Diana

"Seems like it," agreed Vern.

"I don't think we'll have to do too much alteration to their lifestyle," said Elliott. "Perhaps a few mobile homes or campers are the answer. After all, Jason practically lived in one for years until he married Allegra."

"We'll get onto it right away. Our American vampires must be able to travel by day and if possible walk around without drawing attention to themselves. What is more they can start using the death roads for long distance travel. We'll have to check for demon

69

dimensions first, of course."

Sebastian nodded at this likely scenario for the future, but told them the present was what needed some action.

"Vern, you and Diana are alone on this one. We can't risk our own agents, they are programmed into the security systems," said Sebastian.

"We'll manage," said Diana,

They were still waiting for Travis to return when Lucifer, who had arrived again, came from the bedroom, followed by Natalia.

"I thought you were off to do a building check for Old Nick," said Natalia.

"It's not the sort of place you can just breeze into," said Diana, "It's high-security prison from the looks of it."

"Unpleasant comparison," said Vern. "I prefer 'fortress', if you don't mind."

"It doesn't sound a very good proposition," said Elliott.

"Got it in one," said Vern. "It's a high-risk infiltration."

"High risk or not, it's got to be done," said Lucifer, incensed at the delay. "I can't think what you are hanging around here for."

Vern glared at him. "You want a job done right, you've got to have the right credentials. When we've got them, we'll go."

"Fair enough," said Lucifer calming down. "Just don't hang around when you do."

"It seems to me," said Elliott, "we need to get your American assets, organised as soon as possible. Things are moving much too slowly for my liking."

"Where's this vampire from Salt Lake City you were so sure would come? I don't see any sign of him yet," said Pauline.

"Yes, are you sure he's coming?" asked Vern. He turned to Elliott. "I reckon Nick made him up to make us think he'd got more help than he has."

"I'm the vampire from Salt Lake City," said a voice behind them. "Who sent for me?"

Vern and Sebastian turned swiftly to face the door.

A man stood in the doorway. Tall, blond, extremely good-looking, he smiled pleasantly at them all. Vern and Sebastian exchanged a look. Lucifer stepped forward. He had assumed his devilish, cavalier look. No wings, smoke or flames, just the black and red suit and cape.

"Don't be fooled by the blond good looks," said Lucifer. "He really is the most vile evil creature it has been my pleasure to meet.

Just think of the most evil deeds ever done and multiply them by ten. I look forward to getting him, one day."

"You'll have a long wait," he snarled nastily at Lucifer. "What's with the fancy dress?"

Lucifer drew himself to his full height and unleashed a finger of flames towards the vampire. Vern leapt in front of him getting scorched in the process but saving the vampire from annihilation.

"Careful Nick, we may need him," yelled Pauline. "Wait a week or two and then fry him."

Elliott stepped in front of the vampire and helped Vern to his feet. "Go and get Elisande to do some repairs. Enough of the theatrics. Keep a grip on it, Nick." He sounded annoyed.

The vampire looked disdainfully around the room. "Load of amateurs," he said scornfully. "I'm off."

He was immediately seized by Lucifer in a steely grip and held at arm's length. Lucifer looked him in the eye and asked. "Just exactly who do you think I am?"

The vampire shrugged. "You look like the Devil, but I don't think he's allowed on earth."

"Well, you got something right," said Vern, on his way through the door. "But only the first part."

The vampire's jaw dropped, as did most people the first time they saw the Devil in person.

"Speechless are you?" asked Lucifer nastily. "'Fancy dress' is it? Took your time getting here, too! I guess you are having a bad day. WELL! IT'S GOING TO GET WORSE IF YOU AREN'T CAREFUL!" he yelled, incensed. He pinned the vampire to the nearest wall with his right hand. The vampire recovered slightly and pushed himself off the wall, wrenching Lucifer's hand from his throat.

Lucifer in a bad mood is not a pretty sight. His face darkened ominously again and he breathed out fire and smoke, his fingers curled as he forcibly restrained himself from barbecuing the insolent vampire.

The vampire, mindful of his brush with death, now chose his words more carefully. "I suppose those dreams I had telling me to come to New York were from you? How was I supposed to know? I must be the first vampire ever to get a message from hell. It's hardly the place I'd want to get in contact with, now, is it?" he asked reasonably. "You can't blame me for ignoring it. I only decided to come when the ticket for New York appeared on my table and I thought something strange was happening. A voice told me that I was wanted in New York, so I came. When I arrived this morning the same voice told me to come here because an angel was in trouble. I got a picture in my mind of feathers and blood. So, where is this angel who's been hacked about?"

Lucifer put his face right up to the vampire's: the vampire didn't flinch and stood his ground.

"Be careful what you say. That angel was on my business when she got hurt, so this is personal. No one messes with any of my angels and gets away with it, and particularly not this one."

"What's so special about this one?" he sneered. "An angel's an angel in my book. I've never seen one and I don't expect to. I'm going to the wrong place to meet an angel."

"That's my business," said Lucifer sharply as he seized the vampire and once more threw him against the wall, "and watch your mouth!"

Everyone was watching with interest this vampire who seemed to be taking his life in his hands every time he opened his mouth.

"What's your name?" asked Travis gravely. "I like to know the names of those who die in my building."

"None of your business," said the vampire stonily.

"His name's Snake," snarled Lucifer, glaring at the object of his fury. "And death is closer than he knows."

The vampire, now known very aptly as Snake, looked daggers at Lucifer and pushed himself off the wall. "You called me here," he said contemptuously. "Now show me to this angel."

"See for yourself," said Sebastian, opening the door and pointing towards the bedroom. Snake strolled down the hall. He opened the door indicated and, walking into the room, shouldered his way past the witches who tried to prevent him reaching the bed. He stopped abruptly as he reached it and stood very still, looking down at the angel for a long time. After a while, he reached out a hand and pulled down the sheet covering the now naked body and saw her blood seeping into the sheets. For such an unpleasant man he was very gentle as he turned her completely onto her side. When he saw the mutilated wings and bloody cuts on her back, he sucked in his breath and swore quietly and viciously. Very carefully he replaced her comfortably on the pillow and drew the sheet back over her. He placed his hand on hers and seemed to be saying a prayer. The watchers were amazed at these actions, seemingly so at odds with the vampire's previous unpleasant nature.

When he turned away from the bed and faced those standing in the doorway he was in full vampire mode. Elliott and Sebastian were both taken by surprise; he was the most savage and evil-looking vampire they had ever seen and they had seen plenty.

"I wouldn't like to meet him on a dark night," whispered Natalia shuddering. "He's really scary." Elliott gave her a sharp look.

"Snake, my boy," said Lucifer as he noticed the change in the vampire's attitude. "I'm glad to see you appreciate the enormity of this act."

"I had no idea," said Snake harshly. "It's desecration. That's what it is. No vampire would ever do a thing like that, not to an angel."

"Now you know why we are all here," said Lucifer.

"For revenge, I hope," said Snake.

"A little more than that," replied Lucifer, breathing smoke again.

They all adjourned to the lounge once more, except that Elliott noticed, from the corner of an eye, that Snake had slipped back into the bedroom. He strolled back to the door and opened it slightly. Snake was standing beside the bed gazing down at the young angel. He shrugged off the young witch who tried to move him away and, hooking his foot around a nearby chair, placed it beside the bed and sat down without taking his eyes off the angel for an instant. Elliott was rather surprised to see him pick up one of the angel's hands and kiss the fingertips before placing it beneath the sheet. He then touched the tangled hair with a gentle hand and leaned over to kiss the bruised and battered lips, very gently indeed.

Elliott shook his head puzzled for a moment then smiled to himself. Another reformed vampire in the making, he thought. As he turned to go back, Lucifer stood behind him. Lucifer stared at Snake with a venomous look on his face.

"Keep an eye on that situation," he said to Elliott. "I'm not too happy about it."

"About what?" asked Elliott, feigning ignorance.

"You know very well! Bianca's not for the likes of him."

"I'd say he's got it bad," said Elliott. "Why not wait until she wakes up and see what happens?"

"If she wakes up, she'll do as I say," snarled Lucifer.

"But will she really want to?" asked Elliott.

"Don't you encourage him, or her!" warned Lucifer darkly.

73

"Wouldn't dream of it." Elliott told him blandly.

Lucifer was enraged. "I don't like your attitude. Be careful, I still have the edge when it comes to a one-on-one situation!"

Elliott looked contemptuously at him. "You can't be sure of that. Not now," he said meaningfully. "I'm the Dark One, remember?"

Lucifer scowled threateningly as he departed, and managed to get the last word:

"Would you bet your life on it?"

Elliott strolled back to the lounge and noticed some missing faces. "Where's Tally?" he asked Vern sharply

"She's gone shopping with Pauline, there's no human food in the place," said Vern.

"Hell's Teeth!" ground out Elliott bitterly. "Doesn't she ever listen to anything I tell her?"

"Not so's you'd notice," Vern told him candidly. "She doesn't listen to anyone, full stop."

"One day she'll go too far and end up dead." Elliott was livid. "She's got no idea what sort of danger is out there. I told her she could only come if she stayed where I could see her at all times. She deliberately waited until my back was turned and went."

"She'll be okay, she's with Pauline," said Diana, wondering what the fuss was about.

"And how long will she stay with Pauline, if she takes it into her head to do something else?" asked Elliott his rage increasing.

"You should have learned to control the wayward minx, years ago," said Vern caustically. "She runs rings around you and you let her. You have indulged her every whim. No wonder she has no idea of danger, you've wrapped her in cotton wool and shielded her from any harm."

"I promised the Almighty I would never let any harm come to her," groaned Elliott. "How can I stop her?"

"It seems to me that more harm will come to her from letting her have her own way than if you clamp down on her and stop her leaving the confines of heaven for a while. Personally," said Vern strongly, "I lean towards putting her over your knee and administering a sharp smack to her rear."

Elliott looked at him for a minute and then smiled ruefully. "If I thought it would work, I would even try that."

"Try the silent treatment when she gets back," said Diana. "It might make her think twice about doing it again."

74

"Where's the Salt Lake City vampire?" asked Vern, noticing for the first time that he was missing.

"Willing the angel to recover," said Elliott dryly.

"Oh, my! I wonder what Lucifer will do about that?" said Vern.

"He wants me to discourage the association," replied Elliott deadpan.

Vern laughed out loud. "And you with your own angel problem to sort out."

"Quite," agreed Elliott. "I'll be far too busy."

Diana looked at them both. "Why do I get the idea you approve?"

"There's nothing like a reformed vampire for wreaking vengeance on behalf of his mate," said Elliott grimly.

"They have got a bit of a reputation in that department," agreed Vern.

"Tell me about it," said Sebastian coming up behind them.

"I don't think you need to be told," said Elliott.

"No, I changed sides a long time ago," sighed Sebastian. "Now I know why."

"Do I sense a story there?" inquired Vern.

"Not really," shrugged Sebastian. "One day, I woke up and decided it was futile to fight the system any more and started to live as a mortal just to see if I could, and do you know what? It was a darn sight easier that living as a vampire. I already knew Travis owned this building and did tours with his chopper and we joined forces. Soon the witches came to work for us and we became a damned good team. We all earned enough to live in luxury, we like this way of life. We have to have blood to survive, but we have even found ways not to kill. Just take enough to live."

"I rather fancy that your change of lifestyle has been noted and approved where it really counts," said Vern, trying hard to stop laughing at this earnest confession of a vampire.

"I think they have been very strong-minded and brave," said Diana admiringly. "It can't have been easy for them. They haven't had the thousands of years of practice that Jason had."

At the mention of Jason, Elliott frowned, took out his mobile phone and keyed in Alistair's number.

"Where are you?" asked Elliott as Alistair answered.

"I'm here, at Simba. Allegra's in a hell of a state."

"How are you getting on with tracking Jason?"

"I'm leaving it to Ward and this German agent for the time being, I'm waiting for Alex to come back with his disks which may not be until tomorrow. In the meantime I want him to switch on the computer so I can download what he was working on. Jason disconnected from his modem before he left. I've got no phone link until it's re-attached."

"Who's doing it?"

"Alex. He says he thinks he is competent to hook up a disconnected phone!"

Elliott laughed at Alistair's astonishment. Alex now retired had been a pilot in the navy for several years, but few people gave him the credit he deserved for the accomplishments he had acquired during his service. Elliott had the feeling that someone had even told him that Alex had flown helicopters. This, in view of what he had in mind for the American vampires, gave him another of his brilliant ideas.

"When he gets back, tell him to bring Faith and come to New York, but not until he's got a good idea where Jason is headed."

"Don't worry, man. I'll find him for you. But, you will have to bring him back," said Alistair. "Only you angelic types can materialise all over the world, us humans need planes and trains and whatnot!"

"I'll get Nick to spirit you to wherever you want, if you find him," said Elliott obligingly.

"Thanks, but no thanks!" said Alistair shortly. "Every time I see him I get shivers up my spine."

"What makes you think you are the only one who gets them?"

"You too?"

"Often!"

"Very inspiring!" said Alistair sourly. "What a hero!"

Elliott laughed. "Is Daniel back yet?" he asked changing the subject.

"No."

Daniel had gone alone to consult the Oracle when Lucifer had demanded Elliott's immediate presence in New York.

Elliott cut this conversation short as the helicopter was heard overhead. A few minutes later Travis entered the room with a briefcase.

"This is the best I can do at such short notice, but my contact assures me they are genuine visitor permits from the partners. They also gave me a file on the security access to the ground floor. There

76

are several traps for vampires and demons, but they haven't got any for shapeshifters other than the banshee and the Lecc. They may be able to detect the fact that you are supernatural, but let's hope they don't find out what you are. The Lecc are a family of spirits able to pass through the portals to earth from their spirit dimension. They have been around since before time. They are extremely large, not giants but big enough.

"Unfortunately they actively hunt cats. You'll have to be careful."

"Oh, great!" moaned Vern. "I love it when certainties become possibilities."

A low growl came from behind him. Sebastian was still waiting to drive them to Goodman, Goodhew and May, the firm in question. The one, which Lucifer was certain controlled all the evil and criminal supernatural activities in New York. The one containing the men he wanted Elliott and his team to dispose of for harming his angelic messenger.

Diana grabbed Vern and pushed him into the bathroom. She reappeared a short while later dressed as she felt a top female executive should be. She was followed by Vern still looking extremely unhappy.

"Keep that look Vern," said Travis unexpectedly. "You look exactly like the male assistant to one of our top female bosses should look. Downtrodden and put upon. Our female executives have rather nasty reps. Quite evil, some of them," he added with relish.

"Right!" said Diana haughtily. "I can do that!"

Vern assumed a hangdog expression and reached for the briefcase Travis had given them.

"Okay, boss! I'm your lowly assistant, I'll grovel very convincingly when you snap at me!" he whimpered.

Diana flicked his shoulder with her hand and glowered at him.

Sebastian rolled his eyes heavenwards. "Are all shapeshifters like you two?"

"No! We are the cream of shapeshifters," Vern told him. "Lucifer only employs the best, he'd never send out any second class acts."

"Jokers!" Sebastian groaned. "Let's go."

They all three headed for the underground car park.

# CHAPTER FIVE

"This should be fun," muttered Alex as he and Faith walked into the now deserted home of Jason and Allegra.

"Why isn't Katya helping us search for clues to his whereabouts?" he asked Faith, not for the first time.

"How should I know?" asked Faith, "Just tell me where to start. Katya said his office is at the back of the house, through the dining room." They walked down the long hallway, and found the dining room, the office door was open.

"My God, what a mess!" groaned Alex. "Alistair said he was an untidy sod and that's an understatement. Doesn't he ever tidy up?"

Faith was staggered. There didn't seem to be a square inch of the desk and tables that was not covered by papers, notebooks and loose-leaf files. There were papers scattered on the floor around his swivel chair and the fireplace was full of screwed-up, rejected papers and envelopes.

"Perhaps you had better hook up the phone first," she said tentatively. "I'll find a bag or something and put all that stuff in the fireplace into it. You find the disks Alistair wants. Then we'll search the desktop."

Possibly because space is limited on board ship, Alex was a very tidy man. His home was always neat, whilst still being a welcome place for his friends. He was quite frankly appalled that Jason should want to create this mess. He looked thoughtfully at the chaos and decided that Jason must have been searching for something and, having found it, left immediately. To put his theory to the test, he strolled into the dining room-cum-lounge, They were elegant and tidy, but looked lived-in and cared for. He wandered back to the office.

"Leave the fireplace for now," he told Faith as he ran up the stairs. He walked down the hall, opening the doors of several bedrooms and bathrooms as he went. He knew Katya's as soon as he opened it. It was girlish and tidy and empty of any personal belongings. He knew she had been gone some time and had left little of herself behind. The next room was obviously unused and had a computer set up in one corner, possibly an old one kept for emergencies. He found Simon's room and it was a little untidy, evidence of a hasty departure was plain. He looked and found the baby's room. It was beautifully tidy; the baby had not yet used it. He opened the connecting door and found to his surprise that whilst being obviously the room of the vampire and his wife it also contained a carved cradle.

It was not as untidy as he had been led to believe. True, Jason's clothes were rather untidily placed on an ottoman, some shirts hung over a chair, his track shoes were beside the bed and, as the wardrobe door swung open, there was evidence of Allegra's hasty departure. He realised that Alistair had exaggerated the untidiness and now understood that the spartan room he had thought a spare room was in fact Alistair's, and he was comparing his excessive tidiness with Jason's slightly untidy habits. He went downstairs slowly and thoughtfully.

"I think we should disregard talk of Jason's untidiness. It was a vast exaggeration. Jason wasn't anywhere near as untidy as Alistair led us to believe."

"We are going to have to go through every inch of this room, Jason was searching for something and when he found it, he left! I only hope he didn't take the evidence with him."

"It's going to take days," said Faith with certainty.

"I'll start with all this paper around the computer, you start on the desk," sighed Alex.

For the next two hours, all was silent except for the rustle of paper.

Faith went to the kitchen and made tea. She had thoughtfully brought milk and tea bags with her and they ate the sandwiches she had made.

Shortly after they resumed the search, Alistair rang Alex on his mobile and told him to switch off the computer. He had downloaded all relevant data and was studying it. So far he had found nothing of any significance. The resulting conversation brought them no further forward. Alistair was frustrated at not having the disks, and Alex had to keep searching through the papers.

About twenty minutes later, Carlotta appeared in the room and asked for the disks. She laughed as she reported that Alistair had told Ward to send her for them; as she was supposed to be a messenger, she might as well make herself useful.

"Alistair is getting a bit bolshy!" said Alex shortly. "He's been around Old Nick more than is good for him."

"Don't knock it," said Carlotta. "It's good that he is thinking of us all. I like being included in what is happening."

"Well come back here and help us search," said Faith. "We are up to our ears in bits of paper."

"Glad to," said Carlotta and disappeared, only to rematerialise about ten minutes later to help with the search.

Several hours later she gave a grunt of surprise, and smoothed out a piece of paper she'd 'rescued' from the fireplace.

"I've found something," she said, bringing paper to Alex. Faith joined them.

"It's a tracing of a map of Nepal. The pass into Tibet from the Nepalese side," said Alex. "How odd."

"Do you want me to check it out?" asked Carlotta.

"Only if you want Elliott to go berserk," said Alex succinctly. "No angels allowed into danger without his full approval. So, no. Not yet!"

"We need to have a little more than a map to go on. Although Kurt did say he's definitely heading east." Faith sounded mystified. "I'm taking a break."

Alex and Carlotta carried on searching.

"Here's something else." He exclaimed as he leafed through a desk diary.

"What's that?" asked Faith reappearing with a tea trolley.

"It's an entry from last July. He's written a very neat entry about Katya and Charles living together and in big letters it says, 'must find and tell parents – grandparents are essential'." He picked up the phone and dialled Charles's number. Katya answered.

"Katya," asked Alex abruptly, dispensing with preliminaries, "Where are your parents? Are they still alive?"

"Nobody has told us they are dead," she replied not seeming very interested. "We haven't seen them for four thousand years, so anything could have happened to them. Why the sudden interest in our vampire ancestors?"

"I've found an entry in Jason's desk diary for last July, it mentions them and the need to tell them about you and Charles. He's also made a note about them being grandparents."

"Good God, the man's gone off his rocker," said Katya. "Whatever's made him go all mushy after all this time?"

"Nostalgia?" queried Alex.

"Pull the other one," snorted Katya rudely. "He's not the type." Carlotta had been listening to this exchange and shook her

80

head. Alex raised an eyebrow. "Anyone who adores his wife and children like Jason does is definitely the nostalgic type," she whispered. "He's gone to find his children's grandparents," she added sagely.

"You know, she's probably right," agreed Faith.

"I'm bringing these diaries back with me, I've got the last three years. I'm also bringing every scrap of paper in this room."

"It's a waste of time, but if you must, then bring them."

Carlotta left for an exchange of views with Ward and said she'd be in touch.

Faith and Alex locked up Jason's house, switched the alarms on and set off back home.

# CHAPTER SIX

Vern and Diana entered the offices of Goodman, Goodhew and May in the middle of the lunch hour. Quite a number of customers were coming and going, and the staff seemed to be taking their lunch time breaks. The security guards only gave their passes the most cursory glance and waved them through. Diana was nagging Vern for making a hash of parking the car and generally making herself objectionable. As they got into the lift, Vern looked admiringly at Diana. "Clever girl," he whispered. It had been her idea to come at lunchtime. "I just hope that spell Lucifer put on to stop the guilty parties and others from leaving the building doesn't stop us," he added.

The lift ascended to the twenty-eighth floor and everything was just as Sebastian had informed them. Each suite of offices on this floor had an anteroom for the secretary and a large office for each of the accountants. Diana strode briskly down the corridor, her heels tapping loudly on the marbled tiles, followed by Vern attempting to look downtrodden. Halfway to the room the angel had been discovered in, the door opened and a tall but elderly man emerged.

"Get a move on, don't dawdle. You know I hate to be late." Diana snapped irritably to a visibly cringing Vern.

The man eyed Diana appreciatively as she drew level and sneered at Vern as he passed. Vern hid his amusement and hurried after Diana as the man disappeared around the corner to the lifts. She drew level with the door they were seeking, opened it and hustled Vern through.

"Come on," she said loudly and impatiently. She nodded to the bemused secretary, who stared speechless as Diana strode brazenly across to the inner office then waited for Vern to open the door. "I'm never going to bring you again, can't you ever do anything right?" She scowled at him as he edged past her into the office.

"Men!" she said to the secretary. "I don't know why I bothered to hire him!"

By this time the secretary was too scared to even ask why they were there, and hurriedly carried on with her own work.

Diana banged the door shut and raised her voice once more. "Don't hang about, get those cameras working properly!" she ordered in hectoring tones. Vern angled a mirror in the direct line of the observation camera and let it reflect the light from the window into the lens, thus blinding it temporarily.

They were assuming that this room held the secret they sought or at least a clue to it. Vern took out a camera and, opening various filing cabinets with a spell given him by Cassidy, started to photograph anything that seemed interesting. Diana loaded several disks from a locked drawer on to the computer and downloaded it to Alistair. She rifled the desk drawers and found a diary, and got Vern to film the entries for the last seven days and tomorrow. Replacing everything as they had found it and removing the special reflecting mirror they left the room, with Diana still lecturing Vern on the necessity for speed in his line of work. They repeated this performance in the next office and, forty minutes later, they left. Vern followed her past another shell-shocked secretary and down the corridor to the lifts. They reached the ground floor and left the building fifty minutes after they had entered. Diana was still ranting at Vern for dawdling and making her late. They were sure they had attracted so much attention to themselves that no one had even suspected they were in the building for illegal purposes. As they reached the sidewalk, Sebastian drew up to the curb and they climbed in.

Diana sank back in the seat and heaved a sigh of relief, Vern was shaking with laughter as he sat beside Sebastian. "Don't ask me how," Vern told him as he recovered, "but it worked. She was the most objectionable female you could possibly imagine. If I didn't know she was making it up as she went along, I would be terrified of her."

"If I hadn't been so terrified, I might have enjoyed that," gasped Diana. "I want to go home. I still don't feel safe."

Sebastian returned them to Travis's home with the utmost speed.

Vern was still chuckling to himself as they reached the apartment.

Gloomy faces met them as they entered.

"What's up?" asked Vern in dismay.

"The angel's had a relapse," said Travis in a hoarse whisper.

"What does Elisande say?"

"She's gone with Cassidy to find the chief witch in these parts. She's hoping she might be able to help. She's very worried, she needs more potions and spells than she's brought with her to ward off the Angel of Death. The local witches may have some ideas."

"Where's Elliott?" asked Vern sharply. "He's got influence with the angelic realms."

"He's gone to somewhere called Middle Earth to consult with higher authority," said Travis.

"We haven't caught the culprits yet, I don't think that will do much good," said Vern.

"Well someone's got to do something," Snake said, appearing from the bedroom still in vampire mode and seemingly very angry.

Diana looked at him horrified. "You'll scare the poor thing to death if she wakes up and sees you like that." She told him candidly. "You're the most scary vampire I've ever seen."

"Can't help that," said Snake shortly. "My psyche's taken a bashing today. I'm having a crisis of conscience or something. I keep seeing the angel with wings outstretched and her hands pressed together. She's calling for help and nobody can hear her except me. I can't do anything and it bothers me. I even said a prayer myself and I'm not supposed to be able to do that. Is it any wonder I'm in a bad state?"

Sebastian bit off a sharp reply at a frown from Vern.

"Had something very similar happen to me once," said Vern sympathetically, "bloody painful it was, too."

He rubbed his stomach reminiscently and grinned as Diana told Snake. "I hadn't met him at the time, but I heard that there was more blood on the walls and floor than there was in him and his brother."

Snake was momentarily diverted. "Enemy action?"

"You could say that," agreed Vern, "but it was torture at the time."

"Yes!" said Diana. "He annoyed Elliott and paid the penalty."

"I thought he was your friend?" Sebastian was surprised by this knowledge.

"Not then, but I am lucky enough to be alive to call him friend now."

Snake wasn't totally convinced. "He didn't look all that strong to me."

"Looks can be deceptive. He and his friend Jason disposed of seven dark demons in the space of a few seconds not all that long ago. It was awesome!" said Vern.

"You weren't here when he and Lucifer showed up. They've got huge black wings that fill a room. Their eyes are red and spit fire and smoke. They're from the dark side, man!" Travis told him.

"Beware the Devil and all that?"

"I'd say you got that about right," admitted Sebastian.

Snake nodded as he resumed his bedside vigil. The witches had given up trying to stop him.

"He's got it bad," said Sebastian to no one in particular.

"Angels do have this reputation for saving souls. Ours is a busy little bee," said Diana, smiling slightly.

"Yours?" asked Snake, overhearing, and coming back to the lounge.

"Natalia, Elliott's wife, slightly naughty angel," explained Diana. "Leads Elliott the hell of a dance. He lets her; he worships the ground she walks on."

"Never as dull moment in our part of Cornwall," she added happily. "I'm glad I joined the Astral Council. Seeing that angel has brought back to me just why we exist; but don't worry, Elliott will work something out, and if he doesn't Daniel will come up with something"

"What's this Astral Council exactly? One of you mentioned it before," said Travis.

"Never heard of it," said Snake, who had decided the conversation in the lounge was worth listening to, and was keeping an eye on the bedroom from the doorway.

"I reckon you lot are all in by now," said Vern seriously, "you've had contact with the higher echelons when you've met Lucifer and Elliott. Jason and Daniel are off somewhere at the moment, but the four of them are the big guns. Meeting any of them means automatic membership. That's how me and my brother got in."

"Exactly what do they do?" asked Travis.

"Supernatural investigations and soul-saving missions," Diana explained obligingly. "Great fun if you like crawling around in the depths of the earth, falling off cliffs, toting guns through the netherworlds, fighting battles deep underground, saving kidnapped children and helping angels escape from evil demons and hell spawn. Like I said, never a dull moment."

"She loves it," said Vern. "So do I."

"Sounds like a lot of hard work to me," said Snake.

"It'll grow on you," said Diana.

Snake shook his head in disgust and went back to watching Bianca.

Lucifer materialised on the opposite side of the bed and glowered, darkly at him. Snake ignored him.

Lucifer hissed furiously at Cybel, "Why isn't she getting better, and where are the other witches?"

"Gone for more help with healing potions," snapped Cybel. "We are doing our best."

"You are the one who sent her into danger," snarled Snake. "If you can't heal her yourself, find someone who can."

"There's so much damage," said Cybel. "It's taking time to heal."

"Get human doctors," said Lucifer. "I'll dispose of them afterwards."

"You can't do that," cried Cybel. "That's murder."

"Not when I do it," said Lucifer coldly.

"Even you couldn't be that despicable," said Diana, who had listened from the doorway.

Elisande arrived back. Pushing them all aside, she looked hard at Lucifer. "Go away. Leave us witches to do our work. She won't die, but she will be a long while getting well unless you catch the culprits."

Cassidy followed her into the room, assisting a very old lady who leaned heavily on his arm and a stick.

She moved slowly and painfully to the bedside, put her hand on the angel's forehead and muttered a short incantation.

She looked at Lucifer. "She wants to go home," she told him.

Lucifer looked sick, if a demon can be said to do so.

"Tell her everyone is willing her to get better and that we are hunting down the ones who did this. Tell her all of heaven is calling her name. Tell her nothing is more important to me than that she gets well again."

The old crone whose name was Eurydice and the chief witch in America, looked rather weary. "I know the truth, so do you. Tell her what she wants to hear."

Lucifer leaned over the angel and ran his hand lightly down one pale cheek. Bending even further he kissed her forehead gently. What he whispered as he did so not one of them heard, but the crone smiled grimly and nodded her head as, with one last look at her unsmiling face, he disappeared.

"What was that about?" asked Snake.

"Nothing that need concern any of you," the crone dismissively.

Elisande had caught the essence of the thought processes and looked very alarmed, but at a silent command from the older witch, bit back whatever she had intended to say.

"Not in our province," said the crone. "We are here to help the healing process, not to make judgments or to change what is, or shall be."

"That sounds complicated," said Vern.

"Not for us," said the crone.

Vern decided to change the subject and told Diana to get in touch with Alistair and find out where Daniel was. "I think we need him right now," he said.

"Who needs me right now?" A grim voice spoke behind him.

Vern span around. "We do. Elliott's vanished to Middle Earth, and Pauline and Natalia haven't got back from a shopping trip they went on hours ago. They sent their shopping home in a taxi. They've gone off on some business of their own, we can't spare anyone to look for them, and they could be anywhere. Lucifer keeps popping up and he says this angel can't be cured until the ones who injured her are in hell. We all know that's right, of course."

"Anything else I need to know?"

"We'll explain the fine details later. As of now, I think you are in charge," replied Vern.

Daniel moved further into the room and looked at the Angel. He too placed his hand on her forehead and stood immobile as he probed her mind.

"She did it? There must be some mistake!" He sounded surprised.

Vern noticed several changes in Daniel's expression as he continued the mind probe. At first horrified, then concerned, finally relieved.

"Tortured and desecrated, not the final indignity, thank God!" he commented aloud.

A few minutes later he withdrew his hand. "Good Heavens, what a mix up!"

"Well?" asked Vern. "What was all that about?"

"This is not as straightforward as I had hoped," he murmured almost to himself. "I know who did this. I don't know why!"

He turned to the vampires. "You vampires can pick them up tonight," he told Travis. "I'll give you their descriptions"

"They'll soon tell us why," growled Snake. "I can't wait to get my hands on them."

"Just make sure they talk first," said Sebastian harshly.

Snake just looked at him.

Daniel looked at Elisande. "She won't die, she's heard the two voices she needed to hear to stay with us." He sounded relieved.

"Which two?" asked Vern intrigued.

"Not at liberty to say," said Daniel. "Now what about finding Pauline and Natalia?"

Elliott reappeared in the lounge and, hearing voices, moved to the bedroom.

"I'll find them," he said grimly. "There's something I have to take care of."

Vern raised his eyebrows questioningly.

"Tell you later." Elliott sounding really cut up about something.

"You want me to take over here?" asked Daniel.

"Do whatever you must, send for reinforcements if you need them." Elliott vanished.

"Lot of help he was." Snake said in disgust.

"I think you'll find that I can deputise quite adequately." Daniel sounded amused.

"Okay! What's the plan?" said Vern once they were all back in the lounge.

"We've got all that stuff we brought back with us to go through," chipped in Diana.

"Get to it then," said Daniel. "Don't wait for me to tell you."

"Here," said Vern, handing her a file stuffed with papers, "get sorting."

"What are we looking for exactly?" she asked.

"A strong enough reason to get rid of a winged messenger." Travis was alarmed. He recognised the urgency of finding a solution purely by the illustrious nature of those who had arrived to assist.

Silence reigned for a while as they concentrated on the papers and Travis disappeared to process the roll of film Vern had handed him.

Elliott was angry, and deeply hurt that Natalia should have gone without consulting him. He had finally lost his patience with her and had gone to Middle Earth. He consulted with the Almighty on a suitable way to deal with his wayward wife, then asked if there was any quick way to find Jason. The Great One had proffered a solution to the first and had suggested a course of action on the second. He had also told him that Bianca was now free of pain and sleeping peacefully, until the reawakening when the healing would be complete.

He flew over New York invisible to all but other angels, and found no sign of Natalia or Pauline. He was forced to enter many buildings, mainly food halls in his search and found that he was now searching underground having exhausted all other possibilities.

In a fury that the only place left to search was the sewers he was not pleased to hear a scream of rage in a remote location near the buildings of Goodman, Goodhew and May. He heard the sounds of a fight in progress and ran rapidly towards it. He saw Pauline attacking, with every ounce of her strength, four demons who were trying to drag Natalia from her position in an alcove. Yelling at Pauline to get down, Elliott let streams of pure energy flow from his fingertips and annihilate the demons. They disintegrated before he reached the spot and he just looked at the charred remains, before turning fiercely on the two girls, grabbed an arm of each and transported them immediately back to the skyscraper.

Pauline and Natalia, much disheveled, arrived back held firmly by Elliott. Both tried to wriggle free of his grasp. He propelled them into the lounge and threw Pauline towards Daniel. "She's your problem," he told him, "deal with it."

He turned to Natalia. "You have tried my patience far beyond what any man should have to take. I have consulted with the Great One, and until you learn to distinguish between good sense and foolhardiness, you are to be confined within the bounds of heaven. For both our sakes let us hope it doesn't take too long."

Natalia turned white. "But Elliott, you can't come to heaven."

Elliott just looked at her.

Natalia grasped his shoulders tightly. ""But when will I see you again, and what about Nick?"

Elliott's eyes were full of sorrow as he told her, "He will go with you, I can't deprive him of his mother. That's the price I shall have to pay to keep you and our son safe. You wouldn't listen to me when I asked you not to go into danger, and you deliberately went seeking it when my back was turned. I can no longer keep my promise to the Almighty that you will never be put in harm's way. You have shown that you have no regard for my feelings at all. I cannot endure the thought of losing you, but that is better than seeing you die. I hope you realise just what your thoughtlessness has cost us both. When it is safe for you to return and if the Great

One allows, I shall be waiting for you."

Natalia's eyes widened in horror as she realised that Allegra had told her the truth. One day she would try him too far and she wouldn't like the outcome.

"What if I promise never to do it again?" She cried in bitter pain at her loss.

"I can't trust you to do even that, you have gone against my wishes too often in the past."

Her eyes were filled with tears and they ran down her cheeks like a river.

"Not even your tears can save you this time, Tally!" he told her sadly as he lightly touched the golden curls. Forcing himself to ignore the teardrops, he held her face between his hands and kissed her lovingly. "Goodbye my beautiful angel, you will be in far safer hands than mine. You have to go now."

In a blinding flash she was gone. Elliott stood looking at the spot she had been standing for a long time.

Everyone but Daniel had faded quickly from the room when they grasped the nature of the disagreement between the two angels. Daniel had sent Pauline into the kitchen as soon as he realised that something terrible was happening between Elliott and Natalia. He would deal with her later. He alone had been witness to the entire altercation and he now took Elliott's arm and they went to the roof top.

Vern and Diana had remained in the hallway and were shocked at the outcome of Natalia's wilful disregard for danger, but Elliott's reaction to it had been a revelation. As Vern had said to him earlier, she had gone into dangerous situations several times, ignoring Elliott's instructions to wait. The rest of them did as Elliott requested, he had the superior powers to guide him, and them. Twice she had almost lost her life and still she had gone into danger without a thought for anyone but herself. But Vern had never thought he would send her back to heaven and his son as well. He was dreadfully afraid that it was his suggestion on the best way to cure the headstrong angel that had caused Elliott to take this drastic action. He had also, until a few minutes ago, been unaware that Elliott was barred from Heaven itself. He must be in terrible pain.

"Could I have done the same?" he asked himself.

The vampires had escaped to the bedroom and made sure no one left it until they were sure the coast was clear. They now emerged and returned to the lounge to continue the 'paper chase'.

Daniel stood with Elliott on the rooftop. "Did you really agree that she should stay there, until she realises what she's lost?"

"I had to, there was no other way."

"All the years you've been together, I never thought it would come to this. I was sure she would understand what she was doing to you before it was too late," said Daniel quietly.

"I couldn't stand the thought of her dying. The demons here in New York are descended from heavenly outcasts. They can kill an angel. How could I let that happen? She used to listen, you know. She followed me when I said she could and stayed when I told her she couldn't. Sometimes it was necessary to reveal what we were. It worked fine, especially as she was so beautiful, no one ever doubted she was an angel. Me, I look what I am: dark, dangerous and evil."

"Dark and dangerous, yes. Evil? No," said Daniel.

"What's done is done. I love her above all else, even our son, but I shall have to try to live without them both. I hope I am strong enough not to beg him to let her come back too soon. She's just not safe to be let loose in an evil town like this one. Letting her go is the hardest thing I've ever done, but I know she's safe with Him."

"I'm sorry," said Daniel simply, "I wish you had been able to find another way."

"It's worse than you know," said Elliott. "I went to tell my parents what I intended to do and my mother told me she is having another child. She didn't even tell me that. She knew if she did I'd never have let her come. It will be a long time before I see it now, maybe I never will, but He did promise to let me know what it is."

Daniel sucked in his breath, "I don't know what to say to you Elliott, it's a disaster for you and all of us."

"When this is over, I am going back to the Fifth Dimension. Sometimes it's best to get away for a while."

"I hope it helps."

"Having friends helps too!" said Elliott

"It couldn't have happened at a worse time." Daniel sounded worried. "I have this feeling we are going to be overwhelmed with disaster. The Oracles were very cagey about our futures."

"Perhaps Tally is in the safest place, her future will be assured. You'd better tell me exactly what they said."

"They said the forces for evil were in the ascendancy in a high place and that we were their nemesis and the catalyst for change. We should not confuse ancient magic with an even older wisdom. Ancient wisdom still had value if interpreted correctly. New life and new ways were growing from the old. One life is drawing to a close, we should embrace the new as it is meant to be. They said that Jason was on a quest for his roots. They weren't at all forthcoming, but when I pressed them they said that destinies were unfolding and pathways were beckoning, but as there was always more than one pathway, we must be careful how we chose. We don't always stay on the path we start out on; sometimes even immortals have to follow their instincts. They did say that Jason was changing his pathway, when I asked if it was the right path they wouldn't give me an answer. In view of what the vampire sages told him, I think he's on the wrong path." Daniel, unusually for him, sounded rather depressed about it all.

"I had hoped for better than that," said Elliott flatly. "Do you think you know the right path?" He looked searchingly at Daniel as he said it.

"Not yet, but somehow I know I can help him find the right one. But I need to find him first. If only we knew where he was going."

"We'll clear up this present crisis, and then we'll go and sort out Jason," said Elliott.

"I'll be back down in a while, I need a few minutes alone," Elliott told him.

Daniel left him on the roof and went to the kitchen to find Pauline. "Okay, let's have it. What happened?" he demanded curtly.

"I've been a fool," said Pauline harshly. "She wanted to see the shops. We needed food, so I let her come along. I didn't know until later that she promised Elliott she would stay within his sight. She wanted to go sightseeing. When she tired of that, she wanted to see the Goodman building. Then she spotted the sewers that led to Goodman's and was gone before I had a chance to grab her. I had to go after her; I had already sent the shopping home in a taxi. When I caught up with her the demons had already surrounded her. Of course I attacked them, but I'm only one woman not an army. I was losing until Elliott arrived. Oh, God! What will Elliott say?"

"It's too late for any one to say anything now," said Daniel, "She's been returned to Heaven and taken Nick and their unborn child with her. Elliott couldn't take any more chances on letting her stay on earth to get killed. As long as she listened to him and let him decide what was safe and what was not, she was kept from harm. He's taken a hard decision and sent her back."

"He can see her sometimes, can't he?"

"Elliott is barred from entering heaven and Natalia will never leave it again, unless of course she can convince the Great One that she has learned her lesson."

"That's a hellish decision for Elliott to have made," said Pauline. "It must be killing him."

"He's accepted the pain and the guilt, but he is strong and will deal with it," said Daniel gravely.

"I feel it's all my fault." Pauline's eyes were filling with tears. "They were so happy, and he loves her so much. But have you ever tried arguing with her, she just never listened."

"That's the root of the trouble, she didn't listen and she's paying the price. But unfortunately Elliott is paying for her foolishness as well."

"It's so unfair," cried Pauline.

"Life isn't always fair. Look what happened to Jason. Now it seems that Elliott is also paying someone else's price."

"After this is over, I'm never going to work for the Astral Council again," said Pauline bitterly, "there should be some reward for doing good."

"We don't do this for the reward, we do it because it's right," Daniel told her, "and the next time we are called we'll both go willingly."

She reached for his handkerchief and dried her eyes. "What shall I say to Elliott?"

"'Sorry', will be enough for now."

Together they left the kitchen and returned to the lounge, Elliott had returned from the roof and raised an eyebrow at Pauline.

She walked over and placed her hand on his arm. "I'm sorry, Elliott. I wish it hadn't happened the way it did. I couldn't stop her."

Elliott smiled gravely at her. "It wasn't your fault Pauline. She did it all by herself, but I have to live with it. It hurts, but I have to believe she will come back to me."

"Thanks!" She patted his arm and returned to Daniel.

Vern looked sympathetically at them all. "Sorry folks, but we have to get back to business."

Elliott looked at the rest of his team and sank down on his heels to glance at the papers held by Sebastian and Diana. Travis had brought back the developed photos and handed them to Elliott.

"I just can't see anything they would need to kill to hide," said Elliott in frustration. "What's in those files?" he asked harshly.

"Mostly a load of business letters and bills demanding

payment of overdue accounts," said Pauline.

"Let me see them," said Daniel, taking them from her, and flicking quickly through them.

"They're deep in debt to some nasty people," he said, thoughtfully, handing the papers to Travis as he held out his hand for them.

"What does that mean exactly?" asked Elliott cautiously. He left the business side of things to Jason and Daniel.

"It means they've got a strong incentive to commit crimes to get out of debt," said Travis, quickly perusing the papers and seeing the way Daniel was thinking. "But what crimes?"

Elliott got to his feet and, sitting on the edge of the table, pulled out his mobile and spoke to Alistair.

"Have you got anything from those computer files yet?"

"Load of gobbledy gook if you ask me," replied Alistair. "Two almost identical sets of accounts, with different figures for the first six months of this year. Looks very dodgy to me, I suspect a tax fiddle. Several lists of guns and ammunition, rockets and missiles to be shipped abroad, I don't know how they are getting away with that. There are imports from the Far East and South America, listed as industrial samples. Several lists of herbs, medicines and body parts, and a copy of a page of THE DEMON COMPENDIUM. There's a reference to the BOOK OF SPELLS as well as a book with no name. I've already sent copies to New York."

Elliott shot to his feet. "Shut your computer down right now and disconnect it from any phone lines."

Alistair obeyed instantly and called Elliott from Alex's phone. "What's up?"

"The last book you mentioned, don't say the name again. Lucifer will be with you shortly."

Daniel looked worried. "THE Book?"

Elliott nodded. "You'd better come with me this time."

Daniel looked around the room. "Take Vern. If anything happens here at least I've got a chance of preventing disaster, none of the others could. The Book of Spells is bad enough, but the other is catastrophic."

"You are right of course. Vern, we have to go now."

Elliott and Vern vanished.

"Where have they gone?" asked Travis puzzled. "It sounded urgent."

"I can't tell you why, but all our lives may depend on what we

94

all do next. We now know why the spells cast against us are so powerful. Elliott's gone to do some damage control and so must I. You'd better come with me; I need to see Elisande and the Crone."

They all entered the bedroom. Elisande was about to send them away when she saw Daniel's face.

"You look like death," she said softly. "I've only seen one man look like that before."

He went and took her hand and placed it on his forehead. They communicated silently for a minute or two. Elisande's face turned gray and she turned to the crone, who then read her thoughts, the three of them stood in silence, their minds joined.

"I have one," said Elisande, still in silent communication with Daniel and the Crone. "It is a third generation copy and has been passed down through the centuries from the dark ages; I inherited it from my great aunt who lived in Yorkshire in the eighteenth century. She left it to the first girl to be named after her. I have read it."

The crone held up a gnarled finger and beckoned to Cybel. "Take the vampires and go to my home. Tell my granddaughter to give you the lamp which hangs from the ceiling in my bedroom and the chest from the closet nearest the door. Tell her to find her mother. Use no magic of any kind, leave the house at once, go to our relatives in Philadelphia and stay there until I tell them it's safe to return."

Cybel and the vampires left immediately.

"You feel they are in danger?" asked Elisande anxiously.

"Best be safe than sorry," was the reply.

"What's in the chest?" asked Daniel, "and what's with the lamp?"

"The Lamp of Algor," said Eurydice, "is very good at warding off evil demons and it has a magical flame."

"I've heard of it," said Daniel. "I had no idea it was still in use."

"No point having it if you don't use it," cackled the crone.

"And the chest?" he asked her again.

"Just my essentials," she told him. "I wouldn't like to be without them in a crisis."

Daniel laughed as Elisande winked at him. She never liked to be without her 'essentials' either.

When Cybel and the vampires arrived back later, Sebastian told Eurydice that Travis had taken her relatives to the station and

95

that they had gone without protest. The crone had her family well trained. The chest and lamp were handed over and Sebastian was instructed to light the lamp and hang it in the hallway.

He raised his eyebrows in Daniel's direction and was told to get on with it; it was a charm against evil spirits.

Sebastian disappeared with alacrity and soon had fixed a hook to the ceiling and hung the lamp.

Eurydice patted his arm in approval when he had finished. "Extra protection for the angels and us, and my family are safe so I don't have to worry about them," she told him.

Lucifer, Elliott and Vern arrived unheralded at Alistair's side. He almost jumped out of his skin as Elliott spoke to him. "Have you got that disk safe?"

Alistair patted his shirt pocket. "Give it to Nick," said Elliott, "It will be safer with him."

Lucifer pocketed the disk and looked at the computer. "No evidence of its existence left there, I hope."

"Nothing."

"You'll have to come with me," said Lucifer. "Mortals have never travelled the way you are about to, but it is no longer safe for you here."

Alistair looked terrified. "You mean I'm going to hell?" he stammered.

"Safest place in the universe right now," said Lucifer heartily. "Especially with my new resources in place."

"Go!" said Elliott. "I'll sort the rest out."

Lucifer grasped Alistair by the arm and they both vanished.

A few moments later all of his computer equipment disappeared as well.

Vern laughed. "I thought he wouldn't let anyone part him from that, not even Old Nick." Even Elliott's lips twitched at the thought of Alistair's frustration if he were minus his computer for very long as he darted through the rest of the house and found Allegra and the children in the kitchen with Katya.

"Where's Charles?" he asked urgently.

"Gone to check on David and Patrick. They are looking after the business with Vern gone and Charles busy here."

"Damn! Vern, ring him, tell him to stay put with the boys and wait for me. You'll have to wait here for Alex and Faith. Bring them to New York as soon as they arrive."

"Allegra, there's no time to explain, but you all have to leave immediately for Quinn's place. I'm sure you already have everything you need there. If you haven't, Vespazia will have to get it for you."

Elliott opened a portal and pushed the six of them through, "Go on Katya, this path will take you to Exmoor. Drago will be waiting for you when you arrive. He'll take you the rest of the way. Look after Penny and Lucy. I'll tell Pauline and Daniel they are safe with Quinn."

Lucifer had made a tramline available in the tunnels on Exmoor and Drago had made a lightweight trolley car to allow his family a quicker journey to their home. He intended to improve it even further when they took guests as Katya had suggested. The electricity was supplied courtesy of the local electricity company through a meter, in a large house that Jason had purchased nearby, on the premise that the larger the house the larger the bills, though some clever manipulation by Lucifer had been necessary to prevent the electric company querying his excessive bills. Eventually they hoped the hydroelectric plant in the Lost World would take over running the trams.

Quinn and Vespazia intended to use their new Bodmin home as soon as she got permission to leave the Lost World. However the Devon home was big enough for a large number of visitors, from time to time, to cause no undue interest. Meanwhile it gave Jason and his family a good reason to be seen frequently in the area, coming and going from the house at all hours but secretly using the internal tunnels for access to the Lost Word.

Jason had no problem with being thought eccentric; and film stars, even ex-ones, were notoriously so.

Immediately after they disappeared, Elliott departed for Charles's office and found he had obeyed his instructions. Patrick and David looked enquiringly at him.

"Boys, you have to take a little vacation, down underground for a while. There's no time to explain. You can explore to your hearts content, Katya will look after you. You may meet up with her on the way; if you do you can help her with the children."

He opened a portal and told them to follow the trail until they met up with someone from the Lost World who would guide them to it. "You can't get lost, all of the pathways lead to Exmoor," he said, describing Drago to them in case he reached them before Katya did. The boys looked from him to Charles. "Isn't Uncle Charles coming?" asked Patrick.

"I need him to help me," said Elliott. "Trust me, you will be quite safe."

"Okay," said David as Patrick pushed him through. The portal closed behind them.

Elliott used his mobile to call Drago and tell him his family and some young friends were on the way. "You will have to meet them on the surface, I headed them towards the beach. Keep them safe, we have really big trouble up here."

Drago's answer must have satisfied him as he looked less anxious as he turned to Charles.

"Vern is waiting for Faith and Alex, but where is Felicity?" asked Elliott.

"Felicity was at Alex's as far as I know, and although Alex and Faith aren't back from Jason's yet, they were expected quite soon, I believe."

Elliott groaned. "Too many things happening at once, I'm losing track of them. I've no time for messing about." He took Charles by the arm and they arrived at Simba seconds later.

"Vern go and find Felicity, she'll have to come to New York with us."

Vern went to the back door and shouted. He reappeared with Felicity who had been hanging out the washing. "I can't leave the sheets," she said worriedly.

Elliott hissed impatiently and waved his hands in the air. The washing appeared on the kitchen table, dry and ironed.

"Satisfied. Will you come now?"

He opened a portal for them to go to New York. "Charles, you will both arrive on a skyscraper, you will know it's the right one if you see a helicopter on it. Go!"

Charles looked at him mystified. "I hope I'm going to find out what's going on when I get there?"

"Tell Daniel I said he's to tell you and Felicity, but no one else."

"Where are you two going?" He looked from Elliott to Vern.

"Vern will have to wait for Alex and Faith, but I'll check on Ward and Carlotta before I return. Now go!"

They went.

Charles and Felicity arrived in New York two hours later, after a very uneventful trip. It was almost as if the dead knew they needed to get to their destination quickly. They were met by Pauline who had been told by Elliott to expect them.

Lucifer had arrived some minutes before to check once more on Bianca's well being. He wasn't pleased to find no change in her health and even less pleased to see that Snake was still sitting beside the bed holding her hand.

"I told you to leave her alone; I want you out of here," he hissed furiously. "I'll have you flame grilled if you don't get out."

"Shut up," snapped Snake, keeping his voice low. "She doesn't like the shouting. She starts to shake and get agitated when you turn up."

"Me, shut up! You insolent bloodsucker, you leave this room now, or I'll make you."

"You get out." Snake still spoke softly. "You are the one preventing her recovery, interfering with the witches and their spells, shouting at everyone."

"Me, get out?" yelled Lucifer, spitting flames of fury. "You, the lowest form of undead life, a vile murderer and demon, you dare to tell ME to get out?"

"Do be quiet! You're upsetting everyone," said Diana entering the room. "Go and get your new army to infiltrate that building you are so interested in. You have to catch the perpetrators before they attack again. There's no need for you to hang about here causing trouble."

"Things have changed. You and Vern found some very important information in that office and we have to move very carefully. The fiends who are working there are quite likely cast out angels and earth-dwelling demons of very ancient origin. We can't afford to make a mistake," said Lucifer, swallowing his rage at seeing Snake still present and deciding to humour Diana.

"Daniel knows who attacked Bianca now, he will help to capture them," he added, attempting a gracious smile.

"I'm organizing a sortie into the building for tonight," said Daniel from the doorway.

"Well, how about checking those videos we liberated? They may be on them. If you can recognise them he can point them out and we'll go get them," said Diana, unconvinced by Lucifer's crocodile smile.

Lucifer was diverted by this ploy and instructed Travis to play them at once. He was about to join Daniel in the lounge to watch them, but turned for a final word with Snake.

"You keep your hands off Bianca, she's little more than a child; I want you out of here."

Snake just turned away and to continue his watch over the angel.

Lucifer's fingers curled and uncurled as he made a visible effort not to strangle the vampire. Flames shot from his fingertips, singeing the vampire's hair. Snake never moved a muscle.

The Devil walked out in a haze of smoke and flames, his curses echoed around the room for several minutes. His temper simmered dangerously as he entered the lounge.

"Play those videos," he ordered Travis. "You tell me if you recognise anyone," he instructed Daniel.

Cassidy looked at Snake. "I believe you must have a death wish. Only a fool or someone who wants to die would annoy Satan like you do."

Snake glanced briefly at him. "I'm praying she gets better, and for the chance to even the score. No angel should have to suffer like this. You just carry on chanting."

At that moment the hand on the bed began to flutter and the fingers held in his own moved slightly. She opened her eyes and looked straight at him. Great big brown eyes took in the grim-faced man seated beside her. A vampire in full feral mode stared back at her, willing her to stay awake.

"Come on little bird, wake up, you can hold on to me, I'm strong enough for both of us," he whispered. The fingers held in his hand curled trustingly around his fingers and grasped them tightly. She smiled at him, a weak tired little smile, but nevertheless a smile. Then she closed them and lapsed into unconsciousness again.

Sensing the change, Lucifer appeared once more at the bedside, glowered as he saw the entwined fingers, but refrained from commenting. He placed his hand lightly on Bianca's forehead and touched her hair with a gentle hand. A silent communication took place between them and the old crone grinned evilly at Lucifer as she caught the tail end of the conversation.

"Not what you hoped for, but you can't protect them forever," she told him slyly.

"Keep quiet, you old hag," growled out an infuriated Lucifer, "I've got a vacancy for a witch in my palace. Once there, there's no return. Be careful I don't send you there."

"Keep quiet yourself, Nick," said Pauline, "this is a sick room. We don't need you here perpetually droning on. Go and help Daniel sort out the videos. Leave the witches alone."

Lucifer grinned at Pauline and told the witches. "Fortunately for you I have a soft spot for the werewolf and her cubs, so just this once, I'll leave you to it." Pauline grimaced and followed him from the room.

All of the witches moved to encircle the bed and began chanting their healing spells once more. This time their combined strength, allied to Snakes, seemed to work. She opened her eyes again and smiled at them all.

During this triumphant awakening, Charles and Felicity arrived and were greeted with pleasure by their friends. Felicity joined the other witches, and after a quick surprised jolt at seeing a vampire holding the angel's hand, joined in the healing process.

Charles followed her intending to see for himself the injured angel, and was surprised to see that she appeared little more than a child. He observed the way the vampire was holding her hand and was amused at the vampire's dedicated look. Despite his concern at the age of the angel, he knew more than anyone that vampires do have humane thoughts. This one looked as if he had thoughts of atonement.

He thought Felicity was a little taken aback at the sight of the fiercesome vampire, but she hid it quickly and he smiled approvingly at her as she stood at the foot of the bed.

He stayed himself for a short while as the witches chanted together, and he noticed that Felicity was looking very pleased at the way the healing was going. He thought Bianca had dropped off to sleep again.

"Will she be okay?" he whispered.

"We can keep her alive and free from pain. She's just dozing at the moment," said Felicity softly, "but you and I both know the ones who did this have to die before she can resume her angelic form."

"I'm sure Elliott and Daniel are working on it."

As they were speaking, the angel opened her eyes again, and Lucifer, again, darted into the room to see for himself the progress she was making and expressed pleasure at her awakening.

"You'll soon be better," he whispered. "Everything will be fine. Our friends are all here to help you and find the swine who hurt you."

The angel smiled at him and promptly went back to sleep.

Snake heaved a sigh of relief and with his free hand smoothed back the tangled hair from her forehead, then ran his fingers lightly down the pale cheek.

"She'll be fine now, she's sleeping properly and is in no pain," whispered Cybel.

Snake took a last look and left the room, followed by Charles, who wandered off to find the kitchen. Snake joined the others in the lounge.

He was surprised to see the Cornish shapeshifter sitting watching the TV with the female shapeshifter on his knee. "Thought you were in England?" he said to Vern.

"Elliott got into a black mood and wanted to be left alone. They were gone rather longer than he thought they would be, so he decided to go and find them himself and sent me back here. He said he'll come and get me if he needs me. I made an enormous sacrifice and travelled the hard way, by the spirit path, back here. Elliott wants us to go out tonight and get our hands on the swine who beat up Bianca," said Vern. "He thinks we should make that our priority and Daniel is organising it right now."

"I'm in on this one," said Snake harshly. "They overstepped the mark when they tortured an angel. Particularly this one!"

"What's with the angel? How is she now?"

"Getting better," said Snake. "The witches seem pleased."

He went to check that she was still sleeping, and then disappeared for a while. He returned with a large gift wrapped box. He handed it to Elisande.

"Give it to her when she wakes up." He spoke in low tones and left the room again.

Elisande looked at the box and made a guess as to its contents. Felicity giggled and winked at her mother as they came to the same conclusion. The old crone also cackled quietly to herself as she made the same guess. Cybel looked at them as if they were mad and looked at Cassidy who shrugged his shoulders at their incomprehensible mirth.

Charles, finding nothing to eat in the kitchen, made himself a mug of coffee and took it to the roof feeling, if nothing else; that he could say he had seen New York. He stayed quite a while, knowing if he was needed someone would fetch him.

Elisande spotted Charles when, later on, he headed for the lounge. She grabbed him, dragging him to the kitchen.

"There's no human food in this house, we've eaten everything that Pauline got for us. The girls are getting into too much trouble here, you'll have to take Sebastian and go shopping." She sat down at the table and made up a list.

Charles looked at it and groaned. He went to find Sebastian.

"How are you fixed for travelling by day? I've been ordered to go shopping. We humans all eat proper food, you know!"

"Don't worry, I'll show you where to go," grinned Sebastian. "I seldom go in them, but I know where they are!"

# CHAPTER SEVEN

Elliott arrived at the penthouse looking grim and spoke briefly to Daniel before going to find Elisande and Felicity. He spoke quietly to them both and they followed him to the kitchen.

Daniel was already there with Pauline who was making tea. Pauline was looking upset and her hand shook as she poured the water into the pot. Daniel took it from her, and then as Elliott spoke softly to the witches, he handed cups of tea to them both. They accepted them gratefully.

"They are in hospital in Exeter, neither of them has seriously life-threatening injuries. I promise they won't die, but they are very poorly and Alex is in a coma. Faith has a broken arm and concussion but she will recover. I saw them but didn't reveal my presence."

He took Felicity's hand in his.

"I will take you to them. Elisande as well if she wishes. Their car was hit by a piece of metal which fell off a lorry in front of them. It bounced into the windscreen before Alex could avoid it. The lorry driver saw what happened and stopped to call for help and stayed until the ambulance and police arrived. He was very shaken and is in the hospital as well. They have been very lucky, they are both alive and badly hurt, and the coma is very worrying, but they will recover quite soon."

Elisande dabbed her eyes with her hanky and put her arms around Felicity. "Take Felicity, the child will need her mother if Alex is in a coma. Felicity is darn good with healing spells and can sit by her son-in-law's bed and relay news to his wife, without the hospital questioning why she is there."

"Good thinking," said Pauline putting her arms around Felicity and giving her a sympathetic hug. "You go and make them well, Felicity."

Elliott looked at Elisande questioningly. "I'll stay here, Bianca has a long way to go yet, and don't forget I saw what is needed to heal an angel," she told him firmly.

Felicity nodded agreement. "If I need her, mother can be with me in seconds if you bring her."

Elliott took her hand and they vanished.

In Exeter, they materialised in the grounds of the hospital

unseen by anyone. Elliott escorted her to reception, and asked if Mr. and Mrs. Lanyon could receive visitors.

The nurse who stood beside her looked surprised. "We have been trying to contact their relatives for some time. You had better come and see the doctor."

"Felicity would like to see her daughter first," said Elliott firmly, his saturnine features set and cold.

The nurse must have decided it was better not to argue and led them to the intensive care unit where Felicity and Alex lay in beds just feet apart.

Felicity picked up the charts, and examined them, ignoring the nurses look of disapproval and intercepted Elliott's frown of annoyance towards the nurse with a shake of her head.

"You can't stay long," said the nurse, "they are very ill, you know"

"I do know," said Felicity, "and I am staying here until I am sure they are getting better."

"I'll go and see the doctor," said Elliott. "You can take me to him," he told the nurse. "Mrs. Lanyon's mother is a trained nurse and will see they come to no harm whilst we are gone."

The nurse, still apparently undecided, had to follow Elliott as he moved away, leaving Felicity to use her powers to assist the healing process.

Elliott's conversation with the doctor was short but informative and Elliott made sure that Felicity would be allowed to stay at Faith's bedside.

He returned to speak to Felicity and this time the nurse was not there.

"How are they?"

"Faith will soon come around, she is almost awake now, and is going to be fine."

"And Alex?"

"Not so good, there is a piece of glass in his left eye and a multiple fracture of his skull is causing pressure on his brain. I think they know about that but not about the glass in his eye."

Elliott departed for the doctor's office to demand a further consultation. It took a rather delicate mind probe, but he returned with the consultant who had been with him.

"You told me that my friend has very severe injuries and I want to be assured that everything possible has been considered. I want you to check him again and take more X-rays of his head. My friend is a pilot, I cannot take the chance that he could suffer brain damage, or lose his eyesight."

Such was Elliott's powerful presence and his mind control, that the doctors with very little protest did as he asked. Alex was subjected to further X-rays and a consultant was summoned from the eye hospital. Alex was given a very thorough second examination by several doctors and consultants. Elliott and Felicity waited for a long time until the consultant returned.

"A fragment of glass, embedded deeply, has now been removed. Were it not for your insistence," said the consultant with a piercing look at Elliott, "and we had waited until the morning, we might not have been in time to check the damage. Our monitors however have indicated that the pressure on his brain has decreased and is now of less immediate concern. We will, however, be watching it carefully."

He explained to Elliott and Felicity that if it became necessary they would operate at once.

Felicity was very upset as she watched them wheel the bed back into the room. All three witches adored Alex, and she hated to see him so ill.

Elliott reached out for Felicity's hand and pressed it gently. "I'll stay until he wakes up. We will wait together."

"I can't let you. Much as I would like you to stay," said Felicity, "you have too much to do in New York. You still haven't found Jason, and mother told me about Natalia. Go, I shall be fine, this is nothing new to me. I have spent many hours looking after injured friends, you know that. The hospital won't think it strange that I should want to sit with my daughter and son-in-law. You have already told them I am a nurse. Go."

"I'll send James and Drago to take care of you all," said Elliott.

"There's no need."

Elliott left in the conventional way by the front door. He took out his mobile and called James Purcell. There was no answer. All the Purcells were away from home.

He called Drago and was answered by Vespazia. He told her what was wrong and asked her to send Drago to Exeter Hospital as soon as he arrived there with Allegra and the children.

"He'll take hours to get to the hospital," said Vespazia worriedly. "If only I could travel on earth I could bring him myself."

"I'll see what I can arrange," said Elliott. He departed immediately for Middle Earth to speak with the Great One.

"No blanket dispensations, as yet, but she can visit the hospital and the boy's home, when necessary. Wait for Jason's return for anything more."

Elliott accepted the gift and returned to the hospital for a brief word with Felicity, telling her that Vespazia would be arriving with Drago, but she would have to return immediately as he wanted her to help guard all the children and Allegra and Katya. He didn't feel right about putting so much responsibility on the young Fallons, Patrick and David until they were a lot older.

Felicity accepted the extra help with pleasure and told Elliott to get back to New York.

Which, after phoning Vespazia again, he did.

He was still disappointed at not finding James, but on his way to America dropped a note through the letterbox telling him to join Felicity and why.

Back in America…

Bianca woke again several hours later. The crone had retired to the kitchen and Cybel and Cassidy had gone to get a few hours sleep. Elisande smiled at her as she tried to sit up.

"I'm Elisande, Lucifer asked me to come and take care of you. Don't try to move too much, I'll help you to sit more comfortably."

This she did and Bianca now wide awake sat back among the pillows so carefully arranged to ease the discomfort of her broken wings. She handed Bianca the box, "A present from an admirer," said Elisande, her eyes twinkling.

"The Vampire?" questioned Bianca eagerly.

Elisande nodded and smiled to herself as the box was opened to disclose the most elegant and dainty silk nightdresses and matching negligée's she had ever seen. Bianca's eyes sparkled at the thought behind the gift, she was aware that she was naked under the sheets.

"Can I wear one now?" she asked eagerly.

"I'll fetch Eurydice and we'll make you presentable now that you are awake, I'll only be a moment."

Elisande whisked out of the room and returned almost instantly with the Crone who told Bianca her name was Eurydice and the two of them washed her and dressed her in the prettiest of the new nightdresses. They looked at each other as they noticed the Vampire had thoughtfully made sure they were all backless with halter necks,

107

and wondered!

Bianca looked pleased with the result of their labours and looked expectantly towards the door.

Elisande laughed softly and went to tell Snake that someone wanted help to sit up.

Snake, moving with almost indecent haste, darted to the bedroom. Bianca lay on the pillows, dressed, as he could see, in one of the confections he had chosen so carefully. Eurydice beckoned him over. "She would like to sit up a little; you are a strong young fellow, why don't you help her?"

Elisande left the room with an amused smile. These demonic types were pushovers for an angel. Eurydice chuckled to herself as she followed.

Seeing Bianca so much improved, Snake smiled delightedly. The witches had raised the pillows behind her but the vampire lifted her easily to a more comfortable position.

"Thank you for the beautiful present," she whispered, as he lifted her in his arms.

"I'm glad you liked it."

He looked around to see if anyone was in earshot and leaned over and whispered something in her ear. She raised her hand and touched his face; he had resumed his human form when she had, finally, seemed to be recovering.

Bianca smiled serenely at him, and he leaned over and kissed her lightly on the lips. She lay against the pillows and closed her eyes, still smiling.

He watched her until she went to sleep again.

Now that she was properly awake, the witches gave her healing herbs and broth to give her strength, and although she still slept a lot, she awoke from time to time and looked around for the vampire. She had hidden her thoughts from the witches when they had told her his name was Snake although Elisande had given her a rather knowing smile.

It was quite obvious to the witches that she was fascinated by the dangerous vampire. It was also clear to them that she must have known who and what he was before her accident, but it didn't seem to bother her. Elisande and Eurydice were almost certain they knew why.

Snake amused her with tales of the places he had been, the sights he had seen, but never a word of what he was or had done.

Vern listened at the door now and again, mindful of what

Elliott had told him about Lucifer's request to keep them apart. Never once did he even hint at the dreadful deeds he had committed, the murders, and tortures, the crimes against humans and other supernaturals, he had carried out remorselessly in his very long life.

Vern thought that Snake was kidding himself if he was attempting to deny his diabolical past. Everyone should have the chance of redemption, true enough, but by the very nature of his deeds it would be a long and hard one.

Sebastian had told him that Snake was one of the most evil vampires ever to have existed. The most evil vampire had, it was rumoured, been reformed years before, and now lived on the West Coast, attempting to redeem himself with good deeds. His would be a long hard slog as well, Vern had no doubt.

Seeing the influence of these angels on hard men was difficult to imagine, but having seen it for himself, Vern was torn between amusement and sadness at the waste of lives. He thanked God for people like Elliott and Jason and of course Daniel, who had the will and the knowledge to help them all.

Sebastian himself was a reluctant conscript to Lucifer's demonic balancing acts. Lucifer had, through an intermediary employed Sebastian and Travis to infiltrate the company they were investigating, and it was Lucifer who was their client. Vern had given them the bad news as soon as he had figured out what Lucifer was up to. "Sneaky Devil," said Sebastian. He had then told Vern that Snake was unlikely to listen to anything Lucifer had to say, particularly if it included good deeds. "I've heard of him, he is worse than any other vampire – bar one – that I have ever heard of. Do-gooders are usually on his menu. I can't see him changing that much."

"Oh, I don't know," Vern had told him. "Old Nick persuaded you, Elliott 'persuaded' me, Snake will just be a bigger challenge. And you should never discount the influence of angels."

"I can't wait," said Sebastian dryly.

It was quite a while before Charles was able to talk to Daniel and find out exactly what was going on. Pauline had told Charles and Vern about the accident to Alex and Faith, and both were concerned for their friend. Vern had been very cagey when Charles asked for an explanation of the need for their presence in New York, and told him to wait for Daniel to tell him. Seeing Daniel heading for the roof, he followed him.

"Where's Vern?" asked Daniel as Charles came to stand beside him on the rooftop

"He says he's having an hour off, he needs to have a think. He says Elliott is in a very black mood and seems to want everyone here. A show of force or mass spell-casting by the sound of it."

"That will be the last resort," said Daniel. "But I'm not surprised he's in a dark mood in view of what has happened."

"He wants you to tell me what's going on. Vern already knows but won't tell me."

Daniel brought him up to date very quickly. Told him about the cryptic message from the Oracles and a reference to all of their destinies, plus his own feeling that Jason was not thinking straight, and told him about Elliott and Natalia and how she had been returned to heaven for her own safety and the unborn child. "Elliott is very cut up about it of course, but couldn't risk her life in New York," he added.

"No wonder he is in a black mood. We'll have a think about a way out of that crisis for all our sakes," said Charles. "I just wish Jason was here."

"I have to agree. I believe Jason could have found a better way to handle it, although his present disappearance is contrary to his usual way of dealing with problems."

"What, so urgent we all have to be here, or hidden from sight?"

"Alistair found a reference to The Book in the computer files at Goodman's"

"You've lost me! What's 'The Book'?"

"Sorry, I forgot. You haven't any connection to witchcraft or sorcery. We never refer to The Book, by name. The original no longer exists, or at least we are pretty confident it doesn't. We were certain it was destroyed a thousand years ago, but it is well known that copies were made. We must all hope a copy wasn't destroyed by mistake and that they are all well hidden from the sight of man."

"I still don't know what you are talking about."

"Don't say the name out loud for heaven's sake, and I mean that literally; this book is the most dangerous book ever written."

Daniel placed his hand on Charles's head and passed a thought into his mind: 'The MORDEUS MAXIM'.

"Don't say it, and try never again to even think it."

"I've never heard of it anyway," said Charles. "Why wasn't it destroyed and no copies made if it's that terrible?"

"It is only evil in the wrong hands. In the right hands it can do good," said Daniel. "Fear made men destroy it, curiosity made them copy it and hope made some hide it until it was needed again."

"But you are afraid of it?" asked Charles.

"It was mentioned in the same sentence as the DEMON COMPENDIUM, and THE BOOK OF SPELLS," whispered Daniel. "Any sane man should be afraid."

"As should any sane witch!" said a quiet voice behind them. Elisande had arrived silently on the roof to speak to Daniel and had overheard the conversation.

"Daniel knows I have a copy," she told Charles. "It is not hidden very well, and Faith and Alex both know where I keep it. We must get it away from the vicinity at once. Lucifer is the only person who can hold the book in safety."

"Does Elliott know?"

"I am sorry, but he was gone before I could tell him."

"Someone had better call Old Nick."

"Lucifer!" yelled Charles. "This is an SOS, urgent and immediate. Help!"

A flash of light, a puff of smoke and Lucifer stood there. "What's so urgent I have to come at once?"

Elisande told him.

"Curiosity killed the you-know-what!" said Lucifer. "And you've got too many felines around your locality for comfort. Where is it?"

Elisande told him and he departed for her home in an instant.

He reappeared five minutes later. "Got it, hidden it, forget it," he told her, and vanished again.

"He does come in handy once in a while!" said Charles.

"Can you remember what was in it?" asked Daniel curiously.

"Only a little, now. It was a long time ago."

"What about you?" she asked him.

"It's in my ancestral memory banks," admitted Daniel. "I wish it wasn't. I'd rather not have the responsibility."

"You were given those memories for a reason, Daniel. As a druid you have the power to do good. You said in the right hands it can do good. You will be a conduit if required," said Elisande.

# CHAPTER EIGHT

On the upper floors of Goodman, Goodhew and May, the senior executives had been summoned by the chairman and the managing director. They sought an explanation of the incursion into their offices two nights before and the reason why none of the employees were able to exit the building, yet the public could enter and leave at will.

Corazan was still advising the partners on the best way to circumvent Lucifer's intervention in their plans. Balzahar and the witch doctors had taken up residence in a sub-basement and had not been seen for twelve hours. They were preparing a summoning. Corazan knew of it and looked forward to seeing the overthrow of Lucifer and to seeing Balzahar's master taking his place. But Corazan had not been present when the angel had been attacked. He had accepted the accountants' story at face value, but was privately worried that a real angel had been involved.

He was now concerned for his own skin as the Almighty took it badly when his angels were ill-treated. He reluctantly informed the chairman, that a spell had been cast around the entire building. This would have been to ensure that those inside on the night before last would have to remain inside until the matter had been investigated to the satisfaction of the ultimate powers of good or evil, depending on the identity of the victim of the atrocity. He used the word 'atrocity' to bring home to them all the depth of the trouble they were all in. He didn't find it at all strange that he was about to advise Austin Goodman and Erskine Goodhew on the best way to appease Lucifer. He knew that Lucifer would have a powerful ally if an angel had been attacked. His decision to side with Balzahar and his unknown demon master had been spur of the moment and he now knew his ill-considered plan to unseat his uncle was in ruins. He didn't fancy a confrontation with the two most powerful people in the universe. And revised his strategy accordingly. "I'm afraid that the only way to get yourselves out of this mess is to find the real culprits and let me inform Lucifer they have been caught and are ready for his punishment. Otherwise you are all headed for the cemetery." Corazan, while not exactly a coward, was definitely not intending to sacrifice himself on the altar of Goodman, Goodhew and May. He told them that the wrath of the two great and powerful beings was terrible to behold and finite.

The managing director summoned the head of security and demanded the tapes of the night in question be brought to his office, along with a record of all personnel in the building at the time.

Sometime later the man returned looking both worried and embarrassed. "Some of the tapes are missing, but fortunately when the rooftop cameras were disconnected the infra-red digital cameras were activated, and although they were also disabled shortly after, we have got some footage that is usable."

"Let me see what you have," said the managing director impatiently

Sebastian hadn't known when he had arrived that there had been two different sets of security cameras on the roof and he had only disabled one of them. It wasn't until he disabled the alarms that all the rooftop cameras had been disabled.

His arrival on the rooftop by hang-glider and his entry into the building had been noted, but his exit with the angel had not. Fortunately therefore the helicopter had not been seen, or they would have been in trouble. It would have been traced by its identifying letters, a legal nicety demanded by the local authorities for all private aircraft.

Using his demonic power Lucifer's entry and exit had gone unrecorded, but the disappearance of the evidence had not.

This was the matter of such present concern to the chairman and the managing director. One minute the evidence was quite clear on tape, the next it had completely vanished and no sign of who had done it. Lucifer of course had not shown up on the tapes, as they had not been operative during the time he was in the building. They had been reactivated some time after he had left. As no one had owned up to clearing up the mess, the mystery deepened.

The six men involved were not going to admit to their crime particularly as they had disposed of the videos showing footage of themselves and the angel. However, the evidence of the blood and feathers and the hacked-off wings of a mutilated body were there for all to see – as was the sight of the vampire taking photographs. The back-up video had come into use when the accountants had removed the tape of their crime. Sebastian fortunately had his back to it, and it was not connected to the roof cameras, disconnected when he cut the connections as he entered the building. The rest had been deactivated when he cut the alarms. His exit with the angel was not recorded.

The chairman instructed his head of security to see that all cameras and alarms were repaired and reactivated immediately.

Despite the fact that the crime had taken place in their office, the two senior executives refused to admit to the atrocity. The absence of the body caused them only brief concern, so certain were they that the mutant creature was dead. Still none of the six men involved in the attack had any inkling that their victim had been, and still was, a living angel. No one in the building the day after the attack had any idea what it meant to have so misused the heavenly messenger.

That evening as they prepared to leave the building to go home, they began to suspect. During that first night they made several attempts to leave the building, but the strength of Lucifer's spell defeated them. They soon realised that they were contained within a force field, and there was no way out. The rest of the night they spent worrying about their plight. It also appeared that their telephone communications only allowed them to conduct business operations as did their computers. Any attempt to call for help was converted to gibberish or cut off. Rannoth was doing his job well and Alistair was in his element, causing mayhem with the computers.

In the absence of anything else to do they conducted business as usual the next morning. After all, they were there to make money. They were still unaware of the enormity of the crime committed on the premises, but that evening when the same thing happened as they tried to leave, they realised they had offended someone with tremendous power. It was at this point the managing director had sent for the head of security.

Corazan when summoned had told them the source of the power was beyond his capabilities to disable. He had told them that a greater power than his had taken an interest in the building, and that he suspected their 'mutant' creature was an angel.

Lucifer, who had by now got Alistair well tuned in to the firm's affairs on his computer, was highly diverted by the numerous illegal activities taking place, quite blatantly, within the firm of Goodman, Goodhew and May.

Alistair was transferring information from the firm's computers to America's Internal Revenue Service and Treasury Department with the result that these two government bodies were in a flurry of activity to get their hands on the owners of the businesses contained within the building.

He'd found out enough about the executives to keep Travis and Sebastian busy selling information to their contacts for months. He'd downloaded it to Travis's computer as soon as he found it.

He'd found a reference to travel arrangements for two West African witch doctors and a voodoo priest from Haiti. This, coupled with the mention of shamans and medicine men from several parts of the world alarmed him enough to warn Elliott that a number of practitioners of the Black Arts were missing around the world. They had all been bound for New York.

He'd also got a hint that a demon triumvirate was about to rise in the basement of the building. Lucifer hurried to check what was happening.

Corazan, who was orchestrating the rising, was visiting the basement. He was intent on slipping out of the skyscraper's 'back door' when Lucifer, rising through the floor, grabbed him and transported him back to hell.

Rannoth was waiting in the torture chamber with the chief torturer. He smiled evilly as Lucifer handed him over.

"As soon as you've found out everything this idiot knows, I want you to come upstairs with me. There's a possibility you might learn a thing or two about capturing demons on the surface. It's a long time since your permission to visit was withdrawn."

"Thanks, Boss! I've always wanted to visit the surface again!"

"Did you hide that box I gave you?"

"Totally out of sight," grinned Rannoth.

"Right, let's get to work on this one!"

During the late afternoon Ward arrived with Carlotta, obeying Elliott's instructions to travel inconspicuously by the angelic method: instant dematerialisation and rematerialisation. Ward had managed as usual to bring all the essentials to set up computer access to anything he required, and had transferred all the data regarding Jason's travels to his laptop. Vern, after introducing them to the assembled American vampire contingent, casually mentioned that Travis was the pilot of the helicopter they had noticed on the roof. Carlotta looked with interest at Travis on hearing this. Vern frowned slightly as he saw that Travis was watching with a great deal of admiration the Spanish beauty who had accompanied Ward. He was promptly told by Ward that angels were off-limits to vampires.

"*You are* a vampire!" said Travis pointedly.

"She works with me," said Ward shortly.

"There are too many angels around for my liking," Travis commented, as he showed them to his computer room.

"Do you know that there have now been three of you in my home in the last forty-eight hours?" he asked Carlotta as she strolled beside him down the hallway.

"I'm Spanish; I was born and died there. Angels aren't all born in heaven you know."

"There are a lot of us around, these days," she smiled enigmatically at him. "We have been very busy this last fifty years."

"This is my home," said Travis bowing elaborately. "Everything in it is yours to use as you wish!"

Vern, following behind them, groaned silently. "Not another one! What is it with these angels?"

Travis switched on the computer and waved Ward to his seat, "It's all yours."

As Alistair had already accessed it several times before Lucifer had transported him to Hell, there were a number of messages waiting for Elliott. Ward printed them off and asked Travis to give them to Daniel to deal with. Travis went to find him and Carlotta trailed after him, ignoring Ward's warning frown.

Vern watched absently and allowed his train of thought regarding angels to take a leap into the unknown. After considerable thought a crafty look spread across his face. He went in search of Daniel.

Daniel was reading the e-mail from Alistair and frowning heavily.

"Got a minute?" he asked Daniel, a very serious look on his face.

"Is it important?"

"Could be."

"What's the problem?"

"Not here," said Vern, jerking his head in the direction of the roof.

Daniel looked surprised, but followed Vern to the roof where he noted they were alone.

"I need to speak to Lucifer rather urgently, I think I may have a way to overcome a problem he's got and one we've got. But I'd rather not tell you what it is in case he doesn't agree. I want to see him very privately and with no one knowing."

"You want me to get him for you?"

"If you can. I think he will listen to what I have to say."

116

Daniel hesitated only for a moment and said. "Wait here."

He opened a portal and disappeared. He was gone a while, but came back later alone and said, "He'll be along, wait here."

A few moments later, Lucifer appeared in his usual puff of smoke looking extremely annoyed. "I was in the middle of a particularly enjoyable torture session. What's this about solving a problem for me?"

Vern explained his idea to Lucifer, who began to smile and then to chuckle delightedly.

"There's more to you shapeshifters than I thought. I didn't know you had it in you. I shall keep my eye on you in future. You have all the cunning and deviousness I require in my agents. I only wish I had thought of it myself. But of course I never had the full facts until now. I'll be back." With a swirl of his cape and still chuckling, he vanished.

Vern, looking more hopeful than he had two hours before went to rejoin Daniel. He raised an eyebrow in interrogation.

"He liked my idea; he's gone to try it out."

"Is that all you have to say?"

"If it works you will all know," said Vern cryptically.

Daniel asked Vern to join him in looking through the messages from Alistair. Kurt was still following Jason and reported: he had chartered a plane and gone to Istanbul, where Kurt had great difficulty chartering another plane to follow him, but several hours later he landed in Istanbul to find that Jason had already left on a helicopter flight to Qatar. From there he had borrowed a fast launch from a local sheik and left for Bombay. Kurt had followed him to Bombay, but on a normal airline flight and had landed well ahead of Jason. He was waiting there for him to arrive. As he had already spent several thousand pounds, ended the message, he hoped their friend was worth it.

"Where the hell is he going?" asked Vern.

"He could have gone the easy way; in five thousand years he must know where most of the entrances are located. I just don't know what he is playing at," grumbled Daniel.

"Entrances?"

"Spirit paths. They go all over the world, you know."

Vern was unimpressed. "I don't like them; it's too easy to get lost. I'd rather go by plane."

They both resumed reading the e-mails until Daniel went to check on a reference book in Travis's surprisingly erudite library.

117

"Travis had the idea many years ago that if there's any demonic rising in the offing or any weird creatures out there, a vampire should know enough to avoid them," Sebastian had told him dryly. "His motto is ALWAYS TRY TO BE ONE STEP AHEAD."

"An excellent motto for any sensible vampire," agreed Daniel. "I need to check on the true form of this latest triumvirate. There's some question here as to its demonic origins." He waved an e-mail in Sebastian's direction and left the room.

Rannoth arrived in the lounge about ten minutes later, "In view of the nature of the book we mustn't mention, Lucifer has obtained permission for me to check this building for demonic activity, other than your friends of course," he said to Vern. "He also wants me to build a torture chamber in the basement."

"Okay by me," said Vern, "but you had better check with Travis, it's his building."

"Someone want me?" asked Travis as he entered, with Carlotta pushing a tea trolley. She had conjured up tea and cakes, which were seized on by those in the room.

"Good work Carlotta," said Vern enthusiastically as he drank a cup of tea for the first time in days. "I'm fed up with coffee, if we have to stay here much longer you'll have to stay to make the tea."

"I'm sure that can be arranged," said Carlotta with a smile and a sideways look at Travis.

"Stay as long as you like," said Travis agreeably. Then, seeing Rannoth for the first time and noting his black Ninja outfit, turned towards Vern with a questioning look.

"Rannoth here needs to check the building for Old Nick. Some kind of demonic rising is expected shortly. He wants to check it isn't here, and get a reception area organised in the basement for our more unpleasant type of guests," said Vern smoothly.

Rannoth grinned at this masterly interpretation of his presence and gave Vern an ironic salute.

"Feel free to go anywhere you need," said Travis. "You aren't a vampire, you don't need to ask."

"I prefer to make myself known to our clients," said Rannoth with a grin as he vanished to the basement.

"Must be one of Lucifer's trusted minions," said Sebastian.

"I'm his chief assistant," said Rannoth, popping back up to put him right.

About twenty seconds later Vern found himself without any

118

warning, in a large shining white room which appeared to be a waiting room. It had a thick white carpet and white, leather-covered seats surrounding white marble-topped tables. Vern sat at one, before shock made his legs give way beneath him. The sun shone through the windows, its unearthly golden glow filling the room with bright light.

The room echoed to a roll of thunder and a voice boomed out at him.

"So, you are the friend of Elliott and Natalia who wishes to intercede for them?"

"It's a little more than that," stammered Vern, as it dawned on him who was speaking. "I think the punishment is more than Elliott should have to bear, and we shall all miss Natalia dreadfully. The way I see it – er – sir! Natalia needs a couple of bodyguards. Two strong hard men like Snake, who is a truly gruesome vampire, and Drago who can turn himself into an evil-looking troll. Elliott could safely leave her whenever he had to. One look at Snake and anyone would be scared to move.

"Drago frightens her too," he went on. "Carlotta and Natalia were really scared when he turned into a troll. They sat in the kitchen at Quinn's Castle and never moved a muscle. So if you could see your way to letting her return, on the understanding that Snake and Drago guard her day and night when Elliott tells her she is to stay at home, I think it would work. At the same time Snake would be earning some brownie points and Old Nick – er – I mean Lucifer would be pleased to get rid of Snake as he's paying too much attention to Bianca and it's making him really narked. Angry, I mean."

"Young man," boomed the Great Entity. "I admire a man who stands by his friends, even if one of them is the opposition. Lucifer explained the gist of your plan and I find I can agree. Mind you, this is her last chance. She has always been a problem. We all thought Elliott could handle it, but apparently she was too much even for him. But I agree, he should not have to suffer for his wife's foolishness. You can take her with you. Young Nick is already with his godfather, I should let him stay there for a while. Let the angels sort themselves out first. I have also ordained that the other children shall be guarded in the Fortress, where they will all be safe. They shall all be returned when this crisis is resolved. Incidentally, I congratulate my angels on their good friends."

The blinding light vanished and Vern stood alone in the

waiting room. Several minutes passed. There was a flash of lightning and Natalia entered the room. She looked very young and frightened as she stood there. Her face lightened momentarily as she saw Vern.

"What are you doing here? This is Middle Earth, no living human has ever stood here! You aren't dead, are you?" She ran across to touch him.

"As far as I know I am still living," grinned Vern. "I came to fetch you back. Elliott can't bear to live without you, nor can we But you come with strings attached, my girl."

"I know. The Great Entity told me. I'm very lucky that Elliott has a friend like you. I will never take the chance of losing him again. I've learned my lesson. Allegra told me what would happen and it did. I wish I'd listened with my heart, not my head."

"If you've learned that much then we are practically home and dry," said Vern, "let's go."

As quickly as he had come, he and Natalia were returned to the penthouse.

Elliott, who had arrived seconds before, leapt up as they reappeared. Natalia flung herself at him almost knocking him off his feet. He grasped her around the waist and she was engulfed in a tight embrace. "I don't know how you got here, but God knows I need you."

"He does indeed," said Vern as he ushered everyone out of the room, shutting the door behind him.

"I don't know how you managed that, but you have the heartfelt thanks of all of us," said Daniel, holding out his hand and shaking Vern's.

"I shouldn't be taking this so lightly," said Vern. "I have just had a chat with the Great Entity, my insides are still shaking. If I wasn't totally convinced that Elliott and Natalia had to be reunited, I think I might have died of fright."

Daniel looked at him in amazement. "Is that what you wanted Lucifer for?"

"I had this idea for keeping her out of harm's way when Elliott can't be with her."

"And that is?"

"Bodyguards. I know two who scare her to death."

"Who are they?" asked Pauline mystified.

"Snake and Drago. The Great Entity agreed. Whenever Elliott is away, they will stay with her to make sure she does as she's told.

What's more Lucifer is delighted because it means Snake will have to go and live in Cornwall away from Bianca. He's really incensed about Snake, for some reason."

"We should be calling him Machiavelli," said Diana in awe. "The man's a genius."

Vern pretended to preen himself. Being a cat he made a good job of it and Diana gave him a thump. "Don't get too big headed," she warned. "Jaguars have got the edge on a lynx."

Vern morphed and wound himself around Diana's legs purring.

"He's got you there," said Pauline laughing. "That's a verrrry sexxxy purrrr!"

"I'll kill 'im," muttered Diana, as the lynx dragged her from the room, her hand held lightly between his teeth.

"I don't think he's got killing in mind," snickered Pauline.

Charles laughed as they went down the hall.

"I wasn't sure they were suited at first, but she's got him figured out."

"No doubt about that," agreed Daniel winking at Pauline. "It's definitely catching I think my wife would like a breath of fresh air, wouldn't you darling?"

His wonderful werewolf, wiggling her hips enticingly, led the way from the room. Shortly afterwards the lift was heard descending.

"There's another example of animal attraction," said Ward with a grin.

Carlotta looked pained. "The vampire sense of humour leaves a lot to be desired," she said.

Travis was grinning at the English vampire's play on words, "You Spanish angels are too strait-laced for my liking," he told her. "You have to let your hair down a bit now and then."

Admiring the shapely legs and the short red skirt, Travis waited for her sharp retort.

Carlotta looked down her aristocratic nose at him and gave a very unladylike snort of fury.

"American vampires," said Carlotta haughtily. "Don't know class when they see it."

"Oh! That's the name for it now, is it?" he asked with interest. "Personally, I just like to admire the view."

Carlotta eyed him suspiciously, then saw where his appreciative gaze was directed.

"I can't fault your good taste," she told him amused "and of course you do have an advantage over your friends as far as I am concerned."

"What's that?" asked Travis, intrigued.

"Your ability to fly," replied Carlotta promptly. "I find I have just discovered a whole new world, just waiting to be explored, and of course you are immortal, so I should feel quite safe with you."

"Would you like to see New York from my helicopter sometime?" asked Travis, surprised at this ready acceptance of his expertise as a pilot and his vampiric abilities.

"Now that is class," said Sebastian. "Asking an angel to go flying with you."

Carlotta's jaw dropped as Ward and Charles roared with laughter.

"Come into my parlour, said the spider to the fly," they chanted in unison as Travis grinned, unrepentant.

"Beasts," said Carlotta hotly.

"That's what we are," said Charles agreeably.

"I can take you away from all this," said Travis solemnly as he entered into the spirit of things. "We can fly away from this crude lot any time you like."

"You can take me for a flight over the city." She glared fiercely at Charles, Ward and Sebastian. "I need some fresh air and a change of scenery."

"Come my angel," said Travis offering his arm. "Your chariot awaits."

The helicopter took off a few minutes later.

Sebastian looked at Ward. "She'll be perfectly safe with Travis, you know."

"If I wasn't certain of that, she would still be here," said Ward coolly.

Elliott ran his hand lightly over the golden curls as Natalia buried her face in his shoulder. He knew, no matter what she did in future, he could never bear to be parted from her again, even for so short a time.

"I made a promise to Him and Old Nick and to Vern," said a muffled voice into his shirtfront which was already damp with tears. "I'll never go anywhere again until you tell me it's safe and I promised to let this Snake person and Drago stay with me when you are away. Will that do?"

Entwining his fingers in the curls and tugging her head gently from his shoulder, he relentlessly kissed the tear-wet face with love and longing. She kissed him back with equal fervour. They ended up on the couch sometime later with Natalia held firmly in his arms, lying full length on top on him and promising that never again would she risk losing him, by any action of hers.

Elliott smiled to himself and wondered how long the good intentions would last, but was certain the presence of Drago and Snake would be a big deterrent in the future.

"I am absolutely certain, Tally, that no matter what you do, I could never send you away again. But I do beg you to consider how you would feel if I were to die because I went headlong into danger with no thought to you. That is what you have done to me so many times, lately. It is a terrible thing to imagine what might happen to you, because I know what did happen when you rushed in to help rescue Lance and James without any thought to the consequences, even though I tried to stop you. You were kidnapped and hidden from my sight. When eventually I found you, I thought you were dead and I wanted to die with you. I wouldn't have been able to, of course, and immortality without you is a nightmare thought."

Tally's eyes filled with tears once more as she imagined her own nightmare future without him. Forty-eight hours of emptiness and fear had changed her life for ever.

"I'll never rush headlong into anything again. THINK FIRST is my new motto," she promised candidly as she dried her tears on the small piece of his shirt she hadn't cried on.

They shared a very long kiss before he put her away from him, and said, "There is a great deal to do tonight, but I want you to do something rather difficult."

"Anything!"

He told her what had happened to Alex and Faith. "It was a real accident, nothing supernatural about it, but they are unconscious and unable to defend themselves. Felicity will do her best, but I want you to go back to England right now and stay with them. Felicity needs company. I am sending you into danger myself this time, someone has found the Book, and is using it to raise a demon to mortal life. Any one who has the slightest knowledge of it is in danger, the holder is all-powerful and all knowing until stopped. I will send James Purcell to you as soon as I can find him."

"What about Lance?"

"I was really joking when I mentioned sending him and Drago

to America, but I may need him later, to perform an exorcism. After all, he is in holy orders."

"I'll do my best to defend them, and you can trust me not to do anything stupid."

Elliott smiled. "I believe I can. Just do your best."

"You want me to put a force field around them all?"

"It's worth a try. I am going to see if Vespazia can help us reinforce our own powers, but you do what you can in the meantime."

He gave her a final hug and a gentle push. She waved and vanished.

He pulled out his phone again and rang Drago. Vespazia answered and said Drago had already been back with their family. She would guard them with her life, she told him.

"Let's hope it doesn't come to that, but first things first. Did you get Drago to the hospital to guard Faith and Alex? Because if you did I've got a new assignment for him. He has been directed by the Almighty to guard Tally. Whenever I am unable to be with her, he and a vampire called Snake are to be her bodyguards. It is a heavenly command."

"He took up guard duty two hours ago," replied Vespazia. "In view of the public nature of the place, he has assumed his normal human form, but rather taller than usual, I hazard a guess at six foot eight inches. He scared even me, I will tell him of his new assignment." She sounded amused. "Someone called James has also arrived and Alex's mother and father arrived with him."

"James must have managed to track them down, thank goodness. In case no one told you," said Elliott, laughing despite the seriousness of the situation, "all three of the new arrivals are shapeshifters and will be adequate extra guards. I am confident they will stay nearby. It makes Tally's safety more assured."

"I can go to and fro between there and here in seconds, if you wish me to," said Vespazia.

"Whenever it is convenient, I should be reassured if you did."

He went down the hall to find Daniel, less concerned about the British end of the action than he had been ten minutes previously.

"All well?" asked his friend.

"Very well," said Elliott fervently, "I've sent her to England to be with Felicity, and I've got Drago and James to join them as well. Vespazia said she'll nip back and forth between the two places to keep an eye on things. James brought Alex's parents with him A lion and a leopard. That should be protection enough."

"Sounds okay to me," said Daniel.

# CHAPTER NINE

"What's the plan for tonight?" asked Elliott.

Daniel and the shapeshifters had come up with a plan to get into the building. It was actually a two-pronged attack on the building and it was intended that the vampires would attack from the roof and the shapeshifters from the sewers. Daniel and Elliott were to go in through the front door and engage the attention of the guards. They hoped that, by now, the guards would be thoroughly cheesed off at being incarcerated in the building and be rather less watchful than usual and less cautious.

With Travis piloting them, Sebastian and Snake were to use the helicopter to land on the roof and Pauline was to accompany them. Travis would remain in the helicopter with the motor running for a quick getaway, if required.

Vern, Charles and Diana would enter through the sewers and both groups would search floor by floor, office by office for the six faces identified in the photographs obtained by Vern and Diana from the video they'd stolen.

Snake was first out of the helicopter and headed for the camera and door alarms. Within moments he had disabled both.

"I see you're no stranger to breaking and entering," remarked Sebastian.

"Like to keep my hand in," grunted Snake, ripping the door off its hinges with one hand and darting through.

"Nice work, Snake," said Pauline approvingly as she stepped over the buckled door.

Snake was already yards down the hallway, kicking open a locked door and racing through an empty office. The next one was occupied but not by anyone they wanted. Snake hurled the man against the window and shoved Sebastian's photos under his nose. "Who are they and where is their office?" he snarled. "Answer, or it's out the window for you!"

"About twenty-eight floors to the sidewalk," observed Sebastian glancing casually out of the window. "Answer the man, we only have until sunrise."

He screamed in pain as Snake twisted his arm high behind his back and his elbow dislocated.

"Try for the knees," said Pauline from the doorway. "Kneecaps are so useful if you want to walk."

Snake drew back his booted foot for a kick and the man threw himself to his knees. "I'll talk; I'll tell what you want to know."

"Very wise," said Sebastian. "My two colleagues are really not at all nice to know and it makes such a mess when you have to torture someone."

By this time the man was a gibbering wreck and told them anything they wanted to know.

They discovered that two of the men were the firm's accountants and the other four were security guards from several different floors in the building. Two of these shared other duties. One was the chairman's bodyguard and another the managing director's driver when required.

The sales director, who was now their prisoner, told them where they were all likely to be found. Snake knocked him out, tied him to the chair with his own tie and secured him tightly with some parcel tape handed to him by Pauline. "Found it in the secretary's office," explained Pauline.

They all headed for the office where the sales director had told them they could find the accountants.

Snake led the way down to the twenty-sixth floor via the stairs and pushed open the hall doors, looked searchingly on the doors for the office numbers, and headed down the corridor. He crashed through the door of room 2618, catapulting into the room followed by Sebastian and Pauline. Two accountants were lounging in their chairs in apparent unconcern at being held prisoner within the building. Sebastian pointed to the bottles of wine and whisky littering the desks and floor, and understanding dawned. Snake leaped the desk and grabbed them both, smashing their heads together with a cracking sound.

"Ouch!" said Pauline. "I bet that hurt. You didn't hurt your hands did you, Snake?" she added anxiously. "You'll need them for torturing them later."

Snake looked appreciatively at Pauline, "I can see the werewolf genes are in the ascendancy. I hope your old man appreciates you properly."

Pauline grinned back. "No one appreciates me more," she told him.

Both accountants had got the reference to a werewolf and, seeing Snake fully vamped and definitely enraged, they tried to escape by running around the desk and heading for the door. They were too drunk to appreciate the danger. When Sebastian stuck out his foot and tripped them, Sebastian had thoughtfully brought along the parcel tape. He expertly taped their hands and feet, and their mouths, although by now they were past screaming.

"Nice, neat parcels for collection," said Pauline with satisfaction. "I'll stay here and guard them. You go find some more. While you're looking, don't forget Old Nick would be thrilled if you managed to bring the chairman or managing director back with you."

Sebastian nodded his head and Snake grimaced unpleasantly, but agreed to keep it in mind if he should cross their path.

They shut the door behind them and heard Pauline lock it from inside.

"Is she as tough as she sounds?" asked Snake, as they walked swiftly down the stairs to the next floor.

"The Brit witch says she is a holy terror, practically uncontrollable. She said her old man is the only one she pays any attention to. Called Lucifer a moron to his face the first day she was here."

"I've heard about werewolves, never thought I'd meet one, particularly a female one."

"Shouldn't have thought you'd ever expect to meet an angel, and we've met three in four days."

"That's what worries me," said Snake shuddering appreciatively. "All these angels, plus Lucifer and Elliott, makes a fellow wonder if being a vampire is all it's cracked up to be."

"I clocked that one several years ago," said Sebastian. "I make fifty times more money going straight and using my vampire senses to help me in my work than I ever did terrorising and feeding off humans. There are opportunities out there if you want them."

"Perhaps we had better have a little chat about options sometime," said Snake, agreeably surprised by this overt offer.

On the next floor they searched diligently through the offices, disposing of difficult employees by locking them in cupboards and tying up the really awkward ones. They proceeded with caution, but not too much as it seemed they had not been expected. That, or Daniel and Elliott had quelled any opposition.

Daniel and Elliott had strolled in through the main door not sure what to expect. What they found was hysterical employees and demoralised guards gathered in the foyer. Not being able to get out of their building for the last three days had brought home to them all, the price for tampering with the forces of evil.

By now it was known that someone had tortured an angel and that the angel's boss was seeking vengeance. Everyone from the chairman to the office boys had learned of the angel's death and the inability of anyone within the building to leave. To most it was obvious that they awaited retribution.

Daniel had accessed the minds of several of the terrified staff and had found a rampant thread of evil was in the building, particularly centered on the upper floors.

Elliott already realised this and was heading for the lifts to the upper floors when Vern, Charles and Diana emerged from the stairway to the basements.

Charles waved in the direction of the next floor and indicated that they would use the stairs.

Daniel had picked up a thought from one of the guards and headed for the security desk. He leaned over and lifted the man by his tie and jerked him forward over the desk. "Tell me," he said with sibilant menace, "where the managing director is, right now."

The guard, ignoring the soft voice but noting the menace in the tone, pointed to the door to the lift. "Gone to get his car, he's going to try to get help. The banshee and the shamen are with him."

Daniel heard Elliott grind his teeth in fury and together they headed for the basement. The shapeshifters must have come up by the stairs as the managing director went down in the lift.

"He's not going to get away. No banshee can break Nick's spell, and I'm sure a shaman hasn't got that kind of power," offered Daniel in an attempt to offset Elliott's rage.

They ran down the stairs and into the car park. Two shamen and a banshee were standing by a large limousine. The driver and the managing director were about to get in. Daniel sent a thought wave tearing towards the shamen and they collapsed on the ground. Elliott was a little more direct, he enveloped the banshee in a ball of fire and let it burn. They turned their attention to the driver and the managing director.

"This is very nice of you," smiled Daniel pleasantly. "We have been looking for you and here you are, with transport provided. What do you reckon, Elliott, shall we call for back-up?"

Elliott shrugged. "Let's wait and see what happens." He looked at the driver. "This is one of them. We've got the managing director as well. What a stroke of good fortune. After all, the boss is responsible for what goes on in his offices, so he must take the blame."

"Nick will be pleased," said Daniel. "I hope the others are having the same success."

The driver, a large burly looking individual, eyed Daniel's slight form with derision and made an attempt to charge at him. The managing director unwisely took a step in Elliott's direction, stopping short when he saw the grim-faced demon standing menacingly above him. Even without his wings, Elliott in dark form was formidable to behold.

Daniel sidestepped the driver's charge and neatly chopped him at the base of the neck. The man dropped like a stone. Daniel caught him before he hit the ground and threw him into the back seat of the car. Elliott motioned to the managing director to get in with him. Neither moved as Elliott stood, arms folded across his chest, staring at them. Daniel leaned against the open door, examining the captives through narrowed eyes. They waited.

Vern, Diana and Charles emerged from the lift about half an hour later, pushing and prodding three men in front of them. They all looked the worse for wear. Vern had a knife protruding from a wound in his left shoulder, but held a gun on the captives. Diana was nursing a cut hand and also brandished a gun at their captives. Charles had a pained look on his face. Blood was seeping into his shirt from his left shoulder and right side as he helped push the captives towards Elliott.

"Bastard shot me," said Charles, kicking a tall red-headed guard in the back of the knees, sending him onto the floor in front of them. He held his left elbow with his right hand and blood was dripping rapidly on to the floor.

"Seems like he got shot as well," remarked Daniel, looking with interest at the wounds the redhead was bleeding from.

"Diana kicked the gun from his hand, caught it and shot him with it," said Vern proudly, glancing admiringly at her.

"He shot Charles and was still shooting at him," said Diana indignantly. "Vern wouldn't like it if anything happened to Charles, so I shot him."

"Thanks, Sis," said Charles. "Appreciate the thought," he added faintly, before collapsing on the floor.

Diana gave a smothered scream and fell to her knees, feeling for a pulse.

"He's only fainted," she told them thankfully. "Loss of blood I think. We'd better get him home."

Vern and Elliott were watching the captives and they did seem resigned to their fate.

"Can you drive Diana?" asked Daniel.

"Sure."

"Vern you ride with Elliott and the three guards and I'll go with Diana in the Limo. We'll take them to HQ for now and decide what to do with them when Nick arrives."

"I wonder how the vampires are doing?"

"We heard the helicopter take off, some time ago," said Diana.

Sebastian arrived in the basement in a hurry as they were putting Charles on the back seat of the Limo. He helped them arrange him carefully, then got in himself, pointing the gun that Diana had been holding very convincingly at the managing director and his driver, who sat on the floor. Diana drove off with Daniel and Sebastian riding shotgun in the back.

Sebastian told them that Travis had picked up the two accountants and the chairman and was ferrying them back to his place. Snake and Pauline were riding shotgun and had the three of them 'trussed up like turkeys' as Pauline was taking no chances on their escaping.

"She told them how long it takes to hit the ground if you are pushed out of a helicopter at a thousand feet," said Sebastian. "Even Snake is impressed by her ruthlessness."

Sebastian's mobile rang; he spoke for a few moments. "That was Travis, they've arrived safely and they haven't let their captives out of their sight or spoken to them. They are waiting for Elliott."

Vern drove slowly out of the car park and followed Diana back to Travis's home. Elliott just glared at the three guards and kept his foot on the one who had stuck his knife in Vern. They didn't attempt to move. The look on Elliott's face would have deterred Rambo.

131

# CHAPTER TEN

Back at the penthouse the witches were staggered when they saw what had happened to Charles, who was still out cold. They held a whispered consultation as Vern and Diana fussed around him, begging them to stop the bleeding and get him well quickly. Sebastian urged them to get Charles onto his bed and see to him first.

Travis and Pauline had secured their captives in the basement where Rannoth was watching over them, then returned to the penthouse. They were waiting to take the rest down as well, but Charles and the other injured had to be seen by Elisande. No one could agree on what to do next. Elliott watched the circus develop into a comic opera and yelled at them all to be quiet.

"Travis, you and Sebastian, put Charles in one of the bedrooms and you two," he pointed to Elisande and Cybel, "can attend to him."

"Cassidy, you can take Vern to the kitchen and attend to his shoulder, and see to the cut on Diana's hand. You can both come back to the lounge when you have been bandaged. Eurydice can attend to Bianca for now, and Snake can help her. Attend to the enemy wounded when you've done our own."

Elliott turned on his heel and returned to the lounge where Daniel, Snake and Pauline were guarding their captives. Daniel and Pauline were forcibly preventing Snake from tearing all five of them to shreds. In full vampire mode and raging with fury he was enough to make any human die of fright and the managing director already seemed to be having a stroke. Daniel loosened his tie but not his bonds and sat him in a chair. The others cowered in terror as they saw that Daniel and Pauline were taking their time restraining Snake as he attempted to kill them all.

"Sorry, Snake," said Daniel reluctantly, pulling him off them again, "but this is Lucifer's territory. He has dominion over the angels on Astral Council business." Snake reluctantly removed himself to lean against the wall and, simmering with rage, he eyed them ominously. Sebastian returned a few moments later and Elliott told Snake to go and see if Bianca was all right.

Snake disappeared with alacrity, his pleasure at seeing Bianca taking priority over his desire to tear her tormentors limb from limb.

Now that he had time to attend to them, Elliott glowered menacingly at their captives.

"You have no idea of the enormity of your crime," he snarled at them, "and that vampire who has just left the room is the least of your troubles."

"I'm bleeding to death," whined the redhead. "I need a doctor."

"Tough," said Pauline, swiping him across the ear and sending him flying against the wall. "Heck! Sorry Travis, blood on the walls," she apologised.

"Think nothing of it, a small price to pay for seeing him bleed," said Travis. "I'd like to see more of his blood on the walls."

"What about inside you?" drawled Cassidy from the doorway.

"We vampires are fussy about our food," said Travis.

Elliott laughed unpleasantly. "Contaminated blood should be destroyed." He sounded quite evil right then. "The furnaces can be lit quite easily."

The four security guards were looking seriously alarmed by this time. None of their captors appeared to be human. Their dismal fate was beginning to dawn on them.

The managing director, who was the Goodman of Goodman, Goodhew and May was recovering from his ailment and beginning to get the picture.

The callous vampires were congregating in the lounge. "I think we'd all better go down to the basement, no one will hear their screams," said Snake. Assured by Eurydice that Bianca was sleeping he had rejoined them, not wishing to miss the 'fun'.

Pauline and Daniel grabbed the managing director, and Elliott shoved a handcuffed guard towards the door. Cassidy had accompanied them on the pretext that he could make sure than none of them expired before Lucifer arrived, and helped enthusiastically to herd the rest towards the lift. The injured redhead fought wildly and almost managed to get to the stairs, but he was seized by Snake who bit savagely into his neck. "One more try to get away and I'll finish you off with or without Lucifer's permission," he snarled.

It took two trips to get them all to the basement where Rannoth had prepared a small reception. The chief torturer complete with whip and chains, was waiting in the doorway. He locked them in handcuffs and leg irons and clipped each length of chain to a ring at his waist. He dragged them into the middle of the floor where a fiery pit of coals was glowing red hot. He flung them all on to the coals and they screamed agonisingly as they sizzled to his satisfaction. Lucifer appeared in the doorway and walked towards the screaming captives. Elliott and Rannoth exchanged surprised looks. Lucifer was in his full demonic persona, horned and red eyed, dressed entirely in black except for the red, silk-lined cape. He carried the legendary pronged fork.

"This all of them?" he inquired unpleasantly. "They don't look up to much." With a wave of his hand he organised a fiery furnace and a snake pit in the basement. The chief torturer flung them all in the pit, including the chairman and managing director. Lucifer looked down at them with satisfaction. "Painful to watch, but I do enjoy a good snake pit!"

Daniel and Elliott stood aside and motioned to Sebastian, Travis and Cassidy to take front seats. After all, they had saved the angel.

All three strolled over for a look. Vern also couldn't resist and gasped as he saw hundreds of snakes writhing around the eight men in the pit. With a wave of his hand Lucifer had them back on the hot coals once more, and the chief torturer yanked on their chains, tossing them around in the fire. Lucifer looked aggrieved as he said, "They are not suffering enough. Put them in the furnace. The chief torturer with help from Rannoth, flung them all into the furnace Lucifer watched critically from his vantage point.

"Done to a turn," he remarked to Rannoth. "You can bring them out, now."

The blackened and burned semi-corpses were incapable of speech, so Lucifer with a wave of his hand restored them to normal human beings.

They were now kneeling in abject terror before him.

"Before I take you to hell with me, I'll give you a chance to remain in my Pit of Infamy or to go to that place beyond hell where suffering is eternal and terrible. I know you six," he pointed the fork at them, "assaulted my angelic messenger. For that there is no reprieve. But if someone tells me who is intending to call forth the demons from their dimension in hell, their torments will cease after ten thousand years."

The six men who were the subject of Lucifer's revenge shook their heads. "We know nothing of any demon raising," said one, "we admit to attacking the angel. We thought she was a mutant demon."

"NO EXCUSE FOR DESECRATION!" shouted Lucifer. "But

134

a point in your favour for owning up."

Rannoth had been watching the chairman and managing director and noticed them exchange a look of dismay. He nodded his head towards them and Lucifer leapt on them like a tiger onto the kill.

"SO! It's you two who have disturbed my realm once more. Death awaits you no matter what you do now. But it will go down better with my colleagues if you tell us what is to rise."

"It wasn't us," screamed the managing director in terror. "We were only obeying orders."

"Whose orders?" asked Elliott sharply, as he noticed Lucifer about to go up in flames.

"He said he was the Lord of the Universe, he owns our building. We were so deep in debt we had to sell it. He owns our souls, now that he has let us stay there."

Elliott and Lucifer exchanged a look of surprise. As far as they were aware, there was only one 'Lord of the Universe'. They answered to the Lord of the Universe, and quite frequently carried out his orders.

"This is getting monotonous. How many more demons are going to claim the high ground," complained Lucifer. "Elliott, nip off to Middle Earth and find out what's going on!"

Elliott disappeared in a cloud of smoke.

"Copycat," yelled Old Nick.

Lucifer prodded the chairman with the 'toasting' fork, drawing blood, "I'll draw a lot more before I'm through," he told him. "What does this Lord of the Universe look like?"

"We've never seen him," The chairman sounded indignant. "As if such an illustrious personage should reveal himself to us."

"Rannoth," said Lucifer. "Do you think these fools really don't know who I am?"

"Doesn't look like it, Boss," said Rannoth gleefully. "Seems they are in for a shock."

"Do you mean to say that they having been running that building all these years, have supposedly got brains and still haven't put two and two together yet?"

"Well they can't be all that smart," said Snake, who had been watching with interest. "They did bankrupt the business, according to you and Daniel."

"Good point, my boy," remarked Lucifer, prodding the chairman to prove his point.

The chairman winced but remained silent. He was a wiser man than the managing director who looked at Lucifer with contempt. "You can't do anything to us now to make us talk."

"You think not?" said Lucifer.

He signalled to Rannoth who opened a portal to Hell. The shrieks and screams of the blackened corpses were as terrifying as the visual effects of the brutal torments and tortures now seen by the eight captives. The sights and sounds experienced by Charles and Katya as they had passed through hell some months before, were nothing compared to what Lucifer showed his captives, now.

Lucifer showed them the bestial and everlasting torments of the damned. Naked bodies whipped to shreds and flung into the fiery furnaces, corpses hanging from the walls and others being boiled alive in cauldrons of oil. Fires and hot coals covered the floor and a constant stream of bodies was flung into them to keep them burning.

The managing director had a heart attack and died. Rannoth flung him into a fiery furnace and shut the door.

"He'll be done on one side in an hour or so," said Lucifer rubbing his hands. "Take him out and put him in again and do the other side."

Sebastian looked amazed. "Didn't know Lucifer has a sense of humour," he whispered to Vern.

"It's a very one-sided one," Vern whispered back, grinning.

Lucifer spared a moment to frown at Vern. "What are you still doing here? You should be looking after your brother. You've had enough problems with torture to last you for a lifetime. Hop it."

Vern looked directly at him. "Your word is my command, O! Master of the Underworld!" he said loudly, with a significant look from Lucifer to the chairman.

Lucifer nodded appreciatively at this intentional reference to his lordly reign in hell.

Vern departed with a wink at Sebastian who, with a last look at the fiery furnace and the chief torturer waiting patiently for Lucifer to continue the torture, followed him.

Rannoth grinned evilly at the chairman and leaned towards him, spouting tongues of fire. "As you seem to be a little slow on the uptake, allow me to introduce my Lord and Master, Ruler of the Underworld, immortal Satan, Lucifer, the Fallen One."

Lucifer unfurled his great black wings and a fiery halo uncurled around his head, his horns grew larger, his eyes glowed red and fire spouted from his finger tips. His cape swirled in the mighty wind which tore through the basement fanning the red hot coals and brightening the flames in the furnace.

At last the seven remaining captives recognised their tormentor and understood their fate.

"To have tortured and hacked off the wings of an angel has been the greatest sin of all," whispered the chairman, accepting responsibility for the actions of his employees.

The room filled with white mist and a golden light shone brightly in the doorway. "That you know it," boomed a great echoing voice, "may be the first step to your redemption.

"The rest are yours for the next ten thousand years, Lucifer, then they are mine. This one, however has further work to do in this world."

Lucifer bowed gracefully in the direction of the light as it vanished.

"I wish he wouldn't do that," complained Lucifer. "It makes me nervous."

"Sends chills up your spine," agreed Elliott, reappearing and grinning nastily at Old Nick "Sorry I was so long. The Great Entity told me where Old Nick had sent our children. I just nipped down to check on young Nick and the others. You've gone a bit overboard with the guards, haven't you? A full company for five kids and the nurses?"

"No one will ever, infiltrate my fortress and take my godchildren," said Old Nick coldly. "There is no such thing as too many guards. My well-trained troops will patrol those corridors as long as those children are in my care."

"It's a pity I didn't have some to guard Tally the other day," complained Elliott. "You could have offered. We could have been saved a lot of hassle. I could have been spared a great deal of pain."

"Sorry, my boy. If you ever need them in the future, feel free to borrow a whole platoon."

Daniel laughed out loud. "I can see them now, marching around Bodmin Moor on exercises, guarding Elliott's angel."

Lucifer nodded approvingly. A very suitable occupation for his elite troops, he thought, and good practice for any forays to the surface on his behalf in the future.

"So be it!" he said to them both. "They are yours to command, I will so inform them. Mind you, the children will always come first."

137

"Naturally," agreed Daniel. "We wouldn't have it any other way."

Getting back to the business in hand Lucifer turned once more to the chairman. "Any doubt in your mind as to who I am?" he demanded.

The chairman gulped and swallowed fearfully. "No! You are Satan, the Master of the Underworld."

"And any doubt as to who just dropped in for a quick word?"

The chairman seemed incapable of speech by now and just nodded.

"Excellent, so we are agreed then that you should be afraid of me. Not someone masquerading as me?"

"Yes, your greatness," whispered the chairman hoarsely, regaining his voice slightly.

"Now we are getting somewhere. Let's get down to the basics. When did this pretender first appear?"

"About four months ago."

"Did he now? That's very interesting. And when did you see him last?"

"Four days ago," moaned the chairman now shaking in abject terror.

"That narrows the field to one," said Lucifer with a look of fury on his face. "My brother, Azeran has been missing for several months. I thought he was safely occupied elsewhere. He's never interfered in my business before. He's usually too damned lazy to even help me with my problems around the world. Whenever I need him, he's usually off pursuing affairs of his own. He must have thought I was too busy in Cornwall and Devon to notice what he was up to in America."

"I wish you could keep better track of your brothers," muttered Elliott irritably, "they are a constant source of annoyance to us all."

"They are my brothers," said Lucifer coldly. "They have to have a certain amount of licence, but interfering in my domain is not within their powers. Whatever Azeran is intent on raising is not from the demon dimensions."

"Very helpful," said Daniel, "But that still leaves Balzahar unaccounted for, and he can perform a raising ceremony with his powers, especially if he has the reading matter we cannot mention. What's more, I don't believe your brother Azeran is the brains behind this, he's never shown any signs of leadership before. I reckon he's just a smoke screen for someone else. So where do we go from here?"

"Corazan did mention a demon triumvirate, but he could have been trying to mislead. Come to think of it, he was a bit too easy to break. You could be right, maybe someone is pulling their strings," mused Lucifer.

He beckoned to the chief torturer, who moved forward eagerly.

"Fetch Corazan, bring him in irons, hot irons."

The Chief Torturer vanished to reappear moments later with Corazan in smoking handcuffs and chains.

Lucifer leaned towards his nephew confidentially. "I have become tired of your lies and evasions and have come to the conclusion that you should be disposed of permanently. You will be burnt in the Eternal Flame and pay the ultimate price for lying to me. Have you any alternative to this decision you'd like to suggest?"

Corazan looked at Lucifer in disbelief. "I am your nephew, the son of your brother, Demerphon. Would you really destroy me utterly?"

"Have you any doubt that I could?"

"No!" said Corazan. "I will tell you what you want to know."

"Lie, and it's the Eternal Flame," warned Lucifer.

Corazan cowered on the floor as Lucifer leaned over him, his trident raised.

"I haven't seen him, but Balzahar says that Azeran plans to open the portals to the world of infinity and let loose the Hydra and the Behemoth and anything else that slips through."

"And dare I suppose that you know what Balzahar is up to?" asked Lucifer with grim menace.

"You were supposed to be too busy dealing with Azeran to notice what was going on elsewhere when the beasts were let loose. Balzahar has a new master." Corazan cringed as streaks of flame from Lucifer's fingertips singed his ears, and the trident held him pinned to the helplessly to the ground. "And before you ask, I don't know who it is, he never told anyone. All I know is that they intend taking your place in Hell. Balzahar has a large group of followers, as most of the demons in the dark dimensions think you have gone soft and are paying too much attention to humans and are now on the side of the angels."

Lucifer gave a savage laugh.

"They will have their work cut out to remove me. I am the ultimate in evil. No one will ever equal my infamy in this eternity.

All of the demons in hell and beyond cannot muster sufficient power to overcome the evil I can unleash. Beware, nephew, whether I consider your role as his accomplice in this to be worthy of my wrath. Yet for now you will be confined where you can do no further damage to my realm."

Corazan was trembling with fear by now and prostrated himself face down. "I am still your nephew, don't kill me, and I will never trouble you again."

"Let him go," said Lucifer to the chief torturer. "I'll take responsibility for him."

Corazan rubbed his wrists which healed immediately he was released from the chains, but the memory of the pain still persisted. Lucifer waved his hand in a circular motion and Corazan disappeared.

"He's safe enough for now," said Lucifer. "He's in a dimensional cell in the lower underworld. No one has ever escaped from there. Solitary confinement in a coffin should cure him of interfering in my affairs."

"Now we know what is coming, how do we stop it?" asked Daniel.

"First we have to let it rise," warned Lucifer. "It's not an immortal triumvirate, it is a magical one. Daniel will have to send it back."

"Great!" said Daniel. "And how do I do that?"

"You weren't given all that ancient druid wisdom for fun," said Lucifer grimly. "This is just the sort of problem it was intended for."

Daniel looked at Elliott and shrugged his shoulders. "Nothing is surfacing at the moment. Give me time."

"I'll have to deal with Azeran and Balzahar," said Lucifer grimly, "I'll get Rannoth to start searching for them. Wherever they are hiding, between us we'll find them."

"We may have a few days, weeks even, before anything happens," said Elliott. "I don't get any sense of urgency from these morons." He indicated the captives being intimidated by Lucifer and the chief torturer. "What's more we have deprived Azeran, if it is him, which I doubt, of his base of operations and his assistants. He'll have to scout up a few more before the summoning can take place. That'll give us a breathing space. But it is a pity we can't find out exactly what Balzahar is up to."

They all eyed the captives with ill-concealed impatience.

Lucifer was on fire to remove them to hell.

The two accountants had long since become senseless and the other four men were only a little better.

"I think we've seen enough, Nick," said Daniel crisply. "As the managing director died right here, he cannot be returned to life, but I believe the chairman knows much more than he has told us. You might as well take the rest of them back to hell and let Bianca be healed."

Lucifer nodded his agreement and motioned to Rannoth, who herded the six men through the portal and into hell. The portal closed. The chairman remained in the basement; awaiting his fate. The Astral Council members knew that whatever else he had done, he had not been involved with those who had tortured Bianca, but to have incensed the ruler of the underworld was fatal. They didn't think he was going to enjoy his remaining time on earth. Elliott decided that questioning him could wait for a while longer.

Elliott spoke quietly to Snake. "Go back to Bianca, she is waiting for you."

Snake found himself beside the bed a split second after Elliott had spoken and knew he had been spirited there by Elliott's own will.

In her room Bianca was alone; the witches disappeared through the doorway as Snake appeared. A silent command from Elliott to Eurydice had ordered them from the room.

Bianca, looking much better, held out her good arm to the vampire, who sat on the bed and took her into his own. As she put her arm around his neck, the most beautiful sound filled the room. Snake looked around surprise uppermost on his face.

Elisande and Eurydice, beckoned to Pauline and Cybel. Carlotta also joined them. They stood outside the door listening as the heavenly choir sang.

Pauline looked at Elisande, who opened the door a fraction and indicated that Pauline and the Crone should watch. Cybel and Carlotta peered over their shoulders.

The room shone with a golden light as the angelic voices continued singing. Bianca was enveloped in a single shaft of this light. A halo appeared around her head and her dark hair shone like a raven's wings, her face healed to its former perfection, her wings grew and the feathers shone again. Her skin began to take on an alabaster sheen as the bruises faded from her body, and her broken arm and bruised legs healed. Both arms now tightened around

Snake's neck. Her large brown eyes gazed deeply into his blue ones as, with an overwhelming sense of awe, he watched an angel reborn.

A flicker of light touched him as he held her close. He felt a jolt as if he had been hit by a thousand volts of Electricity. He felt as if he and Bianca had just become one person. Bianca felt it too.

"He approves," she said softly. "You have been chosen as my protector. I can go to England with you and help protect the angel Natalia for the Astral Council. You and I have much to do. He knows everything. He knows how we met before and how you saved me then."

Snake replaced her on the pillows. He was overawed. He had not missed the significance of the presence of the heavenly choir, or the fact that he had been permitted to witness the transformation.

"I didn't know then that I was saving an angel. To me you were just a lost little girl who fell from the sky. Now that I know you are an angel it changes everything. If I've been chosen as your protector it will mean we have to live together." He sounded rather shocked. "If we are to go to England to guard that angel, then we are getting married first."

Bianca hid a smile. She had hoped the wicked vampire would have a conscience. He had now proved that he had. She had great hopes for herself and Snake in the future. Although she was very small and dainty, she wasn't as young or as fragile as she looked. She sat up in the bed, in her human form once more.

Catching the tail end of this conversation Lucifer appeared in the room, followed by Elliott and Daniel.

Lucifer was spitting flames as he approached the bed.

"No way am I having a son-in-law called Snake," he snarled at them both then turned on Elliott. "This is all your fault, I told you to keep them apart."

As a deafening silence descended on the room, he suddenly realised what he had said.

Eurydice cackled out loud. "Caught in your own web," she crowed.

Lucifer glared around the room warningly, daring anyone to speak. They all knew now why Lucifer had been so enraged by what had happened to this particular angel.

The one most affected by the revelation was holding the devil's daughter in his arms. He looked horrified. He turned to Bianca. "Tell me it's not true!" he begged.

Bianca hung her head and looked at him under her eyelashes,

142

"I didn't want to upset you before you knew for sure you loved me. It was bad enough that you found out I was an angel, when you got here and saw me injured. Even after I recovered a little, how could I tell you Lucifer was my father?"

"It's a good thing I love you too much to care," said Snake kissing her soundly.

Bianca swung her legs out of the bed and, assisted by Snake stood up. She glided over to Lucifer.

"Everything is all right, Daddy!" she said soothingly. "I shall be well looked after. Snake has been chosen as guardian to angels."

Lucifer was incensed. "That bloodsucking viper has been chosen to protect the angels? Who said so?"

"The Great Entity did," said Elliott. "He told me so himself when I went to Middle Earth to check what was going on. He said he's only once before seen anyone so ready to atone for past sins. He gave the other one a chance as well," he added, thoughtfully.

"He'll have to change his name," said Lucifer, gritting his teeth and capitulating in face of the supreme power of the organiser of this honour bestowed upon his future son-in-law. No child of mine is marrying a man called Snake."

Snake glared at Lucifer and appealed to Bianca. "You can live with Snake, can't you?"

Bianca chuckled at this very public proposal of marriage. "Daddy will have to get used to it."

'Daddy' swirled his cape around a half a dozen times, created a mini whirlwind and disappeared in a mass of smoke, flames and thunder and lightning.

"He's not pleased," said Vern laconically as he leaned against the door jamb.

"Serves him right, he's always annoying other people. He's on the receiving end for a change." Pauline sounded really pleased at the idea.

Everyone laughed.

"How the Hell did he come to have an angel for a daughter?" asked Diana.

"He wasn't always wicked," said Bianca. "He was an angel himself once."

"How long ago was 'once'?" asked Snake cagily.

"A very long time," said Bianca defensively.

"How long have you been around?" he asked suspiciously.

Bianca looked cross. "It's not polite to ask a lady's age," she reproved him.

Pauline hooted with laughter. "She's no spring chicken," she murmured to Diana.

"Pauline!" snapped Daniel angrily. "Shut up! Get over here, right now!"

Pauline's mouth snapped shut immediately.

The American vampires were totally amazed as she slid over to Daniel and put her hand through his arm and never said another word.

They watched in disbelief as they saw the witch's words come true before their eyes. The fiercesome werewolf really was totally under the spell of this slim and elegant druid. They viewed him ever after in a totally different light.

Snake was so diverted by this that he had lost his train of thought and, when he found it again, he decided that it didn't matter anyway. He was a pretty old vampire himself. Maybe he should think himself lucky an angel even deigned to look twice at him.

Bianca caught this thought and held out her arms to him. He caught her close and whispered in her ear. "I don't really care how old you are. You are an angel and immortal. I am a vampire and immortal, if I avoid the sunlight and wooden stakes. Who cares about age. How long is eternity?"

Bianca laughed into his neck as she pretended to bite him. "We have plenty of time in the future to discuss age, if it bothers you that much. But remember a thousand years is a day in the life of the true immortals. Technically, I'm still a baby."

Snake pretended to be horrified. "Do you mean to say that I am cradle snatching?"

Bianca looked at him with a wicked smile. "If you want to be that technical, I am just the right age for you."

"When you two have quite finished," said Elliott in exasperation. "You have a pressing engagement in Cornwall. You can use our headquarters at Simba for the time being. We'll fix you up with somewhere permanent later. If you insist upon getting married right away, and looking at you both it seems a good idea, get Natalia to introduce you to our local vicar and he will perform the ceremony. He is a shapeshifting jaguar and a very good friend of your father's as well as ours. If I were you I'd make sure your father is at the wedding to give you away, or there could be trouble in the underworld!"

Snake and Bianca looked at him in surprise. "You mean we

have to go now? Daddy never mentioned that."

"Daddy," said Elliott coldly, "is not in charge here, I am, and I say you go now. My wife is in need of strong protection, and Snake is it."

"*OOPS!*" said Bianca. "We seem to have offended our new boss, Snake. We'd better be on our way."

She grabbed hold of Snake's hand and they both vanished. A light trill of laughter was heard as they made this dramatic exit.

Elliott ground his teeth in rage. "Another wayward angel," he muttered to Daniel. "I hope Snake lives up to his name and keeps her under control."

"I wouldn't hold my breath if I were you," said Vern sagely. "Angels are unpredictable when they get here on earth, and you demons and vampires are pushovers for them."

"You can say that again," said Pauline snidely, pointing to Travis and Carlotta sitting in the lounge poring over a brochure of the Grand Canyon. Heads together they were deciding whether to go down the rapids on a raft, or to take the easy way and the helicopter, completely oblivious to the by-play between the rest of the people in the apartment.

Elliott frowned as Diana and Vern laughed at this evidence of the earth angels' ability to mesmerise their menfolk.

"Don't even think it," Daniel warned, as Pauline was about to say something cutting to the vampires.

Elliott caught the next thought in Pauline's mind and glared at her

She looked straight at him and thought it anyway.

"I'd keep a strict eye on all the angels if I were you. Just think what the three of them could do if they really tried."

Elliott shuddered, exchanged a horrified look with Daniel and vanished.

"Where's he gone?" asked Sebastian surprised.

"He's gone to make sure that Snake is up to the task of minding a handful of angels," said Daniel cryptically, frowning warningly at Pauline as she took a breath to speak.

Pauline grinned at him saucily and cuddled cosily into his side as, with a toss of her head, she made certain her long black hair swirled across the front of his shirt. Daniel took a deep breath and putting his arm around her waist, steered her towards the largest armchair and pushed her into it. Leaning over her he kissed her firmly and put a strong thought into her subconscious.

"Stay put," he muttered under his breath. "I'll deal with you later."

Pauline tossed her head again, in annoyance, and whispered back, "You won't have the time."

He put his hands each side of her face and told her silently, COOL IT. ELLIOTT'S GOT ENOUGH TROUBLES WITHOUT YOU ADDING TO THEM. AND FOR YOU, MY DARLING WIFE, I'LL ALWAYS MAKE THE TIME.

About ten seconds later, Pauline was fast asleep. Daniel lifted her effortlessly into his arms and laid her on the nearest couch. He ran his hand lightly down her cheek and turned back to the vampires.

"I'm sorry," he apologised quietly. "You must excuse us a rather personal moment. The wolf surfaced and had to be restrained. She will sleep for several hours."

Sebastian looked at him for a long moment and nodded in understanding. "Why don't you put her in the bedroom, she will be quite safe. The witches can keep an eye on her if you need to go elsewhere."

Daniel nodded and picking Pauline up once more followed Sebastian to a large bedroom at the end of the corridor. He noted the en suite bathroom and thanked the vampire for his thoughtfulness. He placed his wonderful werewolf on the bed and covered her with the duvet. One last look and he shut the door very quietly and walked back to the lounge. Shortly thereafter he received a call from India. Kurt Danzigger had finally caught up with Jason, although he had not as yet made contact. Daniel decided to keep the knowledge to himself for the time being.

Elliott meanwhile had arrived at Simba, to find Snake and Bianca still there. He moved silently into the lounge and looked fiercely at them both.

Snake looked coolly at him for a moment and then told Bianca to go into the kitchen and make tea.

"No wave of the hand and a thought or two," he warned. "I want a word with Elliott alone."

Bianca disappeared towards the kitchen. They both heard the unangelic comment about overbearing men who thought they could push people around whenever they felt like it and exchanged rueful looks.

"Don't worry," said Snake. "I've got my angel under control. I don't have to be a nice guy. I've got an evil pedigree going back centuries to enhance my personality, and no one is going to be surprised if I turn nasty. Your angel will be quite safe with me. I promise you."

He strolled over to the door and glanced down the hallway. Seeing that Bianca was still in the kitchen, he said, "She is not certain of me and I intend to keep it that way, until I am sure she will be quite safe when I leave her on her own. The only reason she was in trouble in America was because she was torn between doing what her father wanted and coming back to me. Now she is in no doubt which of us loves her the most, I have a very strong hand to play with."

He hesitated for a moment and then continued. "There is another problem we shall have to deal with in the near future. I know that when Daniel read her mind to find out who had injured her in that office, he also saw who tried to kill her last July. You both told me what he saw, for which I thank you. I understand that for now no one must know but it has made it rather more difficult to guard her. However, she has promised her father and myself that she will never go anywhere without telling me first. I believe her."

"I think you are right to believe her," said Elliott slowly. "I wish I could say the same of Natalia. Only time will tell. Make sure she comes to no harm and I will be eternally grateful to you. At some time in the near future Daniel and I will try to solve the problem of Bianca's little accident, but we really can't spare the time now. You have been chosen for the job you are doing and, if you keep a close eye on Natalia and Bianca, they should be safe enough for the present."

Snake grinned unashamedly at him. "I intend to. It occurs to me that to have both the Dark One and the Prince of Darkness owing me a favour is probably a good idea."

Suddenly Elliott laughed. "I feel that Vern was right to pick you and Drago as Natalia's guardians. I have the feeling you are just the right ones to succeed where I have failed."

"Love can make fools of us all," said Snake. "The trick is to make sure the object of your affection doesn't realise it."

"Too late for me to try that," grinned Elliott. "The object of my affection has me exactly where she wants me: putty in her exquisite hands."

Snake grinned back at him. "It's a shame we didn't meet sooner."

"If you both come with me after we've had that cup of tea, I'll introduce you to Natalia, Alex and Faith and some of our other friends from the witch and shapeshifting communities around here," said Elliott.

Bianca wheeled in the tea trolley and eyed them both suspiciously. "What have you two been up to? You look like smug pigs!"

Snake eyed her silently and she suddenly laughed happily. "It's okay Snake, I'll not do anything to cause friction between you and your new friends. Daddy told me a long time ago how important their work is, and I'm not foolish enough to want to be killed just because I didn't listen to reason. If I think you are wrong about something, I'll argue with you, but I promise I'll never go anywhere that you say is too dangerous, unless you are with me."

Snake grabbed her around the waist and kissed her soundly. "That will do for me."

"You've got an angel in a million there," said Elliott. "Take good care of her."

"You can count on it," said Snake proudly.

# CHAPTER ELEVEN

Later that evening they arrived outside the hospital in Exeter and Elliott took them to meet Drago and James.

When he got to Faith's bedside he was stunned to see very tall dark man, dressed entirely in black, seated on the bed one arm around Felicity and holding Faith's hand in his. He wore a similar outfit to Rannoth's preferred Ninja style, but the black turban draped around his head and hanging in a long fold from his neck told Elliott that he was facing a djinn: a seriously dangerous, high-grade, shapeshifting, half-human demon from the northern borders of the ancient country of Persia, now known as Iran. He was horrified to see such a demon at Faith's bedside. Faith was awake and smiling at something her mother had told her.

"What are you doing here?" he inquired harshly. "Who the devil are you?"

Felicity stood up from her position beside the dark stranger.

She put her hand on Elliott's arm and looked at him warily for a moment. "This is Faith's father," she began, smiling faintly. "It's a long story and not to be told here. Only mother and I knew of his existence until this morning when he arrived to see Faith. He had heard she was in an accident and that she was very ill. He didn't know about Alex's injuries until he got here. He has managed to lighten Alex's coma and he will recover completely and quite soon. Karim has always known and loved our daughter, but it was his idea that she think he was dead. He didn't think he would be acceptable as the father of an English witch. I could never convince him otherwise until he heard she was injured, and here he is."

The djinn looked amused as Elliott eyed him suspiciously.

"I have heard of you," he said maliciously. "The Dark One, servant of Lucifer."

Elliott's lip curled unpleasantly. "If I were you I would be attempting to make myself acceptable to my daughter's friends," he told the djinn coldly. "I have the feeling that my powers far exceed your own."

"There is no doubt of that," agreed the other. "And of course you are right. My daughter's friends should also be mine."

He held out his hand to Elliott who took it firmly. "No point in trying to hide who we are," he told the djinn. "I'm Elliott, this is

Snake, and this is Bianca."

"Never met a djinn," said Snake with interest. "Perhaps we could have a little chat sometime."

Bianca giggled as the djinn raised his eyebrows, at the two of them.

"Angel and vampire. She's Lucifer's daughter," said Snake dryly. "I am here by command." He pointed heavenwards.

The djinn looked shaken for a moment. "I see my daughter and son-in-law move in exalted circles."

He bowed towards Elliott. "I am yours to command."

Felicity took a deep breath. "Karim, you can't stay here, you'll be seen, someone will be bound to report you."

"It's all right, my beloved," said Karim soothingly. "I have a passport and papers to prove I am your husband of long standing and don't forget your passport has many years of entry visas into my country. We have nothing to fear from anyone."

Faith gasped. "*Mother*! So that's where you went twice a year when no one could get in touch with you. You wicked witch, why on earth didn't you tell me?"

"I am to blame," said Karim. "I was afraid you would not want so ancient a demon for your father. But I could not forego the pleasure of my wife's company." He took Felicity's hand and held it to his lips.

"I'm sorry you thought that," said Faith in a low voice, "because I would have loved to have you for a father. But you did come to see me sometimes, in the night when I was sleeping. You spoke to me and told me you loved me, and I have always felt my father was near. Until now I didn't know why."

"Astral projection or materialisation?" asked Elliott knowingly.

"Both, at one time or another, particularly if I wished to visit my wife," said Karim, with a slight smile as Felicity blushed.

"Is there any reason why you can't stay here?" asked Elliott, noting the pink cheeks with interest. "A djinn would be a useful addition to the Astral Council." Felicity looked gratefully at Elliott, "You've already accepted him. Thank you. You've told him about the Council and now he's a part of your organisation, he has no choice."

She turned to Karim and laughed softly.

"Dearest Karim, you are now in the service of the Great Entity and Lucifer. Elliott here is the Commander of the Earth Services.

There is no going back, you are part of it whether you like it or not."

Elliott looked at Felicity with affection. "One day you must tell us all the story, but I agree now is not the time. However there is one thing I must tell your Karim."

He beckoned and the djinn walked with him towards the door. Elliott told him of the likelihood of a magical arising using the Mordeus Maxim and the Book of Spells and the djinn's eyes flashed momentarily.

"You are one of the few in this world with the power to negate the use of the magic called forth by the Book. Your presence in Cornwall is ordained, that is quite clear. Snake will tell you what has been happening in America. My wife will tell you the rest."

He turned back to the bed. "Where is Natalia?" he asked Felicity.

"She went home with James and Drago and the Lanyons," said Felicity, "She is quite safe. She will be back later and so will they."

"Snake has been drafted in to help guard her for me. Either he or Drago will be with her at all times and, as Bianca is yet another angel, I am sure you will have no trouble. As you heard, she is Nick's daughter. Knowing Nick he'll be in and out of this room like a yo-yo. She seems to be daddy's girl. No doubt we shall hear that tale sometime as well. In fact, knowing Natalia, you'll know within minutes of her getting back here tonight."

"Between Snake, yourself and Natalia, you can bring Karim up to date with all that has happened so far. I must get back to Daniel and Vern. Charles has been shot, I need to keep an eye on things in New York. I'll just go and see how Alex is and then I must get back. Snake is in charge here by the way, until Daniel or myself says differently."

He turned to Faith sitting up in bed and talking quietly with her father. "You just concentrate on getting well, I need all my team in full working order," he told her with a smile.

"I'll try and drop by later, when Natalia is here," he added lightly, then vanished.

He looked in on Alex, saw that he was definitely on the mend and went back to New York.

Karim looked at Felicity with concern. "How long have you been a part of this circus, my sweet?"

"A little over a year. I didn't tell you in case you worried too much about us," she told him carefully. "They have such very powerful friends. His wife is an angel you know, and they have a little boy, who is also an angel. His parents live in the Fifth Dimension. His grandfather is a First One."

"I am aware that the First Ones live in the Fifth Dimension, they really are all powerful," said Karim ruefully.

"Mother has met them all," said Felicity proudly. "She was invited to visit the Fifth Dimension about a year ago."

Karim laughed softly, and held her lightly around the waist as they both watched their daughter slide into sleep.

"I fancy my life is never going to be the same," he whispered into her ear. "I have lived a very long time but I have never had the uncertain privilege of working with angels or the Devil."

Felicity laughed happily. "I seem to spend most of my time in hospitals, chanting healing spells," she told him. "They all get into the most awful trouble. I shall tell mother she will have to take over. I need to spend time with you."

"I think I can arrange that," said Karim warmly. "As soon as our daughter is better we shall return to your home and discuss our future together. It promises to be rather interesting."

They sat in companionable silence for some time, just watching Faith sleeping.

Natalia arrived with Drago and James. The Lanyons had gone straight to visit Alex and would look in later. Natalia looked suspiciously at the djinn now sitting on the bed with his arm most familiarly around Felicity and demanded to know who he was. Faith, who was now awake, told her that he was her father and she had better get used to seeing him around as Elliott had put him on the team.

Natalia looked annoyed. "Why didn't he wait to see me?" she said crossly.

"Because, my dear, he expects you to do your duty when he is busy elsewhere, and wait for his return," said Felicity, delicately reminding Natalia of her responsibilities.

Drago told her to sit down and stop being foolish and introduce them all to Felicity's husband.

Natalia did as she was told and before long had Karim telling her all about himself and how he had met Felicity. By the morning Natalia had the full story of the djinn's life, his meeting with Felicity and his fear that he was not a suitable parent for a female human witch child.

She had sympathised and told him her own life story and, as with the rest of her friends, Snake and Bianca had watched

152

speechless and in awe, as Elliott's angel drew Karim's life story from him.

Natalia turned towards Bianca and smiled blithely. "It will be lovely to have another angel living near us," she told her. "Elliott says that Snake is to join Drago as my bodyguard. I have only met one other made vampire and that was Travis, who is in New York. I met him with Carlotta who was with Vern and Diana. Carlotta says that made vampires are very dangerous. I hope you not going to bite any of our friends," she said, only half joking.

"My days of biting humans are now in the past," said Snake tolerantly. "Bianca insists upon it."

"I must say that I am very relieved about that," said Natalia, "but I should like to hear how you met and how Lucifer came to be your father," she added to Bianca.

"Daddy was an angel when my sister and I were born," said Bianca stiffly. "Our mother was killed by another angel in a war in heaven, and father became very unpleasant to know for a long while."

"According to Jason and Elliott he hasn't improved much in the last one million years," said Natalia with a total lack of tact.

"He has always been a good father to us," said Bianca defensively. "We love him anyway."

"Quite right too," said Drago approvingly. "Duty to one's father is most important in my book."

Natalia was diverted by this remark and turned to Drago. "I didn't know you and Quinn actually had a father," she said surprised. "I thought you were the first of your kind."

"Even the first of a species has to have a male parent," said Drago easily. "But my life story is not sufficiently interesting to tell it now."

He exchanged a look with Snake and they grinned at each other. Elliott's little darling was a real eye-opener, she seemed to put a spell on all who came into contact with her.

"No wonder Elliott wants her guarded day and night when he's away," whispered Snake. "I bet she could charm a crocodile into giving her his teeth. We are going to have our work cut out guarding that angel."

Drago winked at Snake as he made this remark and turned into an eight-foot troll. Natalia took one look at him, turned rather pale, and asked him what he wanted. "I want you to stop harassing Snake and Bianca and Faith's father and go and check on Alex," said

153

Drago with a growl.

Natalia disappeared instantly to do as requested.

"How come she's so scared of you?" asked Snake.

"Oh, I've guarded her before on a couple of occasions. She never moved an inch until Elliott came to fetch her. That's how I come to share the guard duties with you."

"She thinks you are a scary vampire," added Drago, seeing Snake's surprise. "Apparently she told Elliott she wouldn't like to meet you on a dark night. If I were you I'd use that to my advantage."

Snake gave a sinister laugh and strolled off in the direction of Alex's private room. He stood in the doorway and vamped as Natalia looked up from the bedside and spotted him. He noted her shudder of horror as she saw him. He had difficulty hiding a laugh as he realised that he had the upper hand when it came to Elliott's angel.

Daniel grabbed Elliott as soon as he reappeared in New York and they went up to the roof, where he was filled in on the call from Kurt Danzigger. Elliott was relieved, but as puzzled as Daniel as to what he was up to. He brought Daniel up to date with Alex's progress, the visiting djinn and his relationship to Felicity and Faith and his reasons for bringing him onto their team.

Daniel was as stunned as Elliott had been. "*My God!* Felicity and a djinn, who ever would have thought it? I'd love to hear how that came about."

"I am certain that as soon as Natalia gets to the bedside tonight, the full facts will be extracted and we will have the story by the morning," said Elliott dryly.

"I can't wait," laughed Daniel, "she does have a particular gift for ferreting out people's secrets."

"I've used that particular talent to full effect in the past, so I can hardly complain when she practices on our friends," said Elliott. "You are right of course, she is a nosy little monkey, but I don't know what I would do without her."

Snake and Bianca had spent part of the night hunting discreetly in the grounds around the hospital and weren't intending to rush back. Drago had taken Natalia and the Lanyons to find a café for breakfast. James was on guard outside the ward as Karim was on duty inside.

Karim, after talking to his wife and daughter for a while, left to check on his, hitherto unknown, son-in-law. He had used his considerable powers to lighten the coma and induce healing. He was rather pleased to see that his powers were as potent as they always had been, and that Alex was awake. Two nurses had just arrived at his bedside when they had observed his eyelids moving.

Karim was there when Alex opened his eyes and looked dazedly around him. He let the nurses do their work and then moved to the bedside.

"Felicity will be here shortly, but Faith is fine and is in another room nearby. I will see to it that you are moved in beside her as quickly as possible," he told him

Felicity arrived within moments of the nurses telling her that Alex had come around.

"Alex," said Felicity quietly. "I hope you are well enough to understand what I am saying to you. This is Faith's father, he came when he heard how badly she was hurt. But she is fine now, a broken arm and bruises, and a fast-healing concussion. You are going to be fine too; a lot of healing and nursing, and you will be okay again."

Alex understood what she was telling him and nodded painfully. "Tell me later, I'm going to be like Alistair, I'm opting to let you sort me out."

Felicity laughed softly. "Karim here is far more powerful than mother or myself, and someday Faith may inherit his powers. What a treat that will be for us all."

"Tell me later," repeated Alex, and went back to sleep.

"He'll be fine," said Karim, "but I think we can get them both into a private ward, don't you?"

"I'm sure you will arrange it magnificently," said Felicity with a laugh.

An hour or so later, Alex and Faith were in adjoining beds in a small private ward, with their parents in attendance. Sophie and Matthew were highly diverted to meet a djinn, who they had heard was part of the shapeshifting community but had never expected to meet. James being James was just watching, listening and learning.

# CHAPTER TWELVE

Kurt Danzigger had caught up with Jason in Bombay. He'd met the boat at the docks and watched for Jason to debark.

He picked him out immediately and laughed quietly to himself, the extremely good-looking young vampire was dressed as Alistair had suggested he might be. Disreputable jeans, magenta T-shirt and denim jacket slung over his shoulder. A green backpack was the only other item of luggage he had with him.

Jason looked around him unconcerned and raised a finger to a rickshaw driver, a bundle of notes changed hands and they departed the dockside.

Disdaining transport Kurt loped casually across the dock and followed them. They were heading for the residential part of the town and eventually stopped outside a very expensive-looking hotel. Kurt was surprised, the vampire looked rather down at heel to him and he began to get concerned. Jason strolled into the hotel and up to the reception desk. He presented a card to the receptionist who, after a very brief glance at it, handed him a key. With a show of thanks Jason headed for the lift and took it to the fourth floor.

Heading for the desk Kurt was surprised to see the receptionist point to what he took to be the register and pick up the phone. He headed for the desk, hoping to hear the conversation. He was very surprised.

Obviously speaking to the owner of the hotel, the receptionist was telling him that Mr. Parkes had just booked in and should she put the Rolls at his disposal, or would he prefer to speak to him himself?

The receptionist preened visibly on being told to do it herself.

Kurt was impressed. The vampire knew the Indian prince who was the owner of this prestigious hotel. Signing in, in his turn, and with one ear on the conversation and one on his own business, Kurt gathered that Mr. Parkes would indeed like to use the Rolls. He thought it wise to obtain wheels of his own. Hertz India was willing to do the honours and, as he now had his own transport, he decided to keep an eye on Jason's transport. He looked around the lobby and found the usual errand boys hoping for a tip from the tourists. He beckoned one over and asked how much he wanted for watching the driver of the Rolls and letting him know when he was about to depart. He handed the boy, whose name turned out to be Imram, a large sum of money and his mobile telling him the number of his room and letting the boy get the merest glimpse of his other self. Imram was duly impressed and being Indian was not too surprised to find himself in the presence of a demon. "No tricks mind," said Kurt. "You and I have a little deal going and you will be well rewarded for your trouble."

Kurt had the uncanny ability of his kind to know when he was in the presence of a believer, and once again had hit the right note. The boy was eager to serve a demon master.

Satisfied that he could keep a long-distance eye on Jason he went to his own room and used the next few hours to catch up on the history of the district and some sleep.

Jason meanwhile, although sorry that he had left Allegra so abruptly, was on a tight schedule. He was racing against time to get to Tibet and then to China before his parents left their summer residence. He had taken almost four months to track them down and wasn't about to miss them now. He had made up his mind, when Katya had mentioned grandparents, that his parents should rejoin the world and help him in his quest for the answer to the riddle set him by the vampire sages, and to be grandparents to his children. He also hoped that Katya and Charles might in the future produce a couple of shapeshifting vampires, thereby starting a new race of vampires.

It had occurred to him several times in the last two years, as he looked at his friends and their mates, that something odd was happening. It was possible that a new race might be evolving and that he was in at the beginning of a species revolution. New pathways, changes, the words the sages had used rang in his head so often now that he wanted to get to his parents and seek their guidance. He was certain that, after their hundreds of thousands of years of existence, they must have gained much of the wisdom and knowledge of the ancients and many of the modern scholars

He was grateful that his old friend was lending him the Rolls, but he also wanted to borrow several horses and pack-mules for his journey into Tibet and China. He hoped he still knew the right people in the right places. He also needed a truck to transport the horses for the first part of the journey into Nepal.

Much as he hated flying he intended to ask the prince for the loan of his plane to get him and his equipment there.

Time was running out. If he didn't catch his parents at their

157

summer residence, he'd not catch up with them until next year. That might be too late to make his reasoned choices. Going anywhere near China was an enormous risk for a vampire. Somehow the Chinese had the ability to recognise his kind and destroy them. Over the centuries only a few vampires now existed in distant and inaccessible enclaves far away from civilisation and consequently were hard to find if you needed them. Why his parents had gone there was a mystery Jason now felt he might soon solve. He felt rather awkward about seeking them out as they had left to find enlightenment nearly four thousand years before, and he had not seen them since. The very last thing they had ever said to him he remembered: "Take care of your sister and remember that life is to be treasured."

He thought he would know them provided they hadn't decided to age too much. He somehow felt his mother would not have bothered.

He had an uneasy feeling as he strolled out to his car the next morning. A nerve twitched between his shoulder blades. Experience taught him to listen to his nerve endings. He adjusted the rear view mirror and saw someone get into a small dark sedan a few car lengths behind his. He drove off slowly and watched as the sedan followed some way behind. He drove rather slowly to the outskirts of the city and stopped several times to effect business transactions. He arranged the delivery of two horses and several pack-mules, tents and mountain clothing. He also bought a supply of food and utensils. He was clearly going to have company on his trip. He smiled wryly to himself, wondering how Alistair had managed to track him so quickly.

He returned to the hotel and, as he went to his room, he again saw the same man enter the lobby and look quickly around him. Jason picked up his phone and spoke to his friend the prince. Within a short time he was in possession of two important pieces of information and a pass key.

He let himself into a room on the third floor and took a leisurely look around. He sat in a window seat to wait. It wasn't long before a key was inserted in the lock and a man who Jason knew at once to be a demon entered and locked the door behind him. He took out a mobile phone and dialled a number. With his excellent vampire hearing Jason was surprised to hear Daniel's voice on the other end. He silently crossed the floor and took the phone from the demon's hands.

"What's up Daniel?" asked Jason coldly. "Why have you had me followed?"

Daniel told him furiously and at length just what chaos his unexplained and abrupt departure had caused.

"There's a letter in the post for Allegra explaining everything," said Jason angrily. "How was I to know she'd leave in the middle of the night and go to Charles and Katya? If she'd trusted me and stayed put none of this would have happened."

He listened in silence as he was put in the picture of the happenings on the other side of the world.

"Well, I can't come back now, I'll miss my parents and I may not be able to find them again for years. It took me four months to track them down as it is," said Jason angrily. "Surely just this once you can manage without me?"

That answer must have displeased him because he told Daniel hotly that just occasionally one's personal dilemmas took precedence over the earths problems.

"You can tell someone to go to my place and find that letter and give it to Allegra. Then you can mind your own damn business until I get back." He swore angrily at Daniel and disconnected the call.

"And just who are you?" He was livid as, in full vampire mode, he turned on Kurt.

Kurt was startled, but, aware that Jason was not violent unless provoked, told him what he had been asked to do.

"It would serve you right if I left you here," said Jason, "but I am going to let you come with me. You can continue to report on my movements to the Council. That should make them all happy," he added sarcastically.

"No need to get upset," said Kurt, "they were all worried about you. They wanted you found and tracked in case you got into difficulties."

Jason had calmed down by now and looked a bit shamefaced. "Not your fault, you were only carrying out orders. I'll make my peace with Daniel when I get back."

"I should do it now, if I were you," said Kurt candidly. "You went completely over the top if he's your friend."

Jason looked at the phone he still held and hit the re-dial button. Daniel answered almost immediately.

"Cooled down have you?" asked the druid, a laugh in his voice. "Ready to listen to reason?"

Jason laughed in relief. "Sorry, Daniel. Forgive me. I had no right going off the deep end. You were right, I should have let Allegra know what I was doing, but I wanted to surprise her with my parents."

He listened as his apology was accepted and he was forgiven. He was also told that Daniel would see that Allegra knew he was on an important mission that concerned her and their children. He would try to let the outcome be the surprise Jason wanted.

After a lengthy update on the current situation, Jason promised to keep in touch and, if he was desperately needed, he would use a spirit pathway and come home.

Daniel was relieved that he could tell Elliott where their friend was heading, but decided to tell no one else for the time being. He had been alone on the roof when his phone had rung and had remained there for a while, confident that Jason would recall him when he had cooled down.

Jason told Kurt that he would see him next morning at breakfast and they would complete his journey together Kurt was agreeable as it was many years since he had last been in China.

"We'll have to be careful," warned Jason. "They have a particular dislike of vampires and demons in China; they seem to have pretty well wiped us out."

"I don't think they have much experience of your kind of vampire," said Kurt, "otherwise I don't believe your parents would choose to live there at all."

"I hope you are right, maybe they can't detect the true vampires."

They parted, agreeing to meet the next morning.

They left for Nepal courtesy of a private transport plane provided by the prince, who had lent them the one in which he flew his polo ponies around the world

Disembarking in Nepal they headed in a hired cattle truck for the Border and, hopefully, a trouble-free crossing into Tibet and thence into China. They unloaded the animals when the road petered out and started the long journey through the mountains with the pack animals. Jason didn't anticipate any immediate trouble as he had arranged to meet a Tibetan monk and a Tibetan farmer with several yaks. These the farmer would exchange for the horses, at a particular shrine just inside the borders of Tibet, only a few hours journey from their present position. The farmer was pleased to do the exchange as horses were a prestigious symbol amongst his friends. The monk, who owed Jason a favour, had discussed with him how they could use a little-known trail into the heart of the mountains.

Twenty-four hours later they were in Tibet. Shortly afterwards the exchange was negotiated and the farmer departed, leaving Jason and his friends encamped for the night. The next morning they were on the trail which the old monk assured them would lead to the monastery where lived the most revered lama in the whole of Tibet. After they had met him he would send someone to guide them to Jason's parents.

A demon and a vampire found no trouble in climbing the mountain trails which led ever upwards. Across the occasional freezing wastes and rivers, deserts of ice and snow, they followed the trail, onwards and upwards into the heart of the mountains. At first they had made slow progress, but after urging the old monk to ride on a yak, they made a much faster journey to the monastery, known as the Monastery of the Golden Light, hidden deep in a far off valley among the icy peaks.

One week after landing in Bombay, high in the Himalayas, they arrived. The entrance was secret and guarded by magical beasts, but the old monk lead them unerring through a maze of tunnels into the very heart of the mountain, and, eventually, turning a corner, they saw before them a great cavern. Its vaulted ceiling curved far above them and, carved into the very heart of its rocky sides, was a monastery. Jason looked around in surprise. It was so very reminiscent of the palaces of ancient Egypt he had lived in long ago, he almost felt at home.

In the doorway of the monastery stood two saffron-robed monks. They beckoned as they saw him looking at them. He walked towards them followed by Kurt and the old man. As they reached the entrance the old monk spoke briefly to Jason:

"I have brought you this far. Another, far wiser than I, will guide you on your way," he said softly, and turned and walked across the cavern into a small door on the far side.

Jason looked after him rather puzzled; the old Lama had disappeared more abruptly than he had thought. He hadn't even said a proper farewell to the old man. He called out to him, but the monk had disappeared into the sanctuary.

"This way," said the older of the two waiting guides. "We have been expecting you."

Jason nodded politely to them and followed them into the

building. It was a magnificent and very old monastery. Surprisingly, it did not feel at all cold. He supposed that being so deep in the mountain the cold did not penetrate.

"The warmth is entirely due to the central heating provided by the hot rocks far beneath us," said one of their guides a hint of laughter in his voice.

"I see you can read my thoughts," said Jason.

"It is a small asset we have acquired over the years," he admitted.

"We do not usually read the thoughts of our friends," said Jason coolly, "but in this instance I shall use my own powers."

He immediately shut down his thoughts.

"Personally," he told the monk firmly, "I prefer to use the spoken word when in the company of strangers. There is less chance of being misunderstood."

"As you wish!" said the other, sounding displeased. He immediately closed his mind to Jason.

Kurt raised a hand in salute as he got the message and did likewise.

Their guides, now quite obviously put out, moved swiftly across the entrance hall towards a pair of ornate doors. They passed through a series of well-lit rooms furnished comfortably in a fairly modern Chinese style, oriental couches and drapes placed near the elderly radiators lining the walls. Electricity provided by generator, thought Jason ironically. These monks don't seen to lack the basic modern comforts.

A few minutes later they were being led down a very long flight of steps, then down a long narrow tunnel carved out of the rock. Torches lit the passage every twenty or so feet. No electricity here, thought Jason grimly, as he used his vampire sight to enhance the dim lighting. He heard Kurt curse beneath his breath as he stumbled over an obstacle and dropped back to assist him.

"Keep your wits about you," whispered Kurt, "this place is not a religious building. I can smell demon activity."

"I know," Jason whispered back, "but I don't sense any real danger here."

One of the guides stopped at a fork in the tunnel and gestured to Jason to stand beside him.

He muttered a short incantation and a shimmering window appeared in the rock face. The guide stepped through, and inviting Jason and Kurt to follow him. Jason hesitated for a moment but, still

162

sensing no immediate danger, and with a sideways glance at Kurt, who shrugged his shoulders in mystification, they both passed through the mystical opening.

They looked at each other warily. This new tunnel appeared to be well lit and rooms led off the passage they now passed along. The guide indicated that Jason should enter one of the rooms. The other led Kurt to the room next door. "Rest a while. A meal has been prepared for you," they were told.

"I don't suppose there can be any harm in that," said Kurt. "I don't know about you, but I am hungry."

Jason was suddenly suspicious. He observed that his 'meal' was in fact a live goat penned in a corner of the room.

Kurt shrugged as he saw Jason's amazement. "They must have been told in advance that you are a vampire. After all, there are a great many seers and sages among the lamas."

Jason yawned and agreed with him. He waved a rather languid hand as Kurt disappeared next door. Feeling unexpectedly tired he sat on an overstuffed and somewhat ancient couch, intending to rest for a few moments.

The next thing he knew a lama was shaking him awake and indicating that he should eat. Tactfully leaving the room whilst Jason dealt with his hunger, he returned a little later with a young boy who led the goat away.

The lama indicated that he should follow him and led the way down the passage. Kurt stepped through his door and joined them as they passed. The passage seemed to lead to a dead end, yet a large carved door opened inwards as they approached.

Suddenly they were in a circular room. A rather comfortable study, in fact. A table covered in papers at one side of the room and bookcases filled with books lined the walls. The room was brightly lit by many candles and a number of lanterns. A large armchair was placed under the brightest of these lamps. A very old and wizened creature sat, almost lost, in the chair, his shoulders covered by a thick shawl and his legs and feet by a blanket.

He looked at Jason and spoke softly. "Come, vampire. You have been expected. Your present quest shall end here, and another may begin."

He gestured towards a footstool and told Jason to sit beside him. This he did, dropping gracefully onto the stool and looking enquiringly at the oldest monk he had ever seen.

He then told the two guides to take Kurt on a tour of the

monastery and come back in a few hours' time. "The vampire and I have much to talk about and also to think about," he said to Kurt. "He will rejoin you later."

Kurt looked for confirmation to Jason, who nodded. "I sense no danger here."

Kurt nodded in turn and left with his two guides.

# CHAPTER THIRTEEN

All of the Astral Council members present in New York were gathered around Charles's bedside. He had slipped in an out of consciousness several times in the last hour. Vern and Diana stood together on one side of the bed, Elisande and Eurydice sat on the other. Daniel and Elliott stood somberly at the foot of the bed. They exchanged a knowing look and a thought flowed between them.

Charles Fallon was very ill, in fact the witches had confided to Daniel and Elliott that they feared he was dying. Vern felt that Katya should be sent for. She would never forgive them if anything happened to him and she had not been told. Daniel nodded his assent to a question Elliott had asked and Elliott left at once for the Lost World and brought Katya to his bedside.

Katya took one look at Charles and threw herself on her knees at the bedside. He opened his eyes and they lit up as they saw her. He tried to speak and touch her face, but his hand fell wearily back on to the sheets. She could tell he was very weak and it was clear to Katya that he was leaving her. She took his hand in hers and felt his fingers weakly grip her own. She felt a steely resolve settle in her heart. Fiercely, she told them all to get out; she wanted to be alone with him.

Daniel looked at her closely and read in her eyes what she intended to do. He herded the rest of their family and friends from the room.

"Leave them alone," he told Vern and Diana. "They need time to say goodbye."

Vern gave Elliott a pained look. "If it's as bad as that, shouldn't we take him to a hospital?"

"We can't," said Elliott. "If he had been anything but shot, we might have risked it. But we are all here in America illegally. We are all connected to the supernatural and have no explanation which would pass inspection by the authorities. All gunshot wounds have to be reported and any of us who went with him would be questioned for hours. The hospital staff would eventually take a sample of his blood and find it abnormal and they would report that as well. Mind control might have been the answer, but even we cannot control that many minds at once. I'm sorry Vern but nature has to take its course in Charles's case. His life's in greater hands

165

than ours right now. Trust Him."

Inside the room, Katya had morphed into her vampire self and sat on the bed. She dare not delay, time was too short. She gathered Charles's weakened body into her arms and without hesitation, bit into his neck. She drank a lot of the small amount of blood he had left. Then she took one of her very sharp fingernails and drew it across her throat, cutting the jugular vein with one delicate razor sharp tip. Gathering him even closer she forced open his mouth and guided his lips to the flow, encouraging him to drink her blood. After the first hesitant mouthfuls he drank more freely and she felt the strength returning to him. After a while he stopped drinking and fell asleep. She sat on the bed and held him, waiting, and thinking.

"You are going to have to forgive me Charles for not asking you first," she told him silently. "But I can't live without you. Not after it took me thousands of years to find you. There's something else you are going to have to forgive me for, but we will talk about that later."

Daniel opened the door very quietly and shut it behind him, locking it. "How far have you got?" he whispered.

"When he wakes up he'll be a vampire," said Katya sounding a little hesitant. "I know he drank enough of my blood. I just hope I drank enough of his. He'd lost such a lot before I got here. The mix has to be just right to make the perfect vampire, and I do want him to be perfect."

"Instinct has more than likely guided you to the correct mix and the right decision for you both," said Daniel, "I hope for both your sakes it has. If not, though, you will have a second chance. You can exchange more blood tomorrow and that should do the trick."

"How do you know all this?" hissed Katya. "I thought only vampires knew that sort of thing."

"You forget how long I have known Jason," said Daniel, still speaking very softly. "I made it my business to check on the process, when I realised he was thinking of turning Allegra into a vampire. I didn't want any mistake to be made. As I don't want you to make one with Charles."

"Thanks for that," said Katya gratefully. "I need a little moral support here; I hope Vern and Martin will forgive me."

"They will be too happy that he is alive to worry about a vampire shapeshifter in the family. This will put paid to any chance of your having a family though, Katya."

Katya smiled enigmatically and touched her abdomen experimentally. "I think not. We shall have one at least."

Daniel smiled delightedly at her. "Does Charles know?"

"It's too new for that, but I will tell him as soon as I am certain," she said.

"So there will be a new race of shapeshifting vampires after all. It seems that evolution may be taking another turn, a step in a new direction," said Daniel. "No wonder the Oracles were cagey about our futures. No wonder they were talking about new pathways and new directions. We all have to make the decisions for our own destinies. You have made one for you and Charles, as I made one years ago for Pauline and myself. I believe you have made the right decision."

"I am sure that I have," said Katya. "I hope Charles thinks the same."

"It will take at least a full twenty-four hours before the change is complete," warned Daniel, "and maybe another twenty four after that before he wakes up. I am going to tell Vern and Diana that you want to be alone with him, but that they can come and see him later. I think it best if we don't tell them what you have done until we have to. I'll come back in an hour or so and see what is happening."

Katya smiled to herself as she leaned over and wiped the blood from Charles mouth and cleaned him up so that no one could tell what had taken place. Her own wound was already healing and, in an hour or two, would be gone.

Daniel looked closely at the fading marks. "I'll tell them in three hours," he warned her as he left the room. "If you need longer, you'll have to come and tell me."

Katya turned back to Charles. "I love you Charles Fallon, and now we can spend eternity together." She smiled to herself. Somehow she knew that Daniel was right, instinct had played a large part in her decision on the direction their future lives would take.

She still held him hours later waiting for nature to take its course.

Vern had come and gone more than once. He had been accompanied by Elliott and Daniel who had both made sure that he didn't actually touch Charles and find his skin cold in death. He just looked for all the world like a handsome Greek god as he lay in Katya's arms. Elliott and Daniel were both confident that a new vampire was about to be born. They preferred to be certain before

167

telling Vern who was unsure why, but somehow knew, that Daniel and Elliott didn't expect his brother to die. He felt a glimmer of hope develop in his heart.

Charles Fallon opened his eyes abruptly. He looked up into a familiar face and anxious blue eyes gazing into his.

Katya breathed a sigh of relief. Charles was indeed going to be a perfect vampire. His eyes told her everything she needed to know, and she held him tightly for a moment.

"Lie there for a few moments, Charles," she told him softly. "There is something which has to be done right now."

Katya whisked out of the room and Charles heard a rumbling of voices. He distinctly heard his brother Vern yelling at Katya:

"You've done what?"

He also heard Daniel's reply as Katya came back into the room.

"He'll live forever now. Would you want it any other way?"

Charles looked puzzled for a second or so, and then sat up. "I know I was dying but I'm completely healed. Was it the witches healing spells?" Katya, feeling a little guilty, was lost for words.

"It wasn't the witches who healed you," she told him at last. "I did it. For us."

"Katya, have you turned me into a vampire?" asked Charles astounded.

She looked at him lovingly. "I couldn't let you die. It took me too long to find you to let you go."

"If I am now a vampire like you and completely healed, why do I feel so weak still?"

"You've been out of it for nearly three days and you are hungry. You need human blood right now," she told him. "Our friends are waiting outside. Just this once they are ready to donate their blood for you. Afterwards, when you are strong enough, we shall have to go hunting together."

Charles looked a bit shocked at this but Katya had already crossed to the door and Daniel, Vern and Diana, came in. Elliott followed but leaned negligently against the bedroom wall.

"No need to ask how you are," said Vern smiling delightedly at his brother. "You had me worried there for a while. Thank goodness Katya decided to take matters into her own hands."

Katya smiled gratefully at Vern and turned towards Charles.

"Just a little from each," she warned him.

Charles was surprised to find himself morphing as Daniel held out his wrist, pointing to the veins that Charles should bite into. "Don't worry Charles," laughed Daniel seeing his hesitation. "I've helped Jason out many times when we couldn't risk him going hunting."

"Sorry I can't offer mine," said Pauline from the doorway, "but I don't think you want to risk turning into a werewolf. You certainly make a very handsome vampire," she added admiringly. "Now you will be a thirty-five-year-old Greek god for ever, but you'll have to take my word for it from now on."

Everyone laughed as Charles looked surprised. "No reflection," she reminded him. "I'll get you a digitally enhanced photo, later," she added, helpfully.

"Could he? Turn into a werewolf, I mean," asked Vern, recalling Pauline's earlier remark.

"Nobody has ever taken the chance of finding out," said Daniel. "It's too great a risk."

Elisande, Cybel and Cassidy now entered the room also offering their wrists for consumption until Katya said that he had had enough.

"I am certainly feeling quite well again," said Charles relieved.

"My brother's a vampire," said Vern. "That should make for interesting shapeshifting in the future."

"That's the least of our worries," said Elliott candidly. "A vampire shapeshifter was always on the cards once he met Katya. The important thing is that you learn how to manage your new powers. You, my dear Charles, are now an immortal shapeshifter."

Vern gasped at this revelation by Elliott. "My brother is immortal?"

"He is the first shapeshifter to become immortal," said Daniel, "None of us knows how this will turn out. We have no idea how this will affect the evolution of your species." He spoke directly to Vern. "It seems the Oracle was right. New pathways are opening up for us all.

"I shall have to think about the rest of what they said. In view of what has just happened, I may be able to piece together what they meant about Jason's pathway," he added thoughtfully.

He turned with a grin to Charles. "As a druid I find you rather interesting. As a senior member of the Council, I welcome a new vampire to our midst, and as your friend may I say that you are now more than equal to Pauline's werewolf strength and instincts, so watch it. She'll be as aggravating to you as she is to Jason. Don't expect me to interfere when she's baiting you, I have enough trouble keeping up with her as it is," he added warningly.

Pauline snorted with annoyance and glared at Daniel. "It's no fun if they know what I'm doing," she complained. "Now I'll have to wait until he's forgotten what you just said."

"Pauline," said Charles, "feel free to annoy me at anytime. It will be an honour to know that you think I am worthy of your talent for aggravating your friends."

Pauline strolled over and eyed him with disfavour. "I'm the one who does the jokes around here, don't push your luck."

Lance arrived in New York the day after Charles had become a vampire, although he was unaware of this. He had been sent by Lucifer, who had arrived to give the bride away when Snake and Bianca were married, two days previously and when Alex and Faith had been pronounced out of danger. Several of the Cornish shapeshifters had been at the wedding. He was sure that Snake and Bianca had enjoyed having Drago as best man and Natalia as matron of honour.

Lucifer had been less annoying than usual at the wedding ceremony and had acted quite properly as father of the bride. But after the signing of the register he had drawn Lance's attention to an entry some eight months before. The entry was completely unknown to Lance. In fact he was certain it hadn't been there more than a few days. It was the record of Katya's marriage to Charles. The marriage certificate was folded in a gold envelope between the pages.

Lance groaned aloud as he realised what had happened. "Another case of holy wedlock I suppose," he said to Lucifer.

"Can't have them reproducing all over the place without benefit of legal bonds," said Lucifer stuffily, "these little niceties have to be taken care of in the proper order. Now would be a good time to go to New York and let them have the good news. There's a hint of a small shapeshifting vampire in the offing. First things first, don't you agree, Vicar?"

Lance gave a hollow laugh. "I wish you could persuade my sister of that."

"Don't worry about it," said Lucifer with a smirk. "There's plenty of time before we need to take care of that particular couple."

"Now I am worried," said Lance.

As he arrived on the rooftop, Travis, who by now was getting used to seeing complete strangers dropping out of the sky, jumped out of his helicopter and walked forward to welcome the latest arrival.

"You from England?" asked Travis.

"That's right," agreed Lance. "Charles around is he?"

"Penthouse flat," said Travis. "I'll show you."

Travis showed Lance into the lounge and he surveyed Lucifer's A-Team. Elliott, eyes closed and obviously asleep, sat with his feet on a glass coffee table. Charles, who had Katya sitting on his lap, lounged alongside him. Vern and Diana were sitting side by side on a large couch and Daniel lounged half asleep across another. Pauline was standing by the balcony window, staring up at the sky.

"Very cosy." Lance was pointedly sarcastic as he looked them over with a very jaundiced eye. "Here was I thinking you were up to your necks in trouble, and here you are lounging around as if nothing is wrong."

Diana waved him to a chair and told him, "Lull before the storm. Come and join us. Good job you've come, this place is full of nasty vampires. They aren't a bit like Jason, and they are increasing in number as fast as you can count them."

Katya choked on the drink she was holding and Charles patted her on the back.

Elliott yawned sleepily, looked up at him, but didn't move. "What's that?" he asked lazily, "Who sent you?"

"Old Nick of course. He said you might need a spot of exorcism here and there. And I brought some news for Charles and Katya."

Lance looked around rather awkwardly at the others, "Is there somewhere we can go and talk privately?" he asked them.

"We'd better use the bedroom, I suppose," said Katya, jumping off Charles's knee and pulling him from the chair.

After he had shut the door, Lance handed Charles the gold envelope. He gingerly opened it and unfolded the contents. He choked on a laugh and handed the certificate to Katya. She looked stunned as she read the contents. "It says here that Vern was best man, Diana was Bridesmaid. Jason gave me away, and Mr. L. Deville was guest of honour."

"I'll never be able to show this to our children," she muttered savagely.

Charles looked at her in surprise. "You were expecting to have children? I thought that was impossible now."

171

"It probably is now," said Katya, but emphasising the 'now'. "But it was perfectly possible before, and I was going to tell you when I was certain. But it seems we are to have a half-vampire shapeshifter before next summer."

Lance had tactfully exited the room when it became apparent that personal revelations were about to take place and, as he was already in the know, he was smiling as he rejoined the rest of his friends.

Diana got up and gave him a hug as she was rather pleased to see him and introduced him to everyone in the room. The witches were still there, as Elisande had thought it wise to make sure that Charles really was okay and that Vern's shoulder and Diana's hand were completely healed. All the witches would have liked to return home, but felt they should stay for the 'rising'.

"What was that all about?" asked a curious Vern.

"You'll have to wait for them to tell you," said Lance with a smile. "They have had a little surprise. In fact more than one, I believe."

Daniel looked at him curiously for a moment and then laughed silently to himself as he gave himself a reasonable guess as to the 'little surprises'.

Elliott received a thought signal from Daniel and shook his head in disbelief. "Are you sure?"

"Wait and see."

Pauline, who was really good at picking up Daniel's thoughts, strolled over and tweaked a lock of his blond hair. "Are you sure?" she whispered.

"About one of the little surprises. Yes, she had to tell me, a couple of days ago. About the other, well, we made an educated guess."

"It made us both more comfortable about what she did," said Elliott silently to her.

Charles and Katya emerged laughing their heads off. "Has he told you?" asked Katya.

"Certainly not," said Lance. "It's your story to tell."

Charles handed the folded licence to Vern who read it and whistled in astonishment as he handed it to Diana, who screamed with delight.

By the time the paper had been all around the room, all their friends were in fits of laughter and Pauline asked when the happy event was to take place.

Katya sniffed inelegantly and stuck her nose in the air, and asked how the hell she came to assume there was to be a happy event.

"Listen sweetie, if Lucifer was at any wedding you can be certain there is a potential godson in the offing," said Pauline. "Look how quickly he got the news to 'you-know-who' about Elliott and Natalia."

"Thanks, Pauline for that reminder," said Elliott sarcastically "It's nice to know you still think I am worthy of your aggravating notice."

"Think nothing of it," said Pauline. "I didn't want Charles and Katya to feel they were any different to the rest of you."

"That's the trouble," muttered Charles. "This is dated the day Katya decided to grow up. I hadn't even thought about anything other than how gorgeous she was."

Daniel laughed. "That would be quite sufficient to have him foreseeing the outcome."

"Well you should know!" said Pauline. She winked at Daniel, who hid his face in his hands at his wife's obvious reference to the day she had agreed to marry him.

Pauline glided over to him and put her arms around him. In a very loud whisper she told him that a couple more werewolves were soon to present themselves, so wasn't it a good job they had such a large house and such a great baby-sitter?

Daniel groaned aloud and pulled her onto his knees. He gathered his troublesome wife into his arms and, in front of all their friends, kissed her soundly and at great length until she begged to be let up to breathe. Looking extremely disheveled and pink cheeked, she looked at him from under her wildly disarrayed hair and told him she adored him, too.

He gave them all a complacent look and did the same again. Pauline was shaken, as Daniel had never made such a public avowal of his love for her before. Although she was absolutely certain of his love for her, she was aware that some of their friends were not. She knew that they were now damned well certain of it.

She sat on his lap with her arms around his neck and playfully nipped his earlobe. Daniel, with one graceful movement, stood up with her in his arms and said to them all, "Sorry folks, this is a druid thing and it can't wait."

Without further comment he strode from the room, leaving them all laughing. They heard Pauline growling throatily as they

173

went out of earshot down the hall. A door closed and there was silence.

"I've never seen him do that before. He's normally a very private person," said Elliott amazed. "You just can't tell what a druid is going to do next."

"I would have thought you knew the answer to that," said Vern. "You being from the Fifth Dimension."

"I'd better read up on the mating habits of druids," said Travis with a grin. "I'm completely new to all these public demonstrations of affection. We vampires are pretty direct but I must say we prefer to be a little less obvious about our private lives."

Carlotta, who had gone to prepare tea, wheeled in the trolley, "I said you American vampires had no sense of humour, now I'm worried whether you'd make good lovers," she told him acidly. "We Europeans are very hot-blooded and much more demonstrative."

Travis leaned over and, with one eye on Ward's reaction, pulled her towards him. With a sly look he tossed her over his shoulder and headed for the roof and his helicopter. "We are off to the hunting grounds," he said coolly. "As I said, we hunters prefer private demonstrations of our prowess."

Diana looked surprised when no one moved to stop him. She raised her eyebrows at Vern, who laughed quite unconcerned. Diana gave a sigh of relief when Carlotta winked at her as Travis turned back to ask Elliott to let Sebastian know where he had gone.

As they left the room, Carlotta looked up waved, and gave the thumbs up signal to Ward, who waved back with every sign of acceptance of the situation.

"You okay with that?" Elliott asked Ward.

"She knows what she's doing; she's been around a while. She doesn't need a nanny where Travis is concerned."

Elliott nodded. He agreed with Ward's assessment of the situation.

Lance looked shell-shocked. These supernaturals led life on a completely different plane to humans, he thought. Totally forgetting he was one of the supernaturals.

"We might as well make use of this," said Vern as he leaned over the tea trolley and helped himself to tea and sandwiches. "I must say Carlotta certainly makes a good cup of tea. She kept her word to keep us supplied."

Everyone helped themselves to what they wanted. Diana handed a cup of tea and a sandwich to Lance .

"What else did you come for?" she asked him.

"I was informed that Elliott and Daniel required a preacher to do some exorcism or other," he told her caustically. "I can't think why. I should have thought they could have managed by themselves."

"We won't be here," said Elliott casually. "We're off to help Jason with his choices. The local talent has the situation well under control and if Nick thinks you can handle the clean-up operation, we're quite willing to let you do it. After all, the whole point of setting up an American operation is for them to do the work themselves."

Diana, who knew her brother all too well, winced as she awaited his predictable reaction to this offhand replacement of the druid by himself.

Lance, for the first time since he had met him, glared furiously at Elliott. "You mean you are leaving me alone with Lucifer and these American vampires and dashing off to the other side of the globe?" he snarled angrily and, morphing into a jaguar, stood there tail swishing angrily and claws tearing great tufts from Travis's carpet.

"Lance!" screamed Diana. "Cool it. You're wrecking Travis's apartment. It will cost an arm and a leg to replace this carpet."

Lance wasn't in any mood to listen to his sister, but she and Vern grabbed him and threw him to the ground and held him until he cooled off.

Once more in human form, Lance pushed them away and got to his feet.

"I'm not staying here and that's final," he said firmly. "I'm going back home."

"I'm sorry Lance," said Elliott, trying, not all that hard, to sound as if he really was, "but if Nick sent you here, he had a good reason. You'll have to stay and find out what it is. Daniel and I will come back at once if we are really needed, but I think we have time to find Jason before anything happens to him OR New York."

"There's something else you need to know," interrupted Vern. "Since we have been here Charles has become a vampire. Katya turned him into one to save his life. So there's a lot more going for us than just the Yank vamps."

Lance looked even more enraged. "Katya turned Charles into a vampire? What's that got to do with our problems?"

"Strong vampires on our side," said Vern. "You know, good

175

omens and all that. According to Old Nick we can manage fine without the head honchos."

"Huh!"

"Our illustrious leaders," said Vern, "Elliott and Daniel, are superfluous to requirements on this mission."

"Thank you, Vern," said Elliott dryly. "I wouldn't have put it quite like that myself, but I see that Lance has got the picture."

"When are you going?" asked Lance grimly.

"As soon as Daniel can tear himself away from Pauline," replied Elliott.

"Why didn't Lucifer mention Charles had become a vampire?" asked Lance, now rather miffed.

Vern gave a snort of laughter. "Since when has Nick told any of us what was going on? He always lets us find out for ourselves."

Lance looked at Vern and his sister and failed to hide a smirk. "He told me he would attend to you two later, so I wouldn't get too smug about deciding your own futures."

Diana and Vern looked at each other in consternation. "He wouldn't dare," snapped Vern.

Elliott swung his feet off the coffee table. "If I were you, I'd decide what to do PDQ, or you will have it decided for you," he told them slyly. "He can't bear to be thwarted, so if you can score a few points off him the rest of us will be delighted."

He sauntered out of the room and down the passage to the kitchen. They heard him speaking to Elisande and the other witches.

A few minutes later, he put his head around the door. "I'm taking Elisande back to Cornwall. I forgot to tell you all, but her son-in-law turned up two nights ago, and she wants to see that all is well with Felicity and Faith. Her son-in-law is a djinn, by the way," he told them blandly. "I don't know the full story, but as Tally is there, I expect to know everything shortly. Tell Daniel I'll be back later or he can join me in Cornwall, whichever he chooses, and we'll go and find Jason."

A few minutes later, he arrived at Exeter hospital with Elisande. She had confessed to Elliott that she had never met the djinn who had married her only daughter. She had, she told him, been horrified to learn of their association and had declined to meet the man who was so ancient that he was totally unsuitable for such a young girl. Yet Felicity, who had been only nineteen at the time, was stronger-minded than anyone had thought and disappeared to Persia with her husband. Apparently she had found a djinn highly

176

compatible. However, shortly before Faith was born she had returned to her mother's home for the birth. Her husband had brought her and stayed with her throughout the birth, but Elisande had left it to her own mother to deliver the child as she could not bear the thought of a djinn in her home.

Felicity and Karim had lived in Boscastle with her grandmother for a while. No one ever mentioned his name in Elisande's hearing. A year or so later he had returned to Persia on family business and had never returned. He had only occasionally been mentioned over the last eighteen years, but Felicity had gone twice a year to his country to visit him. Elliott was sorry to hear this as he felt that Elisande had probably deprived her family of the opportunity of becoming a close-knit unit. The past could not be altered, but maybe he could influence the future?

"As far as I am concerned," he said, his steely gaze fixing her coldly, "his arrival is providential. A djinn is a highly desirable addition to the Council right now. If you want to keep your family safe, I should make a strenuous effort to make him feel at home."

Elisande was taken aback by his icy tones. She realised she had been told to accept her son-in-law immediately. He hadn't actually used the words 'interfering mother in law', but she got the message. She realised at last why Elliott was the acknowledged leader of the Astral Council.

They arrived, cloaked in invisibility. Elliott looked around to see who was there. He whisked them around the side of the building and they became visible. Shortly afterwards they were all at the bedside of the young Lanyons. Both were well on the way to recovery and sharing a side ward, courtesy of the powers of persuasion of a djinn.

Elisande rushed to her daughter's side and looked anxiously at her. "Everything is fine, Mother," said Felicity. "This is Karim, I know you have never met him and I believe you sometimes wondered if he really existed, but he is here now. Elliott has persuaded him to stay for a while at least."

Elisande took a long look at her hitherto unknown son-in-law and held out her hand. "You are Felicity's choice and Faith's father, it's rather late, I know, but what can I do but welcome you?"

"A gracious acceptance," said Karim bowing low over her hand. "I hope to prove worthy of your welcome."

Natalia let out her breath. She had been holding it for some time. She had ferreted out the tale of Felicity and her djinn and hoped that Elisande would find him worthy of her only daughter.

She turned to Elliott, who had been watching her out of the corner of his eye. He had noticed a grim-faced Snake and a worried-looking Drago, make signs that he should remove her from the vicinity forthwith and wondered what the minx had been up to.

He put his arm around her waist and, checking that no staff were around, took them both back to their home on Bodmin Moor. Natalia, finding that he had chosen the bedroom for their reunion was delighted and proved how glad she was to see him with energy eagerness and enthusiasm.

Sometime later as she lay in his arms he turned her head up to his and lazily asked her what she had done to Snake and Drago.

"Nothing," she said indignantly. "I was making sure that we had the full story about Felicity and Karim."

"Anything I need to be concerned about?" asked Elliott with interest.

"Very soppy love story," said Natalia with a light laugh. "Believe it or not they met in university. All of his recent ancestors went to Cambridge, he stayed on to lecture. Felicity attended his courses on ancient and pagan religions. She didn't know right off that he was a djinn, but being a witch she knew that he wasn't entirely human. Of course they all live a very long time, much longer than normal humans. He is actually not all that old for a djinn, he said he is only three hundred and sixty-five. For a djinn that is like being a teenager. Karim told me that his great-great-great-grandfather is still alive and he is nine hundred and twenty years old. His mother is a djinn and she is four hundred and twenty-one next year. He did say that Felicity is his only wife and Faith is the only daughter he is sure he has. Naughty man!" She giggled saucily. "How many have you got?" she asked Elliott.

With great aplomb, Elliott leaned over and put a finger on her lips. "Such thoughts should never cross an angel's mind and definitely not her lips," he told her sternly. "But as far as I am aware you are the mother of the only children I have." He hesitated briefly. "When were you going to tell me about the second one?"

Natalia looked at him in awe. "How did you know?"

"All of heaven knows, as does my mother," said Elliott dryly. "I was soon informed of the next arrival. It was partly the reason I let you go. I had no intention of letting anything happen to you or our unborn child."

"I have been a very wicked angel and a terrible wife," she said softly. "I don't know how you ever managed to forgive me. I don't deserve you, but I will try to make amends and earn you in the future."

Elliott looked down at the repentant face and laughed. "You are exactly what I have always wanted. A beautiful, wayward temptation that I cannot resist. If you change too much I shall not recognise my very own angel."

Natalia put her arms around him and held him tightly. "Just the same, I promise no more adventures without you."

Elliott smiled slightly as he held her close, and if his thoughts tempered this promise with a well-judged question mark, he didn't tell her that.

"What else did you find out?" he asked.

"It seems that they went to Iran and got married, but Elisande didn't go. Partly because she disapproved and partly because James Purcell was about to be born and, as he was an unbound shapeshifter, they had to have a witch as midwife in case of any problems with the birth – and there were. Don't you remember, I told you he said he was born half-changed? If he had been in a hospital there would have been a terrible furore."

"I can imagine," said Elliott amused, and wondering what would have happened if Nicholas had been born with wings.

"Silly," said Natalia catching the thought, "as if he'd be allowed to."

"Go on, what else did you learn?"

"Well, Felicity has been going to Iran twice a year for eighteen years now and, when Faith was born, Karim was there but Elisande still didn't want to meet him and got her mother to deliver the baby. It was very silly of Elisande, because I believe that was partly why Karim didn't let Felicity tell Faith about him being her father. He went back to Iran when she was a year old and used to come to see her when she was very little, but when she got old enough to recognise him he only came at night when she was sleeping. Funnily enough, she does recall his visits in a sort of dream-sequence way. Apparently he also came to visit his wife, as he put it. But he was always gone the next morning. Felicity says her mother either didn't know or didn't want to know, because she never, ever mentioned him. It wouldn't have done for me, I can tell you."

Elliott hid a smile at this laid-back remark from his wife. He was damned sure that his wife would have refused point black to let

179

him disappear every morning. He was very happy with his wife's eagerness to share his mornings.

He now had a very shrewd idea why Drago, and especially Snake, in particular wanted him to remove his nosy wife from the hospital. They both had secrets they would prefer no one made public and they now knew how impossible it was to stop Natalia finding them out.

"Tally," he said urgently "I want you to make me a promise, right now. Promise me that you will never ask Snake how he came to meet Bianca. Even Lucifer doesn't know the full story, but Daniel picked up on what happened when he probed her mind for clues as to who injured her. He told me, but no one else must know. Promise me you will never try to find out."

"I have never heard you speak like this before," she told him. "If it is that important to you, of course I will do as you say."

"It is not that is important to me, Natalia; it is Snake and Bianca who would be in danger and possibly Daniel and his family. You do understand?"

"I promise," she said simply. "Daniel and his family mean too much to me to do otherwise."

Elliott breathed a sigh of relief, Bianca and Snake were safe for the time being, he thought.

"What about Drago?" asked Natalia. "Can I find out what he's been doing?"

"I shouldn't bother," said Elliott hastily. "A million years of history, we can do without knowing."

Natalia giggled wickedly. "I still don't know much about your thirty thousand, I'll concentrate on that."

"And I, my angel, will tell you all you need to know about myself, my adventures and my family." He laughed silently to himself. It would take a long time to tell and by that time they night have several more offspring to keep her busy. He fervently hoped so, and was certain the next few years would be entertaining for both of them. He certainly expected to enjoy the making of his future heirs. Natalia felt him laughing and she held him away from her.

"You are a wicked old demon," she said severely. "Nick will have to build a much bigger nursery if you get your way."

"That reminds me, there's something else I forgot to tell you," he said apologetically. "Pauline let slip, very publicly, that there are more wolf cubs on the way. I was able to come here to you because we had to delay our plans for joining Jason while Daniel showed her his appreciation."

"Sounds interesting," said Natalia. "When can I go and see her?"

"If you can talk Drago into taking you, you can go whilst Daniel and I are away fetching Jason. It's providential that Karim has turned up, he is a match for any magical creatures that arise and any magic that any sorcerers, shamen and black magicians can dream up. Certainly he is a match for any demons around at the present time. We can safely leave the Lanyons and the witches with him and James. Karim also knows how to negate the Book," he added.

"Great," said Natalia gleefully. "Does that mean Snake and Bianca can come as well?"

"If Snake thinks it is wise. Yes, they can."

The next few hours passed in a haze of love and pleasure for the two angels who shut out the rest of the world for just a little while.

Daniel arrived in Elliott's lounge to find the two angels watching television.

Elliott got to his feet. "You get back to the hospital, Tally, Alex and Faith will be glad to see a familiar face. Daniel and I are going to find Jason."

He gave her a quick kiss and told her to get going, he wanted to sure she was safe with Drago before he left.

Natalia sighed and went back to the hospital. She decided to wait until Faith and Alex were a lot better before she asked Drago to take her to see Pauline. In any case she thought it would be rather fun to find out more about the djinn way of life. Elliott wouldn't mind if she did that.

Within minutes Drago rang Elliott to tell him she had arrived and he and Daniel got ready to leave.

# CHAPTER FOURTEEN

Lucifer arrived in a flurry of smoke as they were about to depart.

"I've found him for you," he said with a triumphant grin, "He's been on a tour of the Himalayas and now he is in China. I don't think he's where he thinks he is or where he's wants to be. A fairy watcher chanced on a shift in the Cosmic Flow in the Himalayas last night. You know that I have agents in Fairyland. They keep a constant watch on travellers throughout the Cosmos for fear of discovery. No one believes in fairies any more and they would like to keep it that way. This particular one is very adept at finding the merest hint of an intruder and when she found an unauthorised demonic entry she contacted me. When she knew we were looking for Jason she followed it up, He and your demon friend Kurt are in another dimension. Someone is giving Jason the run around. It's time you stepped in and stopped them."

"I'll give you a head start," he said affably.

He waved his hand in a clockwise movement and they vanished.

Elliott and Daniel materialised seconds later, in the private rooms of the old Lama, just as he was about to start his talk with Jason.

Jason looked at them in surprise, opened his mouth to say something and then closed it again with a snap as the old Lama, spoke angrily to them both.

"This is a monastery, secular guests come by invitation only. Please leave at once."

"Wrong," said Elliott with an edge to his voice. "We can go anywhere in the world that we wish, particularly when we fear danger."

"There is no danger here," said the lama. "This is a meeting between friends"

"In that case we are just in time," said Daniel smoothly. "We are Jason's friends, we need to hear this as well."

The old man held up his hand. "Your presence is not required, you have arrived here uninvited. You are interrupting a personal discussion. This is a decision for the vampire alone," he told them sternly. "Your presence will inhibit the choice he will make."

"Not if we just listen and make sure he is being given good

182

advice," said Daniel. "We are both here to stay, and if you can't agree to that we shall have to take him back home. A true believer will have no problem with an audience who care."

They could all see the old lama's displeasure. He stood up rather agilely for such a wizened old monk and Elliott walked forward and stood in front of him.

"You are no lama and definitely not the abbot of any monastery. You are of demonic origin," he said with certainty. "I can find out who you are without any trouble, but it would save a lot inconvenience if you revealed your true identity."

"Hold it Elliott," said Jason, rising to his feet and speaking for the first time. "You are jumping the gun a little, here. I know who this is and I was just letting him get a little deeper into his act before challenging him. As you have arrived, we can skip straight to the formalities."

He stood beside Elliott and beckoned Daniel to join them. He turned to the old lama and, reaching out, seized him by the shoulders and held him at arm's length.

"This, my friends, is my long lost father. I don't know what name he goes by now, but five thousand years ago he was known as Theron and I suspect my mother Sidonic is somewhere nearby. I didn't expect to find them here, I thought they were in China."

"Lucifer says that you are in China and definitely by demonic means, He has had his agents out looking for you. You passed through a dimensional portal a few hours ago."

"But I only just got here," protested Jason.

"Sorry Jason, but you have been here for at least eight hours," said Elliott, "The Faery Watch noticed the cosmic shift last night."

"Lucifer had his agent find you and then notified us," added Daniel. "We came at once."

"So, I have lost eight hours," said Jason angrily. He shook the old lama he had said was his father, but was forced by Elliott to let him go.

"Let's see what he has to say before you kill him," said Elliott icily. "I'm not going to kill him, I'm going to beat the hell out of him for giving me the run around and messing up my life," said Jason viciously.

Theron threw back his hood, stood erect and changed immediately into a tall, blonde, blue-eyed vampire, so like Katya he was obviously her father. He didn't look all that much older than Jason. A soft footstep was heard behind them and a tall, dark woman, who looked little more than a girl, came forward from a door hidden in the shadows of the room.

"My mother," said Jason ironically, as the woman moved into the light. "It was only after I got to thinking about the vampire sages with a cool head that I began to recall my mother's voice.

"Tell me, mother, would you have told me who you were if I had not recognised you?"

"Your mother wanted to reveal herself as soon as she saw you and your sister," said Theron. "I persuaded her the time was not ripe. By the way, we both thank you for naming your own son after his grandfather. It seems your wife is a very amazing young woman. You are to be congratulated upon finding such a woman to bear your children."

"I happen to love my wife and my children," said Jason sulkily. "I am indeed to be congratulated that such a wonderful woman was able to see past my vampire heritage and love me for myself. Even if we had never had a single child, I would still love her," he added, meaningfully.

His mother nodded her head in approval. "Love should be like that," she said quietly.

"There is a simple explanation for your supposedly lost hours," she added softly. "You seemed tired and hungry and we just arranged a few hours' sleep for you."

"I am quite capable of deciding for myself when I need to sleep," snapped Jason. "I have been looking after myself without parental assistance for almost five thousand years. I resent your interference in my life, and how dare you assume you have any right to take eight hours of my life from me? And what have you done with Kurt, I suppose you drugged him as well?"

"Certainly not," said his mother, sounding shocked that he should think such a terrible thing. "We just used a spot of autosuggestion on you both and you went to sleep."

Jason got more angry that ever and morphed into his feral self. He turned on his parents in a terrible rage.

"I had hoped that you were the same people who brought Katya and myself up to be good citizens of the world we live in. Now I am no longer sure that you are those same parents. No one, not even a loving parent, has the right to interfere in the free will of any adult, unless that adult is about to commit a crime or endanger themselves or others. You have tampered with my mind, I don't know if I can forgive you for that even for the sake of providing my children with grandparents."

"It seems we have made a terrible misjudgment," whispered his mother. "You are angry at our interference, when we only meant to give you a wider choice for a longer future with your family. When we realised you were on your way to find us, we decided to let ourselves be found rather sooner than you might otherwise have done. Oh, you would have found us eventually, I am sure! This way cut a harsh journey a lot shorter."

"I made the journey intending to find you," said Jason. "Now it looks as if you not only knew that, but forced me here, when you could have come to me in England."

"We could have," admitted his father, "but we both felt you should make your choices away from your family. A change of lifestyle and direction should be make without distractions. You are a very old vampire, my son. There are few as old as you left upon the earth. Most have left and gone to a different place long ago. Some to a higher plane, others to the dark dimensions."

"I don't want to leave, I like it where I am. I have got a family now, something I have never had before in all my long life. I love them. I shall always want to be with them. What's more I and my friends have got responsibilities that you could never understand. I have no desire to leave for any reason whatsoever." Jason was vehement in his condemnation.

"This is all very cosy," said Elliott, "but it doesn't answer the question as to why you put Jason, your own son, through this hellish charade. Jason has no need to make choices, his life is not in danger. His soul is his own and if, one day, he has to make a sacrifice and let Allegra go for a while, there is every chance now that she is his soul mate, they will find each other again. The angels are on his side, they will help him find her if it is so ordained."

"That is not why we offered him the choices," said his father. "You of all people know that there are many realms beyond this one. Sidonie and I have gone beyond this earthly realm, and another world has been opened to us."

"Yet you choose to remain in this one," said Daniel, speaking for the first time. "Why?"

"It seems you and your friends do not trust us, my son," said Theron sadly. "Perhaps we should reveal our reasons for testing you. You have earned the right to take the next step in a vampire's evolution. Only those who have lived as long as you have and according to the rules which you have always followed can tread the path of spiritual eternity. Your mother and I both achieved that goal when we left you to search for peace, four thousand years ago. We had tired of our lives on earth. We had lived here far longer than we had to.

"Those whom you called the vampire sages are our spiritual selves. We need no earthly form to travel the universe and the heavens. You can join us if you wish. If you do, you can do as we do and materialise in human form or vampire form whenever you wish and wherever your wife is reincarnated. That is one of the choices we offer you."

"I don't like riddles and I don't like choices, and I certainly don't take kindly to being tested," said Jason furiously. "I came here to find the man and woman who are my parents and the grandparents of my children. That is all I came for. My son and daughter are half-human vampires; they could do with some vampire grandparents. Their maternal grandparents are over a million years old and they are very happy to take on the role. I had hoped my parents would be willing to do the same."

"I'd like to get Jason away from here as quickly as possible," whispered Daniel to Elliott. "Did you notice that his father can shapeshift? I don't believe Jason noticed because he is too angry right now. I don't like being in such a mystical place without knowing just what I am up against."

"You're right," replied Elliott, also in a low voice. "They have contrived this meeting and only our presence is holding them back from whatever mystical act they intended to perform. I get the impression they might have done it without his consent. I don't like this any more than you do."

Daniel stepped forward and put up his hand in a gesture of intervention. "I really don't think that an isolated mountain in China is the place for this conversation. Elliott and I have the power to insist you leave Jason alone. However, as he has gone to such lengths to find you there is something else you need to know, or perhaps you already know, if you are as all powerful as you seem to think. I shall tell you, because Jason doesn't know. Your daughter Katya and her shapeshifter are married and they are having a child. After an accident a few days ago, Katya had to turn Charles into a vampire to save his life. They too could do with some help from the vampire sages who, it now seems, are her parents."

He turned to Jason. "If you are wondering why they didn't wait for you to return for the wedding, it was another case of holy intervention similar to Elliott and Natalia's. Lance found the entry in the register."

Jason laughed. "Can't say I blame Charles, Katya certainly had him going."

"Not too sure that was the way of it," grinned Daniel. "She grew up for Charles and no one else."

"You could be right at that."

Elliott studied the vampire parents thoughtfully and while Daniel engaged Jason's attention spoke swiftly to them. "I hope you are not going to be difficult about this. My parents are much older than you and they live in the Fifth Dimension. I suppose you've heard of it? It means that I still have the upper hand when it comes to pitting my will against a couple of ancient, shapeshifting, dimension-hopping vampires."

Theron stiffened slightly as Elliott made it clear he had got the shapeshifting connection.

"We are familiar with all of the demon dimensions, that doesn't mean we wish to go there, or cross swords with those who do," said Sidonie. "We want only what is best for our son."

"Well, I'm very sorry," said Jason, rejoining them, "but as I told you before, it is what Allegra wants that is important to me. I cannot lose her and I intend to move heaven and earth to keep her with me through eternity."

"This isn't getting us anywhere," said Daniel, impatient to depart, "without Allegra here Jason cannot make any decisions."

"Well, how about using the spiritual travel method to reconvene this meeting in the Lost World?" suggested Elliott.

"We'll have to drop Kurt off in Berlin. He came with me," said Jason. "I can't leave him here."

With Elliott's dark gaze boring into them, Theron and Sidonie were forced to agree and a few minutes later the five of them were standing in the great hallway of the Quinn's castle.

Quinn and Vespazia heard the commotion and rushed to see who had arrived. Allegra just behind them saw Jason and, oblivious to anyone else, flew into his arms. He closed them tightly and thankfully around her, astonished but instantly accommodating. She hugged him hard and, bringing his face down to hers, rained kisses all over his eyes and mouth. After a while she eased herself from his arms and stepped back. She looked straight into his eyes and told him fiercely:

"Wherever you have been, whatever you have done, don't you

ever go off again without telling me or taking me with you. This has been the worst week of my whole life and even the children couldn't make up for not having you."

Jason was staggered by this warm welcome. He had expected a cold reception, to say the least. He wound his arms around his adorable and forgiving wife and gave himself up to the pleasure of her kisses.

It was a while before a discreet cough from Quinn brought them back to their surroundings. They both looked around at their friends. They were quite unembarrassed at having an audience.

"Family reunion," said Jason smiling widely. "Worth the wait."

Allegra cuffed him across one vampire ear and told him to behave. "Do you want to have our reunion here in the hall or go someone more private for a while?" she asked him with a wicked look in her eyes.

"What a woman!" said Jason. His eyes gleamed hotly as, scooping her up, he took the stairs two at a time to their suite.

"We won't see them for a while," said Elliott with a sly look at the older vampires. "We'd better go into Quinn's lounge and get acquainted."

Vespazia shook with silent laughter. She was a little more used to Jason by now and had begun to understand the bond between the vampire and her daughter. She led the way and, being a good hostess, waved her hand around a couple of times and conjured up afternoon tea: sandwiches, scones, jam and cream.

"Great!" said Daniel, "I'm starving! It's hungry work sorting out vampires."

Elliott laughed as Jason's parents looked around in awe at the opulent lounge. They noted the great fire burning in the grate and the enormous chandeliers hanging in rows from the ceiling.

"This must cost a fortune to run," whispered Sidonie to her husband.

"Not at all," said Vespazia kindly. "Jason and Lucifer fixed it up with the assistance of a local building firm, shapeshifting relatives of Jason's, and we find the cost most reasonable."

"We only visited briefly whilst Jason was here before," said Theron. "We hadn't realised that the castle was habitable."

"Done with a wave of the hand and a flick of the wrist," drawled Elliott. "Very efficient, especially if Lucifer is helping."

Daniel thought that the two vampires looked a bit taken aback to learn that Lucifer was involved in the Lost World. He filed their surprise in the back of his mind for later investigation.

After tea Quinn came over all hospitable and offered to show them over the castle. He took them both on the grand tour

"They should be gone quite a while," said Daniel helping himself to more tea.

Vespazia laughed again. "I finally counted all the bathrooms," she told Elliott. "He said why not make it twenty and that's exactly how many there are."

"I told you," said Elliott. "Jason would never let Allegra live anywhere where everything wasn't absolutely modern and perfect. Have you got a dishwasher?"

"I particularly went to look for it when you said there must be one, and of course you were quite right. However, as you pointed out so much more efficient to use the flick of one's wrist."

"Tally still isn't too keen on that," said Elliott. "We had a small difference of opinion about it."

Vespazia looked at him with interest, "Did you win?" Elliott winked solemnly.

Vespazia laughed and changed the subject. "By the way, Elliott, now that Karim is at the hospital most of the time, I left them to it. I felt Allegra needed me more."

"Excellent thinking," said Daniel. "But I think everything is fine again now that Jason is back."

"Let's hope whoever is upsetting Old Nick's apple cart isn't getting things organised again too quickly, we've still got to sort out Jason's choices."

"Judging by the happy reunion there is only one choice," said Daniel, "and I now know how to fix it for her soul to remain with her."

Elliott looked stunned. "My God, Daniel! If you can do that, I can't see any problems. They will be a twenty-first century vampire family with half-vampire children. It's fantastic! How do you plan to do it?"

"I've got some fine tuning to do, but what it boils down to is that I capture her soul at the moment of death and hold it until she wakes up as a vampire. It suddenly came to me when we were in that monastery: all those lama's reincarnating all over the place and the search for the new ones. In the far distant past they didn't always have to search, they held the soul in a casket until the right vessel was born. The memory surfaced just when I needed it."

"I have a strong suspicion that your ancient druid knowledge will always surface in the nick of time," said Elliott sagely. "You have so much knowledge now that it must have to have a trigger before you can access it."

Daniel looked at him ruefully. "We must hope it always surfaces in time."

"You'll soon get the hang of it," said his friend.

"When do we tell Jason and Allegra?" asked Daniel

"As soon as possible. Before anyone dreams up any more choices," said Elliott succinctly. "I couldn't handle another ten days like this."

"And you the leader of the earth forces," said Daniel, tongue in cheek. "I'm surprised at you; I thought you had more fortitude."

"Any fortitude I had disappeared long ago," said Elliott soulfully. "Having an angel for an assistant was bad enough. Having a wife with angelic powers is far worse. I find it very wearing. I must have a much weaker constitution than I thought, because when it comes right down to it, I confess to a cowardly urge to hide deep underground when the word New York is mentioned in the same sentence as angels."

"I hope there's room for both of us," said Daniel, shaking with silent laughter at the though of Elliott being afraid of anything. "With Pauline acting up again, I just might join you. I think we should leave the demon-chasing to Jason for the time being. After all, he did dash off and leave us to sort everything out ourselves. It would serve him right."

Vespazia clicked her tongue in disgust. "The two of you should be ashamed. You are acting like silly schoolboys," she told them.

"Sorry Vespazia," said Daniel, turning on the charm. "We are just relieved to have solved Jason's problem. Letting off a little steam. Didn't mean to upset you."

Elliott grinned at his friend, "Don't worry Daniel, I'll find her a job to keep her out of our hair. She can go to New York and keep an eye on the angels when they go to visit Pauline. She can help Lance exorcise Goodman, Goodhew and May and she can help Jason dispatch the demons."

Vespazia looked suspiciously at him then saw that he really meant it. "I'm not allowed to leave here except to go to Exeter hospital and Simba," she said, suspiciously.

"Oh, Did I forget to tell you?" he said all apologetically. "You are now free to roam at will anywhere on earth."

She leapt from her chair and hugged him and then Daniel "You are wonderful, both of you. Now Quinn and I can travel where we like."

"Changed your tune all of a sudden," said Elliott. "I've grown up again I see."

"Oh, you demon!" said Vespazia. "I must tell Quinn." She dashed from the room.

"You made someone very happy," smiled Daniel.

"I always like to wait for the right moment," said Elliott slyly.

"I'm still a bit concerned about those vampire grandparents," said Daniel, "They seemed a bit too eager to separate Jason from Allegra and his children, and I'm not too sure that they welcomed Lucifer's connection with this place. We will have to watch them."

"I think we have the measure of Jason's parents," said Elliott confidently. "You can get them all tied up with the ancient druid wisdom any time you like, and we both know that Old Nick is more than a match for a couple of vampires."

# CHAPTER FIFTEEN

### *Rannoth's office.*
8,000 years BC

Rannoth was hard at work writing up his latest report for Lucifer. He was fairly new to the demon dimensions, but worked in Lucifer's office complex. He had the tedious job of correlating the various inmates with their punishments. Lucifer liked to keep the books straight.

A flash and a slight draught let him know that someone had entered his office. He finished the line he was writing and looked up.

He rose hastily to his feet, stammered his apologies and came around the desk.

"What are you doing here, Claudia?" he asked horrified.

"Some demons attacked me, when I was in Babylon a few minutes ago," she said, leaning on the desk to catch her breath. "They tore my dress and scratched my arms before I could get away. This was the safest place I could think of on the spur of the moment."

Rannoth led her to a large chair in the corner of the room and told her to sit there, and he'd go and deal with the problem.

He turned into his demon persona and disappeared. Claudia looked at the space where he had been, and gasped: he had turned into a tall, slim, dark-skinned, black-haired, green-eyed horned devil – and vanished.

A few minutes later he returned, two of her attackers held in his grasp. "These two of them?" he queried.

"Yes," she gasped, shutting her eyes to blot them out.

Moments later there were four thuds, one following the other, she opened her eyes and nearly fainted: two demon heads were on the floor and two bodies twitched beside them. Rannoth called the chief torturer, who removed the pieces to the furnaces. "They won't bother you again," said Rannoth grimly. "The other two were vampires, I staked them on the surface. They are already in the snake pit."

"Thanks Rannoth," said Claudia faintly. "I'll be getting along now."

"Don't you think you should wait for your father?" said Rannoth, resuming his normal, rather handsome human shape. "He'll be furious about this."

"Don't tell him," said Claudia quietly. "He'll only get into a temper and everyone will suffer. You've sorted it out nicely, it's over and I thank you."

She looked at him for a moment before she turned to leave, and it was then that Rannoth noticed that she looked sick and ill. She took one last look at the floor where the bodies had lain and with a strangled moan, vanished.

Rannoth didn't actually speak to her again for ten thousand years. Not in his office, anyway. Unfortunately, when he became Lucifer's chief assistant some years later, he quite often found himself in her vicinity. Never once in all the intervening years did she give the slightest hint that they had ever met. Rannoth was rather sad that she had taken such a dislike to him and tried his hardest to keep out of her sight. The fact that she was Lucifer's elder daughter meant that this was not easy. She quite often dropped into her father's office for a brief visit when Rannoth was there. Although it was quite obvious to him that she could not even bear to be in the same room as him. She always stayed beside her father, and although they had nodded rather distantly to each other from time to time, she had always seemed to avoid looking directly at him.

For many of those early years, if there was ever a chance that they might come into personal contact, she had made her farewells and left.

As the years passed she had mellowed slightly, remaining in her father's office and no longer ignoring his presence. On several occasions she had actually spoken quite pleasantly to him. She still, however, kept her distance.

It was with some surprise, then that ten thousand years later – supernatural time of course – a flash of light and a slight breeze had heralded the arrival, in his now much larger office, of the Angel Claudia.

She stood much the same as before with her hands clasped in front of her, and a look of fear on her face.

Rannoth stood, and with lightening speed was around the front of the desk and taking her hands in his. To his surprise they were trembling violently, and she didn't pull away.

"What is it Claudia? Who has frightened you?"

"I don't know," whispered Claudia. "But I think someone is trying to kill me."

Rannoth was staggered. "I don't doubt you for a moment Claudia, but who on earth would dare to attempt to kill Lucifer's daughter?"

"I don't know that either, but four times in the last three weeks I have had a brush with death."

Rannoth led her to his large couch. Sitting beside her and still holding her hands, he gently asked her to tell him what had happened to make her think someone was trying to kill her.

"Three weeks ago I was in London, and I was walking across Tower Bridge when someone tried to fling me over the parapet into the river. There were several small boats nearby, I think I was supposed to be run down by them. I was able to throw myself sideways to the pavement and it looked as if I had tripped, but I didn't; I was meant to fall into the water. I could easily have been killed. A few days later, I was going down an escalator when I distinctly felt a hand grip my ankle and I fell nearly all the way down to the bottom. A man going up the other escalator grabbed me and I just managed to keep my balance or my dress would have been caught in the teeth at the bottom and I would have been badly hurt, if not killed. There was no one around who seemed to have done it, but I know someone did. Last week someone pushed me in front of a lorry as it was coming out of Covent Garden and just now, as I was waiting on the pavement for some lights to change to green for walk, I heard a sort of buzzing noise and something stung my neck, look!" She pulled her hair to one side and Rannoth drew a sharp breath. A raw red gash marred the perfection of her angelic neck. She had been shot.

"Claudia, angel, your father must be told this time," he told her grimly.

"No, he's still angry about Bianca and her vampire and he has to concentrate on this evil rising. You must help me, Rannoth. I know you can find out who is doing this."

"First of all," said Rannoth, "I think we should check that nothing suspicious has happened to Bianca. She is your sister and also Lucifer's daughter."

Claudia gasped in horror. "Ran, I should have warned her weeks ago, we must go right away."

Despite the current crisis, Rannoth noticed with surprise the shortening of his name, and briefly wondered why. Briskly he put this flight of fancy to one side and taking her arm, took them both to Bodmin Moor and the Lanyon residence.

The Lanyon residence was uninhabited, and he headed for Elliott's home to find the same. The Lost World was his next choice and here he learned of the accident to Alex and Faith. He also learned that Elliott and Daniel had gone to find Jason, and that Snake and Bianca were at the hospital guarding Natalia. He didn't think it advisable to appear there as too many strange visitors might attract unwarranted attention. He asked Quinn's permission to wait in his palace as he feared that Claudia's life might be in danger. When he told Quinn that she was Lucifer's daughter they were only too delighted to be able to offer safe haven to her and any friends of hers.

Rannoth smiled wryly, he didn't think he came under that heading but was quite happy to let them think that he was. Claudia smiled charmingly at them and accepted, but as she did so turned to Rannoth and pulled him forward. "Rannoth and I will share a room," she said firmly. "I only feel safe when he is close by."

Rannoth managed to hide his shock at this assertion. "Don't worry Claudia, nothing will happen to you whilst I am alive to prevent it," he told her.

Claudia looked surprised that there should be any question about that. "Ran, I know you won't let anything happen to me. That's why I came to you for help."

"I think you and I had better have a little chat about this right away," said Rannoth hurriedly, as he noticed Vespazia's raised eyebrows.

He hustled her from the room and out onto the drawbridge.

"No one can overhear us out here," he said sternly. "Are you mad, suggesting we share a room?"

"What if they can hear?" said Claudia crossly. "It's not their business if we share a room. I'm a big girl; I don't need permission to share my room with a man."

"I don't happen to want your father breathing down my neck accusing me of sleeping with his daughter," snapped Rannoth. "And, I've got to consider your reputation, even if you don't."

Claudia gritted her teeth. "My father would prefer me alive and with no reputation than dead with it intact."

"Put like that," said Rannoth smoothly, "I accept your offer to ruin your reputation."

They went back to Vespazia. "A room with two single beds if you've got one," said Rannoth coolly. "It has been mutually decided that a bodyguard is more effective in the same room as the victim."

Vespazia hid a smile. "It's your funeral," she said smartly to Rannoth.

"That's what worries me," he said with a sideways glance at Claudia.

"Don't be such a wimp," she said shortly, "you know he can't manage without you after all these years."

Rannoth laughed. "Claudia my sweet, you had better be right."

For the next two days Claudia and Rannoth made themselves at home in the Lost World. Rannoth found Allegra and the boy shapeshifters a complete diversion from the normal people he had dealings with. He and Quinn made several forays into the forest and met with the dragons and rest of the inhabitants. He was given a tour of the small modern village now springing up around the edges of the forest. He was shown the cave where the hatching had taken place when Allegra had eventually walked into it the previous summer, when the King and Drago had decided that the preparations for their birth into a modern world were in place. The new school had taken some time to prepare and the new nurseries had been supervised by Allegra and Pauline. He was even told the story of the baby dragon who had hatched unbeknownst to everyone when it had been caught in the spell which had awakened the King, and had almost killed Natalia and Carlotta in the fossilized forest.

During the two nights that followed these days Rannoth found, to his dismay, that Claudia had no inhibitions about sharing a room with him.

She wandered around their bedroom clad only in the diaphanous dresses worn by all angels when alone. Clearly angels felt no need of underwear, he thought, less than amused. He hoped she had no idea how this affected him – totally unaware that this was precisely what she intended.

He had adored the beautiful creature since the first day he had seen her. It was only after finding out soon after their first meeting when hell became his home in 8,000BC that she was Lucifer's eldest daughter that he had damped down his ardour and kept his distance. Yet he knew also that, after the incident so many years ago when he had thoughtlessly slaughtered the demons in her presence, she couldn't stand the sight of him. Why she had suddenly decided that he was the man to guard her from her present assailant gave him food for thought. He knew very little about angels and less about women, but had the feeling that angels didn't normally wander around tormenting their protectors as Claudia seemed to be doing.

He looked thoughtfully at her as she brushed her hair that night and decided that now was not the time to probe the reason for this new Claudia to suddenly appear, but he fully intended to find out what she was up to at a later date.

To avoid giving himself away he found himself spending time with the shapeshifting young Fallons. David and Patrick were completely in awe of Rannoth. Never having met Lucifer, as Vern had kept them well away from his vicinity, they were thrilled to meet someone who had actually been living in hell for thousands of years. Claudia smiled to herself as Lucifer's chief assistant attempted to give them as watered-down a version of his job as possible. She was well aware that Rannoth was avoiding her and asked Vespazia if she would nip up to Exeter and fetch Bianca down to the Lost World before Rannoth reached boiling point and blew up. Vespazia departed laughing.

She reappeared moments later and told her, "Snake and Bianca have the evening off and have gone to somewhere called Dartmoor to check on the wild life. I interpreted that as to feed, so they won't be here for a while."

"I suppose she'll be safe enough with Snake, after all he was thought good enough to guard the wife of the Dark One," mused Claudia.

She went to find Rannoth and found him still trying to avoid telling David and Patrick what he actually did for Lucifer.

Claudia listening to their many questions on the inhabitants of the lower regions and, seeing his hunted look as they hung on his every word, eventually took pity on him and dragged him off to visit the petrified forest and told the boys they had to stay to guard Allegra.

Shortly after they left, Elliott and Daniel arrived with Jason and the vampire grandparents, and the grand reunion took place. Kurt had been dropped off in Berlin on the way, but told them he would be ready to assist any time they needed him. Snake and Bianca arrived with Drago and Natalia and, about fifty minutes later, all of them arrived practically simultaneously in the lounge – except for Jason and Allegra, who were still enjoying their reunion.

Elliott was seated on a large couch with – as usual – his feet on

197

the nearest coffee table, but this time with Natalia on his lap. Daniel was reading a book he had found in the Palace library, one of Drago's earliest editions. Snake and Bianca were arguing amiably with Vespazia over the merits of underground castles, when Rannoth and Claudia appeared in the doorway.

Snake vamped immediately on seeing them and Bianca let out a scream and grabbed Snake's arm tightly. He pulled her against him and snarled at Rannoth. "What did you bring that murdering bitch here for? Get her out of here. I don't want her in the same room as Bianca."

Elliott pushed Natalia off his knee and got quickly to his feet, and Daniel threw down the book and hurried to his side.

Rannoth held onto Claudia as she would have rushed towards her sister.

"Hold it Claudia, it seems something has already happened to Bianca and for some reason she thinks you are to blame."

"Too right she does," rasped Snake. "You tried to kill her last summer. If I hadn't been there to catch her, she would have died as she hit the ground."

Daniel walked towards Claudia and Rannoth. "Calm down all of you and let's get to the bottom of this, like sensible adults," he told them quietly.

"Whatever Bianca thinks," said Rannoth looking down at Claudia's head buried in his shoulder. "Claudia would never harm a living soul, and certainly not her own sister. So however it may seem, that's not what happened."

Claudia raised her white face and looked fiercely at Bianca. "How could you ever think that I would hurt you in any way? Someone is trying to kill me as well. That is why Rannoth is here, to try and find out who and to warn you. It seems we are too late, someone has already tried."

Daniel and Elliott looked at Rannoth and he nodded his head. He told them what Claudia had told him and how close to death the last attempt had been.

"We have got a small problem with that, and it in no way means we are accusing Claudia of anything, but Bianca quite distinctly recalls that Claudia threw her from the Golden City down to earth. As only angels inhabit the Golden City, the only way that this could happen is if one angel were to cast another down. If this is not the case, the true explanation is not going to be easy to find."

"I don't care what problem you have with it," said Rannoth

tersely. "Claudia had nothing to do with throwing Bianca from the Golden City. For one thing Claudia has been here on earth for the last eighteen months, guarding two babies, and she has never left their sides unless Lucifer or I picked them up to baby-sit. Even then she is never far away from them."

"What two babies?" asked Snake rudely. "Anyone can say they've been guarding babies."

"Not these two," said Rannoth emphatically. "She was ordered to guard them from the moment their mother was injured in a fall before they were born and has stayed with them ever since. She even stayed with them, on the orders of the Great One, when they were kidnapped, to make sure nothing happened to them. She didn't tell anyone until they were safe again."

"You mean Penny and Lucy?" asked Daniel shaken. "They have had a guardian angel?"

"I am their guardian angel," said Claudia calmly, "except when they are in my father's care. No harm will ever come to them when I am with them."

Elliott and Daniel were really surprised to hear that the werewolf cubs were considered worthy of their own guardian angel. "What can I say?" said Daniel. "But thank you."

"It has been a pleasure," said Claudia simply, "they are adorable, I love them both."

"That still doesn't mean she didn't find time to try to kill Bianca," said Snake stubbornly.

"Yes it does," said Bianca, running across the room and throwing her arms around Claudia. "Forgive me for even thinking that you would hurt me. There must be another explanation."

"Indeed there must," agreed Daniel, "but until we find it, Snake and Rannoth are going to have to guard their angels night and day. Rannoth, the best thing you can do is take Claudia back to Hell with you and keep her in the fortress until we find the answer.

"Snake you take Bianca back to New York and take Drago and Natalia with you." Elliott sounded very concerned. "Someone may be targeting the angels. However, you should all be safe enough in New York with the vampires and shapeshifters."

Quinn and Vespazia had listened in silence to all this and now Vespazia came forward with a suggestion.

"I think it is a good idea for Claudia and Rannoth to go back to Hell, but they should tell Lucifer what is happening. He will be angry, upset and very hurt that no one told him of the danger to his only children. But as Bianca was targeted in America for some reason and, what's more, it is rather odd that it happened where Snake is known to hang about, perhaps we should investigate the area more thoroughly? Quinn and I will come to America and I will use my magic powers to help you all."

Elliott looked pleased. "It would make things a lot safer. Very well, that is how we shall play it. But who is going to tell Old Nick?"

"I will," sighed Rannoth. "You are right of course, he has the right to know. It is just possible he may have some idea who has it in for him enough to kill his daughters."

Natalia had been hanging on to Elliott's arm throughout this conversation and reached up to whisper in his ear.

Elliott smiled wryly. "On this occasion, angel you will have to rely somewhat on the shapeshifters and Vespazia to protect you. Rannoth is quite capable of guarding his angel with his demonic powers, but I am inclined to allow Drago to assist Snake in guarding Bianca as she seems to have had the most serious life-threatening accidents. It's possible these incidents are connected. Let us assume for now that they are. All of the team can protect you both. What's more, as Alistair is already in Lucifer's palace, I propose that if there is the slightest hint of danger to any of you, that you all depart for his fortress immediately."

"You mean you really are letting me go to America again?"

"Don't forget the rules. No rushing off without permission," warned Drago, assuming his troll guise. Snake vamped, noting Natalia's shudder with hidden amusement.

"Of course I won't," she said indignantly. "I never intend to be parted from Elliott ever again."

"That's my girl," whispered Elliott, hugging her tightly and giving a nod of approval to Snake and Drago over her shoulder.

"Aren't you coming with us?" asked Natalia anxiously, noting the omission of her demon and Daniel from the travel arrangements.

"In a short while, but we have to tell Jason something very important and we don't want to disturb him right now."

"You won't be long?"

"Not long, Tally, just long enough to make sure Jason doesn't make any decisions until he has heard what Daniel has to tell him."

He pulled her close, gave her a firm kiss and told them all to get going.

Rannoth lingered for a moment with Claudia. "You do

understand that Claudia is not my angel, she is Lucifer's daughter and in trouble. I don't want Lucifer getting the wrong end of the stick."

Claudia standing just behind him and out of his sight winked at them. It was an effort but both of them kept a straight face. If Rannoth imagined that Claudia was not his angel he was in for a surprise. It was obvious to both of them that Claudia thought that Rannoth was her demon whether he knew it or not. They thought Rannoth was a little slow on the uptake. They weren't aware that for thousands of years he had been certain that Claudia could not stand the sight of him, or they might have understood.

Rannoth and Claudia departed for hell and arrived in Lucifer's office seconds later.

Predictably the Devil was incandescent with rage upon learning that his daughters were the objects of some murderous ploy. He ordered Rannoth to guard Claudia day and night and even went so far as to congratulate him on his handling of the matter so far.

"I suppose I'd better not inquire too deeply into why Claudia went to you for help instead of her father?" remarked Lucifer with uncanny insight.

"He helped me once before," said Claudia. "Many thousands of years ago, but I never forgot."

After a few minutes of speculating as to who might dislike him enough to kill his daughters, Lucifer turned to Claudia and gave her a fatherly hug and kiss.

"Well I must say you have far better taste in men than your sister," he told her approvingly. "You had better go and stay with him for a day or two whilst the council sorts this out."

Claudia glared at him. Fortunately after explaining the problem to Lucifer, Rannoth had moved discreetly out of earshot to give Lucifer a few moments alone with her.

"Shhh! He has no idea yet how I feel. I want him to realise by himself, don't you dare to interfere," she hissed at her father.

"Oh, my!" chuckled Lucifer, "the poor fellow hasn't a chance. However I do give you my blessing, my dear. He is quite a suitable catch for the Devil's elder daughter."

He was still chuckling to himself as he told Rannoth, "Clear off to your own office and take this baggage with you. I've got work to do."

Rannoth, looking suspiciously at them both, did as he was told.

Claudia looked around his office, spotted the door to his living quarters and disappeared through it. She was pleasantly surprised. A small hallway led to a large, airy and comfortable lounge, off which led a small but compact kitchen. Another door led to a bedroom dominated by a very large four-poster bed, with dark red velvet drapes. A bathroom adjoined the bedroom. Claudia looked at the bed with its red silk sheets and then at Rannoth who had followed her into the room.

"I thought it looked very comfortable," said Rannoth with a grin. "It is my only extravagance, but I couldn't resist it."

"I think it is wonderful," said Claudia admiringly. "I never associated you with red velvet and four-posters."

Rannoth didn't like to tell her that it was his vision of her in it that had dictated the purchase.

Being a clever girl, Claudia read it in his eyes.

She decided it was too soon to make her move and in any case she wanted him to tell her what she knew had been in his mind for centuries. She knew it was her foolish reaction to his first kill on her behalf which had make him wary of her. She wanted to coax him out of this fear of upsetting her before she let him see her true feelings. She had long ago put thoughts of his brutal treatment of her tormentors behind her. Rannoth's reactions had been those of any demon whose employer's daughter had been attacked. She had managed to insinuate herself into her father's office on many occasions when she knew Rannoth would be around and had made sure that he was aware of her presence. She was, for a long time, quite unaware however that her background presence only reinforced the impression that she could not stand him near her. When she did finally realise this she determined to change his opinion. She had known that it would take considerable time and effort on her part to do this. She had also known it would be worth the wait. She continued to visit her father frequently, and had taken every opportunity to make sure Rannoth knew she was there. She did it often enough to make certain he never forgot her. She was grateful to whatever fate had caused her to be attacked and enabled her to seek his help. His reaction had been all she had ever hoped for.

"You can have the bed," said Rannoth breaking into her thoughts. "The couch is okay for me, I often catnap on it if we are really busy."

Claudia promised herself that this state of affairs would be short-lived, but nodded agreeably.

Later that night, she heard Rannoth curse beneath his breath as he tried to get comfortable on the couch. After a while she crept quietly to the office. He was dozing restlessly as she tiptoed to his side. The covering blanket had fallen from his body and she saw that, although he was wearing his trousers, his chest was bare. She caught her breath for a moment. He really was incredibly handsome and his skin shone healthily in the light from the hall as she leaned over him and whispered in his ear. "I am afraid in that great bed on my own. I want you to share it with me. I don't want to be murdered in my sleep."

If Rannoth had not been half asleep or not been dreaming about being in that bed with Claudia, he probably wouldn't have let himself be drawn into sharing it with her. But events proved too much for him and, a few minutes later, they lay side by side on the red silk sheets.

"This is not a good idea." Rannoth turned his head towards her as he spoke. "I've had dreams of you in my bed for the last ten thousand years. The only thing that prevented me from telling you was the fact that you couldn't stand the sight of me. In fact, it wasn't until yesterday when you thought of me before anyone else that I wondered; and when you called me 'Ran', I confess I felt rather hopeful that you had changed your mind."

"I was a bit behind you in understanding what had happened to me," confessed Claudia apologetically. "It was many years before I began to get the urge to see you around. You kept popping into my dreams and I began dropping by occasionally to see how you were and how you reacted to my presence. But by that time you had started to avoid being near me, and I had to make excuses to father to visit him when I knew you would be there. I have caused you a lot of pain, and myself as well by my childishness. Can you forgive me?"

Rannoth groaned as Claudia leaned seductively over him and ran her fingers across his chest.

"You are a shameless hussy," he told her as he flipped her over on to her back and let her know in no uncertain terms that he had wanted her just exactly where she was for a very long time.

Claudia agreed with him and shamelessly threw herself into the pleasurable pastime of making love with the man she had met so long ago and who, she now knew, had loved her for longer than they both cared to admit. She hoped she could make up to him for the wasted years, when she had not let him know that she had long ago ceased to fear him, but had come to love him instead.

During the night they made their peace with each other and, if an angel or two were listening to make sure that their happiness was assured, no one would ever know. Except of course for the one who was about to organise yet another entry in the register at Reverend Lance Ferdinand's church. Normally this would not have been necessary as, technically, no one knew of their existence; but Lucifer was mindful of his chat with the Almighty regarding Rannoth and his own promise to his chief assistant that he could, one day, be granted permission to live and work on earth. One had to be prepared for all eventualities.

Lucifer smiled complacently. He was not expecting to give this bride away. She had given herself away, thousands of years before. She just hadn't known it at the time.

Certain that Claudia and Bianca were well guarded, Lucifer now departed for the Lost World, making a brief stop at a certain church on Bodmin Moor on the way. Lance, its vicar, wasn't there, but he had no trouble amending the church records. He chuckled to himself as he made yet another entry in the register. This was quite as good as being at a wedding. He was rather pleased with his elder daughter.

He had informed the colonel of his Elite Guards that he was now promoted to brigadier and had the added responsibility of making certain that things ran smoothly in his absence as Rannoth was on an extremely important mission and could not be troubled except in the direst emergency. Such as another breakout. He was to consult Alistair if anything untoward occurred and the earth forces would be alerted. He was also to consult with the Chief Torturer if he, the C.T. had any queries regarding the inmates of Hell, but the palace residents were his prime and sole responsibility.

The brigadier saluted smartly and went to promote his captain to major. They were well pleased with their new responsibilities and were assiduous in their endeavours to carry them out.

Rannoth at this point decided he needed a word with Alistair.

Accompanied by Claudia, who he had no intention of letting out of his sight for a moment, he strolled into the palace and into Lucifer's grand dining room. Alistair was surrounded by mounds of paper and a stack of floppy disks. He looked up as Rannoth and Claudia entered the room.

"Keeping you busy, is he?" asked Rannoth lightly. "Not too

204

busy to do a little research for me, I trust."

"Anything to have a break from these accounts for a while," said Alistair. "Going through the Mafia's accounts would be simpler than this lot."

Claudia leaned over his shoulder. "I don't know how you and Rannoth can possibly decipher all this," she told him admiringly. "Rannoth says you are a genius and, when I was guarding the twins, I heard Pauline say that you are a wizard."

Alistair stared at her in dismay. "You aren't another of those silly angels are you?"

Rannoth laughed at Claudia's disgusted face, and told Alistair. "Unfortunately, she is. I don't want to ruin your day totally, but this is Lucifer's daughter Claudia. She's in a spot of bother and under my protection for the time being."

Alistair looked gutted. "I wish you hadn't told me that. We have enough problems with Elliott's pesky little horror. Don't say you've got another one here. I think I had better go home. These angels are nothing but trouble."

"Sorry Alistair," said Rannoth regretfully. "Lucifer has given orders that you are to stay here and liaise with all the various teams operating on earth."

"Well, what is it you need to find out?" asked Alistair warily. "Nothing too complicated, I hope?"

"I'm not sure what I am looking for, just a feeling that it was not a coincidence that Bianca nearly died right where Snake was standing. I find it hard to believe that she landed, quite by chance, at the feet of the most evil, bloodsucking vampire who ever lived, just as he was about to begin his nightly hunt. I reckon he was supposed to kill her when he found her blood was no use to him and throw her over the cliff. I think someone must have been watching that particular location for some time to have taken note of Snake's preferred hunting grounds. I want you to check your sources for anything unusual about that cliff. Any ancient tribal rituals, any rumours of witchcraft, sacrifices, Indian burial grounds, secret underground tombs, passages or missing persons. Go back into prehistory if necessary. I'll even take an educated guess."

"In other words, you want me to go fishing," said Alistair grimly.

"In a nutshell: Yes."

"You've given me very little to go on. I'll see if I can make it more. Go away, I don't like anyone breathing down my neck when

I'm surfing," said Alistair aggressively.

"Come along, Claudia," said Rannoth. "Alistair doesn't like anyone to know of his criminal activities on the Net."

"You are a fine one to talk," Alistair told him. "I know where you got the money for that four-poster bed, and that nice little villa you recently acquired on a Greek island."

Rannoth laughed. "And who taught me almost everything he knew last year? I just put it to good use."

"I bet Old Nick doesn't know!" said Alistair.

"I intend to give it to Claudia as a wedding present," said Rannoth with a grin. "He'll have a hard job finding fault with that."

"I can see now why you got the job as his chief assistant," said Alistair, glowering. "You are even more devious that he is."

Claudia looked at the two of them and hissed impatiently, "Rannoth, let the boy get on with his work. The quicker he starts the quicker you'll get your answers."

"See!" said Rannoth, sounding hard done by. "I'm henpecked already and we aren't even married yet."

"Oh yes, you are," said Alistair, hurriedly printing out a message which was arriving as they spoke and handing over a piece of paper, with a sly grin at them both. "This is an e-mail from Ward. You were married yesterday afternoon in Lance's church on Bodmin Moor. Just in the nick of time, according to this postscript from Old Nick. He says, CONGRATULATIONS, AT LEAST ONE OF MY OFFSPRING WILL PROVIDE ME WITH HEIRS."

Claudia gave a shocked gasp. "How did he know?" Giving herself away instantly. Rannoth kissed her open mouth to prevent it letting out any more personal secrets, and hustled her from the room to Alistair's mocking laugh and a remark about angels with cotton wool for brains.

Lucifer was conferring with Daniel and Elliott when they were joined by Jason and Allegra.

"About time you rejoined the human race," said Lucifer coldly, "I don't expect members of my organisation to go haring off around the world on wild goose chases, and certainly not without consulting with myself or the Oracles first. Let this be a lesson to you, the answer is always close at hand and with those who have your best interests at heart. Don't do it again. Now Daniel, you tell him what you have found out and how he can safely make Allegra a vampire if she still wishes."

"Thanks, Nick," said Daniel caustically. "You been listening at doors again and put the cart before the horse as usual." Then he told Jason and Allegra what he could do for them to achieve safe transition of her soul from human to vampire.

Allegra threw her arms around him and hugged him, and then Elliott and Lucifer, both of whom were rather overwhelmed by her happiness. Jason looked gravely at all of them.

"How can I ever thank you all, you have given me something no man could ever repay in a thousand lifetimes. Eternity with the woman I love. I hoped for it, I prayed for it, but I never truly expected to have it."

Allegra hugged him tightly. "I told you everything would work out." She smiled happily.

"I should have had your faith," he told her humbly.

"Don't you dare criticise yourself," she said fiercely. "You were searching for a dream, and now you've found it."

"Oh, I certainly have!" he said as he bent over to kiss her tenderly.

"Put her down," said Lucifer sharply. "You've all eternity for that now. I've got serious problems that need immediate attention."

He told Jason what had happened to his daughters whilst he had absented himself, and how the matter had superceded all others for the time being.

"Now you have all the facts, how about some ideas?" He regarded them all in turn.

He stopped short and looked piercingly at Allegra. "Come to think of it you can't stay here, it won't be safe. You can't be left alone with just the youngsters here and everyone else in America. You can join Alistair in my palace. All the children are there and Rannoth can guard you as well as Claudia. What's more, I think Jason would prefer it right now. He, Elliott and Daniel don't completely trust those parents of his. Quinn and Vespazia have taken them to America with them to keep them out of our hair for the time being. You will be quite safe with Rannoth. He is not my chief assistant for nothing and my Elite Guards are on duty twenty-four hours a day. You will be perfectly safe."

Allegra looked puzzled. "I had no idea you were all in such trouble. No one told me what was going on in America until Bianca and Snake got here. Have I missed something else?"

"A lot," said Daniel succinctly, "and I think Nick is right, you should join Alistair at once. You can catch up with all the news from him and Claudia."

Lucifer, once he had decided on a course of action, didn't waste time. He waved a lordly hand and she vanished.

Jason looked annoyed at this cavalier removal of his wife and protested. "You could have let me say goodbye."

"Sorry Jason," said Elliott. "It's very important to us not to risk Allegra until she has been a vampire for quite a while. Incidentally, it was because Katya made Charles a vampire that Daniel had been able to solve your problem. It worked so well it encouraged him to dig into his memory banks for your solution. Katya will fill you in on the details when we get to New York."

Lucifer snapped his fingers and they all arrived in America seconds later.

Almost simultaneously, Allegra, Patrick and David arrived in the palace. Rannoth let out a groan of anguish when informed by Alistair of their arrival.

"You'll have to keep them out of my hair and this dining room," Alistair told Rannoth with unhidden relish. "You can keep them occupied somewhere else."

Rannoth was not amused. "I don't know anything about human children and how to keep them amused," he said in frustration. "Allegra and the angels have got time on their hands, let them help."

Claudia ruffled his hair and told him not to be an old grouch. "It'll be good practice for when we have our own," she told him gaily.

Rannoth looked moodily at her. "I hope you have no immediate plans for that event," he told her suspiciously. "I should prefer a few thousand years to get used to the idea. After all, I had to wait ten thousand years for you to change your mind about me. About ten thousand years of just you and me should be about right."

"Don't hold your breath," said Alistair with the wisdom of experience, "angels are born to do the opposite of what any one wants them to. I reckon it's too late already."

Claudia scowled at him. "I'm not a bit like other angels," she said severely. "I am a very responsible angel."

"You'll be a one-off then," said Alistair.

Rannoth had a strong suspicion that Alistair had been right, it was already too late, his angel WAS very responsible. Responsible for everything that had happened to him lately, and Lucifer's reference to heirs had not been lost on him.

He showed Allegra around Lucifer's palace and all its modern conveniences. He showed her the TV lounge and the reading room.

Allegra told him she would be fine. She could see Alistair had, as usual, made himself at home and she, David and Patrick settled down to watch demon television – censored by Rannoth, as normal demon television was far too violent for humans. He told Allegra he would be in his office and didn't wish to be disturbed for a while. He phoned the brigadier and informed him of his extra responsibilities, then took Claudia's arm and hauled her into his office.

"Okay, let's have it. What did your father mean by in the 'nick of time' and having heirs?"

Claudia actually blushed, and Rannoth was diverted for a moment by how beautiful she looked when flustered.

"Well?"

"He's just guessing!" she told him. "But I am sure he knows we shared the bed last night. He's not stupid, he knew what would happen when he sent me to stay with you. I think he wanted us to. He approves of you; he knows you'll keep me safe."

"As long as it is a guess, then I suppose we can put up with his snide remarks. But we'll make damned sure there are no heirs for a long time yet. Let him damned well wait."

"That's fine by me," said Claudia, "but I think if you don't mind, as soon as all this is over we will find a house near Snake and Bianca and live on earth. But our bedroom must be big enough to take that four-poster bed. I'll never sleep anywhere else ever again."

Rannoth looked at her in surprise. "I hope someone will give me permission to live there or we shall have to stay here."

"I am certain that Elliott can fix it if father can't," said Claudia, winding herself around him suggestively.

At the mention of the bed Rannoth had immediate thoughts of using it and, with Claudia making it clear she was willing, he swung her into his arms, crossed the lounge and, kicking the bedroom door shut, locked it firmly.

# CHAPTER SIXTEEN

Elliott, Jason and Daniel arrived back in New York with Lucifer two days after they had left to find Jason. All Lucifer's available assets now gathered in Travis's lounge.

Vern had a quick word with Jason and got the thumbs up from him. Katya hugged and kissed him. "I was tempted to murder you, for vanishing like that; but I am so happy to see you back, I forgive you."

"I hear you have been busy whilst I was away," he said as he seated himself beside her. "You've created another vampire." Charles was seated on her other side and Jason leaned across her and shook his hand. "Welcome to the fraternity, brother. How do you feel?"

Charles smiled lazily. "I feel just great," he assured him.

"Enough of the welcome home," snapped Lucifer irritably. "I need help solving my current crisis and finding out who's trying to do away with my girls."

"Only a first-class moron would try to do anything to your daughters," said Pauline snappily. "We'd better start looking for an idiot with a death wish."

"That's Snake's prerogative," remarked Sebastian with a humorous glance at the Salt Lake City vampire, "but we can discount him, he's got a hands-on approach to the problem."

Everyone laughed as Snake looked daggers at them all, but stayed on the couch with Bianca snuggled into his side.

"Easiest way to guard them," said Elliott approvingly. He picked Natalia up in his arms and sat in a large chair with her on his lap. "Keep them handy at all times."

"Beast!" said Natalia, though she made no attempt to move.

Elliott turned briskly to Lucifer and the rest of his team. "We are all together in one place at last. Let's get down to cases. Firstly, we need a much closer look at that building of yours. Now that Jason's back, he and Vern can go and see just what is going on there. Sebastian and Travis can go with them."

His eyes narrowed at he continued. "Natalia, Carlotta and Bianca will stay here and be guarded by Drago, Snake and Ward. Eurydice has also decided to stay here. With her family gone she'd be alone at her home, and we are both agreed that the Lamp of

Algor will prove extra cover for the angels. Don't any of you leave this building without my coming here in person to say that you can, unless of course Lucifer or Rannoth come for you. They are the only other people with the powers to keep you safe. Cybel and Cassidy have offered to accompany any of the rest of you who feel the need of magical protection.

"Daniel, Pauline and myself are going to Salt Lake City with Quinn and Theron, something tells us that the heart of our problems might be there. Nick is going with Vespazia to examine every inch of the basement of Goodman, Goodhew and May for demonic interference. Charles, Katya and Sidonie can go to the local witchcraft shop and get everything Daniel thinks necessary in case he needs to do some spell casting. He'll give you a list. Three vampires should be able to look after themselves. It will give Katya and her mother a chance to catch up on their years apart," he added with a meaningful look at Sidonie, who also knew an order when she heard one.

"Where am I going?" asked Lance.

"You can go with Diana and Cybel to the local cathedral to soak up the atmosphere," said Elliott. "I mean it, go and overdose on religion for a few hours. We can't afford to lose you right now and Daniel and I believe you will be safe there. We don't think any of the demons in New York have the power to cause trouble in the cathedral. We happen to know the place is secure. While you're there you can get in a large supply of holy water. Stay there until Jason comes for you. He's got a very large building that will need a wholesale exorcism shortly. He'll take you there when the time is right. Just make sure you've got everything you need."

Daniel glanced from Elliott to Jason, hesitated a moment, and then spoke quietly to Travis and Sebastian.

"I'd just like to remind you that Jason is even higher up the hierarchy than I am when it comes to seniority. If he gives an order it is a good plan to obey without question. Elliott and I do. When it come to smelling a trap, no one is better at it than Jason. He has saved our lives countless times with his uncanny instinct for danger. It also might interest you to know that on the only occasion Jason and Elliott came to blows, Jason won. They both gave me permission to tell you that."

Sebastian and Travis nodded acceptance of this rather explicit order that Jason was now in charge.

They knew he was a vampire, but he looked like a seventies

hippie. Yet there was a suggestion of hidden ruthlessness in his eyes and unleashed power in his walk. They decided that Daniel and Elliott would be unlikely to work with someone who was not their equal, at the very least, and accepted their evaluation of him without comment.

Vern looked amused as he saw them weighing up the hippie vampire and knew they were in for a shock the first time there was any violence.

All four headed for the roof and the helicopter. It took off a few minutes later.

Lucifer and Vespazia had already vanished to the basement of Goodman, Goodhew and May and Elliott and Daniel disappeared to Salt Lake City with their party.

Charles felt they needed a guide to the local witchcraft shops and asked Eurydice if Cassidy could come with them on their search. She agreed and then told them the best ones to go to.

Charles told Lance and Diana to get going with Cybel as ordered because Elliott never made idle suggestions. There was a good reason why he wanted what he did.

They all left on their various assignments. Cassidy took the Limo previously owned by the managing director and drove the vampires on their errands. Charles was quite safe as the limo had very dark windows and blinds. No one knew as yet how his shapeshifting side would accommodate the vampire. They took no chances. As Katya has told them. "One brush with death is all he can be allowed."

Jason, Vern and Sebastian were flown by Travis to Goodman, Goodhew and May. On the way Vern made the introductions and reinforced Daniel's opinion of Jason's superior strength and knowledge by telling them the vampire was over five thousand years old and knew a thing or too.

Sebastian and Travis were decidedly overawed by this piece of information, as neither of them were more than two hundred years old. Travis was only one hundred and fifty and Sebastian, one hundred and seventy-five. Travis had actually been the one to make the most money and buy real estate in the twenties and thirties. Realising that a vampire with a respectable home base was unlikely to be harassed or hounded, he had ended up a multi-millionaire. Also with so many apartments in his building and no one being sure who owned it except America's IRS, no one questioned the age of one of the inhabitants. The tenants came and went over the years, and no one noticed that the penthouse was still owned by the same young man who had bought it in the twenties. It helped that New York was not known as a neighbourly place and visitors were discouraged from friendly advances.

Jason was amused by this tale of the vampire's enterprise. On being told the business they were engaged in, he offered to recommend their services to his friends around the world. He told them he would introduce them to the pleasures of daytime travelling some time in the near future.

Vern looked at him surprised. Jason didn't usually put himself out for anyone but his friends. It seemed that Travis and Sebastian has been accepted by the vampire as his equals.

"You're in," he told them. "You have received the Parkes's seal of approval."

Shortly after this they landed on the roof. Snake's violent assault on the door was still evident and the cameras still lay strewn around.

"No one left in the building with the authority to have them repaired," said Travis, by way of explanation

They descended floor by floor, checking for demons and other supernatural inhabitants. Twice Jason sniffed the air and told Travis to make a note of the office number and remove any evidence of the work the occupants were engaged on. Travis on both occasions downloaded the computer files to his own console.

Sebastian laughed unpleasantly as they got to one office and found a bound and gagged bookkeeper, still in the cupboard he had been locked in several days earlier by Snake. He was a shattered wreck when Travis released him, telling him never to return to the building or he would be sent to hell.

Jason loomed over him menacingly. "He means the hell presided over by Lucifer. Don't come back unless you want to spend eternity there."

None of them had ever seen anyone disappear so fast.

It was going to take a very long time to go systematically through the entire building and Jason was still nosing around the offices on the twenty-second floor when he heard a sneeze and a scuffling sound in what appeared to be a cupboard in the corridor. He turned the handle gently and peered inside.

"Well, my goodness, what have we here?" he asked in amazement.

It was obviously the women's washroom, and inside sitting on the floor were a woman and a small child.

He told the others to stay outside, and moved further into the room.

Both occupants were looking a little tear-stained and rather uncomfortable. This gave way to terror when they saw him.

"Don't be afraid," he said soothingly. "I am here to help you. How did you get into this state? Why ever didn't you go home with everyone else?"

"We did try to get out once, but the front door wouldn't let us through," said the woman weakly. She still looked scared.

"It's a pity you didn't try again," said Jason. "Everything is back to normal."

"There hasn't been anything normal about this building for days," said the woman forthrightly. "I think the whole building was affected by a curse or something. It's been terrible. I've been so scared."

Jason was a little taken aback. He hadn't anticipated anyone human assuming supernatural intervention in the troubles affecting the occupants. "Humph! Just a little electrical problem, caused a force field to be accidentally activated around the precinct," he said lightly. "Nothing too frightening."

"Pull the other one!" said the woman. "I've been working for this firm for five years, some very strange things happen here. But it's well paid and with good pension prospects, so I live with it. But this was beyond strange and getting towards witchcraft, that's completely different. Don't think I don't know about witchcraft. I've seen ghosts appear from nowhere on the twenty-third floor, and there is always a smell of herbs all over the entrance hall."

"I won't try to fool you then," said Jason, changing tactics. "This building does seem to be bewitched and we intend to exorcise it shortly. But I think you should go home. Someone will have missed you by now, I'm certain."

"Right now there is no one who could do that," she told him, quietly.

"Hasn't anyone been to look for you?" he asked surprised. "No husband or father?"

"My brother is in Mexico for a month, that is why I have my niece with me. I couldn't get a baby-sitter last Monday, so I had to bring Janey to work with me. When everyone started to go off their heads, we hid in here. We haven't dared to go anywhere since we tried to get away the first time. We just came back here and hid again. Although I did sneak to the snack bar machine in the corridor once or twice, and we did seem fairly safe here."

"Very sensible," said Jason. "But did you not think of trying to leave again when everything quieted down?"

"It hasn't been very quiet, so far," said the woman, grimly. "Every evening people come along the corridor making a terrible racket. Everything goes quiet for a while and then the noise starts again, and they go past towards the lift. It's even worse in working hours, I have not dared to go out in the daytime."

Jason regarded her thoughtfully. "How very wise of you. But if you can bring yourself to trust us, I will have my friend fly you and your niece to safety now."

He used his mobile and called to Travis, who came in and looked surprised to see two people still in the building who, quite clearly, could have left if they wished.

"Too scared to move," said Jason. "I want you to fly them to wherever they belong and then come back and join us. This young lady has just given me some interesting news. This building has been a hotbed of activity in the daytime and rather quieter at night for the last two or three days. She has also informed me that there is witchcraft afoot and ghostly apparitions on the upper floors, particularly the twenty-third."

"Interesting!" said Travis. "Could be what we are looking for."

Travis, who looked every inch the trustworthy pilot that he was, introduced himself and hustled the woman and child from the room, at the same time ascertaining where she lived. Her name he discovered was Alysanne Lowther and she lived quite near his own building, in Manhattan.

Before Travis disappeared in the direction of the lift, he looked significantly at Jason and suggested, "Shouldn't you find your friend from down below, and tell him about this?"

"First, I think we had better do a more thorough search than ever of the rooms on this floor and the one above," responded Jason. "We've obviously missed something."

"Sebastian, go back up to the roof and wait for Travis, then come down again, searching room by room, door by door and wall by wall. Vern and I will make our way up, doing the same."

Sebastian left to do as he was asked and, once on the roof, subjected that to an inch by inch search as well.

It was a large roof and took a while. Before he had finished Travis came back. He explained to him what Jason wanted.

Together they finished the search of the roof and started on the top floor, with the penthouse.

Jason and Vern had started on the twenty-second floor.

Lucifer and Vespazia were making a micro-search of the basement. They both sensed trouble there but could not pinpoint the origin. There were a great many more rooms in the basement than Lucifer had bargained for.

"Calm down," Vespazia muttered irritably, as Lucifer began to breathe smoke from his nostrils. "I can't think when you start smoking, it makes me nervous."

"Corazan was definitely standing right about here. When I caught him he was about to leave for somewhere, I just can't quite get a handle on where."

"Perhaps there is a hidden room, or an even deeper basement below this one?" suggested Vespazia tentatively.

"Hmmph!" Lucifer looked at her reflectively. "I don't particularly fancy materialising in concrete. I'll have to go and find the plans of this place. I wonder where they keep them?"

"Don't ask me," said Vespazia. "I've been incarcerated in your guest quarters for the last half a million years. I'm only just beginning to understand this modern world. Go and ask Travis or Sebastian, they should know, after all they live and work here. I should think it'd be right up their street. They will have arrived here by now to search the building."

Without further ado Lucifer vanished, reappearing seconds later in the room on the penthouse floor which Sebastian was searching.

"What's up?" asked Sebastian.

"How do we get hold of the plans of this building?" asked Lucifer curtly. "I'm looking for hidden rooms in the basement. I need a ground-plan."

"We're looking for hidden rooms on the upper floors, particularly the top floors," said Sebastian. "I'll give Travis a shout, he should know."

Travis, when consulted, suggested the city planner's offices. "This building is at least seventy years old," he told them. "It'll be in the archives at city hall – and a long and dirty job to find them unless Lucifer can work some spell or other to bring them to us."

"Can't be done," said Lucifer, sounding annoyed. "I've got to know where something is or was to get my hands on it. We'll have to go and get it. Where's city hall?"

He took Travis by the arm as he told him this and they vanished.

The archives at city hall were in a deep basement. It was immense, dark and dirty. "What a shambles," said Lucifer in disgust. "Where do we start?"

"Late nineteen twenties," suggested Travis. "Purchase of plot, planning permission, design and architectural model."

Lucifer concentrated hard on these suggestions and, after a while, gave a shout of triumph as a large box came floating through the air towards him.

It wafted into his hands and he placed it on the floor, waving his hand to disperse the dust of decades, and opened the lid. Surprisingly the contents were reasonably clean, although faded, brown and ageing fast. Lucifer handed each roll to Travis who scanned and discarded most of them, but then looked in astonishment as one of the rolls of parchment unrolled itself and flattened out on the floor. They both got down on their knees for a closer look.

"Well, well, so that's how they did it," said Lucifer admiringly. "They have been up to no good for a very long time indeed. It looks as if someone else has been using those passageways for as long as it has been built."

"Makes you wonder what else is going on in other skyscrapers," said Travis.

"That will be your job in the future," said Lucifer sharply. "Look, listen and learn now."

They returned to the penthouse and Lucifer fetched Vespazia from the basement and Jason and Vern from the roof.

Travis looked shaken. "I can't say I like instantaneous travel, it's a shock to a pilot's system."

"Get used to it," said Jason. "We have to use it a lot in our line of work."

Lucifer was already in the conference room tapping the walls.

"Got it!" he said with satisfaction and, finding a spring catch on the underside of a loose wall tile, lifted it up to find a handle set in the wall. He slid it quietly to one side to reveal a narrow corridor and, in the dimness, a hidden staircase to the floor below.

"This is it," He said in triumph. "Goodness knows what they are hiding down there. You can find out for me on the way to the basement."

Travis and Sebastian exchanged concerned glances. "You want

217

us to go down there? Aren't you coming?"

Lucifer was impatient to go straight to the basement himself and find the secret entrances there. "If you are going to be my agents in this city, you will be entering far more dangerous places than this," he told them sharply. "This is your job from now on."

He gave them a few moments to digest his words. "Well, what are you waiting for? Get going," he ordered.

"All stay together or split up?" asked Jason with a warning glance to the other vampires.

"You and your lot check down these stairs, I'll go to the basement with Sebastian and Vespazia," said Lucifer.

"Shouldn't we check for a similar entrance on the executives' floor?" asked Travis. "It's where all the demonic activity has been taking place, lately."

"We'll work our way down," said Jason. "There's bound to be an entrance in the chairman's and the managing directors suite of offices. We can cheek them on the way.

Jason and his party disappeared into the wall space. Lucifer led his down to the basement in the lift.

"Very appropriate," thought Sebastian wryly. "I'm probably following the devil to hell."

"Don't be ridiculous," said Lucifer, picking up the thought. "If I'd wanted you there, you'd have been there long ago."

"You can't believe how relieved that makes me," said Sebastian.

"Keep your voice down! We don't want them to know we're coming," hissed Lucifer. They descended the rest of the way in silence.

"This has been very cleverly done," said Jason as they descended several floors without finding anything. "It must have taken very clever manipulation of the stairwells and lift shafts to get this one past the inspectors."

"Plus an enormous back hander," added Travis.

"A hidden apartment on one of the floors, entered by the secret stairs going up behind the walls in the stairwells," said Vern. "Very clever." As a builder himself he appreciated the masterful manipulation of the original plans and the brilliance of the architect who had got it past the planners.

"So where is this secret room?"

"Somewhere around the twelfth or thirteenth floor is my guess," said Jason. "That young woman we found was in the vicinity of the managing director's office which is on the thirteenth floor for some reason. The chairman's is on the twenty-third, probably for the same reason, and there's a conference room in the penthouse suite. My guess is that this stairway links all three and the basement. I believe we may soon find out why."

"Most people like to avoid the thirteenth floor, superstition has its uses. What better place to have a secret room? You are walking down the corridor, the office doors are not uniformly spaced along it. One particular wall will just appear to go down the corridor and around the corner and no one will ever notice that there should be a door in the wall. In a building with thousands of doors who is going to notice that one is missing, particularly if the managing director has a suite of offices on that floor," added Vern.

They were still some way from the thirteenth floor when they arrived at a landing with a door in the adjacent wall. Vern cautiously opened it when Jason indicated. They all moved silently into the apartment. A quick survey revealed five small rooms, two with tinted windows. Surprisingly, although clean (and cleaned recently, thought Jason) it was completely empty, except for the vague smell of herbs and possibly incense in the air.

"Which floor are we on?" asked Vern.

"This is the twenty-third floor," said Travis, who had been keeping count. "I was right. Something is happening here. This place smells like a witches' kitchen. Someone has done some spell casting in the last few hours."

"That probably accounts for the noise that secretary was going on about," agreed Vern.

"To account for all that racket, I should think they had coven of witches and warlocks up here," said Jason dryly.

"I hope it wasn't a coven of black magicians or ancient sorcerers," said Vern in alarm. "My blood has suddenly gone icy cold. I don't like this."

"It has gone cold," agreed Jason. "Even I can sense it. Let's get out of here. I reckon Elliott was right. It would be a good idea to have Lance come and exorcise this building as soon as possible."

They backed out of the room very quickly and continued down the stairs.

"This is the thirteenth floor," said Jason as they arrived on yet another small landing.

He opened the door silently, although he didn't really expect anyone to be there. He sensed no presence other than his team.

There were three main rooms, all with tinted windows. An old-fashioned kitchen and bathroom had none. This apartment, rather more spacious than that on the twenty-third floor, had five much larger rooms and, sometime in the past, been luxuriously carpeted and furnished. The apartment seemed uninhabited right then, but Jason had a vague sense of unease as he looked around. Something felt wrong, out of place – maybe even out of time.

It was plain that someone had been living here. It was hard to judge for how long. Most of the furniture was well-worn and beginning to look just a little shabby. The remains of a meal, still fresh, were on the kitchen table. The room was warm and the air conditioning on. The occupant, whoever he or she was, expected to return.

"We need to find out who lives here and for how long. Look for anything of a personal nature," said Jason as he started to roam around the room looking for clues as to the occupant.

His fellow searchers began very carefully to take the rooms apart. They found absolutely nothing of a personal nature to indicate who lived there.

When Lucifer, Sebastian and Vespazia reached the basement, Lucifer unrolled the plans and spread them on the floor.

"Right, you!" he said to Sebastian. "Have a look at these and tell me where the entrance is."

Sebastian oriented himself with the plans and scanned them unhurriedly. A maze of tunnels and pipes, sewers and drains ran under the building. He was actually looking for one that led nowhere. It would be the one he wanted.

After studying the plans for several minutes, Sebastian got up and began to prowl around the basement, in and out of the dozen or so small storerooms, boiler rooms and electrical departments.

After about twenty minutes he returned. "I think I've found something."

He led them to a small storeroom at the end of a corridor. "See that pillar with just one power box on it? It is bigger that all the other pillars down here. I think the staircase goes down inside it. One side of that pillar is a doorway. We have to find it."

Vespazia looked closely at the pillar he indicated and put her hands on the side. She muttered an incantation and jumped back as the side she was leaning on opened outwards.

"Excellent work," said Lucifer as a set of steps was revealed leading down to another level of the building.

Lucifer stepped through and the others followed.

As they neared the bottom of the steps a low murmuring of voices was heard. Lucifer made himself invisible as did Vespazia, who motioned for Sebastian to stay where he was.

The two of them glided silently towards the voices.

Lucifer was extremely put out. Balzahar was sitting on a large chair, holding court with about twenty black magicians and shamen. They were laughing and drinking from large beer mugs. Nearby was a large table filled with food and drinks.

Lucifer gritted his teeth to stop himself from yelling at them. He forced himself to listen to their ravings.

"It won't be long now," boasted Balzahar, "until our new master will be Lord of the Universe and Master of the Underworld. Lucifer has had his chance. He has been losing his hold on the demon dimensions for some years. It is time he was replaced by someone who is more evil that he has ever been."

"Over my very much alive, and your very evil and dead carcass," seethed Lucifer, with thoughts of torture uppermost in his mind.

He considered them intently for a short while and then waved his hands in a box like movement, baring his teeth in an evil leer as he told Vespazia, "I've imprisoned them in a force field of enormous power. They can't get back to hell and they can't leave this room. I've made the food taste like soap and the drink is now vinegar. That should keep them guessing for a while. They'll keep until I get around to dealing with them."

"Some of them are human," said Vespazia doubtfully. "They will die without food."

"Too bad," said Lucifer callously. "I'd get them eventually anyway, this way I get them a bit sooner."

"Oh, Dear!" said Vespazia. "Put like that it doesn't seem quite so awful!"

"Nothing to concern yourself about at all. All in a day's work for me," said Lucifer, trying to sound comforting and almost succeeding.

"Now which of my brothers is stupid enough to think he can pull this off?" his thoughts continued. "None of them," he answered himself. "They haven't got the guts or the know-how. So who in the universe knows enough to negate some of my spells, and hates me enough to go after my only children? Who, in fact, knows that I HAVE children? They were a well-kept secret until now."

Vespazia's thoughts entered his head: "There is of course one person who fills all those requirements. Are you absolutely, one-hundred per-cent certain that my mother is dead?"

"If she isn't," Lucifer replied aloud, "she must be able to regenerate herself."

The two of them shuddered at the thought and then took a horrified look at each other.

"She couldn't be, could she?" asked Lucifer, then answered his own question. "Who else would want to kill my daughters?"

Vespazia was incapable of speech.

"Fifth Dimension," said Lucifer, instantaneously with this thought. "The Oracle, and the First Ones. I'm off. You take the others back to Travis's. Only Elliott and Daniel are powerful enough to be here alone. These morons," he indicated the captives, "can't do any more harm now. I'll be in touch."

He vanished. The absence of the puff of smoke indicating his immense concern.

Vespazia and Sebastian appeared in the apartment on the thirteenth floor. "Stop searching," she said in a hollow whisper. "We believe we've found our answer. It's terrible news."

Jason looked at her in concern. She looked sick and ill. Vern rushed to her side and caught her as she would have fallen, and helped her to a seat. Sebastian filled a glass with water and handed it to her.

"What is it Vespazia?" asked Jason, surprised at her pallor, "Who is it you fear so much?"

Then suddenly he knew.

"Oh, no! It can't be. Not again," he said aghast. "Not Charalder."

"Lucifer thinks so as well. Who else would want to kill his daughters? After all, he helped you and Elliott kill HER sons. I suspect she has turned her attention to them because she now knows that Simon is her great-grandson."

Vern turned white. "You mean, the witch who nearly killed Natalia and kidnapped Simon?"

"Yes," said Vespazia. "It doesn't bear thinking about. I suppose we should have guessed when all those witch doctors and black magicians went missing all over the world, in the last few months."

"How could we guess? Even Alpha and Torquil think she is dead," said Jason equably. "She is obviously even more powerful than we could have imagined. There is only one person now who can deal with her, and he cannot intervene in mortal conflicts.

"Although it may just be that this is no longer a mortal conflict," he added thoughtfully, "She has involved the angels and the devil in her plans. It's just possible she has outstripped her own powers, this time."

"Lucifer says we should get back to Travis's place immediately," said Vespazia.

"Come on Travis, back to the roof," said Jason, "anything else here will have to wait."

They exited the secret stairs on the thirteenth floor and took the lift to the penthouse and thence to the roof. Twenty minutes later they were back at Travis's home and relaying the bad news to the rest of the team.

Jason explained the terrible nature of Charalder's evil to the Americans.

"She was the wife of a former angel, called Zohal. He was the son of Omega, an Archangel who left the confines of Heaven millions of years ago. He wasn't the only Archangel to leave. There were many archangels who were at the Beginning and didn't enjoy the confines of their heavenly abode. Elliott's grandfather, Alpha, was there when the universe was created." He paused briefly as he gathered his thoughts.

"Everyone has always assumed that angels were perfect beings. Not so. There were wars in Heaven but ultimately good prevailed. By then some of the Archangels had had enough. Omega and Alpha created a world they called the Fifth Dimension and holder of the Sword of Xahon, a weapon of peace in the right hands and evil in the wrong ones. Charalder was ambitious and wanted to share this power with Zohal. She was not an archangel and was denied this role. She was the daughter of an angel who stayed in heaven when some of the other angels left. That's why she's got heavenly powers. She and Zohal had many sons but her driving ambitions, to make herself and them the rulers of the Fifth Dimension, turned them against their father."

He hesitated again, "This is not the full story. Briefly, she grew tired of living in the Fifth Dimension, she urged her sons to kill Zohal. The retribution of the Fifth Dimension was swift and terrible. Her sons were thrown into the Eternal Flame and their ashes scattered amongst the stars. Charalder true to form escaped and fled to earth. Her evil deeds became legendary. She gathered up all the knowledge of the demonic worlds and became a by-word for evil. Death and destruction followed in her wake. Her powers increased a thousand-fold as the years went by. She became the most powerful sorceress ever known. She still had many of her heavenly powers; the ability to materialise and dematerialize at will was paramount. During this period she married a demon sorcerer, and had a daughter. That daughter is here with us now." He waved a hand towards Vespazia indicating that she tell her part of the story.

"Although Charalder was my mother, however, she left the blame fall on me for every death and evil deed perpetrated. She forced me to mingle with the dragons to learn their secrets, but I fell in love with the Dolonquin and we had a daughter. To save them both I went back to her but she kidnapped our daughter and her army of demons slaughtered all the dragons except Quinn and his brother. Just before they fell I decided to save them both. I had no choice but to place Quinn under a spell and hide him from human eyes. I allowed his brother to seem as if dead for a short while and to safeguard our daughter's future I sent her soul on a journey destined to last a million years." Here she wryly told them of her horror when she had found out that her daughter was married to a vampire. "Only some one worthy of her could return her to her world. A five-thousand-year-old vampire proved to be just that."

She reflected on Jason's true character for a moment. Then continued, "My mother allowed me to rot in hell for almost one million years.

"Although this all took place long before Lucifer came to earth, even that long ago there was a dimension for the punishment of evil. Lucifer merely took it over and expanded it to accommodate those who fell into his fiery pit of infamy. The tortures became commonplace and his evil spells were cast far and wide. But, so ancient was the place myself, and a few others lived that we were apparently forgotten. If he ever knew we were there he certainly took no interest in us. His chief assistant Rannoth kept a tally of all prisoners but even he had no interest in a million-year old witch. I welcomed the prison of loneliness to a life without my husband and child. However," she said with some satisfaction, "I learned enough over the years to help Lucifer and Daniel destroy her when the time came."

Travis and Sebastian although astounded to learn that Vespazia was a primeval witch hastened to assure her that no one could help who their parents were or what they did. They could see the British contingent thought highly of her and that was good enough for them.

"Nothing much we can do until Lucifer gets back and we contact Elliott and Daniel," said Jason, taking out his mobile and attempting to call Alistair, whose mobile was switched off. He asked Travis to e-mail him with the bad news. He then rang James Purcell and put him in the picture, telling him he had better tell everyone there, as they deserved the truth. He had even begun to wonder if Alex and Faith's accident really was an accident. They too had been in the Lost World at the time of Charalder's demise. He didn't tell anyone else that, but decided to wait for Elliott's opinion.

Travis reappeared some minutes later. "Your brother-in-law is not pleased. His reply should not have been allowed to sully the airwaves. Sufficient to say that he thinks the Astral Council has been derelict in its duty to the universe."

Jason gave a wry smile. "Alistair has always been a bit outspoken."

"Your wife suggests you watch your back for wooden stakes, and don't get in the way of any bolts of fire or lightning. She also suggests that Natalia, Bianca and Carlotta join the other angels under Rannoth's protection. Charalder has already had a go at Natalia, and Carlotta was also in the Lost World with you all when Lucifer helped to destroy her. Allegra is also suspicious about Bianca's accident in view of the latest information."

"Very sensible girl, my wife. Send a message back, tell Rannoth to arrange it. Tell him he can take Snake with him and I'll arrange to have Drago join Karim on guard at the hospital. I'll send Ward back to them as well. We need a vampire in each location for extra protection."

"He's taken charge a bit smartish, hasn't he," whispered Sebastian to Vern.

"I told you. Elliott, Jason and Daniel are the big guns around here. The rest of us obey orders," said Vern grimly.

Ward grimaced at this summary removal of himself and Drago, but agreed with Jason that a vampire at the hospital was a good idea. Travis was disappointed that Carlotta had to leave, but agreed that she must be kept safe. He pulled her into the dining room and said a rather private farewell. She told him she would be back as soon as Lucifer or Jason said it was safe. She had no desire to lose her life, particularly now that she had found it so much more

225

interesting than in the past. She smiled as she saw that Travis was pleased with her reply, and held him tightly for a moment before they rejoined their friends in the lounge.

Jason ordered Natalia to get down to Hell right away and take Carlotta with her. "You've been there with Elliott plenty of times. You know the way."

For once in her life Natalia, who looked surprised at Jason's harsh command, said she was ready whenever the others were. However, Snake and Bianca were still arguing about the necessity of his trip to Hell when Rannoth appeared and glared warningly at them all.

"The safest place in the universe right now is Lucifer's palace. So no arguments, you're going."

He snapped his fingers and they all vanished. He left immediately after they had disappeared, telling Jason that they would be fine with him.

When it came to dealing with angels on earth, thought Jason, Rannoth appeared to have a surprising amount of control over them. He looked thoughtful as he wondered just how much power Rannoth did have.

Ward and Drago left within minutes as Jason opened the portal to the hospital, telling them to keep in touch through Alistair.

Rannoth had moved smartly to carry out Jason's orders and arrived back in Lucifer's palace about fifteen minutes after Jason's message was received, everyone safely in his custody. Snake was less than pleased to be in hell, but Bianca assured him that her father would allow him back when the all-clear was given.

"Now you are here, you had better make the most of it. Daddy likes his guests to be happy," she said with a sly look at Rannoth.

Rannoth valiantly hid his mirth, as normally the last thing on Lucifer's mind was anything connected with the happiness of his guests. Devising awful tortures was more in his line.

Natalia went straight to the nursery to see Nicholas and Carlotta went with her. Allegra was there with Riva in her arms, watching Simon trying to play with Lucinda and Penelope, who were still a little too young to understand that he wanted to play. Carlotta picked him up and sat down by the window and began to read to him from one of the fairy stories with which Lucifer had stocked the bookcase.

Bianca took Snake to meet Alistair, telling to the others to share the workload and leaving them to get on with it. Snake and

Alistair nodded to each other. Alistair indicated the large pile of papers stacked on the table and told Snake he hadn't had time to check through them yet. They were supposed to be a record of everything that had already risen, was supposed to rise or had been prophesied in the last two thousand years. It was unlikely the one they were interested in was there but there was just a chance it was.

"How about it?" challenged Alistair. "You willing to wade through them?" Snake sat down at the table to read through all the papers Alistair had accumulated from sources around the United States and Canada.

Seeing he was now fully occupied, Bianca left to find her sister. She found Claudia prowling restlessly around Rannoth's office, quite obviously getting in his way, and invited her to join her in the nursery.

"It's time you did a check on the wolf cubs as their parents aren't here, and you can introduce me to the other babies."

Claudia was agreeable and they arrived in the nursery to see their father's godchildren. Bianca hadn't seen them before, as she didn't visit hell as often as her sister. She hadn't had quite the same incentive. They spent quite some time getting to know their father's beloved godchildren and Allegra, whom they had never met.

After the children had all gone to sleep the angels gathered in the kitchen. Allegra had decided it was prudent to baby-sit for a while. The two young shapeshifters were there investigating the larder. Because of the current presence of mortal nurses and the witches from the surface, Lucifer had thoughtfully provided a large amount of human food, and Patrick and David had to be fed. This took a while as Bianca and Claudia had never met them before and were very interested in the two of them. The meal was a very noisy one.

Unfortunately, the kitchen was next to the dining room where Alistair and Snake were working. When Allegra brought in a tray of food and drink, she found one, very grumpy researcher. "You can tell those angels to cut out that racket," growled Snake. "It's giving me a headache!"

"Cool it," said Alistair, "Don't be a killjoy. They are enjoying themselves. It's rather nice to see them acting just like gossiping human females. Makes them seem more like us." Yet Snake was not to be mollified. He was trying to read through the mass of information given him by Alistair, and finding it hard to concentrate. He rose to his feet, went to the kitchen and growled at them to shut up.

The angels were all together for the first time for centuries and had started to catch up on one another's love lives and other current and past events. They were making a lot of noise in the process, but they told Snake to shut the doors if he wanted to cut out the noise, they were enjoying their reunion.

Alistair got so annoyed at having so many visitors disturbing his space, he called Rannoth to tell him he'd have to find them rooms on the other side of the palace. Now he couldn't work with all the 'jawing' going on either. Snake tended to agree with him. Whoever would have thought that four angels could make so much racket!

Rannoth too, looked in dismay at the gathering in the kitchen but decided against trying to stop them. He rather thought it would be less than successful, and he didn't fancy being sent off with a flea in his ear. It was always wise for a demon to at least appear to have the upper hand when it came to wives, particularly if they were of the angelic denomination. He decided to separate them by distance rather than force and sought the advice of the Brigadier about the increasingly large number of guests in the palace.

"The Boss's elder daughter will be safe with you," said the brigadier tactfully, "and there's a nice little suite in the east wing will do for Snake and Bianca. Elliott's got a suite in the west wing, as you know, but he'd have my head if I let anyone use that, and in any case I couldn't let the angel Natalia stay there on her own. Allegra, Natalia and the other angel can have the Boss's rooms until he returns, or they can each have one of the nursery rooms and be near the children. That should separate them at least for as while, and the Elite Guard are on duty twenty-four hours a day."

"Do whatever is necessary," said Rannoth. "After all, you will be doing most of the guard duty. Arrange it to suit yourselves."

The brigadier went off to organise a duty rota for his men. Seeing the importance of guarding the angels, he decided to take one watch himself and let the captain and the major take the others. Three eight-hour shifts should be just right.

On returning to his office he sent for the duty officer, telling him to place four men outside the suite where Lucifer's younger daughter was to reside, and four more outside Allegra's room and the other angels' rooms when they had decided which to use. Also he was to double the guards on the human youths and the young children.

Finally he was to discreetly arrange a guard to make sure that no one approached Rannoth's offices without them knowing. He would prefer that Rannoth didn't know either as he might feel this a reflection on his ability to guard the angel Claudia himself. But as she was Lucifer's other daughter he, the brigadier, didn't feel inclined to take any chances.

He would have been relieved to know that Rannoth approved his precautionary measures, but wasn't about to say so. He rather liked the idea that the brigadier held him in similar awe to Lucifer.

Silently and very discreetly all of the men took up their posts. No one could say they weren't the very best at their jobs.

Rannoth rang Jason to tell him everything was set up in his department. Jason rang Elliott to tell him what Lucifer and Vespazia had concluded and what he had done to safeguard their loved ones. Elliott was predictably incensed but applauded his precautions.

Rannoth returned to his office and tried to catch up on some work. This was rather difficult, as Claudia had arrived back after seeing Natalia, Carlotta and Allegra to their rooms near the nursery and Snake and Bianca had retired to their suite. With Claudia now lounging on his couch, one shapely leg swinging idly as she watched him, he felt his blood pressure begin to rise. She knew it too and arranged herself more comfortably onto the cushions, endeavouring to show a lot more flesh in the process. He gritted his teeth and carried on.

Just as he was about to give in and take her to bed, a message flashed across his screen. He read the message from Alistair with surprise and grabbing Claudia by the arm, hustled her off to the dining room.

He and Alistair read with growing dismay the information scrolling down the screen. "My God, Alistair, how on earth did this slip by the Astral Council all these years?"

"I should think they must have used some powerful spells to hide it from view," said Alistair.

"The people who live there must be walking around with their eyes shut," said Rannoth.

Alistair shrugged. "I remember Alex mentioning that Natalia had told him that if something is too awful or weird for people to believe they pretend it has never happened. I expect that is what has happened to this over the years."

"I'll go and find Snake and see what he thinks. After all, he lived there for over forty years."

"Yes," said Alistair, as Rannoth walked from the room. "And nobody noticed he hadn't grown a day older in all that time."

Snake was not in a good mood. Both Jason and Snake himself had overlooked the fact that there was not a lot of fresh human blood in Hell. He had not fed in the last forty-eight hours.

Rannoth was annoyed. "Of course there is. You're not thinking straight. You can take a small amount from each of the humans we are protecting. If you ask them nicely they are sure to agree. You can have some of mine if necessary. I'm a living, breathing immortal demon, I'm not one of the re-born dead. My blood is very similar to human blood and quite tasty, I believe. It would be perfectly safe for you to have a pint or even more."

Claudia and Bianca looked shocked and Snake was positively shaken by this suggestion. "I can't do that. They are our friends and we are supposed to be guarding them."

"A fat lot of use you'll be to them sick or dead," said Rannoth brutally. "If you won't ask them, I will."

He hustled them all down the corridors to the dining room where Alistair was still searching for more information on the area surrounding Salt Lake City.

"We've got a vampire feeding problem. Snake doesn't feel happy at asking his new friends to donate their blood and he doesn't fancy using mine. I told him he can't go to the surface to hunt, he'll have to use the humans already here. Is that okay by you, Alistair?"

"Sure, why not?" agreed Alistair unconcerned. "I've helped Jason out in emergencies before now. You can take a pint and a half in perfect safety. I'll give Allegra a shout and see what she can spare. David and Patrick might take a bit of persuading, they've never done it before. Of course you can't feed off the angels or the wolf cubs. But there are a couple of human witches in the nursery you could ask."

"I'd never touch a drop of the babies' blood," said Snake horrified.

"You couldn't anyway," said Claudia, "the others are an angel and two vampires. Angel's blood would be like drinking concentrated holy water. Instant death."

"I'll stick to humans and animals," said Snake with a shudder.

Allegra hurried in from the nursery and was quite agreeable, as were David and Patrick when asked. She didn't think it necessary as yet to ask the two witches.

"I'll make do with half a pint from each," said Snake. "And if we are still here tomorrow, we'll think again."

Allegra and Alistair held out their wrists and Snake drank slowly and delicately from each of them. The shapeshifters were delighted to take part and also held out their wrists willingly.

"Thank you," said Snake, when he had finished and delicately wiping his lips with a tissue supplied by Allegra. "We vampires have to have our blood fix or we get sick, and it's not pleasant."

"Another half-pint from each of us tomorrow and the next day will be well within permitted limits," said Alistair amiably. "I haven't had a vampire brother-in-law for years without learning a thing or two about bloodletting. Just remember to drink plenty," he said to David and Patrick as they went back to the lounge to watch demon TV, which had kept them absolutely riveted to their seats ever since they'd arrived.

Allegra looked critically at Snake. "You've had barely enough to survive. You need to keep your strength up if you are on guard duty. If you feel at all unwell, you come straight to me. There's nothing I don't know about vampires and their need to drink blood. I go hunting with Jason whenever I can."

Snake looked taken aback. "You actually go with him? But you're a human, it's not decent."

"Why not?" said Allegra coolly. "I'm his wife, he has nothing he needs to hide from me. I find it rather exhilarating to share his night-time hunts."

"Yeah, while I baby-sit!" growled Alistair.

Allegra cuffed him round the ear. "Who asked your opinion?"

Thanking them again, Snake went back to his suite with Bianca, still bemused by their unhesitating donation of blood, but with the firmly held belief that Allegra had quite a bit of the vampire in her already.

Rannoth and Claudia followed them. Alistair trailed after them. He was afraid he might miss something important. Information gathering was his mission on this occasion. He listened intently to the conversation.

"I came to find you earlier, partly because I need to know if you have ever heard of strange horsemen riding around Utah, and also because I need a favour," Rannoth told him.

"I know there has been a lot of talk for a couple of hundred years about a gang of rustlers appearing from the sky on horseback," said Snake. "I always ignored it because no one ever reported any cattle missing that the vampires or demons hadn't killed. I can't think that has anything to do with your problem."

"Believe me, I wish it didn't, but Alistair has found mention of a group of horsemen in your part of America who appear and disappear on certain moonless nights, going back several hundred years. It is part of Indian folklore and even some Spanish soldiers have mentioned it in their journals. There are also a number of references to secret valleys in tribal songs and medicine chants. Alistair has also found a reference to an opening inside the mountain which leads nowhere, but through which people have disappeared never to return. This dates from several hundred years ago, so it was obviously only noticed now that travel and communication are more common. So, discounting the exaggerations of time and repetition, this is still a disturbing thing to find out, just when we are looking for evil to arise. There is a possibility that it could be the Valkyrie or the Horsemen of the Apocalypse, but I doubt it. This is not their style. I need to go to America and check out the area, but I just wondered if you had anything to suggest?"

"The only thing that I have heard recently is the sudden absence of the local Indians from their usual haunts. None of them had been seen for a couple of months. Most people don't bother too much about them as they live quite high in the hills and only come to town if they need to buy provisions. The men come to play pool and have a drink occasionally, but even they have stopped coming. We vampires don't bother with them much. They still have a lot of the native cunning of their race, and they live too high up in the hills to consider walking all that distance just for the chance of a meal."

Bianca and Claudia both looked a little upset at this offhand dismissal of the Indians as 'meals', but Snake hurriedly told them both. "It's all right, I promised never to take human blood again. Unless of course it is offered voluntarily," he added hastily.

Rannoth deemed it wise to change the subject and was pleased when Alistair entered the conversation.

"Jason and Elliott are always going on about any changes from normal behaviour being worth investigation," Alistair told them thoughtfully. "Perhaps you should follow up this change of the local Indians from their usual habits."

"I agree. In view of what has been happening, someone should follow this up. But if you go, who is going to watch over Claudia? The angels have to be guarded. Lucifer will kill both of us if anything happens to them," Snake pointed out forcefully to Rannoth.

"I've thought about that, and that is the other favour. Will you guard Claudia as well as Bianca for a while? I have to go to America for a word with Elliott and Daniel about this. I don't know how long I shall be gone."

Snake looked strangely at him, "You would trust me with Claudia after what I said about her?"

"I trust you to look after Bianca's sister, and to remember that they are both Lucifer's daughters," said Rannoth simply. "I trust you to see that no harm comes to either of them."

Snake was astounded at the demon's show of faith in him. Rannoth was giving him a chance to redeem himself in Claudia's eyes. Snake was determined to show the demon his trust was not misplaced.

"Rest assured. Your angel is safe with me," said Snake.

Rannoth nodded. "Don't leave this apartment unless Snake is with you," he said sternly to Claudia; and, giving her a quick hug, he vanished.

Lucifer had already consulted an immortal Sage who lived on the Astral Plain. Unable to find the vampire sages in any demon dimension, Lucifer had come to the conclusion that they could have progressed to the Astral Plain. He decided to consult an immortal Sage who lived there. However, for the first time in his all-knowing all-powerful immortal life, the sage had nothing to offer by way of past or future prophecies, and no advice on the way forward. This particularly ancient being had no connection with the Oracle in the Fifth Dimension. He and his acolytes lived out their immortal lives amongst the stars. They wandered the Astral Plain and were available only to those whose powers could take them there or had the ability to summon their presence. Lucifer and Elliott, the Archangels and the First Ones were their only contacts with mankind. They did not like being summoned too often. They liked to feel they were the ones in charge of destinies. Having the devil approach them was not a good omen. The sage denied any knowledge of vampire sages and scoffed at Lucifer's fears. Lucifer sensed he was withholding the truth, but couldn't get any further information.

The Fifth Dimension Oracle, when summoned, was disdainful of Lucifer's fears. "I see no change on the horizon. All is as it should be. There is no current prophecy about an evil witch, which has not already been disclosed. You must have misread the signs. They could concern the final fulfillment of past prophecy which has yet to draw a close, or it could refer to an ancient legend which is about to be unveiled. This is of course the third possibility that this is the start of a new era in prophecy, one yet to be recorded. The permutations are limitless but as yet unknown to me. However I can see no terrible evil about your agents on earth."

"Silly old fool. A lot of good you are in an emergency," said Lucifer dismissively, waving his hand and sending the Oracle back to his duties. He went in search of Alpha and Torquil in the Fifth Dimension.

"You are supposed to be the All-knowing," said Lucifer challengingly as he confronted them with his dilemma. "What do you suggest we do, now?"

"At this moment we are too astonished to think of a solution," admitted Alpha, "We will have to convene a meeting of the Council of the First Ones, and ask our children, the Old Ones to join us. We must hope that we can come up with something to get rid of her for all time."

"It's a pity you didn't do away with her when you first had the chance," said Lucifer grimly. "She's had a couple of million years to gather up all the knowledge of good and evil in the universe plus all the ancient wisdom of the gods and the angels. Added together with as many black magicians and their like as she could find, it's beginning to look as if she is now as powerful as we are. I only hope she is not more powerful than the Great Entity.

"She was recently in the Golden City and changed herself to look like my daughter Claudia, trying to kill my other daughter Bianca. Fortunately, or unfortunately as the case may be, she flung her down where a very unpleasant vampire was known to hang out. I suspect he was supposed to kill her but the bloodsucker took one look at her and fell for her hook, line and sinker. When she woke up enough to take a good look at him, and I have to admit he's a handsome devil, she discovered he was just what she had been looking for all her life and decided to reform him. The little monkey has been consorting with him for months behind my back. The only good thing about it is that, now, she has got a strong protector, who can legally stay with her day and night. What's more I find myself looking with some favour on the man who saved her. I must be losing my touch."

Alpha and Torquil looked shocked. "You have allowed your daughter to consort with a vampire?"

"I didn't agree to it. The Great Entity ordered it. Made him a guardian to angels, if you please. I only hope he's going to make sure that evil old hag doesn't go after my girls again. What's more, my elder daughter Claudia has taken a fancy to my chief assistant, Rannoth. Apparently she has been hankering after him for centuries, and now I've had to sanction that alliance. I tell you, you were lucky to have boys."

"You cannot ask Him to intervene," said Alpha interrupting this diatribe. "He cannot take sides in any disputes between good and evil. The game must be played out."

"There you go with that word again. This is not a game, there are no sides. This could mean the end of the world as we know it. He is the architect of all things; he cannot allow some upstart murderess to interfere in his eternal plan. I am off to seek his advice. In the meantime you lot can try to find a solution, just in case."

Lucifer departed for Middle Earth and stood in the waiting room he used when, occasionally, seeking a private audience.

The Great Entity entered. He was in his 'own image', larger, taller and more handsome that any mortal man. He sat down opposite Lucifer, waved him to a seat and looked at him intently.

"Sometimes, Lucifer, you surprise me. Not often, but now and again through the millennia. What do you expect me to do, now?"

"I don't expect anything," said Lucifer. "I know of your eternal plan. If you remember, I was there when you laid it out. I don't expect or even want you to change it. It was a good plan; it still will be when those mortals realise what they are missing. I would like you to give me just the tiniest hint that we will win this confrontation with Charalder. I love all those people, as much as I love my own daughters. I should not like to see any of them wiped from existence. They are doing a good job for both of us. I shouldn't want this made known to them, mind you. I have enough trouble keeping them in line as it is."

The Great Entity smiled slightly at this tribute to the Astral Council members.

"The druid and the Dark One will overcome once more, but this time they will do it with help from one of your people. Make sure you do not interfere. They will never have another chance. Death is not always the way forward, and it is seldom the outcome we seek. Yes, we both know that in most cases, death is a victory, but now and again to give life is a far greater victory." He paused and looked keenly at Old Nick.

"She will not enter any room which contains any of her descendants. In this way, the children can be protected. Rannoth has already seen to that. I shall give him the freedom of Earth once more. His previous transgression is forgiven. He was overzealous in killing to protect an angel, even though she was your daughter, but he has redeemed himself and earned his membership of the Council. The angels were her targets as you have guessed, but you and the vampires have protected them all. Their courage has been recognised. You and I both know that the Dark One and the druid have all the power they need. This battle must be played out in the home of the ancients, and true forgiveness will bring lasting peace to everyone. There are other problems which they must also overcome, but the druid has the answer to them as well."

The Great Entity sighed. "All is not as it seems. Good is not always the victor and evil sometimes gains a strange reward... Even the Oracles can be misled. There are still many mysteries to be solved and life, in the meantime, must continue. No one has all the answers, Lucifer." He looked meaningfully at the Devil as he got to his feet. "As I have told you many times, when free will enters the equation, the end result becomes uncertain."

Lucifer stood also. He bowed as the Great Entity left the room, the consultation over.

He departed at once for the Fifth Dimension to discuss the contents of the message with the First Ones.

Alpha looked at him thoughtfully. "If it were not for the fact that Elliott is immortal, I would say that they are to be sacrificed to save you all."

Lucifer looked horrified as did Torquil. "How do you work that one out?" asked Lucifer. "I didn't read it like that."

"When He referred to death as a victory, my heart told me what He meant."

"Daniel has already been told he will be the last druid, but why give him all that ancient knowledge if he will never get to use it?" asked Lucifer.

"There is no prophecy which tells of the death of the Dark One," protested Torquil. "How can I tell Yohanna, and what will Natalia do without him?"

"Let's not kill them off, yet," said Lucifer harshly. "There are always alternatives to any solution. I don't want to hear another word about this theory of yours, until after the event. I particularly don't want a word of this to reach Elliott and Daniel. We don't want to prejudice their chances before they even start."

"I agree with Lucifer," said Torquil angrily. "No word of this. Let them find their own solution as usual. No interference this time father. You promised Jason you would never interfere again without consulting them, first."

"I did, and I will stand by that promise. The facts and nothing more, just as he asked, but I shall come with you all and if I am asked my opinion, I shall give it."

"Fair enough," said Lucifer. "I won't deny you that right."

The three of them went to meet with the Council of the First Ones and several important facts emerged. Many of its members were almost as old as Alpha and considerably older than Torquil. Two of them put forward the theory that Charalder did not seem to have achieved, as yet, the heights of knowledge of folklore and paganism. Hopefully she still hadn't achieved the dominion over the seasons and forces of nature that the druids had. They suggested that they take Pedn-olva, the First druid, with them to assist Daniel, two heads being better than one. They thought quite possibly the solution lay somewhere more earthly than spiritual. Perhaps they should keep their minds as well as their eyes open for a way to overcome the evil woman. Pedn-olva suggested that they search the archives just in case some ancient prophecy had been overlooked. "The Oracles have been wrong before," he warned.

Torquil was quite agreeable to this. Any solution that might save his son and his friend was acceptable to him. Lucifer and Alpha agreed and the First druid was invited to carry out the search and be ready to accompany them to earth should the need for his services arise.

Lucifer left once more for his palace.

He arrived by Alistair's side about two hours after Rannoth had left for America. He hissed with fury when he found out Rannoth had left the fortress, until he realised that Snake was guarding his daughters and the brigadier had his best men on duty outside their door and the windows.

Reading the information that had sent Rannoth to find Elliott, he disappeared to join them.

# CHAPTER SEVENTEEN

In a deep cavern in the mountains to the east of Salt Lake City, a summoning was about to take place. The Indian shaman, or medicine man as he preferred to be called, was a reluctant participant in the ritual. His was the tribe who had originally held this ground in sacred trust. Its beginnings were lost in antiquity, but the rites were still observed to the present day.

The ancient being who now held his tribe in captivity had threatened him with the extinction of his entire race unless he performed the summoning. Only he, the shaman could perform the ritual. It was unfortunate that this ritual brought forth the evil as well as the good unless done in a certain way; and he had been ordered to bring forth the evil.

He had stalled the proceedings for as long as he had dared, but now began the incantation which would bring forth the Ergoegral, the manifestation of all evil in the universe, in one omnipotent demon. The guardians of the entrance to the secret world had long been aware that to open it would bring terrible retribution upon their tribe. Only the deliverers were to be allowed to enter at a time unspecified, yet foretold. The shamens' sole task throughout the generations had been to keep the secret of the hidden world. For this enormous demon, confined since the beginning of time in a universe so far beyond the understanding of present day humans it hardly registered as a pinprick on the dimensional map, was about to enter the world of mankind.

If the medicine man could have found a way to avoid using his skills he would have. He did not fear his own death, and until the very last moment he had prayed that divine intervention might even now save the world...

He began the ritual very slowly.

As he did so a shadowy figure slipped silently out of the dark cavern and, hardly daring to breathe, made its way swiftly towards the entrance.

Rannoth watched as the shadow left the cave and immediately followed.

With his usual expertise Alistair had conjured up the information they needed. He had told Rannoth that someone had discovered a hitherto unknown and unexplored tomb in the hills north-east of the lake. Alistair had made an educated guess that the anonymous person who put this information onto the Net was the local anthropologist and collector of antiquities, one Steve Rankin, and had lost no time in tracking him down.

Soon he had been able to give Rannoth Steve's address and the demon had hastened to America to check out the area. He had lost no time in finding his quarry and tracking him to the underground tomb. They had both chanced upon the tribal ceremony only minutes earlier. Both realised its significance and Rannoth now hurried to intercept Steve, before he made his findings public.

Rannoth materialised in front of him and – hoping he wouldn't notice that he had appeared out of thin air in the murk – put his finger to his lips indicating silence, and the thought into Steve's head that he should remain silent until out of earshot of the cavern.

Rannoth kept his telepathic message short as he took Steve Rankin firmly by the arm and guided him towards the entrance: "We have to inform some friends of mine of this. We have to stop it before something terrible happens."

He devoutly hoped that they would find Elliott and Daniel not too far away.

Elliott and his party had arrived in Salt Lake City as night fell. Theron and Quinn were quite at home in the dark and wanted to go the lakeside immediately. Elliott hesitated about it as he wasn't certain that Quinn was up to Theron's weight. Seeing this, Theron gave a snort of disgust:

"Quinn and I got pretty well acquainted yesterday afternoon while he was showing us around the palace." said Theron. "I quite understand that you don't trust me with Jason or Allegra, I made a bad move there. But Quinn and I understand each other perfectly. We have no intention of jeopardising our future roles in our grandchildren's lives. We shall search together for the answers to your questions."

"Theron and I are much alike," said Quinn. "We want only what is best for our children. We will work fine together."

"You are both old enough to know what you are doing," said Elliott, frowning at them. "If we don't find anything, we'll meet outside the café over there at ten tomorrow morning."

Quinn and Theron moved rapidly out of sight towards the Lake.

"I hope I did the right thing there," said Elliott. "Jason will never forgive me if anything happens to either of them."

"Where are we going?" asked Pauline. "I'm hungry."

"You're always hungry," grumbled Elliott, "You'll have to wait."

"Not likely," said Daniel. "A hungry wolf is a dangerous wolf, so let's think about this for a moment. For a start, we are going to need a car, and, as you are the one with the fast-track travel, you can go and hire one. I think you forget sometimes that we humans have to eat. I'll take Pauline to that café you spotted; we'll have a meal and wait for you to get back."

Pauline smirked at Elliott. "See, Daniel knows I have to be fed on a regular basis or I get cranky."

"Sorry Daniel, I did forget, and you are right about a car. Good excuse to be in a car park. I'll go right now," said Elliott, and went.

Daniel and Pauline strolled over to the cafe and ordered their meal.

An hour and a quarter later Elliott pulled up outside in a Fourtrak. "Plenty of room for five if necessary," he grunted as the handed the keys to Pauline and told her to drive. He climbed in the back. "Drive up the lakeside until I tell you to stop."

He leaned over the front seat and spoke to Daniel. "We are looking for caves or mineshafts. Something which goes underground a long way."

"Is that what you told Quinn and Theron to look for?" asked Pauline.

"Not exactly. I told them to look for rock formations which looked unfamiliar or out of place to them. After all, Quinn was around at the dawn of time, and Theron since before recorded history. Hopefully they know a thing or two about rocks. We have no idea how long supernaturals have been living here. If they have found a way of hiding themselves from humans, I thought Quinn and Jason's father might be able to find them. I have a suspicion someone around here is trying to hide their presence by magic or witchcraft. After all, Indian tribes have lived around here for centuries.

"Don't be ridiculous!" snapped Pauline. "The locals would notice if strangers kept appearing and disappearing."

"I'm not so sure of that. Remember what happened to the Anasazi Indians? One day they were there the next they were gone. What's more, according to Snake, no one goes up into the hills anymore, there are too many reports of ghosts and mysterious disappearances. Of course Snake, a vampire, naturally concluded

240

that he and his brothers had been responsible for the disappearances. Their feeding habits have caused a considerable number of missing persons over the years. However, most of their victims were found – dead of course – but in the main complete with bite marks, all accounted for. Some they made into vampires like themselves, but it still left a considerable number listed as missing. I checked with Ward and Travis before we left. They did a search of the newspaper files for this state, and the local morgues and funeral parlours." He hesitated briefly, then continued. "There are at least six hundred and fifty people, quite a number of them children, who are completely unaccounted for in the last one hundred years alone. Percentage-wise, in a place this size, that is totally out of proportion with the population count. In the centuries before that with so many migrating tribes, who knows how many vanished and no one noticed?"

"So, that means what exactly?" asked Pauline.

"It means what I said, unexplained disappearances. They could have been the victims of kidnapping or murders, witchcraft or sacrificial offerings. It means we are in the right place," he told her emphatically.

"So we look for a reason out here?" she queried.

"Why not?" asked Elliott coolly. "It's isolated, it's barren and it's supposedly haunted. What more do you want to go on?"

They arrived at a large car park at the north end of the lake. Pauline parked in the furthest corner. The promontory that Snake had described to them as the one he had stood on and caught Bianca was to their left. It was about one hundred and sixty feet high. Elliott pointed it out to them. "I suppose we should start at the foot of that cliff."

"Lead on O, Great and Wise leader," Pauline intoned facetiously, bowing obsequiously in his direction.

"You can lead," said Elliott. "After all, you are the one with the animal instincts."

"Grrrr!" snarled Pauline, baring her teeth, but turning to lead the way.

The base of the butte, the steep cliff referred to, took some time to examine.

"There is no way that anything larger that a jackrabbit could hide down any of these holes," she told Elliott after a while.

"Very well, let's get up to the top. Snake said there is a path from the lakeside," said Elliott.

An hour later they arrived at the top of the cliff. It had been a stiff climb, but all three had survived the narrow path and now stood approximately where Snake had caught Bianca. Elliott could have transported them the easy way but, as Daniel had pointed out, they might miss some important tracks or rock markings on the way up. As it happened they had found nothing out of the ordinary. They started to quarter the ground looking for clues. Hopefully there would be some sign that witchcraft or magic had been done here. Surprisingly, Snake had told them he had caught no hint of any nefarious activities by the local witches, and was in fact certain that they would draw the line at dabbling in any act concerned with disposing of angels. If there had been any demons operating in the area they had been very quiet about it. He certainly hadn't seen any. As to Elliott's idea of human sacrifices: he hadn't heard about them. On the other hand, if there were anything like that going on, they wouldn't be likely to broadcast the events.

Elliott's mobile rang, "Hi, Jason! What's up?" he answered, looking rather surprised. "She did WHAT?" he shouted in fury.

Pauline and Daniel exchanged worried looks. What had Natalia done now?

Elliott calmed down after a minute or so. "Jason, you did the right thing. We'll still carry on looking around here for a while. I like to back my hunches. You handle things your end and wait for Nick to get back. Ring me again when he does."

Daniel and Pauline looked expectantly at him as he put his phone away.

"Vespazia and Lucifer have found evidence that Charalder tried to kill Bianca and Claudia," he told them seriously. "There's a strong possibility she is not as dead as we thought she was. Nick has gone to the Fifth Dimension for a consultation with the Oracle and the First Ones and Rannoth has taken all the angels and Allegra into protective custody in Lucifer's palace. His entire army is guarding them by the sound of it. Apparently Snake doesn't like being there," he added with a grin.

Pauline let out a shriek of rage. "I knew she was too easy to get rid of last time! If she goes after my girls again I'll tear her limb from limb."

"You'll have to wait until Nick has finished with her. His daughters were attacked by her and almost killed," said Daniel grimly. "It's all rather odd. She was definitely dead when she was in Quinn's castle."

"Vespazia thinks she may have reincarnated herself," said Elliott. "That leaves us a horrible problem. How to kill someone who can reincarnate herself Ad Infinitum. I hope the druid memory banks can cope with that one."

"That woman," said Pauline venomously, "is definitely going to get her comeuppance this time. That I swear. She didn't get into the Eternal Flame, did she? She reincarnated at the moment of death and nipped into someone else. We have to find out who."

"Later, we will," said Daniel. "But don't forget she is a shapeshifter, she could be anyone, beast, bird or human. What's more she could be inside anyone who was in Quinn's castle at the time. She could even have taken over one of the shapeshifters who were with Rory Lanyon's company. We can't hope to find her without some help from the Fifth Dimension. We'll have to wait for Nick to get back. For now let's look for a mineshaft or something similar."

"Where's Ward?" asked Pauline after a while. "He could have helped us out here."

"He's in England, at the hospital guarding the Lanyons. Jason and Rannoth decided that a vampire should be available in each location if possible. He will blend in better than an American vampire, and he is not susceptible to daylight."

"Good thinking," agreed Daniel.

For another hour they searched the plateau. They were about to give up when Pauline shouted to them.

They ran to join her. She pointed to a narrow opening in the cliff; it seemed to go back behind two large obelisks, sheltered by an overhang. Daniel drew in his breath as the saw the vague scratching on the stones.

"Those are the remains of a Stone Age painting, and those," he pointed to several other marks on the stone, "are Bronze and Iron Age additions, warning of the devil's horsemen."

"Very odd thing to add to a Stone Age warning," said Elliott. "That reference to the devil bothers me. I don't recall Lucifer concerning himself unduly with America until about a thousand years ago. There weren't enough humans around until then for him to bother with. He let the primeval demons run things for hundreds of thousands of years. Primitive humans, you know them as American Indians, eventually began to inhabit the Northern States. They were tribal and while they were fighting amongst themselves and worshipping the sun, moon, stars and totems they weren't

243

interfering with his plans for the rest of the planet. They had no written or pictorial language it was all handed down by word of mouth. Shamen passed the legends down to their descendants and it became part of their folklore. It took a good few thousand years for them to become just a little civilized but they continued to fight amongst themselves. It was a very violent era. When it got too bad, the demon population took off for other dimensions or blended into the scenery like the vampires and werewolves." He grinned as Pauline growled in disgust.

"Evil is as old as time itself," said Daniel. "There were battles in heaven between good and evil long before Lucifer arrived to rule the earth. Charalder murdered Zohal two million years ago so you are right, evil has been known to exist at least that long. Humans have been on the earth for about three hundred thousand years. Primitive, but here. Lucifer has been here even longer. The Fifth Dimension recorded his first appearance in a Hell dimension six hundred thousand years ago."

"You've never been here before. Are you sure?" asked Elliott, then answering himself. "Of course you are, it's more folklore surfacing. Keep going, Daniel."

"Behind these markers is the opening where the Devil rides out," said Daniel calmly. "On moonless nights and when the sun grows dark. I suspect they mean an eclipse. Well, there isn't an eclipse this year, we have to study the moonless nights theory."

"It's pretty dark tonight," said Pauline sounding worried. "Does it count if the moon is hidden behind the clouds?"

"I should think it very likely," said a familiar voice from the darkness.

Daniel shivered, and a premonition of danger sent an arrow of dread through his heart, as Rannoth appeared from the opening before them, holding a human male firmly by the arm.

"How long have you been here?" asked Daniel. "And who is that?"

"Just arrived," replied Rannoth. "Alistair found some interesting facts about this place whilst doing some research, and I went to New York to tell you about it. When Jason told me you were all here searching I decided I might as well come and try to find you. If I couldn't, I was going to check it out myself." He told them what Alistair has found out about the Wasatch Mountains.

"I found this young fellow in the caverns," he said to Elliott. "This is the local anthropologist, Steve Rankin. He's been investigating the ancient paintings and the tombs in these cliffs for quite some time. Alistair discovered his interest in the tribal burial grounds on the Net and followed up his investigations through his books and publications. Young as he is, he's a noted authority on the cave dwelling ancestors of the present-day Indian tribes. He's a bit off with some of it, but for a human he's made some pretty good guesses and arrived at some very accurate assumptions. I think we are going to need his expertise and knowledge of these caves to show us the portal to what could be either a neighbouring universe, or a previously unknown nether region."

Elliott looked aghast. "Not even the First Ones have ever tried to enter a parallel universe."

"I think you will find," said Rannoth dryly, "that this young man has already been there, and has also seen what lives there, although I doubt myself that it is a parallel universe."

They all looked in silent awe at the young man, still held tightly in Rannoth's grasp.

"Just how did he manage to get there and back without someone detecting the shift in the cosmic flow?" asked Daniel. "Faery land should have detected a shift that big."

"They probably did, but there are so many vampires and demons giving off bad vibes around here it probably never registered as unusual," said Rannoth, sounding annoyed.

"Still, Lucifer or the Faery Watch should have picked it up," said Elliott just as annoyed as Rannoth. "They monitor the Cosmic Flow on a twenty-four hour basis! They found Charalder quickly enough when she hid in the Fifth Dimension last summer, and they found Jason without too much trouble."

"Well they missed this, that's obvious," snapped Pauline, "Too late to cry about it now. Let's deal with it as it stands. 'Stevie boy' here can tell us about this new universe he's found, as he's taking us there."

'Stevie boy' looked dumbfounded as four quite obviously insane people expected him to go back into the caverns and find the opening to another world.

"I haven't found another world," he said sounding alarmed. "I just found a path through the mountains to a secret valley."

"Let me assure you, Steve," said Pauline harshly, "that if Rannoth here says you have been to another world, then that is exactly where you have been. There's nothing Rannoth doesn't know about this world and the next. What's more, he knows all about the other worlds that exist in time, space and any universe. Have you got that?"

Rannoth looked severely at Steve. "Did you understand the lady? I am an acknowledged expert on other worlds. This, however, is a new one on me. Since it apparently survived detection by the Faery Watch, it must have special protection. I intend to investigate it with my friends here. You have been selected to lead us to it."

He looked at Elliott and Daniel with a concerned look on his face. "I think we had better hurry, a ritual summoning was already underway as I left."

Elliott and Rannoth took hold of their friends and materialised inside the cavern where the summoning was coming to a head.

For some reason the shaman hesitated briefly and looked straight at the place where Rannoth and Elliott had materialised. Elliott instantly placed a force field around all of the participants in the ritual, but removed the shaman from the rest a split second before he did so. Rannoth touched Elliott on the arm and they and Daniel moved forward into the light. Pauline held Steve forcibly back as he would have followed.

The three of them, two highly formidable demons of the first rank and a druid who was the holder of all the knowledge of his ancestors, approached the shaman who held out his palm outwards, in the universal gesture of supernatural affinity.

"I prayed for divine intervention," he said sounding vastly relieved. "My prayers have been answered." He looked with satisfaction at the men held within the force field, now unable to move or speak.

Rannoth smiled grimly. "I hope you will still consider us that when you see the true nature of your deliverers," he said quietly.

"How strange you should use that word to describe yourselves. There has long been a prophesy of the three who shall overcome," said the shaman. "The prophecy did not specify who they should be."

Daniel and Elliott had had a good look around. "There is no one here but yourself and these other humans," said Daniel, "We had thought to find the False One with you."

"That you know of the False One proves you are the expected ones." The shaman sounded almost reverent. "Only the true deliverers could know of the False One."

Elliott looked broodingly at the shaman for a few moments. Then he signalled to Rannoth and they both changed to their

246

demonic selves. They both heard a gasp from behind them and knew that Steve was shocked by what he saw. They also heard Pauline tell him to be quiet, as he was in the presence of immortals.

The shaman was unmoved. Probably unshockable if he knew of the pretender to Lucifer's throne, thought Daniel wryly. He beckoned to Pauline and Steve to join them.

Elliott introduced them all. "This is Rannoth, Lucifer's chief assistant and personal representative on earth," Elliott told them forcefully. "This is Daniel, the possessor of all the knowledge of his druid ancestors, and I am Elliott, the Dark One from the Fifth Dimension. It seems you were expecting us?"

The shaman nodded. "I was expecting the deliverers, the prophesied ones. The three who are all-powerful and all-knowing. The three who can open the doorway to heaven."

There was a gasp from behind them as Pauline was unable to contain her horror at this unbelievable statement.

Daniel turned and held out his hand to her. She came forward and he put his arm around her shoulders.

"My wife," he said simply. "She is as horrified as we are to hear what you have to say. We have been in contact with Heaven for centuries. The Great One is known personally to some of us and Elliott here has actually met him. His wife is an angel. Several angels work with us and for us. We know that the gateway to heaven is not on earth. It is only opened to those who have earned the right to go there. Whatever this gateway is you want us to open, it is not the gateway to heaven."

The shaman was unmoved. "The Prophecy is not explicit in naming heaven. It states that three shall come who can lead the way into the eternal realm. Those who can show they have led blameless lives shall join the immortals in the golden land. If that is not heaven, what is?" he asked simply.

"We don't normally involve ourselves in local disturbances," said Elliott. "We usually work on a global scale, but we were informed that there is to be a ritual summoning of an evil entity in a high place, and this seems to fit the bill. So how about it? What were you summoning?"

The shaman looked embarrassed. "My humble apologies to you all. I was indeed performing a ritual summoning. The False One has imprisoned my tribe in their homes. They cannot leave them as they are held within a force field, much the same as yours." He waved his hand towards the imprisoned men. "It is preventing them

247

from leaving the village. They will all die if I do not perform the ritual. Unfortunately, the summons to open the portal is also the signal for the evil malevolence held within the mountain to come forth. I have delayed as long as I dared, and now you are here to save us."

"Such faith," murmured Pauline to Daniel. "I hope you can prevent this."

"According to Lucifer, it is for just such a crisis that I have been given my powers. With two extremely powerful demons to assist me, I expect we shall prevail," he said softly to her.

"Perhaps we had better hear this prophecy in full," said Rannoth. "It might give us a clue as to what we are expected to do."

"I should have thought of that myself," said Daniel. He looked at the shaman. "Okay, we'd better hear this prophecy."

The shaman did not hesitate and intoned it forthwith:

'On moonless nights shall they come forth, the faceless horsemen from the north.

Down the mountain paths they ride, immortals from the other side.

When the horsemen shall appear, then their hoof-beats ye shall hear,

As they seek and find, those injustice has confined.

All who join the ghostly band, shall pass into the promised land,

For as the sun shall rise once more, the riders pass though heaven's door,

Into the realm of peace and light, forever hid from mortal sight.

And yet shall Evil one day rise, and take the guardians by surprise

But three unknown, all-powerful men shall deliver them then.

A wise one and two young, yet old, shall step into the realm of gold,

The secret of this place unsealed, the truth at last will be revealed.

These three who are from worlds apart, shall bid the evil one depart.

She who speaks with evil tongue, the false one shall be overcome.

By justice she shall be confined, with the first ones of her kind.'

Pauline gave a low moan and sank to the ground. Daniel knelt hurriedly beside her.

"It's her. It's Charalder," she said chillingly. "She's the false one. She's the one who has been trying to kill Lucifer's angels. This is the high place where evil has to be overcome, but it's Charalder who is the evil. Elliott, you and Daniel and Rannoth have to stop her."

"You know," said Rannoth thoughtfully, "I think that prophecy has lost something in the mists of time. It didn't ring true, somehow. If she knew of this prophecy all this time, why has she never tried to get in there before? Why try to raise some evil demon in New York when she is trying to penetrate this world? We know this is not heaven's door, but it is the door to somewhere, and we still don't know what evil is being summoned. I think we are here for some other reason. Let's ask our young friend here exactly what he saw."

He reached out a hand and pulled Steve into their midst. "Tell us everything you saw, whilst you were in the secret valley," he told him. "I rather fear that you have had a vision of the future, rather then an actual experience. I do not believe a mortal has the power to enter another world unaided."

Daniel nodded his head. "A prophecy such as that one might very well be preceded by a mystical portent."

Elliott frowned as he considered the facts. "Maybe he did accidentally uncover a secret entrance. A prophecy merely foretells the future; it doesn't always make it clear how it will actually come about. I think Steve should show us the entrance he found."

Steve thought for a minute. "I know you are demons, how do I know you are good ones?" he asked suspiciously. He looked at the shaman, "How do I know you were doing this against your will?"

"You don't!" said Daniel softly. "But are you willing to take the chance of letting pure evil out upon the world, without at least trying to stop it?"

Steve sighed and told them what they needed to know:

"There was a valley, green grass as far as the eye could see. Herds of buffalo and horses as far as the horizon. Forests, rivers and distant mountains, a lot of blue sky, a few small white clouds. A perfect summer's day. I heard distant voices, and I saw a large building like a glass castle in the distance. I saw several old men walking on a pathway near the river, and they had children with them. There were women with babies setting out a picnic. It really did seem like the heaven Mountain Walker, here, told you about. If

249

it was a dream, it was very real."

During this report, Daniel and Elliott had looked at each other in consternation. "It can't be. But it is suspiciously like it," Elliott was dumbfounded.

"One of us has to go in there. I think it's going to have to be me," said Daniel. "According to the Oracle. I have the knowledge to defeat the evil one. But did they mean Charalder, or someone else?"

"I think one of us should go to the Fifth Dimension right away." Elliott sounded alarmed. "I didn't like that reference to the first one of her kind. That's either Alpha, Torquil or myself. As I'm here and they aren't, it's a little disconcerting, Quite frankly, I'm a little too young to die; or to be incarcerated in the valley beyond for a hundred years."

As Elliott was about to take off for the Fifth Dimension, a flash of light and a puff of red smoke caught their attention. Lucifer materialised in the cavern.

Daniel and Rannoth looked relieved to see him and even Elliott let out the breath he had been holding for a long moment.

"No need to go now," Lucifer told them. "I've just been there. Alpha, Torquil and Pedn-olva, that's the name of the First druid, by the way, are all willing to study the situation. They are searching through the ancient prophecies right now.

"You all look like mourners at a funeral," he added candidly as he surveyed the long faces. He nodded at Pauline sitting on the floor leaning against a boulder. "What's up with her?"

"We've found that Charalder is the subject of yet another prophecy and she's already here," said Pauline with a dangerous note in her voice. "And the prophecy mentions Daniel, Elliott and Rannoth. It's very strange and unsettling."

"Not really," said Lucifer. "The last few years may have been leading up to this day. Or so the Oracle has suggested. He said that this could be the final stage of a prophesied event, and the Great Entity agrees. We just have to figure out the meaning of the prophecy and compare it with what has been happening."

He looked at the men contained in the force field. "Who are they?"

"Black magicians, sorcerers, Charalder's helpers," said Elliott.

"We don't need them?" asked Lucifer.

Elliott shook his head and, with a wave of his hand, Lucifer dispatched them to Beyond Hell.

"I've put in a new laser containment field. Very mystical and magical, but modern," he said, sounding pleased. "Every time someone tries to cross it they get fried, and then put in the Snake Pit, so I know who's attempted to escape. The Chief Torturer is very pleased. It's given him a new set of tortures to try out.

"Now to get down to business," he went to say, but broke off abruptly as he noticed Steve, trying to hide in the shadows. "What's that human boy doing here?" he asked Elliott sharply.

"He's helping us find the way into the secret valley," said Elliott lightly. "We probably wouldn't have found it if he hadn't been inside already. Quite by chance," he added hastily, as Lucifer sent fireballs careering around the cavern.

"You should know better than to allow some human to learn about us," he said furiously.

"He's been quite useful and amenable so far," said Elliott cautiously. "His knowledge of this area is quite exceptional."

"Hmmmph! Well, if he's making himself useful, he can stay for now," agreed Lucifer reluctantly.

"He seems to have had a portent, a dream, so maybe he should be here at this point in time. Perhaps he has a role to play. I think we should wait and find out," said Daniel mildly.

"If he turns out to be a problem afterwards, if I think he can't or won't keep his mouth shut, I can always wipe his memory, I suppose," he added darkly.

The 'human boy' shivered as the Devil gave him a very black look and frowned as if reconsidering his decision.

"Well we can't do anything until we are inside, so let's get going," said Lucifer. "You," he pointed to Steve, "how did you get in the last time?"

"I stood right here and touched the wall here and an opening appeared," said Steve.

"It can't be that easy, can it?" asked Rannoth.

"Do it," ordered Lucifer.

Steve did as he was told and as before a section of the rock face slid to one side and they all walked through.

Pauline held tightly on to Daniel's arm. For only the second time in her life she was afraid of what they would find. She had an awful feeling she would never see her daughters again, and what if they didn't get out and her other children were born here? She could scarcely control her emotions as they walked into the secret valley. It was just as Steve had described.

Elliott was immediately struck by the similarity to his own

world, as was Lucifer who had been there a lot recently. Even Daniel, who had only visited there a couple of times, was taken by surprise by the familiar sights. So, it wasn't a dream, they exchanged the silent thought.

They felt even more surprised when a tall, elegantly dressed man came forward and, holding out his hand, said, "Welcome my sons, it is past time that you came."

He looked at Lucifer. "We were not expecting the Lord of the Underworld, or the humans."

"Less of the humans," growled Pauline. "My lupus genes object."

"My apologies, my dear," he said charmingly. "Your beauty hid their presence."

"Silver-tongued old rogue," said Lucifer. "You look a bit familiar. Who are you, anyway?"

"Forgive me once again." He bowed in Elliott's direction, "I am of your kind. I am Zohal, the son of Omega. You are the grandson of Alpha, and you have brought with you the last true druid and the son of Varfael. He looked at Rannoth as he spoke. Rannoth looked alarmed. "Only Lucifer knows who my father was," he said shortly. "I do not wish to hear his name."

"My son, you do your father a great injustice," Zohal chided him gently. "He was never guilty of the crime he was accused of."

"Why did he run away, then?" asked Rannoth.

"To save the one who really did it," said Zohal. "A foolish gesture, but one he has never regretted, except of course to know that his son thought him guilty. We will talk about this later. This is not why you have come, although it is why you are here," he added cryptically.

"I think it would be a good idea if you told us how you come to be here, in this hidden world so like the one you left so many million years ago," said Elliott forthrightly. "You are supposed to be dead. Murdered by your seven sons, who, incidentally, suffered the death of the damned for their sins. They have now been consumed by the Eternal Flame and are no more. Their mother, Charalder, still lives and is making life a misery for everyone who had anything to do with wiping out her sons, and yours of course. I am sorry you had to hear about it like this, but she is the most evil woman who ever existed and twice we have attempted to get rid of her, and each time she escaped our retribution by her magical spells. The last time she may have reincarnated herself and escaped into another body, unfortunately we don't know who.

"We are partly to blame, we should have known. After your presumed death she became consumed with the idea of finding your sons and bringing them back. A million or so years ago she allied herself to a black magician. As their daughter is an immortal witch and her granddaughter Allegra is an Old Soul who has been reincarnated thousands of times, we should have guessed Charalder could as well. Fortunately her daughter and granddaughter are on our side, and she realised last year than her granddaughter has a son who is the only living male descendent of her line. It has caused her to transfer her attentions elsewhere, and it seems that you are her target. It is a mystery how she knew about this place. Even the Fifth Dimension is unaware that it exists."

"That is not quite true," said Zohal gently. "The Great One helped me to set up this dimension, although he has never paid us any attention since. I confess I thought he had forgotten about us."

"Well!" said Lucifer, rendered almost speechless for once, "The cunning devious old... Entity. He told me to keep my nose out of this, and he knew all the time what was going on."

"It is even more strange than you are aware. No one in the Fifth Dimension sought to question my supposed death. I am just the same as you and your father and grandfather," he said to Elliott, "I was and still am immortal. I cannot be killed even by another of the First Ones and certainly not by my own children. Only an archangel or the Great One himself can destroy the First Ones, and only they could kill the Old Ones. Lucifer himself is proof of that. Many have tried to kill him over the millennia, yet he is still here.

"No. I left the Fifth Dimension voluntarily, when I realised what my sons had done. I had no wish to stay in a world where the children I once loved had tried to kill me. Their mother hated me enough to encourage them. Even now I still love her. Love does not die because the beloved has proved false. It becomes tempered with sadness and a sense of loss, but it still remains. She has enormous power if she has found this world. Although the Indians who own this land are the guardians of the entrance, I suppose it was inevitable, after all this time, that a hint of our existence should have surfaced. No doubt some rumour fuelled her imagination and she tracked us down. Even so, as you were foretold, so was she, and I shall remove her from your world for all time quite soon. But she has to enter my world for me to remove her from yours. It would seem that she has a hatred for one or all of you, or you would not be here."

"All of us have had dealings with her in the past two years," Elliott informed him. "My friend Jason and I killed her sons and consigned them to the Eternal Flame. She and her sons had tortured and almost killed my wife who is an angel from the heavenly realms, and she was about to kill my friend's son, her own great grandson. The Flame consumed them and every trace of them destroyed. She escaped at the last moment and sought vengeance again. Daniel sent her into oblivion the second time. She had attempted to interfere in the lives of the ancients, and meddled in the affairs of Lucifer's dimension. Daniel and her daughter killed her and summoned the Eternal Flame to consume her natural body. Lucifer and I distracted her whilst they did it. After she died she must have been reincarnated. She almost immediately turned her attention to Lucifer's daughters, they are both angels. One is married to Rannoth, and that must be why he is here. Pauline is Daniel's wife and was also present when Charalder was burned in the flame.

"Steve Rankin was the instrument through which we found your world. Our young researcher found him on the Internet and followed up his line of work and, eventually, we found him and he led us here," concluded Elliott.

"It is just possible that Rannoth is also here to meet his father," said Zohal. "Many of the people who now live here are innocent exiles from life's injustices, or suffered untimely deaths at the hands of others. They live out their lives in this spiritual paradise and, very occasionally, we venture into the land of the humans to see if there are any lost souls out there who wish to join us. We have also gathered many animal species here which would otherwise have been lost. This is a big world, there is plenty of room for all who wish to live here."

"All I can say is that I hope having Charalder here doesn't place an evil black cloud over your perfect world," said Pauline feelingly. "Better she should live in ours and be hunted forever than spoil yours.

"What am I saying," she said aghast. "She'd be after my girls again, they'd have to live in hell, full time. Even so," she said frankly to Zohal, "I feel it my duty to warn you that she is evil incarnate, and you should think twice before bringing her here."

"Your warning and your graciousness are acknowledged," said Zohal. "You have a generous heart, your reward will be in heaven and on this earth," he told her sincerely.

"I have my reward right here," said Pauline as she looked lovingly at Daniel. "He is my reward."

Daniel smiled at her and ran his hand lightly down her hip-length hair. "You are my life," he whispered in her ear, "and this is my reward." He gently tugged the black tresses.

Zohal smiled benignly at them both. "I see that you truly appreciate each other."

"Just a second," said Elliott. "Before you change the subject, what's all this about Rannoth's father? If there is something odd about his death, I think we should hear it right now, particularly if it concerns Charalder."

"It only concerns her indirectly," said Zohal. "The story of the way in which she urged her sons to kill me, their own father, has led to the disposal of other fathers in much the same way. She has a lot to answer for. She encouraged the first murder amongst the First Ones, and thereafter down the ages. That it didn't succeed was not her fault. She certainly intended that it should."

Zohal closed his eyes for a minute or so, obviously communicating with someone. A tall dark demon materialised before them.

"You sent for me?" he asked Zohal.

"Your presence is required for a short while," said Zohal. "You need not stay after I have introduced your son to you."

The demon was taken aback. "One of these demons is my son?"

Rannoth stepped forward. "It seems that I am your son. I had no idea you were still alive," he said stiffly. "My mother and your brothers, my uncles, told me you were dead."

"The choice was mine," said his father. "I disappeared, thus apparently proving my guilt, but it meant the real culprit could remain at liberty. As you see, I still live. I did not die."

"Who was the real culprit?" asked Rannoth curiously. "I know that you could not be accepted here if you were indeed guilty, and I, more than most, know how the innocent can be made to appear guilty. This strikes very close to home for me. My own angel Claudia was thought by her sister Bianca to have tried to kill her, when it was Zohal's wife Charalder who did it."

"Maybe that is why you are here, today," said Varfael. "You now have a first-hand appreciation of how injustice can arise. Your own experience gives you understanding." He hesitated briefly, and continued with a slight catch in his voice. "It was my wife, your

255

mother, who I had to shield. It was Dewaela who killed her own father, and made it seem as if I had done it. To save her, I left to prove I had."

"I cannot disbelieve you," said Rannoth surprised, "but she has always mourned you, and has always defended you to everyone. She hasn't spoken to her own brothers for over ten thousand years, because they say you killed him and she should refuse to stand by you. That doesn't sound like she did it either. I do wish I had known about this sooner. I'm sure there is another explanation."

"If Rannoth thinks there's another explanation," said Daniel, "then I would like to test his theory. So far he has been very helpful in his diagnosis of our problems and Lucifer relies on his expertise to sort out problems in the underworld. Some time soon we will check this out. It would be a pleasure to help him prove his father's innocence."

"Right now," said Elliott, "we need to get this prophecy sorted out."

Daniel looked around and realised instantly that someone was missing from their group. He tapped Elliott on the shoulder. "I thought it was a bit quiet around here. It's not like Nick to keep his opinions to himself. Where did he go? I didn't notice him disappear, did you?"

Elliott frowned, "No, but I don't suppose it matters all that much after all we three seem to be the only people required at the moment."

"Well, I don't like it. He's not normally so quiet when he vanishes. It bothers me more than a little," said Daniel.

"I don't like it either," said Rannoth, "It's not like him at all. His usual pattern is to blame everyone else for what's gone wrong and moan about having to put it right. Then he'll vanish in a puff of smoke, or thunder and lightning depending on how furious he is."

"He's the devil. He can do whatever he wants. I haven't the time to worry about him right now," said Elliott.

# CHAPTER EIGHTEEN

Lucifer had returned to the Fifth Dimension.

He materialised once more in the palace and yelled for Alpha and Omega. Torquil and Yohanna as usual came running the instant they heard his voice.

"Not you again," said Torquil. "What's up now?"

"Depending on the answers to a few questions," said Lucifer, overlooking this, less than gracious welcome. "I may have some good news for all of you."

Alpha was the next to appear and Omega arrived shortly after.

Lucifer looked around and waved his hands towards the chairs circling a low table and they all sat down.

"I'd like to ask you a question," he said to Omega. "What led you to believe that your son Zohal, who I must remind you was an immortal, was actually dead?"

"He was killed by other immortals," said Omega. "He could not have survived. Why bring this up now the subject is still very painful to me, and to us all?"

"Too bad," said Lucifer callously, "I need answers. Now bearing in mind that Zohal's children were not of his generation and nor was his wife, as she was the daughter of a friend of his own generation, what made you assume that the third generation could kill the second generation?"

Alpha and Omega looked appalled. "Just what are you telling us?" inquired Alpha.

"I'm telling you that I have just come from an unknown dimension, which can only be entered from earth, and that Omega's son, Zohal, is the ruler of that dimension. I actually met and shook hands with him less than an hour ago. It is clear to me now what the Oracle meant: it is Zohal, not Elliott, to whom the prophecy refers. This should please you all, I hope. It means our boy is safe."

Torquil started to smile again, and even Alpha looked a little pleased. Yohanna, uncertain what they were talking about, looked a little puzzled. Omega was speechless.

"My son still lives?" he asked Lucifer.

"I thought I'd just finished telling you that." Lucifer sounded annoyed. "Your grasp on reality must be slipping somewhat. How much plainer do I have to be. Your son lives."

257

"I must see him for myself," said Omega firmly. "You must take us all there. Quite possibly we can control the outcome of any trouble there."

"You cannot interfere," said Lucifer. "I've already told you that, and I have Alpha's word on it. Elliott, Daniel and Rannoth are the ones who have to dispose of Charalder, who we now know is the pretender to my underworld crown and not some male upstart demon. The prophecy refers to her as the false one. My idiot nephew Corazan put us off the scent. Probably on purpose," he mused. "She's a very smart woman. Pity she's so evil."

"Pedn-olva the First druid is ready to accompany us," said Torquil. "He is looking forward to being on earth again. This new world will really be an adventure for him and for all of us."

Lucifer grinned evilly, an ominous sign. "You're in for a surprise, all of you. Zohal has built his new world as a mirror image of yours. It's uncanny how alike they are. Elliott was having a bad time of it until he realised that Zohal was one of his own kind."

He looked at Yohanna, "Are you coming?"

"No," she told him. "I don't mind a small adventure now and again, but I have a feeling that Elliott would rather his mother didn't see him in action. He does prefer that Natalia and I don't see the terrible things he has to do. Torquil can tell me afterwards."

"Okay, then, let's be off!" said Lucifer, waving his cloak to encompass them all and vanishing. They all appeared moments later in the meadow.

"So that's where you went," said Daniel to Lucifer. "You had us worried for a while." He nodded civilly to Elliott's relatives and greeted the First druid with a smile.

Elliott looked surprised to see his father and grandfather, but Zohal was even more surprised as he saw his father.

Omega stepped forward and grasped his son's hands. "You should have let us know, my son," he said. "We still mourn your absence."

"I'm sorry, father, but to stay would have been a continual reminder to you and to me of what should have been. It was better this way."

"For you, yes. But not for us," his father chided gently. "However, glad as I am to see you still alive, there is work to do here."

Daniel and Pedn-olva stepped forward. "We've put our heads together and we think the only way we are going to resolve this situation is to complete the summoning and see what happens," said Daniel.

"I don't like the sound of that," said Pauline. "We've never deliberately brought evil into the world before. I don't think we should start now, Daniel."

Daniel beckoned to the shaman who came forwards, reluctantly.

"I have prayed for divine intervention to prevent the evil from being brought into our world and now you plan to call it forth," Mountain Walker protested.

Lucifer stepped forwards and assumed his legendary, devilish persona. "You have the divine intervention of the Council of the Fifth Dimension. The First Ones and their assistants," he said regally. "I, too, am here to oversee the summoning. Have no fear. Nothing evil can arise of which I am not the master. This concerns us less than the intervention of the so-called False One. She is so evil that it will take all the knowledge in the universe and great cunning and strength to overcome. So get on with the ritual and see what happens."

"I cannot do it here," said the shaman. "This is the Promised Land. The spirits of our ancestors dwell within."

"Let me assure you, Mountain Walker, that this is definitely not the Promised Land. It is a dimension of the netherworlds, hidden from view for millions of years. It has no special significance, except that it is where the exiles from this and other worlds appear to have gathered in safety over the millennia. That's not to say that your ancestors aren't here. Perhaps some of them are, but most of them will be in a dimension far from here and much safer," said Lucifer, "providing of course they are not in my realm."

"That is quite true," said Zohal. "Some of your ancestors are here, and some in Lucifer's realm, but most of them passed to a greater dimension thousands of years ago. You may perform your ritual right here. I see the most powerful beings in the universe are all gathered here right now to assist you."

Alpha held up his hand. "We of the Fifth Dimension have sworn not to interfere as has Lucifer. The solution is in the hands of the druid, my grandson and Lucifer's son-in-law."

"We can, however offer advice. Whether or not you take it is entirely up to you," added Pedn-olva.

The shaman looked around him and took in the solemn faces of the men, who he knew were not of his world and the woman who was obviously highly regarded by all of them. He knew he had to obey their silent command to go ahead and he began the ritual summoning once more.

"Hear the words of your tribe. Hear the cries of your people. Open the gate and ride forth ye horsemen, those who live in the shadows await thee. Take back to your home, the oppressed and the fearful. Give sanctuary to all who do not hide from thee." He looked nervously around and then carried on:

"Not of this world, not of this time, not of humankind. I call you. I call you by name and by the powers of the ancients who lived in this place." He threw a bunch of herbs into the air and waved a small pouch to and fro and, as they fell to earth they caught fire and he threw powder from the pouch on the ground as they fell. They fell in a small circle and seemed to feed the flames.

"From the earth I summon thee, from ancient memory I summon thee, from the world unknown to men, I summon thee. Ergoegral, I summon thee. Come forth, show thyself to thy servants. Come forth to reap the harvest of souls who now await thee."

He walked three times around the circle and the flames grew higher and higher. The earth shook as, out of the flames, walked a giant. He looked down upon the men gathered watching and bent down to look more closely. Mountain Walker leapt back in fear. Elliott, Daniel and Rannoth walked slowly forward looking up at him in surprise.

Daniel looked at him and laughed. "It's one of the giants who built the causeway," he told them. "Everyone thinks they were a myth. Now here is one of them."

The giant bent down once more. "You know me?"

"I know of you. You are Finn McCool. I have seen your face in my dreams and those of your companions," said Daniel. "You are not supposed to be an emanation of evil. Whatever have you done to these people to make them think you are an ogre?"

The giant winked at him. "Nothing like the hint of evil to keep unwanted visitors away, and no point being this big if you can't throw some weight around. I'm all for a quiet life and I don't like trouble, but I do pop out every thousand years or so to remind people I'm still around," he said humorously. "By the way, I think some one else followed me here." He pointed at the flaming circle and stepped away from the group as if to disclaim any connection with the coming events and faded into the background. Steve Rankin had also done the same and the giant and the human onlooker watched as the end of one era and the beginning of another unfolded before them.

There was a flash of light and a blue flame rose from the circle. A figure formed within the flames and a woman stepped forward.

Pauline screamed at Daniel. "It's her. She's here!"

"She looks just like Charalder has always looked. This is no true reincarnation," thought Elliott, instantly becoming the Dark One.

As Rannoth morphed into his demon form, the three of them confronted Charalder.

She hissed with rage as she saw Elliott standing before her. "You!" she screamed in fury. "You killed my sons, and you," she turned on Daniel. "You helped my daughter destroy my earthly form."

"You should have stayed dead," said Elliott coldly. "There is no place in the universe you can escape our wrath. Three times now you have attempted to kill the angels, we cannot allow another. There is no place now you can hide, nowhere we cannot find you. Our combined powers now far exceed your own."

Rannoth stepped forwards. "You attempted to kill the angel Claudia, on several occasions. She is mine and I, too, have vowed to end your evil ways. I will hunt you to the ends of the earth, and beyond, to keep her safe."

Charalder sneered at them. "Your power can never equal mine, you cannot kill me. I will make your lives the hell that you made mine. I will kill your children as you killed mine. One by one I will destroy them, you will never know when I will strike next. I tried to kill Lucifer's children, but they still live. I will kill your son," she pointed to Elliott, "and the druid's twin daughters, but not yet. In my own time I will end their lives."

"No you won't, you wicked old hag," screamed Pauline throwing herself at Charalder. "I'll kill you or die trying before I let you touch my daughters."

She clutched Charalder around the neck and hung on grimly, Charalder tried to throw her off, but the werewolf strength was well to the fore and she found it impossible to undo the stranglehold.

While she was engaged in fighting Pauline, Daniel had begun to chant a ritual enchantment in a strange tongue. No one could understand it, but as the words flowed from his lips, Charalder began to grow limp and eventually sagged in Pauline's grasp. Pauline loosed her fingers and let her fall to the ground. Daniel continued to chant.

Zohal came forward and looked at his wife lying, still as death, on the ground. He knelt beside her and took her hand. "She is just as beautiful now as she was then," he sighed. "If only she could have been satisfied with her life in the Fifth Dimension."

Daniel finished his chanting and beckoned to Elliott and Rannoth to join him.

"You have to forgive her," he said to Zohal. "I have given her a new dream life. It can only become real when everyone she has harmed, who still live, forgive her. You she harmed the worst and you must be the first to forgive. Vespazia will have to forgive her, as will Quinn and Jason and Elliott. The angels will have already forgiven her, that is their duty and their nature. Torquil she wounded, and he will forgive for Omega's sake. She almost destroyed the shapeshifters. One of them must forgive her for all of them. I think that will have to be Lance. Pauline and myself, we also have to forgive her. By doing what I have done, I have already forgiven her." He turned to look at Pauline, a question in his eyes.

Everyone except Zohal and Lucifer were looking at him in horror.

"What are you saying, Daniel?" asked Elliott sounding shocked.

"Death is not always the answer," replied Daniel. "A new life, from the old, and a new start in this world will end Charalder's reign of terror. Do you truly want me to kill Vespazia's mother for a third time? The great-grandmother of Jason and Allegra's children? Or do you want me to give her into Zohal's keeping for eternity?"

Zohal stepped forwards. "Ancient wisdom has given your friend the solution," he said quietly. "I will see to it that she never leaves this world again. Lucifer shall seal the opening for ever. This is a good world to live in. It has great potential, and can last for as long as the earth and the universe exist. I still have my powers and so have many others who live here. She will never remember what she was. But I believe she will be happy here with me."

"I hope I have done the right thing," said Daniel. "I have allowed her to believe that she had just met you. She knows your name. Anything else she knows will be what you tell her. There's just one thing," he smiled wryly. "I think you should avoid having any children. She has new memories, not a new personality."

"I think I shall be able to avoid the pitfalls of the past," said Zohal sounding amused. "One should always learn from one's mistakes."

"Quite," said Daniel.

Pauline laid her hand on Daniel's arm. "Are you sure?" she asked him

"Yes!" he told her simply. "This is not the only way, but it is the right way."

Pauline looked at Zohal. "I trust my husband with my life and our children's," she said softly. "If he asks me to forgive, then I must and will do so."

She walked over to Charalder's supine figure and looked down at her for a long moment.

"If it means an end to all our fighting and leads you to peace, then I forgive you," said Pauline, and she turned and walked away.

Elliott followed her example and, leaning over Charalder, said, "I find this hard to do, but I know Natalia would want it. I forgive you, for Natalia, for Nicholas and myself. Live here in peace."

Lucifer, who had disappeared for a short while, returned. This time he had Vespazia with him. He told Elliott to go and find Quinn and then fetch Lance.

"I can't be expected to take care of everything around here," he grumbled irritably. "It's bad enough to have to forgive the evil harpy."

He led Vespazia towards her mother's unconscious form. "Daniel has found a way to get rid of her yet not to kill her. I told you what happened here. You too must forgive her, for her to rise again as an immortal."

Vespazia looked dispassionately at her mother. "Daniel is right of course. He couldn't kill her again, and I can't either. I can't speak for Quinn or Allegra and Jason, but I too forgive her. It is hard for me to do this. I do it for Zohal and the First Ones."

Daniel beckoned to Rannoth who walked forward and looked down at Charalder. He looked unhappily around at them all.

"On behalf of my wife, I forgive her. After all, that is what Claudia would want. I didn't even know her. But I do know what she did to you all. If you can forgive that, then so can I. I forgive her also on behalf of Bianca and Snake."

Omega stepped forward.

"My son has forgiven her, then so must I. But I am going one step further. I have no other children, and I cannot lose this one again. I shall remain in this world with my son and Charalder. This time maybe I can help them both. We First Ones have been too wrapped up in our ancient ways and beliefs for too long. It is time we joined the world again. This world could be just the place to start afresh."

Zohal clasped his father's hands as they were stretched towards him. "Your wisdom is far greater than mine. Together we can make this world a wonderful place to live for us and all future generations."

Alpha and Torquil looked at them both and nodded. "I should want to be where my son was," said Alpha. "Although it is many years since he heard me say the words. I have a great love for my son, my grandson, and my great-grandson. I should not wish to live in a world apart from them."

Elliott's jaw dropped as he stared at his grandfather. "I mean it," said Alpha. "A man takes great pride in his offspring. However headstrong their behaviour down the years," he added, with a sly smile.

Torquil laughed at Elliott's discomfort as his grandfather gently chided him for leaving his home to seek adventure in other worlds and running around the universe at the beck and call of Lucifer.

"I'm off to fetch Quinn and Lance," he said gruffly and vanished.

Rannoth's father had been silent throughout this discussion and now stepped forward. "I should like to return to my world, if that is possible," he said. "I see now that running away was not the answer."

"No problem, that I can see," said Daniel calmly. "We will do our best to find out the truth of what happened to your wife's father, but even if we don't, we can accept Zohal's word that you were innocent. It looks as if Old Nick has a clue as to what happened or he wouldn't have employed Rannoth for millennia, and I certainly don't see him letting Claudia run around with a demon with a doubtful pedigree. We can twist his arm later for answers."

Lucifer gave Daniel a sour look. "Trust a druid to ferret out the secrets of the underworld," he said in annoyance. "I'm not ready to reveal the truth of that one as yet."

"It's waited ten thousand years, it can wait a bit longer," agreed Daniel.

Varfael looked at them both. "So there is another answer? Very well, I shall return with you and my son and seek it for myself."

"Much the best plan," said Lucifer enthusiastically. "No need

264

to betray a confidence if you do that."

"What are we doing about Charalder?" asked Pauline impatiently.

"We are waiting for Elliott to return with Quinn and Lance."

Elliott arrived back as they spoke. He had Quinn and Theron with him and was about to leave again to fetch Lance and if possible Jason and Allegra when Rannoth stopped him and said that he would fetch Jason and Allegra. He needed to tell Claudia and Bianca what they had done. Elliott nodded his assent and departed for the cathedral to fetch Lance.

Quinn walked towards Vespazia and held out his hands. She took them, a sad look on her face, and told him what Daniel had done and what she had agreed to.

"She treated me badly but she almost destroyed you," said Vespazia. "I'll understand if you cannot forgive her."

"How can I be less generous that you," he said softly. "You, she allowed to be imprisoned in Hell for almost a million years. I slept throughout, knowing nothing. If you can forgive her for that, then I can forgive her for bringing about the prophecy which brought you and our daughter back to me."

He joined Vespazia and Zohal and stood over her. "I forgive you, for your daughter's sake," he said firmly.

Rannoth arrived and with him were Allegra and the children and Jason, who he had collected from New York on the way. Jason carried Simon in his right arm, his left arm around Allegra who was carrying Riva.

They walked towards Daniel and Pauline, standing beside Zohal. "Rannoth told us what you want," said Jason harshly. "You ask a lot. I shall let Allegra decide."

"There's no choice, really, is there?" asked Allegra, looking at Vespazia and Quinn, "I cannot condemn my grandmother to death if there is another way. Especially if Daniel says that it is the right way." She looked down at Charalder. "She doesn't look evil any more." Simon wriggled in his father's arms and demanded. "Down, down!" Jason put Simon on the ground and he toddled towards the witch who was his great-grandmother and put his small hand on her face. "Pretty lady, sick," he said to his mother. "Make it better."

"Out of the mouth of babes," said Daniel with a sigh. "We are doing the right thing Jason. Forgive her, both of you."

Jason squatted on his heels beside Simon and Allegra knelt beside him with Riva. He held out his hand and Allegra put hers in it. "We all forgive you," said Allegra softly. "We all hope you have a wonderful life in this world. We are going to have such a wonderful life ourselves, I could not enjoy it quite so much if I knew we had condemned her to eternal death, and Zohal to this sterile immortality." As she stood up, Jason looked at her for a brief moment and, putting out his hand, touched her lips gently with his fingers. "Wise words for one so young." He smiled proudly at her. "I made the right choice when I picked you."

Lifting Simon onto his shoulders, he put his arm around Allegra and all of them joined his father who was still talking to Quinn.

Lance and Elliott arrived next, and Lance viewed the assembled supernaturals with amazement.

"You didn't tell me everyone was here," he said to Elliott.

"Only those who Charalder has harmed in some way," said Elliott firmly, "and you know what you have to do."

Lance didn't hesitate. He was, after all, in the forgiveness business. To be on the safe side he waved his incense burner over Charalder and, sprinkling her with holy water, uttered the words of exorcism just in case. He glanced uneasily at Zohal and Omega, as he did so. They actually nodded in approval.

"On behalf of all shapeshifters, especially those who you caused such pain and agony around the world, I forgive you. May you never cause any further disharmony in the universe."

Then, unable to help himself, he uttered the words that were to complete the ceremony. "Go with God! May you always walk in sunlight!"

As he spoke them a small shaft of light, much the same as that which had healed the angels, fell upon Charalder and she opened her eyes. The first face she saw was Zohal's smiling gently at her. She held out her arms to him and with tears in his eyes he lifted her into his arms and, turning away from the assembled throng, walked swiftly towards the tall edifice in the distance.

Omega and Alpha watched them go with a smile at each other. Torquil and Elliott were totally dumbfounded.

"All we went through the last two years and they walk off just like that," said Elliott, sounding bemused.

A pained look crossed Jason's face as he watched them walk away. He looked down at Allegra and felt a momentary pang of immense sorrow as he realised that once she became a vampire, she would never again walk in the sunlight. It was a terrible sacrifice to make. He told himself that he should make it quite clear to her before she accepted the new life just what being made a vampire meant.

Theron walked away from his son and family and joined Elliott and Daniel. He looked askance at Daniel, who swiftly brought him up to date with what had happened.

"It makes what has happened to us vampires over the millennia pale into insignificance," he said wryly. "The First Ones have a great deal more power than any of us ever knew."

Daniel looked at him thoughtfully, "You know of their powers, then?"

"They were our forebears also," said Theron. "One likes to think one knows all about one's ancestors. It seems that, even so, a lot of the truth was always hidden from us. Still some of us do retain our racial memories and our shapeshifting abilities," he said with a grin, and changed into a dragon.

"Elliott and I wondered when you would admit your heritage," said Daniel. "I'm not sure Jason has noticed as yet. But we've a little surprise for you!"

He beckoned to Quinn who was gazing wistfully at the dark forest.

"Quinn!" he shouted. "Come and meet one of your descendants."

Quinn looked up and gave a start of surprise as he saw Daniel standing beside a large dragon. He morphed immediately and flew across to them. Vespazia followed more slowly, looking rather surprised. Jason had looked up as well and gaped at his parent, who stood beside Quinn, a little smaller perhaps, but definitely a dragon. He grasped Allegra's hand and walked towards them.

Theron changed back and laughed as he turned to Quinn. "I see we got a little smaller with each generation, and we seem to have lost our wings." He looked warily at his son, then turned back to Daniel, and carried on with his explanation:

"Jason and Katya have never shown any shapeshifting abilities and there never seemed a right time to tell them of what was, possibly, their inheritance. Sidonie and I felt neither of them were ready for it when we left. In any case, as Sidonie is descended from the demonic line, and cannot shapeshift, there is no certainty that either of them could shapeshift. Of course they both have the ability to age whenever they wish.

"We always meant to go back and tell them of their heritage

but we never got around to it. Both of them decided on their own what age to stay at, and I'm afraid that Katya would not have used the powers wisely if she had known too young and the ability had manifested itself. It seems that now we must stay and guide our descendants. Our grandchildren may have inherited the ability to shapeshift, particularly as Allegra is also descended from the same line. Maybe now Sidonie and I should tell them both. Perhaps you and Vespazia should be with us when the time comes?"

Jason gazed in thunderstruck silence as all this was revealed. He shook his head in bewilderment.

"I didn't even register what he had done!" he told Allegra. "I must have a son-to-father talk with him sometime. It seems to be about five thousand years overdue."

Allegra giggled as she caught his arm and drew him over to where their children were sitting in the care of Alpha and Torquil.

"Did you know he was a shapeshifter?" Jason asked them.

Alpha shook his head. "They are generally thought to be of purely demon origin. Torquil can look up your family tree sometime when we have some time on our hands. It should be an interesting search."

Quinn and Theron strolled off towards the nearby forest. They now had something else in common, to draw them closer together. Vespazia watched them go with a thoughtful look on her face. Perhaps the two vampire grandparents should be invited for a lengthy stay in the Dolonquin's castle. The vampire sages were at long last showing some signs of the wisdom they had gathered over the centuries.

Daniel's eyes were sparkling as he strolled over to where Pauline was standing.

"I think I have an even better idea of what the Oracle and the vampire sages were trying to tell Jason," he said to Pauline. "Come for a walk and I'll try my idea out on you."

Pauline tucked her hand into the crook of his proffered arm and they strolled off towards the river. "Go on tell me," she said. "What brilliant idea have you come up with this time?"

"Did you notice Jason's face when Lance was giving Charalder his blessing? It was the 'always walk in sunlight' bit that got to him. He suddenly realised that if Allegra becomes a vampire she will be allergic to sunlight and never be able to go out in it ever again. The thought hurt him badly, yet he knows he has to turn her and soon."

"So? What can you do to help them?"

"I have this sudden urge to search the archives in the Fifth Dimension. I know, without any doubt, that there is a spell amongst the ancient writings that will make a vampire almost human. I can't let Allegra become a vampire until I have found it. I hope you don't mind, but I shall have to stay there for a while whilst I complete the search."

"You clever old druid," said Pauline kissing him fondly. "I knew you'd come up with a way for Allegra to live normally. Now we won't have to cancel our shopping sprees. What's more I can come with you and visit Yohanna. She told you she'd love to have us all visit and told you to bring the twins. We can all be together there. Won't that be wonderful?"

"You, my darling wife, are a very wicked werewolf. You knew I was worried about their future together if she could only join him at night."

"You forget," said Pauline with a grin. "I can read your thoughts after all these years just as easily as you can read mine."

"In that case," said Daniel smoothly, "you have probably selected a nice secluded spot for what I have planned."

"There's a rather nice shady spot underneath that tree over there! I thought it looked rather pleasant," said Pauline leading him towards a large weeping willow.

Elliott had watched amused as the two of them disappeared around the bend in the river and turned back to Theron. Out of the corner of his eye he observed Finn McCoul and Steve deep in conversation.

The giant had just finished telling Steve all about himself, the others of his race and his life in the netherworlds. Steve was utterly overwhelmed to find out that the people in the stories he had always assumed to be fairy tales were in fact real, but had been withdrawn from human sight tens of thousands of years ago, when the humans had begun to persecute them for being different.

"It's the same now," said Steve moodily. "Anyone who is the slightest bit different from the norm is ridiculed or persecuted. Things haven't changed at all in all those thousands of years."

"You should come to my world," said the giant. "You'd probably enjoy meeting all these people who supposedly 'don't exist'."

"I would like to," said Steve eagerly. "It would be an adventure. I have always wanted an adventure."

"You are having one now," said Elliott overhearing him. "And even if you went you could never tell a living soul what you had seen. Faery Land is top secret. Fairies are totally unable to defend themselves against this world. They are gentle creatures and very small. Even the giants are gentle giants. Only if you were prepared never to reveal that you had been there could we sanction your going. What is more, now that you have seen the beings who inhabit this world and my friends and myself and our powers, you have inadvertently stepped into another world, The world of the supernatural, vampires, shapeshifters, demons, angels witches, wizards and many more. You can never talk about us, either. In fact, once someone is aware of our existence, they are automatically included in our organisation. If you are willing to swear the oath of allegiance to the Astral Council, then the giant will be allowed to escort you to his world for a visit."

Seeing Elliott in earnest and rather tense conversation with the human, Lucifer strolled over to find out what was going on. Elliott informed him of the inclusion of Steve in their organisation. Only the third human ever to have joined them.

Lucifer frowned sternly at Steve. "You realise that this is a great honour which has been granted to you? Do you know who I am, and who this is?" He indicated Elliott.

Steve looked a little alarmed. "I think that you must be the Devil," he said cautiously in a hushed voice. "I know this is Elliott and he is the leader of these people."

"Very observant of you," said Lucifer assuming his devilish form complete with red, lined cape and horns. "See that you remember, who metes out retribution if you are ever tempted to talk about our little adventures. However, you are much too young to be allowed on earth with all the knowledge you now possess. I shall have to find a safe place for you to learn how to handle yourself in my service." He exchanged a knowing look with Finn McCoul. The Giant nodded shrewdly. He knew he had been given the task.

Steve nodded speechlessly, his worst fears confirmed. He was now firmly entwined in a web of intrigue which included the Devil and a number of otherworldly beings whose powers seemed limitless. He had just witnessed a woman brought back to life and the instantaneous appearances and disappearances of a number of those present. He was clearly in the presence of immortals.

"That's one problem settled," said Lucifer jovially. "Off you go, then. When we need you back, we'll let you know."

He smiled benignly on the giant. "Go on. Don't hang about. We don't need you here. We've no use for a giant at the moment. Don't call us, we'll call you," he added facetiously.

The giant, knowing an order when he heard one, took Steve by the arm and they both vanished through the portal conveniently opened by Old Nick.

"By the time he gets back to civilization, he should be just about ready to work for us," he told Elliott with satisfaction, "and he'll know all about the netherworlds. We won't have to train him at all. If there is any doubt at all about his suitability, I shall just wipe his memory. Amnesia is not uncommon after a fall from a great height," he added thoughtfully. "Very dangerous it can be, messing about in these mountains."

"And of course if he does join us, he'll know all about the Astral Plain and be sure no one will believe a word he says," said Elliott with a grin. "Thanks, Nick. You've solved one our most immediate problems: what to do about him.

"My next problem is the exorcism of your building. We hauled Lance away from New York to take his part in the rehabilitation of Charalder, and to do an extraordinary exorcism here, but I think we should get back as soon as possible. Just because Charalder is taken care of in this world it doesn't mean that Balzahar won't go on with the summoning. You know what an evil swine he is. He'll enjoy trying to take your place in hell. He won't succeed at that, but he could still upset the balance of power in the world, if he goes ahead. If he is the one who has The Book he can do untold damage.

"Daniel has really finished his job here. We need to get back to New York and sort out the mystic risings."

Lucifer looked speculatively at Alpha and Torquil, talking to Omega, Rannoth, Varfael and Pedn-olva.

"Come with me," he said to Elliott and they both walked over to Alpha. "Can I leave you to clear up here?" Lucifer asked Alpha the leader of the Fifth Dimension. "I want you to close this world to outsiders for the next ten thousand years. No one in, no one out. By that time humankind may be ready for the knowledge that it exists. We'll have to see what happens."

"We were just discussing the necessity of hiding it permanently," replied Alpha. "Omega and myself feel that it would be more like eternal imprisonment than hiding the existence of a secret dimension."

"Ten thousand years is fine by me," said Omega. "It will give us a goal, something to work towards. Alpha and Torquil can hold the key and in ten thousand years we can discuss this again."

"We should do this very soon," said Rannoth. "I feel uneasy about the portal being open for too long. Not so much for what might get out as what might get in."

"Good thinking, my boy," said Lucifer. "He's not my chief assistant for nothing," he told the inhabitants of the Fifth Dimension.

By now Elliott had rounded up the rest of his team and had already sent Lance back to New York with Vespazia. "Get set up to exorcise the empty room on the twenty-third floor," he had told her. "Jason didn't like the feel of it and neither did Vern. While you are at it you can do all the floors between twelve and twenty-four."

Daniel and Pauline were walking back along the river bank and still some way from the others when he appeared beside them. "It's time we went back to New York. Wait here while I have a word with Rannoth," he said.

As he spoke to Rannoth he noticed that Mountain Walker was looking very concerned and he and Rannoth both went to speak to him.

"I should like to be sure my people are safe," he told them.

"I'll take you there right now," said Rannoth as he and the shaman vanished.

"He's very relieved to find them all in good health and released from the spell. He assures me of his good faith and assistance should we need it in the future and will weave this experience into his memory tales. He says his tribe is all set to continue the guardianship down the ages and will make sure that non-intervention is forcefully recommended," said Rannoth with a grin as he reappeared.

"I told him to make sure the tales are a bit obscure and hard to decode. He said he'll make certain that it will take them ten thousand years at least."

"Good thinking, Rannoth. Now, I want you to take all your responsibilities back to hell," said Elliott. "We aren't out of the woods yet. There's still the little problem of what's about to rise in New York, and Daniel and myself must both be there."

"You take Jason, Daniel and Pauline with you, and I'll sort out the rest," said Rannoth in full agreement with this plan.

Elliott took him at his word and, allowing Jason only a brief farewell to his family, left for New York.

Theron told Rannoth that he and Quinn would return under their own steam and promptly vanished with Quinn back to the Lost World.

Rannoth gathered up his charges and returned them all, including his father, to Lucifer's palace.

Lucifer, with a studied look at Alpha and Torquil and an authoritative word on the speed of their exit and with one last glance at the marble edifice, left for hell, to check that all was well.

Alpha and Torquil began the spell which would hide Omega's new home from existence for the next ten thousand years. They stood in the cavern at the newly sealed entrance, knowing they were now the only ones who held the key to open this world. They committed it to memory ready for when it was needed.

Her husband and his father regaled Yohanna with the story over afternoon tea, shortly after they arrived home. They never did tell her how they had feared for Elliott's continued existence, or how relieved they had both been to find that the prophecy referred to Zohal, not her son.

In the cavern, now lit only by the flickering torches left by the shaman, a number of Indian medicine men from ages past watched as the two ancient beings left the scene. They looked solemnly at each other and then at the sealed entrance to the now forbidden land they had inhabited in spiritual harmony for hundreds of years. They'd learned a lot in the ancient world they'd been living in. Their spirit forms were capable of taking on corporeal form at will. They looked guiltily at each other. "Being immortal has its advantages but ten thousand years without seeing our true heritage, our descendants, is too great a sacrifice. Even when the prophecy mentioned a thousand years it seemed too long. I hope we don't regret our decision to leave," sighed the Cheyenne Chief Running Wolf, the oldest of them. "We shall have to learn to adapt to the modern world we have heard so much about."

"We shall have to reveal ourselves to Mountain Walker," said Grey Cloud of the Sioux, who had joined them just over a hundred years before and benefited from their great wisdom.

"We shall have to learn to use our human forms once more," said Running Wolf. "No doubt our children will help us to adapt."

"I fear that we shall be disappointed in the world as it is now," said Three Rivers, of the Kiowa tribe. "The last time we rode out there was a great deal of killing with terrible machines. We have, I suspect, with insufficient knowledge of this world and in haste, exchanged paradise for purgatory. Yet time is on our side. We have ten thousand years to repent our hasty decision to leave before the door closed."

"Well, no use complaining now," remarked Grey Cloud philosophically. "We must start our new lives with a visit to Mountain Walker. Shall we go, my friends?"

Without further hesitation they walked from the cavern. As they walked into the sunlight, Running Wolf looked down at his deerskin suit and moccasins. "I think we had better assume similar apparel to those who visited us earlier," he said dryly to his friends, "We will blend into the landscape more easily."

Grey Cloud laughed, as he and the others assumed modern-day jeans and plaid shirts, very similar to those worn by Steve Rankin and Daniel who, they had uncannily known, were correctly dressed for the present day.

"You know something?" he said thoughtfully, "I think there very well may be a place for us here. Once we have accustomed ourselves to this new age, of course. We will have to use our powers very sparingly, we cannot afford to draw attention to ourselves."

They could have transported themselves spiritually to the village, but thought it more interesting to cover the ground on foot to see just how the world had changed from the days when they had walked upon it.

They were unaware that Elliott and Daniel had only remained for a brief moment in New York before returning to make sure that Alpha and Torquil obeyed Lucifer's commands. They had hidden in the shadows and had overheard their entire conversation. They exchanged a thoughtful look.

"Could be they might come in handy in the future. They could be really useful to the American organisation," said Daniel. "We'll keep an eye on them."

# CHAPTER NINETEEN

Back in the tower block of Goodman, Goodhew and May Lance and Vespazia had almost finished the exorcism of the entire twenty-third floor including the secret room. Lance had started with the rooftop and worked his way down. He and Vespazia were both convinced that Charalder had been the perpetrator of the evil contained within the building. She had gathered up the most obnoxious creatures to do her bidding, including Balzahar and Lucifer's nephew Corazan, who was now confined for his own protection.

"It's a pity we can't find Azeran," said Vespazia. "I quite liked him. He wasn't nearly as bad as the rest of Lucifer's brothers. I hope Lucifer isn't too hard on him when he finds him."

"I just hope he hasn't caused too much trouble for Elliott and the rest of them to put right," said Lance, who didn't care two hoots what punishment Azeran had to suffer.

Balzahar, as Vespazia had told Lance, was in a sub-basement and had several black magicians and other demons with him. Lucifer had confined them in a very strong force field until he could deal with them.

Lance was keen to get the whole building exorcised if that was what it took to please Elliott.

They descended to the thirteenth floor. Lance sprinkled Holy water generously on the walls, doors and stairwells all the way.

When they reached the thirteenth floor, the location of the second and much larger hidden apartment, Lance hesitated on the threshold.

As he prowled around the furnished rooms, he began to look worried.

"I have the strangest feeling that someone still lives here. I have no sense of an evil presence at all. Just an overwhelming sadness."

"How very odd," said Vespazia. "Do you suppose someone has left their essence behind on earth and that is what you sense?"

"If I interpret your remark correctly, I believe you mean in modern terms, a ghost," replied Lance, somewhat amused at Vespazia's oddly old-fashioned phraseology.

"If you mean an ethereal being, then yes," she said crossly.

"Don't be upset, Vespazia. Quite possibly in your day there

275

were no such thing as ghosts. Only nowadays they are accepted quite readily by a vast number of people as visitations from those who are trapped between heaven and earth. We priests are often called upon to exorcise a wandering soul and send it on its way."

Vespazia was rather surprised. "Oh, we did have a few in my day, but they were certainly not trapped; they stayed willingly to cause as much trouble as possible. Take my mother for example, she was an ethereal being who thoroughly enjoyed being as evil as possible."

"I'd prefer not to even think about your mother," said Lance stiffly. "She caused us shapeshifters a great deal of grief."

"Well, you are probably right anyway," continued Vespazia. "This building is quite old enough to have its own ghost, although I have never heard of one that owned its own apartment."

"There are a lot of things neither of us had ever known or suspected until we met Elliott and his friends," said Lance with a sigh.

"I don't think I will exorcise this apartment until I have checked with the chairman and Elliott. We'd better just carry on with the stairs to the basement."

Lance continued his exorcism until they reached the ground floor, when his supply of holy water ran out.

"What should we do next?" he wondered out loud.

"How about the basement?" asked Vespazia. "Shouldn't we exorcise that?"

"Not yet! We'd send Balzahar back where he came from if he is still there. In any case Elliott and Daniel said the mystical arising should be allowed to take place and then they will deal with it, and that is supposed to take place in the basement."

Lance grimaced at another unpleasant thought. "What's more Lucifer quite fancies being able to take Balzahar and whoever is with him back to Hell himself. He is there now, devising his new torture chamber for those who tried to usurp his kingdom."

Vespazia shuddered and winced. She had had experience of Lucifer's torture chambers. She wished Daniel could erase her memories of that time as he had Charalder's.

She took them both back to Travis's apartment.

Elliott and Daniel were already there, having arrived several hours previously. They were rather amused to hear that it was possible that a ghost was the inhabitant of the secret rooms. But less pleased to learn that Balzahar had been using them as well. That Charalder had quite possibly coached him in his role was also on the cards. But none of them could visualise her overall plan.

"What on earth did she think she was playing at?" asked Jason.

"You've got me," said Elliott. "This is a real puzzle. She's left us with. Pity you didn't hop into her mind for a few minutes Daniel before you zapped her with the dream life."

"Sorry, Elliott," apologized Daniel. "I really thought we had the entire story."

"The trouble is we are not even certain that it is Balzahar who has The Book," added Elliott.

"Even after we've got rid of her for all time, she's causing us hassle," said Pauline moodily.

"We can't be sure that Balzahar was referring to Charalder either," pointed out Daniel. "I recall quite clearly, Lucifer said he mentioned a master, not a mistress."

Elliott groaned, "Now you tell us. In that case, it must be Azeran after all. I can't think of anyone else who would know about The Book."

In the absence of Lucifer, Elliott and Daniel decided to check on Balzahar and the other captives in the basement of Goodman, Goodhew and May. They took with them the chairman, who had been a prisoner in the basement of Travis's building since Rannoth had confined him in a small, yet tastefully furnished cell in a corner of the boiler room. The chairman had promised not to try to escape and, as he had told Rannoth that he had no desire to meet Lucifer or Elliott again until the Day of Judgment, Rannoth had not bothered to have him guarded. Yet he had taken the precaution of sealing the room from the rest of the building, and setting it in a nether region all of its own. To all intents and purposes the chairman was alone in another world.

Elliott strolled down to the boiler room and after lifting Rannoth's spell, opened a window to the chairman's cell.

"How are you today?" asked Elliott, in his most charming manner. "I don't suppose you feel like a short stroll over to your offices?"

Daniel chuckled as the chairman nearly fainted from shock at seeing them both. "Are you sure it's allowed?" he asked doubtfully, "I believe Lucifer's assistant arranged this accommodation."

"Rest assured," said Daniel grimly, "Rannoth has to defer to Elliott when it comes to pulling rank."

Elliott opened the enchanted locks on the door and beckoned to the chairman to join them.

In seconds all three were in the chairman's office on the fourteenth floor of his building. Lance and Vespazia were waiting for them.

"Now, we can have a little business chat," said Daniel quietly. "I have to tell you that our young computer expert has fed the contents of your accountants' computer files and disks to the IRS and the Treasury. Both those government departments are on file to come down and deal with the fraud and illicit arms and drugs deals that your firm has been engaged in for many years.

"However, our young friend tells us that he can find no clear proof that you yourself had anything to do with it. Quite clearly you have been extremely adept in keeping your name from being associated with the criminal actions of your accountants. In other word, you have been either rather naive or cleverly covered your tracks. We'll let the government decide."

"Don't think you are getting off that easily," said Elliott nastily. "You will be working for us in a rather unusual capacity from now on. Nominally you will still head this firm, but we shall be running it. Legitimately, of course, once the criminal element have been disposed off. We expect the Federal agents to do that for us. But of course you will be very helpful in pointing the finger at the guilty parties."

"We shall be appointing one of our own as managing director," said Daniel, "and our associates from Knight and Hunter will be overseeing all of this firm's interests from now on."

"You will of course give them every assistance and in that way we shall be able to gain control of the building and exorcise any remaining demons who attempt to evade our agents. You take care of it," said Elliott to Lance and Vespazia, "Demonic exorcisms are your department. Daniel and I are off to deal with our problem."

He and Daniel disappeared to the basement.

In the basement, Balzahar and his henchman were drunk and incapable, and seemingly had been for some time. Elliott looked grimly at them and raised the force field. He and Daniel dragged Balzahar from its confining beams and dumped him in a corner of the basement, and lowered the force field again.

They stood looking down at Balzahar for a while and spoke briefly to each other.

"To think that this moron has access to the darkest secrets of all!" said Daniel. "In his hands anything could happen."

"Well," said Elliott wryly, "there is only one way to find out."

Daniel noticed a fire hydrant in a corner of the boiler room and knew there must be another water supply somewhere. In a short while he had found a small washroom and filled a bucket with cold water. He stood over Balzahar and tipped it over him. The icy cold deluge caused him to sit up with a bellow of rage, which was abruptly silenced as he spotted Elliott and Daniel.

Balzahar had a nasty shock when he recognised the Devil's emissary and his druid friend. He had heard of their powers and knew they were at least equal, if not superior, to his own. He glared with glazed red eyes at them both.

"You're too late, our new leader has left to perform the summoning. We have already called the Behemoth and the Hydra and they are on their way."

"Too late?" said Daniel dispassionately. "Your leader is already in 'chains' of her own making and confined to a world far beyond this. Unfortunately she didn't leave any instructions regarding your disposal so we thought we'd leave it to Old Nick. He's got a whole raft of new tortures lined up for you. What's more you've annoyed Rannoth as well, this time. Somebody tried to kill his favourite angel and he's gone to town with the torture rituals. He must have a least five completely new ones lined up for you."

"No one could have killed our new leader, he's immortal like the angels," scoffed Balzahar.

"There he goes again," muttered Daniel softly to Elliott. "He didn't hesitate to say HIM. Even though you indicated it was a woman."

Elliott looked thoughtfully at Balzahar. "How do you know your new leader is a man?"

"I just knew the voice was that of a man!" said Balzahar grittily. "I saw him as well." He certainly looked like a man to me."

"Well, it's possible it was a woman in disguise," said Elliott. "She had a very harsh voice."

"Well if you say so, maybe it is, but I think you are wrong and it doesn't change anything. He or she has limitless power and expects to win," said Balzahar,

"I told you she's already history. I don't suppose she told you that she'd upset the Great Entity when she tried to kill the angels?" asked Elliott raising his eyebrows in pseudo-concern.

Balzahar deflated like a burst balloon. "He never told us that," he said aghast. "We're done for. Toast!"

"Yes, indeed you are," agreed Daniel. "But it might ease your punishment slightly if you told us exactly who you called forth from the world of myths and legends."

Balzahar almost choked on the words as they issued at great speed from his mouth. His words tripped over themselves; in his haste, he was getting the details a little mixed up, but essentially accurate as he told them what he and his allies had done.

"I wonder if it is worth our while bothering with the Behemoth and the Hydra?" said Elliott. "After all, they don't seem in any great hurry to come forth. Let's just send Balzahar back to hell and let Nick deal with him."

"Then he might just escape again and do this all over. After all, we have to assume he has The Book," sighed Daniel. "Let's do what Alpha said and wait for them to appear. You and I are supposed to be able to deal with them. I wonder if Vern and Charles would like to see this?" he suggested as an afterthought.

Elliott laughed. "No way. If this goes wrong the less people who see our downfall, the better. We'd suffer a huge loss of face and we'd never get our street cred back."

"There is that," agreed Daniel. "Okay, we'll do it your way."

"Let's hope they aren't in too bad a mood at being called forth to enter the world of humans," muttered Elliott moodily. "They are all so ancient, it's a wonder they are still alive. They must have had to stay hidden a hell of a long time to avoid the pitfalls of human society in the past. I hope they don't blame us for their plight."

"I hope they don't attack before we have a chance to explain our policy of non-intervention in the netherworlds and make sure humans never find out they are real," replied Daniel.

"This waiting is getting me down," said Elliott perversely. "I wish they'd come so we can get it all over."

"Get what over?" asked Balzahar.

"Nothing to concern you," said Elliott furiously, putting him back inside the force field with the demons and sorcerers.

Seconds later the earth heaved under their feet and a green scaly arm sliced through the veil between the worlds. A large green creature, a cross between a lizard and a snake with arms and legs, stepped into the basement. Its three heads weaved back and forth on three extended necks as it looked around. Its three pairs of evil red eyes squinted in the bright light as it swayed unsteadily on its feet. It uttered earth-shattering roars as it stamped its way towards Daniel and Elliott.

The Hydra was followed seconds later by an enormous animal with an almost human head. The eyes shone like purple headlights and its face was a mass of red, scaly skin. It stood at least fifteen feet high and had to sit down quickly as the basement was only twelve feet high. The Behemoth had the legs and feet of a large animal, possible a lion or a tiger. It pounced on Elliott and Daniel, who immediately put a force field around themselves and stood looking impassively at the two, huge creatures.

The Hydra knew Elliott. They had met thousands of years before when the Hydra still ventured out on occasion to play and have fun. Elliott and the Hydra had run a race in which Elliott had won and the Hydra didn't fancy a rematch. Ancient demigods had cursed the Hydra when it had been young, and dooming it to live forever. When its heads were cut off they grew again. Even after its confrontation with Hercules in the depths of the past it had still, after a lengthy period of healing even though cast into the depths and confined, grown back its heads once more.

Summoned once more into the mortal realms it was angry, and looked for revenge. When it spotted Elliott, it roared with rage and attempted to reach him through the force field.

"Who has had the temerity to call us from our sleep?" spat the Hydra. "Was it you, demon? Why do you need to confront us again? Have we not suffered enough at the hands of immortals?"

"We are not the ones who summoned you," said Daniel loudly and forcefully. "If you will listen to me for a minute, I will send you back where you came from if that is where you want to go. First of all, though, I should like to ask you a favour."

The Hydra stopped short and peered curiously at him. "No one has ever asked us a favour." The Hydra sounded puzzled. "They always want to kill us."

"That's the favour," said Daniel. "I would like to know why you refer to yourself as 'us'? The world believes that you are one being."

The Hydra abruptly sat down on the floor, bringing itself to Daniel's eye level. "How long have you got?" it asked. Rather humorously, thought Elliott in surprise.

"As long as it takes," said Daniel. "We haven't any immediate plans."

The Behemoth gave a snort of disgust. "Confession time is it?" He moved towards then and seated himself beside the Hydra. "I might as well hear this myself," he growled.

The Hydra glared at him. "No interruptions you ignorant hulk," it snarled.

Daniel and Elliott exchanged concerned glances. "I hope you two aren't planning on fighting each other," said Elliott caustically. "We don't want to send you back without hearing your story."

"If you sit down and shut up," said the Hydra impatiently. "I'll tell you."

The middle head started the tale:

"It all began in Utopia, about a hundred and fifty thousand years ago. We were a fairly peaceful race of people. Humans like yourselves, but with magical powers and almost immortal. We lived very long lives. We, that is my two brothers and myself, were warriors, protectors of our prince and lord. We lived well and prospered according to the laws of our land. One day we met three beautiful creatures, females, the daughters of the gods. We fell in love with them and they with us. We were all very happy for a while. Unfortunately we didn't know which god was their father. We soon found out!"

"One day their brother found us all together and told his father. He came to our prince and ordered him to kill us, as his daughters were not intended as brides for human males. Our prince refused. He said we were free to choose who we should marry and so should the daughters of the gods.

"Their father was enraged and brought terrible plagues upon our prince. We saw how the people were suffering on our behalf, and went to Mount Olympus and promised to give up the daughters of their god, the great Zeus.

"This was not enough for him," he went on bitterly. "He turned us into what you see before you. One monster with three heads. We have been joined so, ever since. It is a terrible thing to be together in this way. He told us that only if his three daughters came to us, and offered to give their lives for ours, would we ever return to our human form. We would spend eternity as we are now. No one can kill us, and if they cut off our heads, we should lie dormant for a while until our new heads grew.

"Many have tried to kill us and many have almost succeeded. Hercules once caused us the most anguish. You," he pointed to Elliott, "sent us back to the netherworlds and told us never to return. Until the summons, we never have."

Daniel looked a little alarmed by this story. "There is a faint memory surfacing," he said to Elliott, "but I cannot for the life of me see the connection. But something is telling me to summon the Three Graces."

"Do it!" Elliott directed. "They were supposed to be goodness and beauty personified. I can't see any harm in that."

Daniel looked around the basement and eventually found what he was looking for: earth, water, and fire.

He refilled the fire bucket and placed it in the centre of the room. He gathered several handfuls of dust from a corner and pulled out his box of matches. He scattered the dust particles in a small circle and sprinkled the water in the centre, then he tore a large piece from his shirt and set fire to it. Very carefully he placed it in the centre of the circle and held the matches ready in case it went out. It didn't.

"From the elements I summon the daughters of the gods, from the dark places of this universe I call upon the Three Graces to appear before me. In the name of justice and mercy I call you forth."

When nothing happened he repeated the incantation and suddenly a mist appeared in the circle and three females took form. Elliott and Daniel stood transfixed and the Hydra let out a low moaning sound. Three beautiful women stood before them. A tall willowy redhead, a statuesque blonde and a petite black-haired elfin creature. They stepped from the circle and looked enquiringly at Daniel.

"You summoned us from our imprisonment?" said the tallest in a sweet musical voice. "Why do you call us?"

"I believe you are here to right a terrible wrong," said Daniel. "Tell me do you know the Hydra? Did you ever know three young men from Utopia, long ago?"

All three Graces turned towards the Hydra and began sobbing. They cast themselves to their knees before it and begged its forgiveness.

"We didn't know. How could we know what a terrible fate our father would visit upon you?" they cried as one. "He imprisoned us in the clouds for our disobedience, but we have never ceased to beg for your release. He has never forgiven us or you. But can you forgive us?"

"We never blamed you," said the Hydra. "We have never even considered that."

"Well!" said Elliott, "I thought I'd seen everything, but this is a new one on me. I wonder if Hercules knows about this?"

"Probably not. But since we do, what are we going to do about it?"

"I think we were told the answer to that," said Elliott, "but the solution is as bad as the problem. Only by offering their lives in exchange, I believe, can they cure the Hydra. It's hardly a viable alternative."

"I think you are wrong, Elliott. The word offer is the crucial one. They don't have to make the exchange, only offer it," whispered Daniel. "Something tells me that will be enough to undo the spell."

Elliott considered this idea for a while and then nodded. "Okay! See if they are willing."

Daniel explained his solution to their problem and the three women agreed without hesitation.

The Hydra was shocked. "We couldn't possibly let you risk being changed as we were," it said sadly. "Better we stay as we are for ever than let you make such a sacrifice."

All three heads nodded assent in a forcible manner. The Three Graces stood gravely in front of them.

"We couldn't live with ourselves after seeing you like this, knowing how long you have been bound to that form, if we didn't at least try to release you," they chorused. They turned to Daniel. "Do what must be done."

Daniel looked over their shoulders at the Hydra, and hid his surprise. At that very moment, the Hydra vanished and three handsome young men stood in its place. He smiled at the Three Graces and told them to turn around.

Elliott told their friends afterwards that he felt a bit choked as the six of them fell into each other's arms. He and Daniel walked away and left them alone for a while.

"I don't know where that surfaced from," said Daniel. "I somehow knew it was the right thing to do."

"Keep up the good work," Elliott said with a grin. "We'll soon get the world sorted out."

The Behemoth grunted and coughed gently to attract their attention.

"This is all very well," he said morosely, "but it doesn't help me at all. What am I going to do? There's nothing in this world for me."

"You are right, and there is nothing for them either," said

Daniel. "But I think I may have a solution for all of you."

"The Lost World," he said to Elliott, who had raised his eyebrows at this statement. "We have some friends," explained Daniel to the Behemoth. "They live some way from here. On earth, but deep below the surface - miles below in fact. No one knows they are there. But they live very comfortably and in extremely up to date surroundings. You would soon get used to the place. We visit there often and one of our friends practically lives there. Of course you would have to get used to Lucifer turning up for tea every so often, and the Fifth Dimension tends to ignore any boundaries between them and the Lost World. The King there a close friend and you should get on very well with him and his brother. They are both rather large dragons, shapeshifters of course. They are considering the suggestion that they open a hotel and holiday complex for people such as yourselves, who have need of a sanctuary for a while. One day you may be able to blend in with the humans on earth, but you will need a little practical experience, first."

"If you let me see it first, before I make a decision," said the Behemoth. "But almost anything will be better than where I have been for the last few thousand years."

"We'll see you get a good look around before you decide," said Daniel cheerfully. "In any case you are not restricted to this dimension; all of the supernatural dimensions are open to all of you. You may prefer Faery Land or The World of Myth and Legend or even the Land of Mystery and Magic. Of course, it just may be that the Fifth Dimension will allow you to enter their world, as you are all so very old."

"I should say they are!" said Elliott amused. "They were gone from the real world before my father was born."

"I'd never have guessed," said the Behemoth with gentle sarcasm. "No doubt it is your grandfather who is of my generation?"

Elliott and Daniel grinned at each other and turned to the Behemoth and the now restored Hydra with the Three Graces. "You have certainly saved us a lot of grief with your friendly acceptance of our terms," said Daniel. "So, Elliott and myself now feel very obligated to you. Enough that we shall personally sponsor your entrance into the supernatural dimension of your choice."

After a short discussion they accepted Daniel's offer, and were told by Elliott that they should accompany him to Travis's home where they could, for the time being, make their home in his now extremely comfortable and private basement-level apartments.

Elliott told Daniel to hold the fort whilst he transported them there and got Travis to take over. This only took a few minutes and he arrived back to assist Daniel in the disposal of Balzahar.

"Something tells me that we have only scratched the surface of Balzahar's deception of Lucifer, and there is still no sign of Azeran," said Daniel thoughtfully. "I have this awful feeling that we have missed something important and it's going to catch up with us when we least expect it."

Elliott sighed theatrically, "When did we ever have it easy?"

Then he indicated Balzahar and his cohorts in the force field, "What do we do with them?"

"We need to find out if he's had his hands on The Book and where it is now," replied Daniel.

"I can't believe he's the one who has it," muttered Elliott. "He'd have used it by now."

"It's very worrying that he hasn't," agreed Daniel.

Elliott brought Balzahar out of the force field and told him to sit on the floor. He stood looking broodingly at him for several minutes. Daniel waited patiently for him to decide what to do.

Elliott stood threateningly over him and pulled him to his feet. Throwing him against the nearest wall, he caught him on the rebound and pushed his face up against Balzahar's, his eyes blazing red and his mouth spouting flames,

"Where is it?" he asked abruptly. "Where have you hidden it?"

Balzahar glared furiously at them both. "I haven't hidden anything."

"The Forbidden Book, you must have had it," said Elliott impatiently.

"What would I want with spells?" scoffed Balzahar "I am a first-generation demon; I have all the power I need. In any case, I know which book you mean and I'm not saying the words either. The writer of the original is still somewhere in the Cosmos. To use the name of the book is to invite retribution. Leave me alone, I know nothing I tell you!"

"He sounds as scared as we are," muttered Daniel. "I don't believe he has it. Now I am really worried."

"I agree with you," whispered Elliott. "What if he has hit on the truth? What if the original owner has retrieved it?"

"I can scarcely bring myself to even think it," said Daniel, aghast.

Both of them contemplated the awful prospect. "He couldn't have it, could he?" asked Daniel after a lengthy silence.

"It doesn't look as if Balzahar can tell us any more," said Elliott getting back to the business in hand. "What shall we do with him and his accomplices? They are no further use to us."

"I lean towards sending them to where the Hydra and the Behemoth have been languishing for centuries," said Daniel, with an unusually evil glare in their direction.

"I agree. Let's do it," said Elliott.

With a wave of his hand he sent them there and Daniel with a short spell, locked them into the depths of the dark dominion where the Behemoth and the Hydra had been cast so long ago.

"I hope Lucifer didn't want to punish Balzahar right away," said Elliott. "But what's done is done."

"I'm not going to concern myself with Lucifer's feelings on the subject," said Daniel swiftly. "He should be watching his charges more carefully. He's got one less to bother with now. In any case, if he wants him back he can go and fetch him. After all, he is all-powerful."

Elliott clapped him on the shoulder. "I admire your bravery, Daniel. Let's get back to the real world."

# CHAPTER TWENTY

Daniel was right to be worried. They had indeed overlooked something. Two things in fact.

They had been very remiss, they had totally ignored a vital piece of information. One they should have dealt with days before. They had in fact considered it of no immediate concern.

On the other side of the Atlantic, in a rather old building not unlike a medieval Palace, someone was poring over the contents of The Book. It was well over a thousand years since he had last seen his life's work. He was well aware that the original was lost to him, but this mystical copy from the dark dimensions was equally potent. The one who had placed it in his hands had known exactly what she was doing and had exhorted him to do his worst. He was filled with enormous pleasure as he turned the pages. There was a considerable number of evil torments, dark deeds and disasters which could be let loose upon an unsuspecting world. He had plenty of time, half the pleasure was in the anticipation; let them stew for a while.

In New York Jason, with time on his hands to bring himself up to date with events, sat down to read the e-mails from Alistair. They relayed the information he had extracted from the files retrieved by Vern and Diana from Goodman, Goodhew and May. He reached the page that mentioned the DEMON COMPENDIUM – and the book with no name.

He read it a second time and his face grew dark and furious. He leapt into vampire mode almost without realising it. He took out his mobile and rang Elliott.

"Elliott Black," said the Dark Angel. "What's the problem, Jason?"

"You are," snarled the vampire viciously. "Get back here right away!"

The shapeshifters and American vampires looked surprised at Jason's extremely irate comments and wondered what on earth he was so mad about. They began to get alarmed, especially Vern who knew Jason only got angry when something had gone seriously wrong.

Elliott and Daniel appeared in Travis's apartment seconds later.

Jason pounced on them angrily. "You are a couple of idiots.

288

Which one of you read this message from Alistair?"

"I did!" said Daniel. "There's nothing I could do about it until we find the thing."

Jason ground his teeth in rage.

"Where did they get it from? Didn't you think of that? We all know the original was destroyed. After all, we destroyed it. There's only one authorised copy – and where is it? In the Fifth Dimension amongst the sum of all knowledge! Or it should be. What's the betting it isn't there any more? Don't forget, Charalder has been back to the Fifth Dimension recently. I bet she stole it from them. That would account for everything that has happened in the last twelve months. That's why she knew so much and was able to escape our magical spells and enchantments. That's how she found out about the world of Zohal.

"My God, Daniel, I hope you really wiped her memories completely or we are in trouble. Someone right now may have enough power to bring forth another Dark Age. I've lived through one and so have you. I don't want that for my children and neither do you."

"She didn't have it with her in Zohal's dimension," said Daniel firmly. "That I would have been able to detect."

"If anything that makes it worse," said Jason, his rage undiminished. "Now we don't know who she gave it to, and having the Fifth Dimension copy is as good as owning the original with its full power. It could even be in the hands of the one who wrote it in the first place."

Elliott and Daniel were dismayed at hearing what Jason had to say. They had already shared the same thought. Having it put into words by their friend was not what they wanted to hear.

"She certainly had enough time to find it and bring it back to earth with her," admitted Daniel.

"No! She couldn't have," protested Elliott. "My father would have missed it."

"Don't be ridiculous," snapped Jason. "One book among billions?"

"We'll go and find out," said Elliott calmly. "We can't make an informed decision without knowing."

He opened a portal and all three stepped through.

The onlookers were horrified. They had got the gist of the conversation and realised they could be in big trouble.

"What about the Elisande's copy?" whispered Vern to Pauline.

"It's only a fourth- or fifth-generation copy, it has very little power only information about spells and suchlike," said Pauline, "and in any case it is safe with Old Nick.

"There must be other copies," said Sebastian. "What about them?"

"Daniel and Elliott are relying on the fact that no one would ever admit to having one and has hidden it, with strong spells, generations ago. Hopefully where it can never be found," said Vern.

"Sound a bit 'iffy' to me," said Diana. "Very careless of someone."

"Yes," agreed Sebastian sardonically. "Very careless."

"Should we tell the witches?" asked Diana. "I think they should know what Jason thinks. He doesn't normally get all twitchy and feral unless something ghastly has happened."

"He certainly went into overdrive," admitted Vern. "And he certainly does have an uncanny knack of sensing danger."

Sebastian now seized upon something Jason had inferred, he could scarcely believe that he had heard aright. "What did he mean; they lived through the Dark Ages? I thought Daniel was a druid? He would have had to be alive over a thousand years ago," said Sebastian in a low voice to Vern. He looked strangely at Pauline. "How can he have lived so long? I'm sure he is human, he gave blood to Charles."

"I wondered about that as well. Is there something about him we haven't been told?" Vern looked askance at Pauline.

She looked at them all, hesitated for only a brief moment and spoke to them very softly.

"I can't tell you the full story, it isn't mine to tell and anyway it would take too long. Only seven people know about it and Lucifer is one of them.

"Daniel was born in Wales in 33 AD. Something happened when he was twenty-eight that changed his life. One day, when we have plenty of time, I will get him to tell you the story. To put it bluntly, he cannot die. He can be killed, but he will never grow old and die. That is all I am prepared to tell you right now. Please believe me when I tell you that Elliott, Jason and Daniel have been working together for nearly two thousand years."

Sebastian and Travis drew deep breaths of astonishment. "Why is it such a secret? Why couldn't he tell the rest of us? We all know about Jason and Elliott being immortal, what's the difference?" asked Sebastian.

"There's a lot more to it than that," said Pauline, tears welling into her eyes. "Trust me when I tell you it is not easy to explain. But I will give you a small hint. My destiny is now tied to Daniel's. Just how old do you think I am? I know I look about twenty-eight or so. I hate to admit it but, I was born forty years ago. I haven't aged a day since I met Daniel twelve years ago. It looks as if I never will."

Everyone silently digested the knowledge that Pauline, owing to some unknown supernatural or magical cause, could not age." Vern looked searchingly at her and nodded. He thought he understood.

He and Diana went to the kitchen to tell the witches the latest developments.

With the outcome of the visit to the Fifth Dimension in doubt, no one had anything to say. An air of gloom descended upon the apartment.

In the Fifth Dimension Jason had stormed into the castle and shouted for Torquil. He and Yohanna came running as usual. They stopped short on seeing his feral visage and the gloomy faces of their son and Daniel.

"Something else gone wrong?" inquired Torquil in alarm.

"It all depends on whether you still have your copy of the Book we do not name," snarled Jason. "Go and find out."

About to chide the vampire for his audacity, Torquil, on seeing Elliott's frown and Daniel's shake of the head, changed his mind and vanished. He reappeared seconds later looking shaken.

"It's gone!" he told them faintly. "Do you know who took it?"

"We made an educated guess," snapped Jason. "Your unauthorised visitor must have taken it when she was here last year. We've been suffering for your carelessness ever since."

Yohanna intervened. "Come into the Lounge and you can discuss this like civilised men," she told them crossly. "I'll ask Alpha to join us."

A few moments later Alpha, accompanied by Pedn-olva, appeared in the doorway and joined them. Both were in ethereal states.

Alpha looked at the three senior members of the Astral Council and saw his son's shaken look and immediately assumed his corporeal form, as did his companion.

"Only a disaster could have brought you all here. What has happened?"

Torquil told him, fearing that Jason would use his full powers on them all if he did not.

"I think we should be rational about this," said Alpha. "I share Daniel's view that she did not have it in the new dimension. I also believe Jason may be right, she has given it to someone who will make use of it to create a new Dark Age. However we cannot assume that the original author has it. There are a number of masters of the Black Arts who would not hesitate to use it if they got their hands on it. We must try and narrow down the field."

"I suggest you hurry," said Jason impatient at any delay. "The world may be in imminent danger of destruction and eternal darkness and it will be your fault."

Alpha gave him a pained look. "Condemnation of our laxity is understandable, but recriminations will not help. Right now we need answers."

He conducted them all to the conference room. Daniel recognised it as the one he had been in when he had first met Pednolva. The computers were humming quietly. As Alpha and Torquil appeared most of them started to print out lists of names and places.

"I told them what we wanted as we spoke," said Alpha. "Soon we should have an idea who has it."

All those present turned as an unknown voice spoke grimly from the doorway:

"There is a darkness about to fall upon the demon dimensions. Mordeus Maxim has been restored to its original author. I have had a vision. He is not going to use it yet, he is enjoying your fear and despair. He is toying with you. Everything that has happened so far has been to distract you from his true purpose. He intends to play with you for a while longer. But in time he will unleash his poison on this world. I have left my home for the first time in a hundred thousand years to join you. All the knowledge that we have acquired in our lifetimes will barely suffice to overcome the disaster about to befall!" said the Most Ancient of Oracles in a doom-laden voice.

"Lucifer already knows and will remain in Hell and oversee the events. He cannot leave for even a short while in case his full powers are needed to avert disaster there. In this case we can hope for no help from him. He and Rannoth have their hands full guarding your loved ones and making sure no one intervenes in his domain. He was certain that would be your wish as well."

"Of course it would," said Jason gruffly, "we agree with his decision. Look what happened last time he left for more than a short while. All hell broke loose, literally."

Elliott and Daniel nodded their agreement.

Daniel looked at the Oracle, who read his mind.

"You three," he looked directly at Daniel, Elliott and Jason, "have met him before. You destroyed his copy of the book and took away much of his power. For centuries he has waited. He had rewritten much of the original material and remembered much more. He has regained a great deal of his former power, but as you are all aware, total power comes only with possession of The book.

"By now you have realised that the former owner has recovered it. Lucifer will keep your families safe. He intends to guard them himself, this time. There is no one on this earth with more power than he. But he can't take the chance that several sorcerers, reading from The Book, could rip apart the dimensional veils and unleash the demons now contained. Before he could restore them untold harm would have been done to the earth.

"You will find the dark sorcerer, but great cunning will be needed to overcome his power," the great Oracle continued. "I saw a black shadow waiting to dispatch the evil one, but it had no face or substance.

"I saw no more in my vision. I did not see the outcome. So be careful, the results are in doubt, unless all the right decisions are taken when you meet the holder of the book."

"Another riddle," rasped Jason. "Don't you Oracles ever give straight answers?"

"When the outcome is uncertain," said The Oracle. "No one can give a definitive answer for fear of prejudicing your decision."

"He has told you all he can," interposed Alpha. "But the total sum of knowledge of the Fifth Dimension is at your disposal."

"Well, you promised never to interfere again," said Jason with a grim look at Elliott's grandfather. "I cannot fault your reasoning this time. I would only request that perhaps you will accompany us when we meet with our nemesis, and lend your powers to our own."

Alpha looked surprised and pleased at this request and nodded his head graciously. "I shall be there if you need me."

"It looks as if we have to let disaster find us again," muttered Elliott angrily. "I know we destroyed The Book but we never did find out for certain the identity of the author. We were pretty sure it was Mordred but we could never catch him. He used his powers to get away. It was really only because Jason is so fast on his feet that he was able to snatch The Book from his hands as he stepped through a portal. Doesn't anyone know for certain who wrote the damned thing in the first place?"

"Unfortunately," said Torquil with a frown, "The Book is made up of the most ancient spells of a number of different sorcerers and magicians. They were gathered together and written in the book we know as The Book of Evil, a long time ago. We would be only guessing at their identities. The original material came from many sources, now lost in antiquity. We never knew ourselves. Although it was always thought to have been gathered into one volume by the great Merlin, in his heyday.

"He used it merely as a reference book. He really was a great sorcerer, far greater than he was ever given credit for. And now, sadly, he is often treated as a figure of fun.

"We in the Fifth Dimension know that it was first used when he was just a young magician. He used sorcery to gain power for King Arthur and to defeat his enemies. He used it occasionally in the years after Arthur died. When Merlin himself eventually died, and he was many hundred of years old when he did, The Book, which was in fact a collection of scraps of paper on which were jotted the magic spells and potions known to the demonic sorcerers of times past, disappeared for a while. We are fairly certain that this was when Mordred got hold of it rewrote the entire volume and had it enclosed in a mystical binding that gave The Book its great power. When it resurfaced in Mordred's hands a great foreboding of disaster hung over the land, We have always suspected that its use led to the Dark Ages and not vice versa. A great deal of evil abounded in those times and the three of you were sent to bring about the destruction of The Book. It was last used in the early 9th century when you disposed of it.

Torquil smiled thinly, "I think I had better take you up on that offer."

"Nothing further we can do here," said Daniel. "Let's get back to New York."

They arrived back in New York, to find Vern patting Pauline on the back as she cried into his shoulder. Diana stood beside them looking helplessly at the witches who looked very worried.

Daniel hurried across to them and Vern relinquished Pauline to him. He gathered her into his arms and lifted her face to his. "What's the matter Pauline?" he asked quizzically. "Who has upset you?" He placed his hands each side of her face and joined his mind to hers.

After a few minutes, he laughed aloud.

"Sweetheart, I never thought to keep the secret as long as I have, and particularly not now we have so many new friends and relatives to consider. Of course I don't mind you telling them. Jason made it quite obvious that we have been together for centuries. They were bound to pick up on the connection."

Everyone gave a concerted sigh of relief that Daniel had not been angry with Pauline for telling them about his extraordinarily long lifespan and how hers was tied to his. Pauline had suddenly got cold feet after telling them and had started to worry that Daniel would disagree with her. Vern had been comforting her with the thought that Daniel seemed to love her enough to forgive her anything she might do wrong. He was, of course, quite right.

Pauline reverting quickly to her normal aggravating self, grinned at them all. "Sorry folks for getting all weepy. It must be the hormones all confused about the next set of twins... or triplets... or...!"

"Pauline!" said Daniel. "Do be quiet, this is not the time to discuss our personal domestic arrangements."

"That a new name for it?" queried their vampire friend with interest. "Personally, I find an expectant wife very sexy, and I don't care who knows."

"Your vampire preferences are no concern of mine," said Daniel glaring at him, "and I prefer to keep my personal life just that. So mind your own business."

"Shut up you two," said Vern. "You can argue about your domestic arrangements some other time. We want to know the facts about 61 AD and Daniel's extended lifespan."

The entire New York membership of the Astral Council seated itself expectantly around the room, waiting for the revelations.

Elliott and Jason grinned at each other. Daniel had avoided the issue for centuries and now he had an audience hanging on his every word.

# CHAPTER TWENTY-ONE

## *MONA,*
## *Anglesey, 61 AD*

"Let me set the scene...

"The druids who still remained in Wales during the Roman occupation of Britain were now living in the last druid stronghold of Yns Mon – the present-day Island of Anglesey. They had gathered in a small settlement on an inlet on the far side of the island. Having been driven from their birthright and homes in Britain and Wales they were now almost entirely isolated on the island. They hoped the stretch of water between them and the mainland would deter their oppressors. They were wrong!

"Druids moved quite openly amongst their people. They were their leaders, elders of the tribes. In those days before the advent of modern communications, we Celts had an oral tradition, a dislike of the written word. Knowledge of our history and traditions and laws were passed down to our descendents by word of mouth, through poetry, songs and chants. We were a secretive people and the memories of these storytellers, known as Bards, were vital to the continued history of our race.

"However, although a little known fact, the Celts did have a form of writing long before the Romans arrived. As far back as the first century BC, Ogham script, or the tree alphabet as it was often known, was a rare but recognisable written record mainly on Celtic crosses or memorial stones of the birth and death of kings and leaders and not necessarily the history of their people. Inscriptions can be seen on memorial stones that stand to this day. Occasionally we used hide or cloth. Unfortunately they were lost over the years as were those records written in later years on Papyrus which eventually rotted. Any other records of ancient druid writings are lost in the mists of antiquity. Only the Fifth Dimension has any record of its existence. In these dangerous Roman times druids mainly used word of mouth to communicate over long distances. A runner was used to take messages to other tribes.

"Don't think of pre-Roman Britons as an ignorant race of

people, there were quite a lot of scholars amongst us. We weren't averse to gaining great knowledge of the Greek and Roman Empires. I was born in 33 AD. I was fit and healthy, and my father had raised me to one-day take his place as priest or elder of our tribe. I had travelled widely and knew how to read and write, as had many of the elders. It was our duty to pass on the history of our people, not just the folklore and racial memories of distant ancestors. I learned well from my teachers; the learning came easily to me. Some friends and myself travelled to Rome and to Egypt and learned the art of writing on Papyrus, a fragile parchment. We learned the language and studied Egyptian hieroglyphs. We learn the secrets of their pyramids and their mystical religious gods. I spoke with philosophers and alchemists. My knowledge of spells and magic increased enormously. For reasons I didn't understand for many years, I was allowed to move freely amongst these learned men. I was there when a Christian religion started to spread. I learned about that as well. Although at that time I had formed no opinion as to its truth or the origins of this new religion, I had no idea how it was to impact upon my future.

"When I returned to Britain, I was only twenty-four but I was allowed to attend meetings of the elders and even then they told me that I had mastered the duties of a druid and had a great deal of wisdom for my age. To be fair, there was not a lot to do in those days except to learn what one could about the world about us. We kept a great deal of what we knew to ourselves. Our leaders discouraged the use of the written word. The fact that some of us could read and write was kept well hidden. At the time I lived in Anglesey it was actively discouraged. No one wanted a written record of what we thought and did to fall into Roman hands. Bad enough that they guessed what we thought and did.

"The elders held meetings in places of worship, in woodland clearings, on cliff tops and on hills, on mountains and in stone circles. There were festivals to celebrate various seasons, and amongst these were the Spring Equinox and the Summer Solstice held at Stonehenge. This was the most sacred site known to the druids who came from near and far to attend. The festival of Beltane held on May first was another of our four great annual festivals. Druids lighted bonfires the night before to mark the beginning of summer. They observed a number of rituals designed to acclaim the great Earth Mother, and were in fact the environmentalists of their day and were held in great awe by the people they lived amongst.

297

We held the festival of Samhain on November the first. It marked the end of one year and the beginning of the next and was thought to be the night that the mortal world opened to the Otherworld of the supernatural. Even in those days the existence of a supernatural dimension was taken for granted. With druids organising and presiding over all these festivities, it was not surprising that they were feared by the Roman conquerors of their country. It was about this time that they came under scrutiny from their leaders. They were sure we had enough power over the people to lead a rebellion."

Daniel looked around at his audience; they seemed to be spellbound by his story. No one said a word. He shrugged his shoulders and continued. "For the next two years I discreetly practiced all the things I have learned.

"If my people had known of such things in those days, I would have been considered a Philosopher or a doctor. I knew enough about herbs, potions, and the human body to be thought to have the gift of healing, but using it too often drained my strength and I used it sparingly. I knew more than enough about magic to be considered a warlock in later years; in those days however it was considered a gift. I was also adept at something only a few of my fellow druids aspired to, and to my knowledge, none have achieved. I found at a very young age, I seem to remember I was about fifteen, that I could read minds. Apart from that, I didn't consider myself to be any different to the rest of the elders; I could just do things they could not. I never let them know I could read their minds. It seemed to me they would never understand.

"Suetonius Paulinus, current ruler of the Roman Empire, had in AD 60 consulted with his Generals. He had listened to his advisors and had agreed with their estimation of the power of the druids over the people of Britain. He sanctioned an expedition to destroy the Welsh villages where the druids held sway."

He paused briefly to collect his thoughts.

Pauline leaned over and handed him a glass of water, which he sipped thankfully as he carried on with the tale. Jason and Elliott had been standing near the window, but now came and stood behind him and leaned on the back of the couch he and Pauline were seated on.

"In the early spring of AD 61 several strange things happened.

Although at the time they had no special significance, I knew afterwards they were ordained. A young dark-haired stranger appeared in the village. He was rather quiet and withdrawn. Almost overnight he built himself a small stone dwelling roofed with thatch, and earned his living by herding sheep for a local farmer.

"A few days after he arrived another stranger appeared. He had black curly hair and dressed somewhat strangely in bright clothes. He carried a strange musical instrument slung around his shoulders, and a pack on his back. No one had ever seen anyone quite like him before. I certainly hadn't.

"He smiled and joked as he wandered around our village. He brought a bit of colour to our lives. He had no visible means of support, but as he strolled around playing his strange instrument, he accepted hospitality from the local inhabitants in exchange for a tune and a story.

"He became a familiar sight around the area and soon blended into the background.

"Only a few weeks passed before both these strangers started to attend the meetings in the local woods and gathering places of the villagers. They seemed to want to talk to me in particular and asked me many questions about the life of a druid and our beliefs and even our history. I found myself quite often in their company and as they seemed anxious only to learn, I saw no reason to deny myself the pleasure of their company. Because that is what is was. A new experience, an exchange of ideas and views with men from outside my enclosed little world. It was a while before I realised I was being questioned by experts. Because, although I found out a little about them, they soon discovered all about me."

Jason tapped him on the shoulder. "Not all!"

Daniel momentarily turned to look at him, "I did manage to keep the odd secret!"

He turned back to the others, "I did keep from them a vision I had had some years before of a beautiful woman with long black hair. She wandered through my dreams for several nights running – I had it again, quite often, down the years. It took me almost two thousand years to find her – but I did." He took Pauline's hand and held it to his forehead for a moment or two. Pauline kissed him fondly on the top of his blonde head and growled softly.

"I know," she told him. "I love you, too."

"I don't know how I knew, because even in those days, the true nature of supernaturals was hidden from us, but I somehow

299

knew they were different. They were not ordinary men, they had an air of amused authority about them, as if they knew something no one else did.

"Don't get me wrong, shapeshifters or shape-changers were part of our culture. There were many tales about Gods or people with supernatural powers who could change into crows and ravens and visit battlefields. Another about a woman who gave birth to twin wolfhounds. There was a song about three brothers who changed into swans. As in so many myths and legends a hidden truth was revealed. There must have been quite a few real ones around, but fear of discovery by the Romans had led them to make their homes in very remote parts of the country. I know now of course that they lived on the vast moors of Scotland, Cornwall and Yorkshire. I had heard about vampires but they lived in parts of the world we Britons had scarcely even heard of. Europe and Russia were their main hunting grounds. With the population of Britain, Wales and Scotland so sparse and gathered mostly in small hamlets a vampire would have stuck out like a sore thumb; at least a made one would have. They would soon have been discovered, and despite our respect for gods and deities I suspect they would have been driven out.

"It is a great shock the first time you learn they really exist.

"What I didn't know then, but they did, was that the soldiers were even then marching to annihilate us.

"The Roman army descended upon our peaceful druid-led populace in great numbers. It led to the massacre and mass extinction by the opposition we so feared. The druids and their pagan religion and their hold over their people, was broken. Eventually only our village on the island of Anglesey remained. In 61 AD he ordered his generals to begin an assault on this last and rather remote stronghold.

"Our druid leaders were men and women of strong beliefs and powerful minds. There was no way they were giving up without a struggle, but first they felt they should attempt to reason with the generals. As news of the approaching army reached us they decided to seek a meeting with them and try of find a peaceful solution. I was considered too young to be with the elders on this occasion, but they allowed me to accompany them to the meeting place and watch from outside the encampment.

"No one is quite sure what happened at the meeting, from what I could see and understand the generals told them they would have to give up their pagan religion and worship the gods of Rome if they wished to live. Naturally they refused, expecting to speak further on the issue, but they were immediately seized and slaughtered on the spot.

"I saw the whole thing," said Daniel steadily. "My own father was amongst them. For a moment or two I was unable to move. I was about to return to the village to warn them when a hand was clapped across my mouth to stop me calling out. A very strong arm pushed me to the ground and a man pinned me beneath him. A voice in my head told me to 'stay down or you'll get us all killed'. I was half-dragged, half-carried to a nearby ditch where he threw me in and fell on top of me.

"Oh, I struggled with him! But he was uncommonly strong. Then the first voice was joined by another. 'It's not your time to die. You have much work to do. If you promise not to struggle or cry out, we'll let you up'.

"I was rolled on to my back and was strangely unsurprised to see the two strangers who had taken such an interest in me, leaning over me, looking rather grim and strangely inhuman.

"'Yes', said the dark curly-headed one as he read my thoughts. 'You are quite right. I am not human as you know it, but I assure you I am, in my own way, most humane'.

"'And I,' said the other, 'am not of this world, but I can live and work on it, whenever it is necessary. Not work as you know it, my duty is to safeguard the human world, to see that all the good and decent aspects of it survive. You, a druid, are now to be amongst the survivors of your race. You have been selected to preserve your druid heritage'.

"As he spoke the words his face changed and darkened, his eyes glowed yellow, his mouth opened, fire shot from his tongue and he seemed to grown taller. More impressively, his clothes changed to ones I had never seen, black and red flowing robes and gold amulets hanging around his neck. He looked like a demon from hell."

Elliott smiled enigmatically as Daniel got to this part of the story.

"This demon held out his hand towards me and said, 'I am Elliott, servant of the Astral Council, this is my friend and associate Jason. You will never have seen his likeness before either. He is not like other men, he is a creature of the supernatural, a vampire, he will tell you all about himself one day. For now, believe that he is a good man to have on your side'.

"At this point Jason turned into his feral self and I confess to being frightened. To see a handsome youth change before your eyes into a wild and dangerous animal was a terrifying experience."

Jason vamped and glared wildly at them all with the most evil grimace he could manage.

"He got me that way the first time I saw him," said Charles, speaking for the first time. "If I hadn't known about vampires I would have been terrified as well."

"I knew about vampires and I was scared stiff," said Vern with a grin at the leering vampire.

"Get on with the story," said an impatient Sebastian. "It's just beginning to get interesting."

Daniel laughed and resumed:

"Well, Elliott told me that in the future I would travel with them and learn of my destiny. I found it difficult to believe, at first. What of my village and my people? I must warn them, I told him.

"'Too late,' he said sadly. "What was your village and your people are no more. They are in greater hands than yours. Even as your father came here the soldiers were destroying your village'.

"'Why didn't you warn them?' I asked him. I was almost speechless with rage and despair.

"'That is not why we are here,' he told me. 'We are here to save you'.

"'You can't go back', said Jason, 'You must come with us. You have much to learn from us and we have much to learn from you; but we have to go far from here. Somewhere you will not be recognised for, believe me, for such a young man you are rather famous. Your knowledge and honesty are known far and wide in this land, and for a while you must lay low. The Romans have heard of you and they are afraid of you. They feared the power you druids have over your people and have now destroyed them. They are no longer a threat to them, but you still live!'

"'We cannot risk your life,' said Elliott, 'We three are unique in this world, a force for good. We are here to fight evil in an expanding world. This is a turning point, where the good must start to overcome evil. Up until now we have been scratching at the edges, learning the ways of the world. Now we must begin to fight'.

"I held up my hand to stop the flow of words, I needed to know more about them, who they were, who sent them. 'Why me?' I asked them'.

"'Even we do not know why. We have been sent to fetch you to join your destiny to ours,' Elliott was quite explicit on that point.

"'It's almost three thousand years since Elliott and I met.' Jason told me, "'You are our new partner'.

"Right then Elliott reached out and took my hand, and Jason placed his on both of ours. That's when it happened. I felt as if I had been struck by one of the bolts of lightning that sometimes seared and felled the trees in summer storms. I felt my head fill with strange images. I saw places and things that I had never even dreamed of. Tall stone buildings, horseless carriages, iron bridges, planes and a lot more I didn't understand at the time; and I saw the three of us walking together down the centuries towards a white light in the distance. No matter how far we walked the light stayed far ahead of us. For a brief moment I had been given a vision of a future far beyond my understanding, but which I knew was mine.

"When my mind cleared again, Elliott and Jason were looking at me and I understood they had seen the same vision.

"'How can I live that long?' I asked them. 'With all our knowledge a druid cannot extend life for more than a few years'.

"'You have been given a gift', Elliott told me. 'You will live as long as the Great Entity, the one who commands us all, has decreed that you can be of service to him and to the universe'.

"'You could live forever provided no one kills you,' Jason told me. Then he told me even more. 'I'm a vampire, I have to steer clear of wooden stakes and spears, and fire of course, but as you are human, I'm guessing swords and axes and iron spears'.

"'I'm immortal', said Elliott, 'and I live in our Otherworld. It's a little different to yours. I've been living there for many years. We call it Hell. It's a place of punishment for those who committed evil deeds when alive and in the Afterlife are tortured for eternity. It's ruled over by Lucifer, the fallen one. He's pretty evil himself'.

"'You can say that again', muttered Jason, 'Lucifer makes the Morrigan look like a new-born lamb'.

"Hell!" I was staggered. "The Morrigan is an unpleasant goddess who rules over the spirits of the dead. If an evil one rules these and is worse than her, I certainly don't want to work for him!

"'He's not all bad', Jason told me. 'We'll probably never meet him. He hates vampires and he isn't all that keen on humans. He only deals with Elliott'.

"I was very relieved but I'd rather not have known that little item of news. I was still a bit worried so I asked them straight out.

303

'Are you sure you are on the side of good'?"

"And I," said Jason, grinning as he leaned over the now tired and thirsty druid and gripped his shoulder, "told him that of course I was, my mother and father brought me up to be a good little boy."

Everyone laughed as this remark lightened the atmosphere in the room. They had been really bound up in the druid's life story, but they now came down to earth again.

"They never did let me go back to Mona. The Roman soldiers were everywhere. It was then I had my first experience of astral travel. I am not too keen on it even now," said Daniel as he finished his story. "We went to live in Scotland, as is, for a while. I was welcomed there, some Caledonians were Celts as I was. The Romans were really afraid of them.

"It was a very long time ago, and I no longer remember it as clearly as I once did. We have worked together ever since. I believe we have made a difference. In fact, on most occasions I am certain that we did. We don't just work here on earth you know. Sometimes we find ourselves in other worlds, doing there what we do here. I don't like space travel either," he added gloomily. "Still, there's so much to do here on earth now. I may never have to leave it again." He brightened up at the thought.

Elliott also leaned over and punched him lightly on the shoulder. It had been a strange time for Jason and himself, hearing their meeting with Daniel told in such detail.

Daniel stood up and, walking around behind them, put his arms around their shoulders. "Don't worry, I wouldn't have changed a single day. It has always been a privilege to work with you both."

Jason and Elliott laughed as he finished. "He's too modest," said Elliott. "He's been invaluable to the Astral Council over the centuries. As you now know we were very active in the Dark Ages, but that story will have to wait for another time."

Jason's mother stood up and walked over to them all. "Thank you for letting me hear this. Theron and I are really pleased to know that our teachings in his youth have brought such rewards to our son."

Jason then did something he hadn't been able to do for over four thousand years, he took his mother into his arms and hugged and kissed her. She patted his cheek gently. "You have no idea how much a mother misses a hug and kiss from her son." There was a suspicion of tears in her eyes.

304

"Stick around and you'll get plenty more," said her son with a wicked grin.

"Knowing all this is going to make what you expect us to do the heck of lot easier," said Travis, "but I can see we have a lot to live up to."

During the telling of this tale Pauline had sat quietly on the arm of the couch just giving her support to Daniel. Now she stood up and walked to stand beside him. He slid his arm around her waist and drew her tightly against him, kissing the top of her head.

He turned to the rest of their friends. "In the last two thousand years I have aged about five years, even that could be put down to the stress and strain of the job I do. After all, I am still human. I expect Pauline has already told you, but in case she didn't; when we were married, my powers were extended to include her, for which I am eternally grateful. I cannot imagine how I ever managed without her."

Pauline tossed her head and looking straight into his eyes, in a very sexy growl, told him, "And I intend to make certain that you never have to."

Elliott and Jason both laughed again, as Daniel very definitely blushed.

"Thanks for the history lesson," said Vern sincerely. "It answers a lot of questions Alex, Charles and myself have not dared to ask. You were all three so sure of each other's reactions in any given scenario and spoke of things in the past as though you had all been there when they happened. We wondered. Now we know for sure. You were."

"There's another little item needs answering," said Sebastian, "You said we have some time before anything else happens, but what about that book?"

"According to the Oracle, we have time to prepare ourselves for the eventual appearance of the madman who has it," said Elliott. "The author is toying with us at the moment, probably trying to get us to make a move before we are ready.

"It's possible we have cards to play he doesn't know about. I suggest we all go home and wait for him to make a move."

"What about us?" asked Travis.

"Vern and Diana have agreed to stay in New York to guide you through the next few months. James Purcell will join you until we find a suitable replacement for Snake. He and Bianca will have to live in Cornwall from now on.

"Well, don't forget no one is sure what Azeran is up to. He may be Nick's brother, but he is still a loose cannon. Daniel and I are rather concerned that no one can find him. I am making myself nervous saying all this – I just hope I am not asking too much of you all," replied Elliott.

"Oh, great! Hop off back to Bodmin and leave the Big Apple to the locals," said Travis with an exaggerated sigh. "Still, what more can you expect of dimension-hopping demons who drop from holes in the sky at all times of the day and night. I think a little extra assistance would be in order."

He added slyly,

"How about sending an angel to help out? I reckon I could make a good job of looking after Carlotta for the Great Entity. I really would have a personal incentive there."

"I'll run it by Lucifer next time I meet him," said Elliott blandly, "I can tell you that your personal interest in the item has already been noted."

"Make sure you give me a first class reference," said Travis with a grin.

"I may see him quite soon," said Elliott. "I'm off to his Palace to join my wife and son for a few days. He's bound to drop by to visit us."

"When you get there, you can get him to send Allegra, Simon and Riva back," said Jason. "I'm sure their witch and vampire ancestors can keep them from harm for a while. I want them with me right now. Charles and Katya can come back to my place as well. There's plenty of room and safety in numbers. If we feel at all threatened, we can move to Quinn's place."

"I'll agree to that on one condition," said Elliott. "Vespazia stays close to Allegra, Simon and Riva if you aren't."

"Good plan. I like it," agreed Jason.

"Well, that's you lot all settled," said Daniel satisfied. "I think Pauline and I will just get off home ourselves for a while, but to keep them safe we'll leave the twins with Nick."

"Don't go yet," said Sebastian, whose vampire hearing had heard his doorbell ring several minutes before, and Cybel going to answer it. "I have got a little surprise for you all. It came to me when Pauline mentioned your extremely large house and a baby-sitter."

As he spoke Cybel ushered three women into the room. They rushed across to Sebastian and hugged and kissed him in turn.

306

"My sisters," said Sebastian proudly. "Susan, Carla and Janine, all trained nurses," he added significantly. "Just what you and Pauline need to look after a large number of wolf cubs. Who better than a trio of vampire nurses for young werewolves?"

"We'd love to give it a try," said Carla eagerly. "We've already met Sophie Lanyon and heard a lot about England. It seems just the right place for us New Age vampires."

Daniel looked stunned, but Pauline looked thoughtfully at the three female vampires.

"Trained nurses? Vampires?"

All three obligingly vamped. They were strangely beautiful. Not quite as lovely as Katya, but Pauline didn't think they would stay single if they lived in England for long. She laughed.

"I think Sebastian has hit on a great solution," she told Daniel. "I was wondering how I would be able to go with you wherever you go, with five or six babies to look after. This will solve that problem. I really can't imagine letting you go into danger without me, but I couldn't bear to let our children be drawn into it as they have in the past. How about it Daniel? Will you let them come with us?"

"Nurses, and Sebastian's sisters? How can I refuse. We shall be in Sebastian's debt for years if this works out."

"It will, if I know my sisters," said Sebastian. "What's more, I shall feel they are really safe in England under the eye of one of the supremos of the Astral Council."

Daniel endeavoured to look modest at this tribute to him and his companions, but failed lamentably.

Pauline laughed throatily as she told him. "We'd better go the short way as they are made vampires."

"You know how I hate this." He protested forcefully as he opened a portal on the roof a few minutes later and they all stepped through.

"Don't worry so. I'll be holding your hand all the way!" said Pauline.

Faith and Alex had left the hospital the day before all this took place. It had been decided they were well enough to travel home, provided they took it easy for a few weeks and had their parents to look after them. The district nurse would be calling to check on Alex, but he was expected to make a full recovery.

Matthew and Sophie drove them home the day before Christmas Eve. Sophie had arranged a very quiet family Christmas with just the two families. Ward had been invited but told them his secretary had invited him for Christmas for the past five years and he couldn't let her down.

"I'm very fond of her, and wouldn't want to offend her. She's an excellent secretary, I can't afford to lose her. I enjoy her company," he added simply.

"Sounds to me as if he is more than fond of her," said Alex to Faith as Ward departed via spirit path to Inverness.

"Perhaps he is, but it's not our business," said Faith firmly.

Drago decided to go with them as extra protection. He looked forward to a family Christmas; he had never taken part in one.

James and his parents drove Drago and Elisande to their respective destinations as Felicity had taken her car to go Christmas shopping. Karim had accompanied her.

Elliott was waiting for James and his parents when they arrived home and arranged with James for his immediate departure for New York. James was not best pleased as he loved a family Christmas.

Elliott was adamant. James was needed in New York.

James had refused point blank to go by a spirit path, and grumbled for some time about being uprooted at Christmas. But Elliott noted that he was packing as he did so.

He then went to visit the Lanyons and made all the necessary arrangements for Karim and Felicity to join James. Felicity grimaced, not all that thrilled at missing Christmas with Faith and Alex.

Elliott ignored their protests, telling them that New York was in desperate need of their assistance. Karim nodded his assent and prepared for an immediate departure.

Wishing them a speedy journey, Elliott vanished to join Natalia.

Elliott joined Natalia in Hell, prepared to enjoy a well-earned rest and a few days spent with his son and heir. There would be a long wait before the arrival of young Nick's sibling and he looked forward to a few days alone with his family. What's more he intended to see that he got them. He wasn't in the slightest bit concerned that he was staying in Lucifer's palace. He had his own suite of rooms and now made his family at home in them.

He smiled wickedly to himself as he told Natalia, "Penny and Lucy will be much be safer in our apartment with both of us to guard them."

Natalia frowned. "I can see through your machinations. You think I'll be so busy with the twins and Nick, I won't have time to do anything else."

"Oh, I can think of one or two things you will have time for, and I'm one of them." He laughed at the indignant look she cast him.

"Beast! I may arrange to have a headache!" She attempted to flounce from the room. As she passed him he seized her around the waist, pulled her firmly into his arms and with his fingers twined firmly in the golden curls pulled gently until her mouth was exactly where he wanted it.

A few minutes later a breathless Natalia was released and a demonic Elliott looked coolly at her.

"What was that about a headache?"

Natalia wound her arms around his neck. "I'll have it tomorrow."

Claudia, Carlotta and Bianca materialised in Elliott's apartments and each retrieved an infant, returning with them to the nursery. Claudia let Natalia know telepathically what they had done as they did so.

Lucifer, his eyes and ears everywhere, decided the twins had better go home for Christmas. He'd send them tomorrow as he already knew about the three new nurses about to arrive in Salisbury.

The soldiers on guard duty outside the various apartments looked grimly at each other. The captain groaned when informed of the various movements of their charges and quickly altered the rota to temporarily include the latest movements of the godchildren.

The brigadier smiled grimly as he was informed of the moves and arranged yet another duty rota for the new arrivals. He might have to increase his intake of recruits if this mass influx of Lucifer's friends and relatives were to continue. He called the major to his office to discuss the problem. The captain had the current duty shift and was far too busy.

Back in New York there was one last surprise – albeit in two parts – for Travis and Sebastian. Six hours after Elliott and the rest had departed, a dark shadow in a corner of the room moved forward into the light.

Travis caught sight of the shadow and half turned to face it. For a moment he nearly lost it, but quickly recovered.

"Peace be unto you, my brother," said a soft calm voice. "I come as a friend. My name is Karim. Possibly Elliott has spoken of me?"

"He did mention a djinn being available to help us out," said Travis coldly. "A little warning wouldn't have come amiss, you startled us. Are you alone?" he added suspiciously as another shadow seemed to move behind the djinn.

Karim laughed and beckoned to the figure in the shadows. Felicity moved fully into the lighted room and smiled at them.

"Here I am again. Our daughter and son-in-law are almost well and after Christmas are going to convalesce with Karim's family in ancient Persia. They will be well looked after and quite safe and, as Elliott was really anxious that we came, here we are."

"My wife," said Karim softly, "has told me of your changed lifestyle, rather different to that of the vampires that I have known. I am pleased to meet you.

"I have met the angel whom you saved. My world is not so different to yours. We consider that to have saved an angel is a wonderful deed to have performed." He bowed gracefully to them both. "Allah be with you always for such a great service."

"Elliott wants us to stay here until he tells us we can return," said Felicity. "Karim is a very powerful djinn and Elliott is confident that he can negate any demonic actions which may arise here in the future, at least until the others arrive back."

"James is coming as well. He will be arriving in a few hours time. He refused point blank to travel the supernatural paths and insisted on coming by plane, train and car." Felicity smiled enigmatically at them all. "You mustn't be taken in by his seeming disinterest in what goes on around him. He's much more than he appears to be. He is so easy-going, and looks half asleep most of the time, yet he knows everything that is going on. It's amazing what he can arrange and get away with."

"Alex and Faith will join us as soon as they are well enough to travel, but Lucifer has forbidden them to come here until they are completely well, and none of us care to disobey his orders." She looked directly at Travis as she spoke.

"Except Jason," muttered Vern to Diana, as they re-entered the room on the tail end of this conversation. "Did you notice he was first to decide to go home and to demand the return of his family to his own custody?"

"Who is Jason?" inquired Karim, "the name is familiar."

"One of the head honchos," said Vern. "Senior partner in the Astral Council, very sure of himself, likes to have his own way. Isn't afraid of anyone or anything."

"He wouldn't be a vampire by any chance?" asked Karim.

"As a matter of fact he is," said Vern surprised. "Have you met him?"

"If he's rather dark skinned, with a mop of curly black hair, a penchant for bright colours and a dreadful dress sense, then, yes, I believe I have," said Karim. He frowned. "I had believed that meeting all of you was a coincidence, a result of Faith's accident. Now I am not so sure."

"Knowing the celestial powers, I should accept that you are where you are meant to be. I no longer believe in coincidences myself, nothing happens to us without a reason. By the way, if you know Jason how come you didn't know Elliott and Daniel?" asked Vern.

"I met Jason some years ago in Tibet, when the Dali Lama still ruled there. We were both acquainted with the then current great Lama, a very wise and intelligent man. We learned a lot from our friendship with him. Jason was on holiday at the time. I had no idea he had a connection to the celestial realms. He wanted to climb a mountain; to be, as he said, the first to climb Everest. Of course, being a vampire he succeeded. He was the first vampire to climb it and the first being ever to set foot on the top. Being a vampire he doesn't need oxygen as we humans do, and he didn't feel the cold. It was no more than an exercise to him, but an achievement nevertheless. He just wanted to climb the highest mountain. I know for certain he did. I was at the top with him. I didn't climb it, I materialised there. That was over a hundred years ago. In all we spent a month or so in the mountain retreats. I haven't seen him since."

"Well, well! So our bosses do have their little vanities after all," said Vern. "I'm very glad to meet you Karim. Have you been to New York before?"

"It's not a place I feel comfortable in, but I do have to on occasion," said Karim ruefully. "My father and I have business dealings with some of the more prestigious stores. Persian carpets are still in demand. Genuine antiques, of course!"

"Oh, Yes!" scoffed Diana. "Made last month by six-hundred-year-old genies, I bet!"

"How clever of you to figure that out my dear, I can see we

311

shall get along beautifully."

"You'll have to watch your step," said Travis. "She's a vicious jungle animal when it comes to business." Felicity choked on a laugh as she remembered that Diana was a jaguar in her supernatural state.

She eyed Travis suspiciously, he was getting very much like Jason in his ways, and she wondered if Travis was going to be the leader of this bunch and not Sebastian as Lucifer had suggested. She decided to very quietly have a word with Vern about Travis. He certainly had potential.

Leaving Vern and Karim deep in conversation, Felicity allowed Travis to show her the room she and Karim would occupy whilst in New York.

"No luggage?" inquired Travis.

"It's coming with James," she told him. "Karim's idea of luggage is a toothbrush; he is used to travelling light."

She looked around the large en suite bedroom and separate lounge, and exclaimed with pleasure:

"This is wonderful, Travis! Karim and I will enjoy being here." She looked at him with a twinkle in her eye. "Have you got a car I can borrow? I intend to see all the sights whilst I am here. Karim can show me where to go."

"How about a helicopter tour?" asked Travis. "You know I'll take you anywhere you want to go."

"I shall look forward to that," she told him gaily.

They returned to the lounge to find the rest of the party enjoying a friendly drink. Travis and Felicity joined them.

They sat in animated conversation for quite a while. Making new acquaintances is a lengthy process when long lives are under discussion.

Diana and Vern left after an hour or two to take in the night-life of the city they had offered to stay in for a while.

"We should familiarise ourselves with the layout," said Diana, "and we have got the Limo. It's probably mine now anyway, if I'm going to be the new managing director."

"I'm entirely in your hands," said Vern in a low voice. "I hope you can find your way to Central Park, I fancy a hunting expedition in New York!"

They had not yet returned when James arrived six hours later.

Two taxis drew up outside the front door disgorging a vast amount of luggage, parcels and James. Right behind them was a large van with the name of a rather prestigious store emblazoned on the side.

All three drivers assisted James into the foyer. On production of a large tip they helped him to load half of the packages into the lift, and accompanied it to the penthouse. They unloaded the lift and returned for a second load.

A stunned Travis watched as a large tree, already completely decorated, was carried into his lounge and placed in a corner. The men made several more trips, supervised by James who nodded to Felicity and Karim before returning to the lift to supervise the unloading of the rest of his baggage.

The three men accepted an extra tip and departed.

"James! What on earth have you brought with you?" cried Felicity in astonishment. "How long has Elliott sent you for?"

"Christmas Tree, presents and all our luggage," said James succinctly. "I'm not giving up my Christmas just because Elliott says I have to come to New York and do some guard duty. Mother and father are here, too. They won't be long they are down at Wal-Mart getting the food and drink."

"James! This is the famous James Purcell?" asked Sebastian sounding surprised. "Daniel said he was a nice quiet young fellow, no trouble to anyone."

He eyed the mountain of suitcases and parcels piled up in the hallway with horror.

"I'm not," said James indignantly. "But I'm not missing out on Christmas and that's that."

"And why should you?" said Felicity calmly. "It will be really nice to share Christmas with you and your parents and our new friends. Won't it, Karim?"

"I am certain that if you enjoy it, my beloved one, that I shall also," said an amused Karim.

Travis looked at them all and shook with laughter. These English shapeshifters were something else. He could see life was never going to be quite the same ever again.

# CHAPTER TWENTY-TWO

*Salisbury.*
*Christmas Eve*

The day after Daniel and Pauline arrived home, Rannoth appeared with the twins. "The Boss reckons they'll be safe enough now you've got the vampire nurses. You need to spend Christmas with the whole family. He'll have them back when things hot up again. By the way, he's ordered half a dozen soldiers to do guard duty around the house just in case. But they won't be any trouble to you. The Brigadier has arranged to change the guard every four hours."

"Doesn't anything slip past him?" asked Pauline in exasperation.

"Unfortunately, no! I must say I wish it did," muttered Rannoth. "He keeps mentioning heirs whenever he visits us. I don't want to, but I reckon I'm going to have to give in just to shut him up."

"Don't you dare!" said Pauline. "The rotten know-all needs someone to stand up to him now and again, just to let him know he's not totally in charge of our destinies."

Rannoth laughed. "Just for you, I'll try and hold out a bit longer!"

He vanished back down under.

Carla's jaw dropped. "Who on earth was that?"

"Lucifer's chief assistant, also his son-in-law!" Daniel told her. "We think a lot of him, he's a good friend."

"You mean: he's not afraid of Lucifer?"

"Let's just say that they respect each other's abilities and that being married to the Devil's daughter gives him an edge."

"Darling, did Rannoth just mention Christmas?" asked Pauline anxiously. "What is today's date?"

Daniel looked at his watch. "Oh, hell! It's the twenty-fourth."

"Christmas Eve!" screamed Pauline. "What time is it?"

"Don't panic! There's plenty of time to get organised," said her husband calmly. "Check the freezer, see what you've got."

Pauline darted off to the kitchen.

314

Daniel went out to the garage, found the Christmas decorations and rang the local nursery to arrange to have a large tree delivered. He also ordered holly, mistletoe and dried flowers.

He showed the sisters to their rooms and the linen cupboard. They said they would help get Christmas organised first and then make their rooms ready. "Working together it should not take long to organise everything that needs to be done," said Susan cheerfully. "We are used to Christmas in the hospital. We know what to do."

Pauline dashed past them and out of the front door. "I'm off to the shops, we'll need loads of food and things. Get the place decorated while I'm gone!"

The brakes squealed and the tyres threw up gravel as the car tore down the drive. "Slow down, Pauline," muttered Daniel, sending a thought wave towards the car: "I do prefer you all in one piece."

Don't worry, thought back his wife. I'll be careful. I like me in one piece as well.

Several hours later, the house decorated, the food stowed in the fridge, the turkey stuffed, the presents wrapped and the excited twins fast asleep in their identical cots, Daniel, Pauline and the nurses sat down to enjoy what was left of Christmas Eve. They were all exhausted but pleased with all they had achieved.

Elliott and Natalia had the benefit of angelic heritages; a wave of the hand and a thought or two saved them a lot of hard work. Pauline, although a werewolf and Daniel, albeit awash with magic spells and ancient folklore, could not equal their expertise. Even Jason and Allegra had Vespazia to help them.

Susan, Janine and Carla had been delighted to be asked to come to work in England. They looked forward to meeting Sophie again and the rest of the shapeshifters, particularly Sophie's family. They had the feeling they were in for a very interesting future. They had decided to ignore their brother's warning that it could be dangerous as well. In their rather long lives they had not been strangers to danger and had managed to survive so far. They were aware of the protection of the local witches and knew the druid and the Dark One had powers that even vampires only dreamed of.

Christmas Day was the first the Jefferies had spent with children to consider. A hilarious time was had by all. They had a great time every day of the holiday.

Carla, Susan and Janine had their first taste of an English Christmas, which was made a lot more of than in America. They

315

confessed to a desire for any future Christmases spent in England to be as good as this one.

Pauline was delighted. She had help with the twins, help in the house and plenty of time to spend with her husband. She also whispered to him, when no one else was listening, that it now gave her more time to spend the vast sums of money he kept placing in her bank account.

He quietly told her that it would probably take her a lifetime to spend it, as it seemed to keep growing without him even lifting a finger.

"Well, you keep on letting it grow and I'll keep on trying to spend it," said Pauline with a grin. "Just as long as you keep a couple of million on one side to put the girls through university, some day."

"Aren't we having any boys?" asked Daniel amused.

"I just don't want you to be disappointed if there's no male heir to your throne," said Pauline, with an unusually serious look on her face.

"I promise that nothing you could do would ever disappoint me," said Daniel kissing her soundly, "and I feel that I have already been forewarned that we shall have all-female children. If you remember Pedn-olva said I should be the last true druid of my line, and hinted that I should eventually train Patrick to take my place."

"Still he did say the last TRUE druid," Pauline reminded him. "Any son of ours, if we have one, would be half werewolf."

"Well if we do, and he is, that will be fine by me," said Daniel.


Winchester – Christmas Eve:
Jason was rather pleased with himself. His family had been returned into his care that very morning. Rannoth had escorted them to Alex's home where he had picked up his car and been joined by Charles and Katya in theirs with Theron and Sidonie. Vespazia had used her powers to arrange everything and was now waiting with Quinn at his home in Winchester.

He had reached an understanding with Allegra that she would soon join the ranks of vampires. He had a son and a daughter he adored and had provided them with a couple of ancient vampire grandparents. His wife had forgiven him for rushing off without telling her where he was going and his sister was about to make him an uncle. He felt on top of the world and no one was going to upset his apple cart, not even the unknown author who supposedly held their fate in his hands.

Followed by Charles in his own car with Katya and the new grandparents, he drove his Mercedes up his elegant private driveway and stopped with a flourish outside his highly polished front door.

Smiling proudly he escorted them all into his vast lounge and grinned at his mother as his wife handed her the baby. Allegra headed for the kitchen to make tea, followed by Simon, who knew his mother and the kitchen meant food and by Charles who, for some strange reason, was still addicted to coffee and did not appear to be over the moon at drinking blood.

Katya flung off her jacket and dashed after them.

"Charles! Too much coffee is bad for vampires; they get over excited and cause trouble. Don't touch that coffee pot. There's a nice pot of chilled ox-blood in the fridge."

The voices faded but Jason could hear Charles complaining loudly that it was no fun being a vampire. He wanted a Cornish pasty and not raw meat.

"You are not human any more!" yelled Katya. "You are a vampire now."

"No, I'm not. I'm a shapeshifting vampire and my feline genes like their meat cooked and washed down with tea, coffee or beer," said Charles, sounding quite reasonable about it all.

Allegra entered the argument. "For heaven's sake Katya, give him what he wants. He'll soon find out whether it's good for him or not."

Theron raised a questioning eyebrow.

"He hasn't changed in the slightest even though he is a made vampire," said Jason "I'm still not sure what it is that has made him able to walk around it daylight without any ill effects. It's very odd. He's a new type of vampire, descended from a long line of shapeshifters. He may be right; his shapeshifting genes could be in the ascendant. I hope it is permanent for both their sakes. We'll soon find out. I told the witches to stand by in case he has a bad reaction," said Jason

"Should you be allowing him to make the decision for himself?"

"He's a grown man, it's his decision to make. Anyway, Allegra is usually right. He knows what he wants and how he feels."

Sidonie was laughing as she re-entered the lounge. "Our son-in-law has a mind of his own. I don't envy Katya, trying to keep up

317

with that one."

"She needed a strong-minded man," said Jason, "and believe me, she's got one. I have great respect for his strength of mind and muscle and so has Elliott. He is the only man I know, apart from Elliott, who is anywhere near to my weight."

"It's nice to see a brother who respects his sister's choice of husband," said his mother with a smile. "Such a good foundation for family values."

Theron smiled complacently, he was quite resigned to rejoining his vampire family for the next few decades. It rather looked as if they led almost too exciting a life for two reclusive grandparents. He and Sidonie would have their work cut out to keep up with them all.

Jason leapt to his feet as a shriek of horror came from the kitchen and Allegra rushed in to the lounge.

"With all the excitement and danger and meeting your relatives, I completely forgot the date. Do you realise today is Christmas Eve? We've got to do something about it."

"I know," said Jason relieved that the shriek was nothing serious. "Tree, presents, turkey, food for a feast for the returned hero!"

Allegra laughed at his resigned voice and pushed him from the room. "Take Katya and Sidonie, it will be fun for them. Off you go, the shops will close at four, it's ten past one now."

"Grrr," he growled as he shepherded his mother and sister through the door. "Orders is orders, missus," he whined as he passed his laughing wife.

The car disappeared down the drive rather faster than usual.

"Anything I can do?" asked Charles as he strolled in from the kitchen with Simon at his heels.

"You can practice baby-sitting for the afternoon," said Allegra, "You still have to take it easy. A nice quiet afternoon with Simon and Riva will do you good. Theron and Quinn can help you. Vespazia and I have a lot to do."

The Hoover appeared on its own in the hallway and began to clean the downstairs rooms. Theron raised his eyebrows enquiringly.

"Vespazia, Allegra's mother, a very superior witch, does everything with a wave of the hand and a flick of the wrist," said Charles.

Theron nodded in understanding. "Should we make ourselves

scarce, take the children for a walk or something?"

"Good idea," said Charles and shouted to Vespazia in the kitchen.

"We are off for a stroll with the kids. Where's Riva's pram?"

The pram appeared beside him seconds later and Vespazia settled Riva into it and made sure she was well covered and warm. She put a warm puffer on Simon and Theron picked his grandson up in his arms. They headed down the drive towards the park which Allegra had pointed out on the way to her home. They did not intend to return for some time. Vespazia and Allegra had the look of two females who could do without men around for a while.

Quinn was made of sterner stuff. He followed Vespazia as she opened cupboard after cupboard in the kitchen.

"You had better tell me what is so important about Christmas," he told her. "I've never heard of it. I don't want to make a fool of myself or spoil it for everyone for the sake of a few hints from you."

"I only know what I picked up over the latter years in Hell, and from things the shapeshifters have mentioned from time to time. When they were rebuilding the castle they did mention that the ceilings in the main rooms would be difficult to decorate and we had better stick to trees and standing ornaments. I believe it is traditional to have a pine tree or a holly tree in a big house like this or our castle. In fact, I should think several might be appropriate. I heard that lights in the windows and candles on tables are another necessity. I'll check with Allegra, she's gone to find the tree ornaments and the hanging lanterns. Apparently Jason brought them back from Japan some years ago and they look quite wonderful hanging from the ceiling."

"What about this turkey and what feast?" asked Quinn beginning to get alarmed.

"That's another tradition," said Vespazia smiling a little herself at his worried look. "A stuffed turkey and roast potatoes and other vegetables are eaten on Christmas Day, followed by something called a Christmas pudding which is set alight before consumption."

"It sounds rather dangerous to me," said Quinn.

"Don't worry," said their daughter gaily as she rushed into the room carrying a large box on which several more were precariously balanced. "These are all ready for when Jason brings the tree. He does love to decorate it himself. You wouldn't think a vampire would be interested in Christmas. But he really loves it!"

"I have to get everything ready the night before. He insists on

319

us all opening our presents and having breakfast whenever he wakes up. Daniel says that ever since Christmas was invented he's enjoyed every moment of it. Honestly, Mum! He's just like a big kid every year at this time. As he's so marvellous all the rest of the year, everyone indulges him."

Quinn and Vespazia looked at her with pleasure. "Do you realise that this is the first time you have ever called me Mum?" Vespazia couldn't hide her happiness. "I feel that I have just been given my first ever Christmas present. You are my only child. You have no idea how long a million years can seem. But that is how long I have waited for this moment."

"Mum, I shall call you that from now on, every chance I get." Allegra gave her an extra loving hug and kiss. "You too, Dad," she said as she turned to her father and did the same.

"My child," said the rather choked Dolonquin. "Truly, Christmas must be a delightful festival if this is anything to go by."

"We are going to have a wonderful time as soon as Jason gets back with the goodies," said his daughter. "Although we don't have to wait for him to get back to have a Christmas drink."

Fetching a bottle of wine from the cupboard, Allegra and her parents toasted each other several times. Then several times more after that…

The Hoover continued cleaning and the dusters got in on the act. And the occupants of the kitchen opened yet another bottle of Jason's very fine wine.

When the shoppers got back several fruitful hours later, three very tipsy people were lounging in the kitchen and very little work was done. By now there were three empty bottles of Jason's finest wine on the table and Allegra was leaning back in her chair with her eyes closed giggling at a rather involved story being told by Quinn.

The Hoover had bounced upstairs and the dusters had followed. No one had thought to stop them. They were having a high old time.

"Where do you want the tree?" asked the deliveryman from the local nursery. "Put it in the hall, shall I?" He grinned at Jason as he saw the state of those in the kitchen. "Started a bit early I see! One of them yours?"

"The redhead," sighed Jason. "Oh, well! I don't suppose they'll be much help for the rest of the day."

He reached into his pocket and slipped a large denomination note into the nurseryman's hand and reached into the cupboard for a bottle of his best wine.

"Enjoy your Christmas. I rather think I shall be enjoying mine." He indicated his giggling wife.

"Best of luck, pal and a merry Christmas to all of you." The man saluted the grinning vampire and laughed all the way to his van.

Sidonie and Katya were hysterical with laughter as they witnessed this exchange.

"What do you want us to do?" asked Katya when she was able to speak.

"It looks as if we are going to have to unpack the car and put everything away without the benefits of Vespazia's hand," sighed Jason. "We'd better get a move on. We passed Charles and father about three miles down the road. Kat, there's a large red carpet in the utility room in a box marked 'Christmas carpet'. It has to go down wherever we put the tree to save the needles falling on the cream one. You weren't here for Christmas for the last twenty years, but you should remember where everything is kept. And for heaven's sake, Mother, try and stop that Hoover."

"Don't worry, brother, I'll find whatever is needed. Allegra's already got the decorations down," said Katya as their mother vanished upstairs.

"I was relying on Vespazia for this," muttered Jason as he eyed the boxes. "Now I'll have to get the ladder and do it myself."

"We could try coffee to sober them up," offered Sidonie tentatively as she arrived downstairs once more. "I got the dratted Hoover to stop and put it away. I had to speak very severely to it. I suppose your father could manage enough magic to hang the decorations, provided we tell him where to put them. He's not terribly interested in interior decoration, I'm afraid."

"I think we had better try and get it done without his help," said Jason, remembering his father's ham-fisted attempts at building and decoration far in the past. They had lived in Egypt when he was very young, as it was the most civilised society of that time. His father had not been much help with interior decor even then.

Jason and his mother headed for the car and started to unload the shopping and presents. Katya disappeared to find the red carpet.

Allegra peeped from under her eyelids at the doorway and saw they had all gone. Quinn and Vespazia, not quite as tipsy as they appeared, looked at her.

"What are you going to do about that?" asked Quinn.

His wife and daughter winked at him and moved quickly and

quietly to the lounge. Allegra showed her mother the box of decorations and took a couple out to show her what they were like and where they had to be hung. Quinn sat down to watch.

Vespazia looked thoughtfully around the large room and waved her hand in the air several times. Allegra giggled hysterically as the decorations poured out of the box and the streamers hung themselves artistically from the walls and ceiling. Katya appeared in the doorway with the red carpet and that too slipped out of her grasp and laid itself in a large space in front of the French windows. The tree floated majestically through the door and planted itself in the floor, exactly in the middle of the red carpet. The tree decorations floated out of their boxes and hung themselves on the tree.

By this time Jason and Sidonie were standing open-mouthed in the doorway. The fairy doll, rather tattered from frequent use, suddenly appeared bright and shining on the top, and seemed to smile at everyone.

"Are you sure that's not a real fairy?" asked Katya suspiciously. "It looks very like the ones Charles and I saw in Faery Land when we passed through. I'm sure it winked at me just then!"

"It's a speaking likeness," said Vespazia smoothly. "In any case fairies wouldn't dream of standing on a tree all Christmas, they'd want to come to dinner."

"Well, just in case," said Katya, "I'm inviting this one to dinner, and to stay for Boxing Day as well."

The fairy smiled and nodded.

Allegra gasped. "*Mother*! What have you done? That fairy is real!"

Vespazia laughed, "I assure you it is not. Just a little special magic for Christmas, just for you."

"Thanks Vespazia," said Jason appreciating his mother-in-law's little joke. "I think we'd all better have another drink to celebrate putting up the decorations and of course the tree."

Amidst much laughter and Christmas spirit – whisky for the men, wine for the women – a festive air soon pervaded the Parkes's household.

During the seasonal festivities that followed, Katya went several times to check on the tree fairy and put a small plate of food and drink beside the tree at every meal time. The food was always gone when she went to fetch the plates. She left a glass of wine on three separate occasions, but it was ignored. Even after the holiday was over and everyone had settled back into the everyday routine, she wasn't certain the fairy had not been real.

Charles and Theron had arrived, to find the entire family, including both of their wives, totally incapable of any serious thought for the next few hours. Charles gave a resigned sigh and began to put the perishables in the fridge and freezer. The turkey was left on the worktop until Allegra or Jason sobered up enough to stuff it.

Simon got terribly excited when he saw the tree and had to be forcibly restrained by his grandfather from climbing up to see the fairy. After being told that he could only look and not touch he sat down to enjoy the sight. Theron kept an eye on him, but he was agreeably surprised to find that Simon only needed to be told once. His grandchildren were being brought up in a way he approved of.

Later, Charles took over and attended to Simon and Riva, whilst Theron made a valiant attempt to sober up his family. They refused to co-operate so he left them to it.

Fed, watered and changed, his niece and nephew were put to bed by Charles. The afternoon air had tired them out and they quickly went to sleep.

Theron raided the fridge and found Charles and himself sufficient food for their tea. Theron knew that Charles did not enjoy blood and cut them both ham sandwiches. He left the coffee for Charles to make. He too was used to a more varied diet than most vampires.

Several hours later, Allegra and Jason wandered into the kitchen. Charles and Theron had prepared the feast for the next day, and sat at the table in silent contemplation of a pile of wrapping paper and presents. They had no idea what was for who, as Theron put it.

Charles with a sly laugh told him. "We'll wrap them up and give them out with no names on, and we can have a game of pass the parcel before breakfast."

"No you won't," said Jason. "You can wrap them and I'll tell you who they are for and Allegra can write on them."

Allegra laughed happily. "I'll just sit right here and do them." She pushed Jason onto a chair and slid onto his knee. He put his arms around her waist as she almost fell off onto the floor.

"You'd better get on with it," said Jason holding her tightly. "I don't know how much longer she'll stay upright."

Charles and Theron started to wrap the presents. It took them several hours, by which time Allegra had fallen asleep and been put to bed. Jason and Katya finished off writing on the parcels and Charles and Theron made sure than everyone had at least one present and even wrapped their own.

During the next three days a hilarious time was had by all. Fortunately, Charles, Jason and Katya were sober enough to cook the food and look after the children. Both sets of grandparents pleaded ignorance of modern appliances and the mysteries of the festive season and concentrated on making sure their grandchildren had a good time. Allegra was wrapped in a mildly alcoholic haze for a lot of the time and drifted around the house, showing everyone the sapphire and diamond necklace given her by Jason who let her show him her appreciation several times. Katya said he was wearing out the stair carpet.

"I could help to wear it out a bit more if you want," said Charles obligingly.

"You've had enough exercise for the time being. You mustn't wear yourself out on my account," said Katya slyly.

However, right at that moment Charles spotted the saffron cake which Allegra had instructed Jason to buy for him and decided eating it took preference over Katya and their bed.

"It's a good job I absolutely adore you," said Katya, "or I might have seconds thoughts as to the suitability of a husband who prefers food to me!"

Charles laughed. "I still have the greatest desire to help wear out the carpet, you'll just have to wait until I've eaten, anyway I need to keep my strength up," he added virtuously.

Jason heard all this as he entered the room. "Never let the sun set on a good idea," he told him, "and it's nearly sunset right now."

Charles grinned as he finished his tea and cake. Then, picking Katya up, slung her over his shoulder and departed.

"Good advice," he said to Jason as he passed him.

Jason looked complacently around the lounge. His entire family was here in his home for the first time ever, "This is the best Christmas I have ever had," he told them all.

His family looked at him and smiled.

"It has been wonderful," his mother said with a smile. "Let's hope we have many more."

Theron and Quinn smiled at each other. "Our children have certainly embraced the twenty-first century with open arms," said Theron.

"I fear Vespazia and I have an awful lot to learn," said Quinn.

"Never fear," said his new friend. "Sidonie and I will help you. With Vespazia's powers a trip around the world is the best way to learn. Sidonie and I haven't always been on the Astral Plain and we certainly didn't spend all our time there. We have spent quite a lot of time on terra firma, or should I say the waters of this world? We have been sailing since the earliest times. Long before the Vikings crossed the Atlantic Ocean to America, we were sailing with them around the coasts of Scandinavia and down to the Mediterranean. Why, we lived there until we went to Egypt in 3,400 BC. Jason was born there. We have kept up to date with our skills; we sailed across the Atlantic several times in the fourteenth and fifteenth centuries. We gave up for a time in the sixteenth and seventeenth, too many pirates around. We went again several times in the eighteenth and nineteenth. After 1950 we went often in our own yacht and took several maiden voyages on the new ocean liners. We went across the Atlantic several times in the seventies, and we took an anniversary trip around the world in 1980. I think we should leave as soon as possible; we should all enjoy the experience. Our children are more than capable of taking care of any demonic risings or threats to the end of the world as we know it."

Jason looked suspiciously at them as this historical account of their sailing exploits were detailed.

"How come you never dropped in to see us? And how come nobody noticed an extra boat sailing along with them across the Atlantic?"

"Dear boy," said his father with a pained look. "Invisibility spell of course. Doesn't detract from the experience of the acquiring of modern skills, just doesn't draw attention to the fact that an unknown couple are sailing with them."

"Seems a bit odd to me," said Allegra. "You could have dropped in to see your only son."

"We did hear about him from time to time, but never seemed to able to catch up with him. He always seemed to be one step ahead of us," said Sidonie hesitantly. "It was only when your large party of supernaturals disturbed the cosmic energy fields deep underground that our friends alerted us to the fact that it might be him and his friends. We decided to see whether he was involved. We knew he had joined with a demon and a druid, two thousand years ago; we just didn't ever catch up with you all until you entered the Lost World. Theron now thinks we were meant to find you," she added thoughtfully.

"That wouldn't surprise me," said Quinn. "Elliott thought everything went too smoothly for his liking, and of course he was right about that. Maybe someone put another ingredient in the pot that none of us suspected."

"Well, it doesn't matter now," said Theron. "Here we all are, and ready for a trip around the world. As soon as Jason fixes us up with a nice ocean-going yacht, we'll get going. We'll decide where to go when we get to sea."

Sidonie and Vespazia exchanged a conspiratorial glance. They had their itinerary already mapped out. Sidonie had read Theron's mind two days before and she and Vespazia had made their plans.

Jason sighed in resignation and picking up the phone spoke at length to a friend in Southampton.

On New Year's Day everything changed.

# CHAPTER TWENTY-THREE

*Early on New Year's Day Thomas got a frantic phone call from his mother:*

"Thomas, where's your father?" she asked without preamble. "I need to see him right away."

"What's up?" asked Thomas, alarmed by the slightly hysterical note in his mother's voice.

"Quite possibly nothing, but as your father is the only man I know who knows about the supernatural world, he's the only one I can think of to help me."

"He's still in America," said Thomas more calmly than he felt. This was the first time ever that his mother had admitted out loud that such a world existed. "I know just as much as he does and we both know a lot more than we did a year ago. I told you all about our battles with the ancient sorceress and finding the Lost World."

"I know and I appreciate your truthfulness," said his mother. "It gave me a lot more courage to face the future and it made things a lot easier for me. But you are my son, I need to speak to your father."

"I'll see what I can do, but can't you tell me what's wrong?"

"It's not the sort of thing a mother can discuss with her son," she replied firmly.

"Sit tight, I'll find a grown-up to help!" said Thomas, amused rather than offended.

He disconnected and immediately dialled Elliott's number.

"Black here," said Elliott tersely.

"My mother seems to be in a spot of bother connected with the supernatural. Something she can't discuss with her son," said Thomas. "She wants to speak to Dad, and got quite agitated when I said he was still in America. I have this strange feeling it involves some man and that's why she doesn't want to talk to me. Probably thinks I'm too young!"

"So you thought of me!" said Elliott.

"Well, no one could call you young," said Thomas laughing.

"I'm on my way."

Seconds later Elliott appeared and, grasping Thomas's arm, told him to think of his mother's home. In a flash they appeared in the kitchen of her home in Kent.

"The kitchen? I should have known," said Elliott ironically.

"I can't help it if I see my mother doing the cooking," said Thomas defensively. "You know how I love home-cooked food."

Hearing voices, his mother came running. She looked surprised but not horrified to see them.

"You were quick," she said to Thomas. "Who is this?"

"It's Elliott, you said you wanted someone older. And he is definitely older!" said Thomas with a grin.

"Go and find something to do outside for a while. Go and take a walk," Elliott ordered Thomas. "Your mother and I will get along fine." He opened the back door indicating with his thumb that Thomas should disappear.

Thomas snorted in disgust, turned into a lynx, and stalked off down the path.

His mother smiled for a moment then turned back to Elliott.

"He has spoken so much about you all that I feel I know you. I am probably being foolish, but something has happened which I think needs explaining.

"You must know that Vern and I divorced a few years ago. I just couldn't live with the fear of them all being discovered any more. I still love them all, I just couldn't stay and wait for something terrible to happen every time they went hunting.

"I came here. Not too close, yet not too far away. I see the boys often and Vern comes now and again to make sure the house is quite safe and in good repair.

"I know he has Diana now, Thomas and Patrick both like her and told me about her. I must say I was rather pleased.

"I recently met someone myself. He looks quite young but he says he is much older than I am. He said," she blushed, rather charmingly thought Elliott, "that he has always preferred rather more mature women as they have a greater knowledge of men than the young girls of his acquaintance. He seems to think I am very attractive and just what he has been searching for. I'm not wholly sure I believe him, but it is a very nice thing to have said about one."

Elliott nodded, not quite sure where this was leading but prepared to wait for her to get to the point.

"Last night he vanished," she said abruptly. "During the night, one moment he was by my side the next he had gone. I'm sure he was spirited away without his consent, at least I hope so," she said fervently.

"Anything else I should know?" inquired Elliott laconically. He had a shrewd idea, now, where this conversation was heading.

"He didn't stop to get dressed," she said shortly. "His clothes are still where he left them."

At Elliott's raised eyebrow she avoided his eyes and said, "On the chair by the bed. My bed!"

"Very disconcerting," drawled Elliott suavely, "and how wise of you to send for an expert on the subject."

"Don't you start," said Margaret Fallon. "It looks as if I've jumped out of the frying pan into the fire in a big way. At least Vern was always there in the morning."

"I am quite certain that whoever spent the night in your presence fully intended to be there in the morning," said Elliott soothingly. "The man would be a fool if he didn't."

"I'll take that as a compliment," said Margaret, relaxing a little as she realised that she was definitely talking to a man of the world.

Thomas opened the kitchen door. "I can't see that there's anything you have told Elliott you couldn't have told me," he said peevishly. "I have had the odd girlfriend, you know. I do know about the birds and the bees."

"I'm sorry," said his mother, "but it's not the sort of thing I could confess to my own son. Although the nosy little blighter had the nerve to listen at the door to find out anyway." She gave him a whack across the nearest shoulder with a hard right hand.

Elliott grinned at this well-aimed punishment and laughed as Thomas put the width of the table between himself and his mother, fearing further retribution.

"Oh, do sit down Thomas!" said his mother irritably. "Now you know there's no point in hiding the fact."

"Not really," said Thomas. "I'm sure that neither Patrick nor myself begrudge you the company of a man who quite obviously thinks you are the cat's whiskers."

This time his mother got up, walked around the table and hit him hard across the shoulders, tweaked his right ear and clapped her hand across his mouth. "Any further mention of cats and you won't have any whiskers," she said warningly.

Thomas pretended to cower away and put up both hands in surrender. "No more cracks," he promised.

"Can you tell me something about this new friend of yours?" asked Elliott now that the by-play was over.

"He's quite tall, has jet black wavy hair. He is very elegant and wears very smart black suits and royal blue shirts a lot of the time. But he also wears jeans and red shirts and sometimes a black and red tracksuit around the house. He has the most wonderful golden eyes and he looks rather Arabic. He likes walking and we often walk for miles along the beaches and footpaths.

"He was very pleased when he found out that I knew about the world of the supernatural. He said it made it a lot easier for him to tell me that he was a demon. A good demon, and he wanted to prove to me that some demons are good."

Elliott heard Thomas's indrawn breath and frowned at him to keep quiet.

"Well, of course I knew they were and said so. Thomas had told me about you and Jason and about Lucifer. Although I did find that a bit far-fetched. But I had to believe him when Martin and Erin wrote to tell me that they were both saved by Jason and Thomas and cured by Lucifer.

"Of course Asa said he could have read my mind and found out, but he preferred to keep everything above-board and honest between us. I don't think I did anything wrong in telling him because if he was a demon he would know and if he wasn't he would think I was barmy and leave. As he stayed, and he was here for almost four months before he vanished, I think he understood."

Picking the bones out of the story and making two and two add up correctly, a strange thought crossed Elliott's mind. The description of Margaret's demon matched almost uncannily with Lucifer's missing brother Azeran, a noted ladies' man for millennia, and the name Asa seemed the clincher.

Elliott didn't dare to tell her. He had a feeling that Azeran might just have been interested enough in the shapeshifter's human mother to have tracked her down and, finding her both attractive and fairly young, had marked his territory. It was up to him to tell her who his brother was.

He made eye contact with Thomas.

"We'll get onto this right away," said Elliott. "There's no way I'm leaving Thomas's mother alone here, though. You'll have to come back with us."

"No!" she said firmly. "If he comes back I want to be here."

"I'll stay," said Thomas. "If he comes back I want to see him for myself. You go and do your stuff. But I tell you what you could do, you could send Elisande here. She's at a loose end with Felicity in New York and Faith gone with Alex. It'll give her something to do."

"I'll send her along as soon as possible," agreed Elliott. "I'll make inquiries about your Asa. I've a couple of calls to make in the demon dimensions. I'll get back to you."

Thomas nodded knowingly as Elliott left for Lucifer's palace.

# CHAPTER TWENTY-FOUR

*New Year's Day.......*
*AD 2003*

NEW YORK

Sebastian had suggested, rather forcibly Vern and Diana that they should go and meet with the chairman and talk about her new duties as outlined by Daniel and Elliott.

"He's expecting you to come and discuss the business of helping the Feds root out the criminals in his organisation. You have to make sure your stories don't conflict and make them suspicious of Diana.

"You are both going to have to familiarise yourself with all the firms in the building. It's going to take a great deal of time and effort to find out which are genuine and which are the subsidiaries of Goodman, Goodhew and May who are laundering the drug money and gun running. What's more, you are both the right kind of people to find and get rid of the demons and witch doctors and other supernaturals who were working with those crooked accountants. Travis and myself, in your shoes, would be investigating the lawyers who work there. They would certainly have a legal team protecting their interests."

"Okay, okay, I get the message. We'll go today. It will be quiet and we can ferret around the offices without any one knowing." Vern was irritated but knew they had to go.

"It can wait until tomorrow," Sebastian said grudgingly, satisfied that they knew the urgency of the problem. "No one will be there today."

"That's why we'll go now. We can nose around the offices without anyone knowing." Vern was keen to get going now that he had made up his mind.

Travis nodded assent. "You could be right." He turned to Sebastian and indicated his approval of the plan. "There is probably only a skeleton staff there today. It sounds ideal."

Sebastian shrugged. "It's their move."

Vern spoke quietly to Diana, as the vampires conferred.

"Felicity had a word with me the other day, she reckons Lucifer got it wrong when he suggested Sebastian taking charge over here. He's too argumentative and emotional. She thinks Travis is the one he should be looking at. I'm sure she's right. I'd better tell him myself, I suppose. It can wait until I next see him. We'll leave them to it for now. You'd better drive me to Goodman, Goodhew and May to get started on your new job. Have you got everything you need?"

Diana pretended to search her briefcase and closed it with a snap.

"I have, and my Limo is waiting whenever you are ready," she said haughtily, getting into the part a little early as she strode out of the room.

"In my position I should have a chauffeur, so you can drive! You might as well make yourself useful for once. Hurry up, I'm late as it is!" she hurled over he shoulder to Vern as he followed her.

Overacting with a vengeance, thought the vampires as they caught sight of Vern's irate glance at her back as she sailed towards the lift.

Vern drove Diana to work, and in case the staff were watching, gave a very convincing impression of the perfect chauffeur, getting out to open her door and closing it very gently before darting to the entrance to open that as well.

Bowing elegantly as she nodded her thanks, he said in his most ingratiating tones, "At what hour would madam like to be picked up tonight?"

"You can pick me up at five thirty and for once try not to be late. You can go and park the car, but don't go far away, I may need you later. I'll page you, so do try to stay awake. You know how I hate to be kept waiting," Diana hectored him loudly, hiding a grin as he looked livid at this last remark.

"Madam had better watch it," he muttered softly, "or she'll find it difficult to swish her tail in the morning!"

Diana smiled smugly as she turned away and strode towards the lift. Vern did rise nicely to the bait; it really was fun being a female shapeshifter.

Tonight, my girl, Vern promised himself, a sleek black cat will regret every one of those words.

Vern parked in a reserved space in the underground car park and took the lift to the fourteenth floor.

Nodding to the secretary he walked through to Diana's office.

It was empty so he presumed she was with the chairman discussing her role in the firm's affairs.

He strolled along to the room they had stolen the tapes from a few days before and entered without knocking. He was surprised to see a secretary at the desk and the door to the accountant's office open. He silently crossed the floor and pushed the door a little wider. He was astounded to see a couple of demons and a witch doctor taking several items and a large book from the safe. He and Diana had not had time to remove the safe or its contents on their brief sortie and he had no idea that anyone knew that the accountants were no longer in this world.

Considering himself outnumbered he backed silently out of the room, beckoning the secretary to accompany him and silencing her with a finger to his lips.

Once outside the door, he hustled her into an empty office – one of many now that Lucifer had taken over.

"Who are they and where did they come from?" he asked her quietly, not wishing to frighten her.

"They are part of the security detail; they said they had to collect secret files from the safe. Was I wrong to let them in?"

"No, you were quite right," said Vern soothingly, realising she would probably be dead otherwise. "You didn't happen to see what book they were holding?"

"If you mean the one in the safe, I saw it when my boss brought it into the office a few months ago. It had such a strange name I remembered it, the DEMON COMPENDIUM," she said triumphantly. "Was that what you wanted to know?"

"Yes. But if I were you I wouldn't go back into that office not even to fetch your handbag. I'll see you get it later. Now, I happen to know that the chairman and new managing director will both be needing a new secretary," said Vern. "Why don't you trot upstairs to the chairman's office and say that Elliott sent you to be his new secretary. He will be pleased to see you, I have no doubt."

She disappeared so quickly; Vern wondered what he had said to alarm her.

Not wishing to confront any demons or witch doctors, as he was not equipped to deal with them, he left to tell Diana what he had found out and to get in touch with Alistair. It rather looked as if there was more information to be found in these offices and on the various computers than he or Diana knew enough to find. He had the feeling that they might be encrypted way beyond his ability to crack.

He wanted Alistair to come to New York for at least as long as he and Diana were there. He trusted Alistair's expertise and his own gut reactions to danger.

Diana wasn't in her office and Vern was beginning to get alarmed. She should have arrived by now. He fetched a secretary from another office to ring around and find out where she was. She paged her on the intercom, but there was no reply. Vern got really concerned and rang Travis who hadn't seen or heard from her either.

Realising that he needed mystical assistance, Vern rang Felicity and asked her to bring Karim over to the office. They materialised two minutes later right in front of him.

"I'm probably over-reacting, but she's not the sort to test my reactions by vanishing. She knows how I feel about missing relatives. She'd never do that to me. She's been kidnapped or taken hostage."

"Where did you see her last?" asked Karim.

"In the foyer, the front office!" said Vern. "She told me to park the car."

"I'll start there. Are you coming, Felicity?"

They left the room in the conventional way and headed for the ground floor via the lift.

Shortly afterwards, the helicopter landed on the roof. Travis hurried into the office a few minutes later.

Vern brought him up to date and decided to call Alistair in the underworld. He brought him up to speed as well. Alistair was surprised to hear the Diana was missing. There didn't seem any reason for it.

"I'm still patched in to their computer files, but there are no archives referring to the purchase of the building. They must be on paper records or possibly microfilm done in the seventies. You'll have to find them to give me something to go on. Ward knows a lot about paper records, I'll get in touch with him, then I'll find Old Nick and see what he thinks."

"I'll leave that with you," said Vern. "I'm getting really worried."

Karim and Felicity materialised in a quiet corner of the grounds surrounding the building and entered through the same door as Diana. Karim strolled around the foyer as Felicity approached the front desk.

After a few minutes' chatting to the security guard she

returned to Karim.

"He says she took the left hand lift to the twenty-fourth floor. He particularly noticed her as she was arguing with her chauffeur at the entrance. He said she looked a bad-tempered bitch," said Felicity. "I think we can safely assume she got in the lift."

Karim said nothing but took her arm and crossed to the lifts.

"I think we'd better try the same one," he told her as he assisted her into it. He pressed the button to take them upwards to the twenty-fourth floor. "We will also assume that she never left the lift."

He looked upwards at the escape hatch. "One moment, my dear!" He pressed the emergency button and the lift shuddered to a halt.

He dematerialised and reappeared a little later looking perturbed. He carried a briefcase, which he opened, showing the contents to Felicity.

"Those are the clothes Diana was wearing this morning," said Felicity looking ashen. "Surely she didn't take them off herself?"

"No, I don't think she did," said Karim. "Only a man would throw them in like this."

"However are we going to tell Vern?" whispered Felicity, sounding sickened by her thoughts.

"We must tell him the truth of what we found," said Karim. "But we would be guessing if we voiced any other suspicion."

"She didn't have any other clothes with her, she wouldn't walk around with nothing on. She would have to shapeshift; she couldn't in daylight, it would be too dangerous." Felicity looked helplessly at him.

"Unfortunately the other alternative is that she had been abducted for some nefarious purpose," mused Karim. "In which case I don't think they know she is a shapeshifter, or they wouldn't have bothered to take her clothes leaving her, as they might suppose, vulnerable to being terrorised, or tortured."

"Oh, how awful! She must be terrified. We must find Vern and Travis at once and tell them."

On the way to Lucifer's palace after reassuring Margaret that he would looked into the mystery of her missing demon, Elliott got sidetracked.

On Bodmin Moor, the Lanyons and Drago were sitting around a roaring fire, enjoying a lunch-time drink. Alex and Faith had delayed their trip to her Father's relations until the mystery of the

Book was solved satisfactorily.

All the shapeshifters had returned from a morning spent on the moor, as they needed the exercise. Faith had declined to venture out in the cold.

Without warning a terrible storm darkened the skies, thunder and lightning ripped across the moorland. In the middle of the day it became as black as the darkest night. Lightning filled the rooms at 'Simba' and other homes on the moor. Rain fell in sheets; the thunder was constant and overhead for hours. Lightning strikes felled the power lines, the phones were cut off and the television and radio masts were destroyed.

Candles were lit all over the moor and the residents took to their cellars, if they had them, to get away from the noise of the thunder.

The Lanyons escaped to their cellar for a while, they were wrapped up to keep warm and had been reluctant to leave the fireside. It was only a little less thunderous in the cellar.

"We need Elliott," shouted Matthew above the noise.

"The phones are out," shouted Sophie.

"Try the car phone," yelled Alex. "It might work."

Matthew motioned to his still-recuperating son to stay put, made a dash for the garage and dived into the car. He called Elliott, who was about to materialise in Hell and reached him right away. Elliott heard the noise from the receiver and, realising it was Alex's mobile, materialised in the house before Matthew got back from the garage. He found his way to the cellar where the Lanyons were gathered and was joined, a couple of minutes later, by Matthew.

"Black magic, definitely," pronounced Elliott soberly. "Very unpleasant. It's meant to strike terror to all those in our circle. Can you stick it out a bit longer? We've got a bit of a crisis on our hands. Diana has been kidnapped; we can't find her. Vern's going berserk, and Lucifer is yelling at everyone in sight, because we still can't find his missing brother either."

"Can we help?" asked Matthew.

"Not right now. Just hang in there and remember, this is just a bad storm right now. I'll get the Faery Watch to monitor the area for any cosmic activity, but for now sit tight."

"Can you bring Elisande here? She's on her own at Aurora. She'll be better off with us."

"I'll take her to Kent. Thomas and his mother need the company," said Elliott, and did just that.

"Elisande, stay here until I give the all-clear," said Elliott as he left her with instruction to Thomas to tell her all that had happened. He vanished once more.

"I feel better just seeing him," said Sophie, laughing at the quick exit. "He's got such a commanding presence, you just know everything will be all right."

Alex laughed. "I know just what you mean."

The room suddenly got very cold.

"Lets go back to the lounge," suggested Sophie. "I think I could put up with the noise, just to be warm."

Everyone agreed.

It was fortunate they couldn't see what was going on outside and Elliott didn't tell them, but the moors were becoming a jungle of gorse and brambles, hedges and trees were growing at a tremendous rate. Before long everything would be overgrown and hidden from sight. Water ran off the moors like a river and the roads were now feet deep in water channeling between the hedgerows and overflowing into the fields. The valley bottoms were about to become lakes as the enchanted rain still fell in torrents.

To avoid utter disaster and possible loss of life, Elliott used his powers to secure all the homes likely to be affected with sandbags and then used a dispersal spell to keep the waters out of the houses. He was reasonably certain the inhabitants would find a rational explanation for the miracle of their deliverance from the flood waters.

Unfortunately, until he found The Book, even he couldn't negate the spells it invoked.

All across southern England the rain fell from darkened skies, inundating the land. It rained until the land could soak up no more and the floods spread across it like ancient lakes. Elliott was certain that only black magic could cause disaster on such a scale. He went to find Jason and Daniel.

The three of them stood in Daniel's office studying a map of southern England.

"It must be Mordred. He's surfaced again, and sending us a message. He knows it was us who destroyed his book and made him just another black magician. He's taken advantage of Charalder's knowledge and thinks he's all-powerful again. He doesn't realise how the world has changed in the last one thousand years. It must be him."

Daniel looked positively ashen as Jason put their thoughts into words.

"I agree," came Rannoth's voice from behind them, "and so does the Boss!"

"We'd better try and figure out which deeds are down to Charalder and which to Mordred," said Elliott. "We might find a pattern."

"He doesn't have the knowledge to infiltrate the Fifth Dimension," said Daniel, "and anyone who tries to get into hell without Lucifer knowing has a death wish. They might get out now and again, but in six hundred thousand years no one has ever got in."

"But to raise Balzahar and a few mythical beasts is within his powers," said Elliott.

"Maybe those black magicians should be questioned again," said Rannoth. "I'll go and do it."

"As usual, we have too many leads to run down and not enough agents available," snarled Jason. "The world is running out of control. No wonder 'Old Nick reckons he needs more help around the world! I've got a lot of reorganising to take care of when this problem is solved."

"What do you have in mind?" asked Daniel.

"For a start, tightening up security in the Fifth Dimension, they have too many holes in their defences. Then I'm checking Lucifer's got his domain sewed up tight. Then I'm off to check the witchcraft in America is up to scratch and the American vampires have full access to the celestial realms. They need another angel besides Carlotta. A man to hold down the position of chief messenger."

"You are going to be busy," agreed Elliott, eyeing him sardonically, "but I have a feeling someone has anticipated you just a little."

"Proves I'm right," said Jason triumphantly.

"Any other little gems of advice for your fellow council members?" asked Elliott sarcastically.

"If Vern and Diana are going to stay there, I think it would be a sensible idea to send Alex and Faith to America. It is so much bigger than England we need a whole network set up. Alex can fly our agents around when Travis is busy elsewhere and he can help with the legwork for their firm. Matthew and Sophie can hold the fort at Simba, they should be good for a few years yet. Charles and Katya can keep the Fallons' firm going. Snake and Bianca will be living nearby and you and Natalia will be just down the road. Daniel can keep Pauline under control as usual."

"I see you've got it all worked out." Daniel frowned as Jason laid their futures before them.

"You two haven't done much good lately," said the irrepressible vampire.

They both looked at him in disgust, turned on their heels and walked away.

"You can't really argue with the truth," thought Daniel.

"I can," said Elliott, "I'm in charge."

In the underworld Lucifer, his cape swirling around him, was pacing around his office causing a mini-typhoon.

"For heaven's sake Nick, sit down. You are making the hell of a draught," yelled Pauline. "If I've got to be here, I want at least to be comfortable."

Nick glared at her, but stopped pacing and sat down. "What else has he done that I don't know about, yet?" he rasped.

"Wait for Elliott and Rannoth to get back and you'll find out," she snapped.

Nick looked at her and smiled, a slight lifting of the lips, more of a grimace really.

"I'm not good at the waiting game, as you know!"

"Who is?" replied Pauline. "But as you said, we all have to stay here. That's the price you have to pay!"

Lucifer resumed his pacing. Pauline growled furiously at him and went to join Allegra in the nursery.

Elliott and Rannoth arrived together in his office to discuss events.

"You don't know for sure it is Azeran," said Lucifer dismissively when informed of Elliott's suspicions. "It's not like him to leave a seduction unfinished. Until we do know, as far as I'm concerned he's on the loose, possibly with The Book."

"Well I think you are wrong," said Elliott. "He's been captured by someone who bears you a lot of ill will."

"I bear them even more," snarled Lucifer, "for putting me to all this inconvenience, and if it turns out to be Azeran, I'll be thinking about the Eternal Flame."

Smoke and flames spewed forth with each embittered word.

"Now get out there and find that Book at all costs," ordered Lucifer, "before disaster spreads to the whole world. You know the Great Entity can't intervene in human affairs. However I can, so find it, and sooner rather than later. I'll see what I can do to put

340

things right."

"I know it's odd, but it seems to me that this is directed particularly at Elliott, Jason and Daniel. After all, they did destroy the original in the first place. Now he's got it back he's after them first and foremost," pointed out Rannoth.

"All the more reason for them to find him in a hurry before he does away with them altogether," said the know-it-all of the demons. The water is creeping up towards Daniel's place and Jason's isn't all that safe. Elliott's is already surrounded by moorland everglades."

"Well what are you hanging around here for, get going," he added furiously. "I'll take care of everything around here."

"Okay, Boss!" said Rannoth and all four vanished.

# CHAPTER TWENTY-FIVE

Diana groaned as she lifted her throbbing head from the cold stone floor she lay on.

"Stay where you are and don't move a muscle," whispered a low voice into her mind. "Try not to make a sound, you are being watched."

She couldn't tell if it was male or female, but did as she was told. She lay there, in the pitch darkness, holding her breath for what seemed like several minutes. She was aware of bone-deep cold and a dank, musty smell.

"It's okay, he's gone," said the voice. "You can get up now."

A rattle of chains and a strong arm, helped her to her feet. She was lifted clear of the floor and placed on a stone ledge which appeared to do service as a seat. She was aware of a figure seated beside her.

"I'm sorry," continued a male voice, now speaking normally, "but the amenities are a trifle basic. May I suggest you take your supernatural form? You will find it warmer and also less embarrassing."

Diana suddenly realised what he meant. "Oh, hell: I wondered why I was so cold," she thought, and changed immediately into her jaguar form. She felt warmer at once.

"Very elegant," said the man, sounding a little amused. "I am afraid I cannot change my form so easily, I must apologise in advance for my lack of attire. I believe our captor feels we shall be more amenable minus our dignity."

"Think nothing of it," replied Diana politely as she projected her thoughts to his. "I have seen a naked man before; but I'm very sorry, you must be really cold."

"Not really," said the man evidently holding back his laughter, "I am not human either; I am in fact a demon. My name is Azeran, you will have heard of me. I am sure you know my brother if you are who I think you are!"

Jaguar eyes studied him closely.

"You are a prisoner here? Lucifer thinks you were helping Balzahar and the author of The Book. He isn't all that sure you haven't got it. Seems he got you all wrong."

"Lucifer judges everyone by his own standards," said Azeran

wryly. "I have nowhere near his capacity for evil or ever wanted it. I came to earth with him because he is my brother and for no other reason.

"Unfortunately these chains are enchanted, and we are both within a mystical barrier. Neither my brother nor your friends can hear our thoughts. Fortunately the barrier is within this room, so neither can our captor.

"A momentary lapse of concentration and here I am, and now so are you. I am not sure why he has imprisoned us or even where we are."

He was silent for a minute or so.

"It occurs to me that he may not know what you are. He has left you unchained, but unclothed in order to keep you here. He wouldn't have bothered to take your clothes and would have chained you with a neck collar if he knew. He obviously thinks you will be unable to escape or to help me escape."

"I need to think," muttered Diana. "Here we are in some cold damp musty old dungeon, somewhere Old Nick can't see or hear us, freezing cold and naked. Is there anything else I should know?"

"I think you have summed up our predicament quite nicely," said Azeran.

"Absence of clothes won't hinder my escape, but what about you?"

"If you get the chance to escape, take it. Once Lucifer knows where I am, no one, human, demon or sorcerer, can prevent him saving me."

"I still wish I had some idea where we are. I was kidnapped in America. Where were you?"

Azeran hesitated before speaking.

"As I said, a momentary lapse in concentration. I was on earth, I am not prohibited from it like my brother. The pleasures of this world are not denied me."

"You were in bed with some woman," accused Diana. "Why didn't you just say so?"

"Hardly the thing to discuss in our present state of undress," said Azeran stiffly. "I was afraid of embarrassing you."

"Good heavens, you and Lucifer are a fine pair! He's going around making sure all his friends and relatives with children are legally married and you can't mention a romp between the sheets like an any normal male. Nothing to get embarrassed about, men and women have been doing it since time began. You and your

343

brothers must be living way in the past. I thought you demons were proud of being so sinful. In any case where were you?" she said, abruptly getting back to the subject.

"I was in England, a small village in Kent. A rather charming woman who didn't seem to mind that I was a demon." He sounded rather defensive, thought Diana. "She had a great deal of knowledge of the supernatural. I hope she will one day forgive my abrupt departure. Everything happened to suddenly, I was taken by surprise. I didn't even have time to get back to hell before I was captured."

"I hope it wasn't too much of a surprise," said Diana meaningfully, "there are some things no one should interrupt."

Azeran made a choking sound and the chains rattled violently.

Diana's mind was hit by a thought-bomb.

"That's a very private matter for myself and the lady only!"

"Well I hope she does forgive you, but if she doesn't you send for me and I'll give you a marvellous alibi."

"Can we change the subject?" muttered the acutely embarrassed demon.

"Why did he need you anyway? Did he think Lucifer would do anything to get you back?" asked Diana, determined to find the answer.

"If he did, he doesn't know my brother," said Azeran ruefully "Even a brother wouldn't stand between him and his prey. No! He wanted to use my body to hide within, until he could use The Book. He probably thought it highly amusing to use the Devil's brother as a host. Fortunately for me, my body was unsuitable. I have all the powers of my heavenly connections, unless mystically chained, and a captive body is of no use to a sorcerer who needs to move around. He couldn't let me go, he couldn't be sure I didn't know him."

"So if we can get you out of those chains, you can get us both out of here?" queried Diana.

"Without these chains, I have my full powers."

"Let me see them. I can't do anything to them with paws," said Diana in exasperation, changing back to herself and shivering in the cold damp air.

Azeran held out his hands, which shook slightly as Diana took hold of then and looked closely at the chains. Demons have excellent eyesight.

"He was in league with your old enemy Charalder, until she used The Book to find Daniel and Elliott and quite by chance found the world which was sheltering Zohal. She left in a rage and hasn't come back. Our captor is in a real temper about it. He couldn't resist telling me where she had gone and why."

"She won't be back," said Diana. "She's confined for the next ten thousand years, where there's no chance of her getting out, even with the nameless book. Good riddance to the old harridan!" she ended.

"Nice for you all. One less evil to worry about," said Azeran, attempting to recover his composure.

He really didn't like being naked with this rather exotic female in such close proximity. He might be ancient age-wise, but he was still a man. It took every bit off willpower he had to appear unconcerned as she bent over the handcuffs.

"Who is the author of this dratted Book?" asked Diana as she pulled a hairgrip from her untidy French pleat, intended to impress the chairman's employees.

She began a gentle prodding of the keyhole. "Fancy him using handcuffs with a key," said Diana. "You'd think he'd manage something computerised in this day and age."

"Just be grateful that he didn't," said Azeran evenly.

"Okay, so who did write the darn thing?"

"Telling you will put your life in even more danger than it is now," he warned her.

"I think someone besides you should know who he is. I know Vern won't rest until he finds me, but I could manage to escape on my own. So you really should tell me."

"The contents were gathered together by the greatest sorcerer of all time the great Merlin. The spells he'd collected were the combined knowledge of a number of sorcerers and alchemists. It was not however they who used them for evil.

"Here I must digress a little, to put the facts in some perspective." He paused...

"In the same century as Merlin lived in Camelot, another great sorcerer, two in fact, if you count his mother lived there also.

"He was known as Mordred. His mother was Morgan Le Fay, they were disciples of evil even then. They gathered around them many black magicians, learned all their secrets and then disposed of them. All this knowledge made them the most powerful sorcerers in the known world. They were reputed to be immortal. Many thought they had the secret of eternal life, they had a dark following. In time Mordred's knowledge surpassed that of his mother, but somehow

345

their magic was still unequal to the power of King Arthur, and his sword Excalibur. Only the Oracle of the Fifth Dimension and the Lady of the Lake know why.

"It was about time Merlin started to write his book of magic. Throughout his extremely long life – it was rumoured that he had been reincarnated at least three times – he had been gathering material. He was now ready to inscribe it all into one volume. During the reign of Arthur he used his knowledge to help Arthur and the Knights of Camelot and other Western Kingdoms, he was a very frail old man when he finally decided to write it all in one book.

"It would have been the greatest book of magic ever written but he was hundreds of years old when he decided to write it and he never finished it. A number of my associates wondered why he didn't try another reincarnation. It is possible that he used such a vast amount of his own power to help Arthur keep his kingdom; he drained his strength in the process. Who knows?

"This may have been why Mordred was able to capture him and extract not only his great knowledge but also possession of the material for the Book of Spells. Why he didn't dispose of Merlin is a mystery. Merlin did escape eventually, but his powers were never quite as great as they had been, his great mind never quite as clear. He died of grief and shame when his great book was used against Camelot and in a final terrible battle Arthur was vanquished. Soon after the death of Arthur and the return of Excalibur to the Lady of the Lake, the magical powers bestowed upon Camelot were lost. Because of my connection to Lucifer and therefore to the Hell dimensions I can tell you that Arthur is in none of them. I know that he has departed this world and his Knights of the Round Table with him for another dimension where he awaits a summons to return. I suspect that the prophecy regarding this return is not likely to be fulfilled in the immediate future.

"Soon after this Mordred killed his mother, Morgan Le Fay, making himself all-powerful. Many worshipped him as a God as he led them to great conquests and great evils in one guise or another. Attila the Hun and Genghis Khan may have been his disciples. They are now in Lucifer's deepest pit of infamy. Their punishment will be eternal.

"Because Mordred had stolen the information to create the magical book, after a while everyone assumed that he was the author. In a way he was and in his hands it was evil incarnate. He used it many times to raise himself to power. But although he was immortal, he was not omniscient. There were times he was outmaneuvered.

"In the Dark Ages he was known as the Red Monk, possibly for the vast amount of blood shed in his name. In those darkest of days books were not exactly forbidden but they certainly weren't available to anyone but the few educated humans around. In those early years the church discouraged the reading of books particularly those they considered of pagan or non-Christian origin. Personally I saw no evidence that these books were actively destroyed but because of the fragile parchment and thin cloth they were written on they soon disintegrated and would have been lost forever but for the efforts of a number of learned monks. Mordred took advantage of this and hid his book in a remote monastery in the mountains of Italy. He hid it among thousands of other books in their library. But the monks there were also copying all that came into their hands to preserve the knowledge contained therein. Even sending them to other countries in an exchange of knowledge. They copied the book of Mordred, by now known as the Mordeus Maxim. No one who handled it lived very long afterwards but it was a while before a visiting monk declared these deaths to be the work of the book and ordered it to be burned. Unfortunately it disappeared before this could be done. If I were a superstitious man I would suspect the book of removing itself."

Diana groaned at his witticism.

"It sounds to me as if it had become so powerful it probably summoned Mordred to remove it from danger."

"You may be right. Certainly no one dared to say its name. To admit it existed would mean that the Christian monks had copied a book of magic that the Church would have undoubtedly have destroyed, it being considered the work of the devil. It was widely rumoured to be so evil that to own it meant death.

"It was thought that he had discovered the secret of Eternal Life centuries before, he went into hiding. Thus the myth of his continued existence persisted throughout the ages. In the Dark Ages your friends, Elliott, Jason and Daniel, caught up with him but only by a fluke were they able to destroy the original book written from Merlin's material. They were even luckier that one of the monks at the monastery where it was copied was a vampire and an associate member of the Astral Council. He recognised the first copy of the original for what it was. It was removed to the Fifth Dimension for safekeeping. As to the other copies already made, the monks would never tell where they had sent them and they died taking the secret to their graves. The first copy was almost as powerful as the original. Mordred searched for it, but never found it. At that time it was beyond even his powers to discover the existence of the Fifth Dimension. I don't think even they knew they had the first copy ever made and that merely by having it they gave it untold power.

"There were other copies, and copies of copies, but the original was gone forever, and with it the awful power of its combination of evil potions, spells and incantations. It was the book itself that had the power. Somehow it took on a life of its own. Without it the author was just another sorcerer, albeit, a very powerful one.

"He has surfaced from time to time over the centuries in various guises. Lucifer thought that Rasputin or Vlad the Impaler might have been him. But he was proved wrong. A number of dictators and Kings have shown signs of Mordred's evil presence in their lives. He could have been any one of them. Lucifer is certain that he took over the bodies of many of the evil men of this century and the last. He did wonder if Hitler and Stalin were taken over. We shall probably never know. He probably exited any bodies he inhabited long before they died and escaped into someone else. He was difficult to track, as he never attempted to poach on Lucifer's preserves until now. He interfered with the Hell dimensions when he accepted the Book from Charalder and attempted to raise a demon. Then he was ours."

"Lucifer would never countenance his interference in his domain or with the Astral Council, so his days are numbered, I hope we are still alive when he is annihilated. I fancy the Eternal Flame has been waiting to receive him for some time."

"It was Charalder who gave him the first copy. She gave it to him to do with as he would. Once returned to him he became omnipotent, although her power was still far greater than his. But now you say that she is confined, then only the Fifth Dimension can deal with him, unless my brother decides to intervene."

"I don't think there's much chance of that," said Diana. "He's too concerned about his own world. Drat it! I almost had it that time. Anyway," she continued, "Elliott and the others have enough power to dispose of him, but they have to find him first."

"Someone's coming," hissed Azeran. "Lie on the floor, quickly!"

Diana flung herself on the floor as the door opened at the light from the passage shone directly on her body and Azeran chained behind her.

"Not with us yet, my dear," sneered a male voice, prodding her back with a rough hand. The hand ran down her back across hip and down her thigh. She held her breath and kept still as the hand came back up, but stopped abruptly as Azeran spoke calmly. "It would be unwise to damage the goods. My brother has a special interest in the woman and the owner is known to have enormous powers at his disposal when crossed. Your former accomplice feared him, so if I were you I would wait until you are certain he is no longer with us before you enrage him even further than you have."

"You are probably right," sneered the voice. "This druid has powers I have never supposed them to have. No need to tempt fate too soon."

Footsteps crossed the floor and the door slammed, darkness descended on them again. Diana waited for Azeran to tell her the coast was clear.

"You can get up now," he told her a few minutes later. "He's gone."

"You made him think I am Pauline. Why on earth did you do that?"

"The black hair fooled him in the first place. I just never corrected him. The werewolf is a particular favourite of Lucifer's and Daniel has already routed Charalder with his knowledge. It didn't hurt to remind him and I am sure you didn't want his hands to roam any farther."

"Damn right I didn't. Thanks, Azeran."

"You can thank me by getting me out of these chains."

Diana resumed her lock picking.

"I think I should tell you that Lucifer isn't about to leave his domain, right now. He's determined to guard his fortress himself this time. He told Elliott he's not leaving it until The Book is destroyed. There are too many lives at risk, The godchildren, the angels, Allegra, Katya and Alistair. I wouldn't be surprised if he hasn't got Pauline down there now. He'd never let her be harmed."

"It seems we must rely on the demon and his helpers," said Azeran resigned.

"I hope he has his radar on full alert," thought Diana.

Azeran made no reply. He didn't want her to know he couldn't see a way out of their prison.

"I can't quite get this last bar to drop," said Diana. "Tell me, is this Mordred human, demon or spirit in human form?"

"It's very hard to tell, I haven't had a good look at him. As I said, he is supposed to have the secret of eternal life. He's been around for thousands of years."

"Could he be a vampire, hiding his true nature? Or maybe a spirit who takes over bodies?"

"He could be anything he wants, according to legend."

"Discounting legend and immortality, could he still be a demon? Because if he is we can beat him. He's got everyone convinced he's immortal but what if he isn't? What if he had done it to make people think he is? After all, vampires have convinced people they have no reflection, whereas it is only the made vampires who have none. They don't actually get killed by wooden stakes, only poisoned by them – a nasty death if not treated, but curable. When it gets right down to it, anyone would be killed by a stake through the heart, wooden or otherwise, and sunlight only affects very young or new vampires for a few decades and then they gradually become immune. These myths just run on and on if no one corrects them."

"I see what you are getting at, but I shouldn't want to put it to the test before we have some proof," said Azeran

"Got it!" exulted Diana as the handcuff she was working on opened. Azeran quickly pulled his hand out before anything happened to close it again.

She handed him another pin and told him to work on the other wrist, whilst she did the ankles. She averted her eyes as she bent down.

"Put your feet on the bench," she said gruffly. "I won't have to bend so far."

Azeran smiled to himself as he obeyed.

It took them another half-hour before the chains were removed. Azeran stretched and waved his hand in the air. Immediately he and Diana were clothed in warm track suits and fleeces.

"Thanks!" said Diana. "I feel better already. Now, let's get out of here."

"I have to remove the mystical barrier," said Azeran quietly. "It may take a few minutes."

It took ten. Then they were outside the building, courtesy of Azeran's powers.

"I have a little surprise for our captor," said Azeran thoughtfully. "We can now confine him in one of my brother's force fields. I'll let him know we are here."

A few seconds later Rannoth materialised in front of them.

"We just got your message. You've caused a furore in America," he told Diana. "How did you get here?"

"Long story," said Azeran. "We need one of Lucifer's force fields put around this entire area."

"Done!" said Rannoth. "Whatever you are up to, keep the boss informed. I'll tell the others where you are."

He vanished as quickly as he had come.

"Useful fellow to have around," approved Azeran.

"Well, where are we?" asked Diana.

"In Venice. This is a medieval palace, we were in a dungeon far below water level. That's why we were so cold and damp."

"How about zapping us back to America?" said Diana. "I'm not happy about being in Italy. It's where the monks copied The Book, isn't it?"

"I believe we should stay here, we can get Vern and the others to join us."

Before she could open her mouth to reply they both materialised in Lucifer's office. Rannoth grinned at them as Lucifer rose majestically to his feet.

"Well, get on with it. What have you found out?"

Lucifer listened in silence until Azeran had finished the tale. His face turned blood red as he looked from one to the other.

"Get back there right away, put everything back as it was. The chains, the mystical barrier and yourselves. At last he has made a mistake, it gives us an edge."

He spoke to Diana. "Are you up to this? I'll tell Vern you are safe and I'll make sure he's in the rescue party." He turned to his brother. "No time to lose. No recriminations, no post mortems, you've done well, but I need you both to hang in there a little longer! This is the chance we've been waiting for. I'm sorry about the indignity and the embarrassment you have both suffered, but strength of mind and character are called for now. This is no time to be squeamish, I have faith in you both. Azeran will look after you," he told Diana. "You are every bit as smart as that man of yours. I've got my eye on both of you."

"We'd better get back before we are missed," said Azeran, and in a flash they were back in the dungeon. Diana shivered as the warm clothes disappeared. She turned into a jaguar, as Azeran had said he would let her know if anyone came.

"I just hope that Mordred or whatever his name is turns out to be a demon and you can dispatch him quickly and permanently," moaned Diana. "Are you sure you couldn't tell?"

"Until he brought you in here, and I saw him in the light from the passage, I didn't know who had thrown me in here," said Azeran dryly. "He didn't stay around to introduce himself. I just happen to have seen him in the early years of this millennium and remembered his face. I need a much closer look at him before I can be certain what he is."

"I plan on giving you the chance at the earliest opportunity," said Diana, flexing her back legs and practicing a leap across the floor.

"*Don't!*" said Azeran. "You are our secret weapon. If I hear him coming you must resume your human form. Unpleasant though it may seem, his view of you as a human female for him to play with could be the edge my brother mentioned."

"Ughh, don't say that! You are asking a lot of a mere mortal," shuddered Diana. "But okay, if you think I should, I will!"

"Don't worry! These chains are no longer enchanted, Rannoth exchanged them for ordinary chains whilst we were talking to Lucifer. The mystical barrier can be overcome in seconds now I know the key. If he oversteps the boundaries you have set for his unwarranted attentions I will intervene. Otherwise we just have to wait for the signal to escape.

"I am an extremely ancient demon; I have travelled the earth throughout its history. I am no stranger to the human female form, I find it delightful to behold, but I have never felt the need to force myself upon one. Do I make myself clear?"

Diana giggled, as far as a jaguar can do so. "Don't worry, I'm not going to go all girly and hysterical about it. I have it on good authority that my figure is quite superb."

"I have to agree with that observation," said Azeran wryly. "I'll try not to let it influence me in any way." He rattled his chains to reinforce this remark. They sat for a while in companionable silence.

Azeran noticed she had gone to sleep. He was glad; sleep would ease her anxiety while they waited. He had no idea what Lucifer was going to do. Just that he had to be ready when the time came.

Several hours passed, twice the cell was inspected by their captor and twice Diana endured the indignity of being inspected closely by him.

Azeran promised her the final say on his punishment in hell.

"After I've torn him to shreds," she told him frostily.

"Having seen the claws, I suspect it will be a painful end to his career!" was the only response from her fellow captive.

Rannoth appeared in New York. James was at the computer, trying to find his way around city hall records. When asked he said Sebastian was showing Marsh and Selena around the city. They had agreed to work for Travis until he could find more permanent assistants, and the others were in the lounge.

Vern, Travis, Karim and Felicity were sitting around the room in various stages of gloom and despair.

Vern leapt to his feet. "What have you found out?"

Rannoth told him.

Vern was enraged. "I want her out of there now!"

"You can't. Elliott and the Boss have a plan."

"Sod Elliott and Old Nick," shouted Vern, "it's Diana who is in danger."

"Calm down. Azeran will keep her safe now he has his full powers back."

"Safe? Safe! You call what she's been through, 'safe'?"

Karim raised his voice slightly to be heard. "I will go and check on them for you, I will stay until all is well."

He vanished and appeared, seconds later, silently and invisibly in the Venetian dungeon.

Seeing Diana asleep with Azeran watching over her and sensing no other presence, he materialised.

"Oh, it's you!" said Azeran recognising an acquaintance of many years' standing. "Greetings et cetera."

Karim smiled grimly. "I had no idea my demonic friend was Lucifer's brother. Perhaps it is just as well you kept your birthright a secret. I fear my family would have been a lot less welcoming over the years."

"I know," said Azeran. "Why do you think I kept silent on the subject?"

"Quite understandable," agreed Karim.

"So why are you here?" asked Azeran.

"Vern is anxious about Diana's safety. I am staying to give you extra protection, I shall remain invisible. Don't let her know I

353

am here. I am going to take a look around the rest of the palace, I intend to search for Mordred's Book. I have a good chance of finding it."

"Go for it!" said Azeran. "I can look after Diana."

Karim nodded and vanished.

Jason, Elliott and Daniel were in conference with Lucifer and Rannoth. It was the first time Jason or Daniel had been to his palace. They sat in his office, listening to his explicit instructions. The brigadier was also present. He understood the honour done him by this meeting with the heads of the Astral Council.

"I want him disposed of once and for all. Use the Eternal Flame if you have to. No messing about: final destruction."

"We will do whatever is necessary; we don't want any more trouble from him either. It's eleven hundred years since we last crossed swords with him. I do wish we knew where he's been hiding himself all these years."

"Who cares?" said Lucifer. "After the Eternal Flame has had him, he'll be gone forever."

"We are leaving right now. Sit tight until we get back and keep the girls safe," said Elliott.

All three vanished, reappearing seconds later around the corner from the home of El Duce.

"Fetch Vern and join them Rannoth, I want Diana back in one piece," ordered Lucifer as they left. "Make sure she is."

Rannoth obeyed.

"Who is going in first?" asked Daniel

"I am!" said Elliott. "Invisible of course! Give me five minutes and come in making as much noise as you can."

Jason and Daniel walked briskly towards the building.

Once inside, an invisible Elliott moved from room to room searching for Mordred and his assistants.

On the third floor he sensed a familiar presence, and materialised. Karim did likewise.

"Where is everyone?" asked Elliott.

"Either hidden by enchantments or they are simply not here," replied Karim. "I have the strangest feeling that we have only one adversary, who has been pulling our strings all along. You and I should have no trouble finding him."

"With his prisoners in the dungeon, he shouldn't be too far away!" agreed Elliott.

"There are too many damned rooms," said Elliott after a while.

"We'll let Jason find him for us. He should be crashing in any moment now. He's got it down to a fine art."

Karim winced as a door crashed open some way below him, loud bangs and the sound of breaking glass followed by more crashes and more breaking glass.

"We'd better get down there," said Elliott.

They arrived together in the great hall as Daniel strolled in through the wreckage of the huge front doors. These were hanging by their hinges and looking as if they had been hit by a tank. Karim looked in awe at the vampire rampaging through the ground floor rooms.

"He does love to smash down doors and jump through windows," said Daniel tolerantly, as Jason leaped through a window between the dining room and the hallway and tore up the stairs to the first floor.

"Shall we follow? We don't want to miss anything!"

"I think Karim and I will stay out of sight," said Elliott as they both vanished.

Daniel followed the trail of destruction upwards.

Jason arrived in a first-floor dining room, chandeliers hung from the vast ceiling and expensive drapes hung at the windows, the walls were covered in precious arts and tapestries in excellent repair.

"Nice," approved Jason, as he ripped apart a thousand-year-old wall hanging and pulled the curtains from the windows.

"Careful Jason, this may not be his own place," warned Daniel. "Don't do anything too drastic."

"I'm looking for a hidden cupboard, a safe or strong box," said Jason. "This is the easiest way to find one."

Karim was astounded. The vampire's trail of destruction already amounted to millions of pounds' worth of damage. He hoped his new allies knew what they were doing.

Eventually they reached a large study at the end of a wing on the third floor. As they ran down the long corridor, the door was flung open and a very angry man confronted them.

"How dare you invade my home!" he raged. "The police are on their way. You will pay for this vandalism."

"I think he really means it," said Daniel as Jason leapt towards the man.

He grabbed him by the throat and shook him violently. The man seemed to shrink and cower away.

"I do believe he really is a human. Do you think he is the real owner?" asked Jason, seeing his quarry's extreme fear and failing to detect any demon possession.

"Of course I am," stammered the terrified Duke of Montesentia. "But you are not the fiend who took over my home and kept me a prisoner here."

"Sorry," said Jason, helping the Duke to a chair and handing him a drink. "Mistaken identity. It's your captor we want. Badly," he added. "Where is he?"

"He has gone to the attics to check that I have not released my family. I think he has others in the cellars," stammered the Duke. "He goes to visit them every few hours. I don't think he feeds them, he never takes food with him."

"He's a sorcerer," said Daniel coldly. "Surely you realised that?"

"I hardly dared to think at all," replied the Duke. "He has my family imprisoned. I must go to them."

"I'll go," whispered Karim, returning to Jason's side but still invisible. He returned seconds later with the news.

"They are all well," said Karim. "Hungry, frightened and cold, but well. I have told them help is on the way."

The Duke got terrified all over again as the invisible voice conveyed the message. "I think you and Elliott had better show yourselves," said Daniel. "The voices need a body to give a little confidence to our friend here."

Karim materisalised first and the Duke went even paler at the sight of the djinn.

"Tell me," asked Elliott, materialising in his human form, "did you call the police?"

"It was just a threat," said the Duke, looking relieved at the appearance of an apparently human male. "The phones are cut off."

"Excellent, we do so hate having to dispose of them," said Jason, "it's such a waste."

Daniel smiled grimly as he spoke to the Duke. "Has your captor been reading a very old and heavy book whilst he has been here?"

"Yes! It's in his room."

"And where would that be?" asked Karim softly.

"The third door down the hall!"

Karim disappeared and returned with The Book several minutes later. He handed it to Elliott who immediately vanished.

"It's safe," he told them on his return. They all breathed a sigh of relief.

"Now for the author," said Jason.

As one they made for the dungeons. Even the Duke followed them. Elliott and Karim materialised outside the door as Rannoth and Vern arrived.

"I'll go in with Vern," said Rannoth. "The Boss's orders."

Azeran and Diana were beginning to wonder what Lucifer was up to when Rannoth appeared in the doorway.

"All clear, you can leave now."

"Thank heavens for that," muttered Azeran, then watched amazed as Diana took a flying leap at the man who had followed Rannoth through the doorway. She bowled him over onto his back and started growling throatily. The man morphed immediately into a lynx and stayed put as she nuzzled his face with hers.

"They seem rather friendly," he observed to no one in particular.

"Cornish cats," said Rannoth succinctly. "No inhibitions."

He and Azeran, who had swiftly discarded his chains and clothed himself, discreetly exited the dungeon. Azeran placed a track suit on the floor by the door, closed it quietly behind him, and left them together in the darkness.

The jaguar growled softly as, courtesy of Azeran's powers, dim lights eased the blackness. Diana resumed her human form and Vern, realising he held a naked female in his arms, morphed back to human. He held her closely, waiting for her to speak. His arms warmed her cold body and she felt safe once more. After a while she eased herself out of his arms and put on the track suit. She smiled at him as he zipped it up. He kissed her upturned face and, speaking for the first time, whispered, "I'm sorry I wasn't there when you needed me. Forgive me?"

Diana held him tightly. "Nothing to forgive, you couldn't have prevented what happened. It was my fault for sending you away. Do you forgive me?"

"How about we forgive each other?" said Vern.

"I'm going to kill him," said Diana conversationally, as they left the dungeon and walked towards the stairs. "As soon as they tell me where he is, I'm tearing him limb from limb. You know Vern," she told him, "it wasn't so much being naked. Oh, I minded that, don't get me wrong! But it was the cold, the bone chilling, freezing damp cold. He thought I was human and knew I could freeze to death. If I hadn't been a jaguar I would have. When I had to change back so he could see I was still there, I have never been so cold in my life. That's why I'm going to kill him!"

"You certainly have the right," acknowledged Vern, hiding his fury at the terrifying ordeal suffered by his loved one. "But we shapeshifters have never been premeditated killers of the human race, couldn't you try for ALMOST kill him?"

"I'll see," said Diana, reluctantly acknowledging this point. "But I'm making no promises. In any case, I have this feeling he is a demon, so it won't apply."

"Let's go and find out." Vern took her hand and they crossed the ground floor.

"Looks as if Jason has been here," observed Vern. "Vampire vandalism on a grand scale."

Diana laughed. "I wish I could have seen it."

"Don't worry, I'm sure we'll see him do it many times in the future."

They climbed the stairs to the first floor. In the dining room vandalised by Jason they met up with Daniel, Jason and Karim. The Duke was still powerless to speak, he was overwhelmed by the identities of his 'guests'. Elliott had disappeared again to try and find Mordred. Daniel spoke quietly to the Duke.

"I know you have realised who we are. You are a believer who has encountered the supernatural. I also know you are never going to tell anyone. After all, who would believe you? Your family know only that they have been kept prisoner. You can see that it stays that way. We can arrange for your home to be put back as it was before. Tomorrow someone will arrive to do so, on your instructions. The price of your silence will be that from now on your home will be protected. Will that arrangement satisfy you?"

"It is more than I could have hoped for two hours ago." He replied, gratefully. "I will see to it that my family think this is the work of vandals and drug users."

"You can report it to the police as just that," said Daniel. "They will never find the culprits, but it will allay any suspicions your neighbours may have and quite possibly the insurance will be useful. We, however, will make complete reparation for the damage."

The Duke nodded, but pointed to a side wall where an unearthly scream was followed by a loud crashing and banging.

"I think I had better join my family in the attics," he said with a sigh of relief. "I believe it will be better for all of us if I don't see what happens next."

Daniel nodded and the Duke rushed from the room.

A section of wall swung open and Mordred appeared from his hiding place. Followed seconds later by Elliott in demon form. Mordred had been so taken up with taunting those before him, he neglected to check behind. He had no idea that Elliott had followed him from his hiding place.

"Now I have you where you can't get away," he gloated. "You are alone and your demon friend cannot help you."

He pointed a finger at Jason. "You, a mere vampire, you shall go first." He unleashed a streak of lighting towards Jason.

Daniel and Karim instantly placed a force field around themselves and Jason – and the fire rebounded on Mordred.

He screamed abuse at Daniel. "You are the druid touch me and your wife dies! I have her in my dungeon, she cannot escape."

Daniel feigned surprise. "I'm afraid you have made a mistake, my wife is safe in Lucifer's palace. I hope you haven't kidnapped some poor innocent female and expect us to worry about her?"

Jason snorted in rage. "Let me at him!"

"Sorry Jason," said Azeran from the doorway. "Someone else has a prior claim."

Mordred saw Vern and Diana standing beside the man he knew to be Lucifer's brother and it unnerved him. He backed away as Azeran, followed by Rannoth, was joined almost immediately by a demonic Elliott, and all three paced towards him.

Mordred, cornered, tried desperately to escape. But the combined power of the Astral Council was too great for him. He threw lightning bolts and fire streams towards them all, but they were fended off by the three demons. Those he aimed at the force field bounced off and hit the walls and ceiling. The room became a disaster area.

Mordred looked towards the door seeking escape and gave a horrified gasp. Then screamed in terror as an enraged jaguar sprang across the room. With a howl of rage, claws extended, the jaguar ripped him from neck to thigh. His clothes in tatters and blood pouring from deep gouges, he fell back across a small table. Diana leapt upon the terror-filled Mordred. Her powerful teeth almost ripped his arm off as she wrenched it from its socket. She sank her teeth into his neck and gouged his face with her claws; then she sank them into his wrist and flung him onto the floor. A wild, snarling beast stood over him, jaws dripping his own blood onto the face of her captor.

"Diana, darling, do leave some for the rest of us," said Vern plaintively.

Diana stopped chewing on Mordred's arm and turned towards Vern. She pawed the ground and swished her tail furiously. Then suddenly calmed down as Vern walked towards her.

Azeran joined them and spoke briefly to them both in a low voice. All the rest of the onlookers were spellbound as the three of them left the room.

Elliott was the first to recover. "I doubt if I shall ever have the nerve to challenge anything she ever does," he said in amazement.

"I don't think I would like to fight with her," admitted an awed Jason.

"I'd better warn Pauline not to cross her," said Daniel. "I'm not sure who would win."

Mordred, almost at death's door, said nothing; he was a beaten man.

Lucifer, hearing from Azeran that it was all over, appeared in the room.

"He was not human, his mother was a witch and his father a demon. Death is too good for him," he said. "He should be suffering an eternity of pain and torture in Beyond Hell."

"You would have to keep a strict eye on him or else wipe his memory. I wouldn't trust him an inch," said Elliott. "The Flame would finish it for all time."

Azeran interrupted, "I promised Diana the final say in his punishment. You must ask her."

Everyone turned to Diana, who had now returned with Vern. She looked pale as she saw her handiwork, but didn't flinch as she viewed the body.

"I want him to suffer," she said viciously, "for a long time."

"Very well, Lucifer shall arrange it," said Azeran, looking at his brother.

"I want him naked for eternity and boiled in oil at frequent intervals, and I want to watch!"

Azeran looked at Vern and raised an eyebrow.

"If that's what she wants," said Vern. "She earned the right, after all she could have killed him."

"So be it. He'll be tortured around the clock, that will give him no time to plan an escape," said Lucifer evilly. With a wave of his hand he dispatched the shredded body of Mordred to Hell. "The chief torturer should have great pleasure in incarcerating him in the worst possible torture chamber in Beyond Hell. I'll review the sentence in ten thousand years."

"Come to view the remains whenever you wish. Rannoth will arrange it," he told her cordially. "You can bring your shapeshifter with you; I'll be expecting you both."

# EPILOGUE

Elliott finalised the American end of the Council.

In consultation with Lucifer, and after hearing what Felicity had to say, he, Daniel and Jason had appointed Travis head of the New York Branch and Vern had agreed to be his second in command.

Sebastian would continue to run their business with Cassidy and Cybel. Travis would ferry everyone around whenever he could.

Jason pointed out that it wasn't Travis's fault that Snake and Bianca had to live in Cornwall, thus depriving him and America of a strong right arm. They had to replace him with someone equally as good. That was Vern.

Travis then suggested that Diana should take over permanently as managing director of Goodman, Goodhew and May and make sure the business was run honestly and legally. Vern was all for it and Sebastian seconded the plan. Diana was delighted; she'd enjoyed her venture into the world of commerce and enthusiastically agreed. Lucifer had already given orders that once all the firms in the building had been sorted out the profits were to be diverted to run the American end of their affairs. Jason and Daniel had both laughed at his ploy and told him that Travis and Sebastian were almost as rich as they were. They could fund it all on their own.

"I have to have a contingency fund!" said Lucifer loftily, "I can't keep diverting money from the US Mint to fund all your escapades, There's a finite number of methods of cooking the books and I've used most of them twice.

"I've got a small uprising to arrange in Central Africa, another to encourage in South America, and several more tortures to oversee. I can't stop my other enterprises just because you are all running out of money."

When fully recovered, Alex would share the piloting duties with Travis and help Sebastian with the leg-work. Faith would join with her mother, Karim and Eurydice, to provide the witchcraft and magic they would need until such time as a fully organised network was set up. Elliott and Travis had decided that they needed time to gather around them the kind of supernatural agents they were bound to need in the years to come, on the American side of the Atlantic and who better to help in the meantime than the shapeshifters from Cornwall.

"It should give the remainder of the shapeshifters a rest from the newspapers and television," muttered Daniel to Pauline, "with most of the cats working in America, they'll have nothing to photograph for a year or two."

Charles arranged for Snake and Bianca to live with Thomas until their new home was built, a few hundred yards from Elliott's. Natalia and Bianca were thrilled. Elliott and Snake weren't sure if they were doing the right thing.

Azeran? Sufficient to say that Margaret gladly forgave him. He was a very personable as well as persuasive, demon.

After a few weeks, living in the same house as Snake and Bianca, Thomas packed his bags and went to live with Jason. Lucifer's frequent visits were too much for the artistic young shapeshifter. Lucifer had come over all paternal and full of good advice.

Jason, who had completed his plans for the revision of security in the Fifth Dimension, had laughed when asked and told him to come right away. Lucifer wasn't his idea of a Dutch uncle either.

Jason now felt they had covered all angles and left for the Fifth Dimension with his family to introduce them to Alpha and the First Ones and to check their security as he had promised. Thomas accompanied them. Alpha and Torquil awaited his arrival with trepidation. His reputation had gone before. Yohanna thought it would liven up the stuffy old fogies and do them all good. Daniel and Elliott went to see them off.

Elliott laughed to himself as his friend stepped through the portal. "The Fifth Dimension had no idea what was about to happen to it," Daniel chuckled as he read his mind.

They returned to their homes to await the next crisis.

Lucifer, having made certain all the families were reunited and all where they should be, returned to Hell to oversee the punishment of Mordred and the Black Magicians. He retrieved Balzahar from the dimension he had been sent to by Daniel and Elliott, seated himself in his smoking chair and sat back to enjoy the entertainment.